Please return or renew this item by the last date shown. There may be a charge if you fail to do so. Items can be returned to any Westminster library.

Telephone: Enquiries 020
Renewals (24 hour service
Online renewal service available
Web site: www.westminster.gov.uk

2 3 MAY 2017	QUE	
		City of Westminster

ALSO BY
Chris Beckett

THE HOLY MACHINE

'Beckett examines the interface between
human and machine, rationalism and religious
impulse with the sparse prose and acute social
commentary of a latter-day Orwell'
GUARDIAN

'Incredible'
INTERZONE

'Beckett can stand shoulder to shoulder
with Orwell and Burgess. A triumph'
ASIMOV'S SCIENCE FICTION

DARK EDEN

Chris Beckett

CORVUS

Published in E-book and paperback
in Great Britain in 2012 by Corvus, an imprint of Atlantic Books Ltd.

3 5 7 9 10 8 6 4 2

A CIP catalogue record for this book is available from the British Library.

Paperback ISBN: 978-1-84887-464-0
E-book ISBN: 978-0-85789-671-1

Printed and bound by CPI Group (Ltd), Croydon, CRO 4YY

Corvus
An imprint of Atlantic Books Ltd
Ormond House
26-27 Boswell Street
London WC1N 3JZ

www.corvus-books.co.uk

For *my* family
– Maggie, Poppy, Dom and Nancy –
with much love

Acknowledgements:

Special thanks to my dear daughter Nancy
who first suggested that I write this book.

Thanks also to Tony Ballantyne, Una McCormack,
Nic Cheetham, Mathilda Imlah and John Jarrold,
who all contributed in various ways to the final form
and indeed existence of this book.

And many many thanks to my dear wife Maggie.

DARK EDEN

1

John Redlantern

Thud, thud, thud. Old Roger was banging a stick on our group log to get us up and out of our shelters.

'Wake up, you lazy newhairs. If you don't hurry up, the dip will be over before we even get there, and all the bucks will have gone back up Dark!'

Hmmph, hmmph, hmmph, went the trees all around us, pumping and pumping hot sap from under ground. *Hmmmmmmmm*, went forest. And from over Peckhamway came the sound of axes from Batwing group. They were starting their wakings a couple of hours ahead of us, and they were already busy cutting down a tree.

'*What?*' grumbled my cousin Gerry, who slept in the same shelter as me. 'I've only just got to sleep!'

His little brother Jeff propped himself up on one elbow. He didn't say anything, but watched with his big interested eyes as Gerry and I threw off our sleep skins, tied on our waistwraps, and grabbed our shoulder wraps and our spears.

'Get your arses out here, you lazy lot!' came David's angry spluttery voice. 'Get your arses out fast fast before I come in and get you.'

Gerry and me crawled out of our shelter. Sky was glass-black,

1

Starry Swirl was above us, clear as a whitelantern in front of your face, and the air was cool cool as it is in a dip when there's no cloud between us and stars. Most of the grownups in the hunting party were gathered together already with spears and arrows and bows: David, Met, Old Roger, Lucy Lu . . . A bitter smell was wafting all around our clearing, and the smoke was lit up by the fire and the shining lanterntrees. Our group leader Bella and Gerry's mum, my kind ugly aunt Sue, were roasting bats for breakfast. They weren't coming with us, but they'd got up early to make sure we had everything we needed.

'Here you are, my dears,' said Sue, giving me and Gerry half a bat each: one wing, one leg, one tiny little wizened hand.

Ugh! Bat! Gerry and me pulled faces as we chewed the gristly meat. It was bitter bitter, even though Sue had sweetened it with toasted stumpcandy. But that was what the hunting party was all about. We were having bat for breakfast because our group hadn't managed to find better meat in forest round Family, so now we were going to try our luck further away, over in Peckham Hills, where woollybucks came down during dips from up on Snowy Dark.

'We won't walk up Cold Path to meet them,' said Roger, 'we'll go up round the side of it, up Monkey Path, and then meet Cold Path at the top of the trees.'

Whack! David hit me across the bum with the butt of his big heavy spear and laughed.

'Wakey, wakey, Johnny boy!'

I looked into his ugly batface – it was one of the worst batfaces in Family: it looked like he had a whole extra jagged mouth where his nose should be – but I couldn't think of anything to say. There was no fun in the man. He'd hit you hard for no reason, and then laugh like he'd made a joke.

But just then a bunch of Spiketree newhairs arrived in our clearing with their spears and bows, walking along the trampled path that linked our group to theirs on its way to Greatpool.

'Hey there, Redlanterns!' they called out. 'Aren't you ready yet?'

Bella had agreed with their group leader Liz that some of them could come along with us and take a share of the kill. They were the group next to us Redlanterns in Family and, for the present, they were keeping the same wakings and sleepings as us, which made it easy for us to do things together with them (easier than with, say, London group, who were having their dinner when we were just waking up).

I noticed Tina was among them: Tina Spiketree, who cut her hair with an oyster shell to make it stick up in little spikes.

'Everyone ready then?' Bella called. 'Everyone got spears? Everyone got a warm shoulder wrap? Good. Off you go then. Go and get us some bucks, and leave us in peace to get on with things back here.'

~ ~ ~

We went out by a path that led through a big clump of flickering starflowers and then into Batwing. A whole bunch of Batwing grownups and newhairs were in their clearing banging away at a giant redlantern tree with their blackglass axes, working in the pink light of its flowers. We walked round the edge of their clearing to Family Fence, dragged away the branches at the opening, and went out into open forest. No more shelters and campfires ahead of us now: nothing but shining trees.

Hmmmph, hmmmph, hmmmph, went the trees. *Hmmmmmm,* went forest.

We walked for a waking under the light of the treelanterns, slashing down whatever birds and bats and fruit we could get as we went along, and finally stopped to rest at the big lump of rock called Lava Blob. Old Roger handed us out a gritty little seedcake each, made of ground-up starflower seeds, so we could have something in our bellies, and then we settled down with our backs against the rock, so we didn't have to worry about leopards sneaking up behind us. There were lots of yellowlantern trees round there, which we didn't get so much back in Family, and also yellow animals called hoppers that came bouncing out of forest on their back legs and wrung their four hands together while they looked at us with their big flat eyes and went *Peep peep peep*. But hoppers were no good to eat and their skins were no use either, so we just chucked stones at them to make them go away and let us sleep in peace.

When we woke up, Starry Swirl was *still* bright bright in sky. We ate a bit of dry cake and off we went again, under redlanterns and whitelanterns and spiketrees, with flutterbyes darting and glittering all round us and bats chasing the flutterbyes and trees going *hmmph, hmmph, hmmph* like always, until it all blurred together into that *hmmmmmmmmmmm* that was the background of our lives.

After a few miles we came to a small pool full of shiny wavyweed and all us newhairs took off our wraps and dived into the warm water for crabfish and oysters to eat. All the boys watched Tina Spiketree diving in, and they all thought how graceful she was with her long legs, and how smooth her skin was, and how much they wanted to slip with her. But when she came up she swam straight to me, and gave me a dying oyster with the bright pink light still shining out of it.

'You know what they say about oysters, don't you, John?' she said.

Tom's neck, she was *pretty* pretty, the prettiest in whole of Family. And she knew it *well* well.

In another couple of hours we reached the place where Peckham Hills began to rise up out of forest of Circle Valley, and started to climb up through them by Monkey Path, which isn't really a path, but just a way we know through the trees. The trees carried on up the slopes – redlanterns and whitelanterns and scalding hot spiketrees – and there were flickering starflowers growing beneath them, just like in the rest of forest. Streams ran through them down from darkness and ice, heading towards Greatpool, still cold cold but already bright and glittering with life. And small creatures called monkeys jumped from tree to tree. They had little thin bodies, and six long arms with a hand on the end of each. Handsome Fox shot one with an arrow, and was pleased pleased with himself, even though they were all bones and sinews and only give a mouthful of meat, because they move fast and are hard to aim at with those big blotches on their skin that flash on and off as they swing among the lanternflowers.

As we climbed up it got colder. The starflowers disappeared, the trees became smaller, and there weren't any monkeys any more, only the occasional smallbuck darting away through the trees. And then the trees stopped and we came out from the top edge of forest onto bare ground. Pretty soon, when we'd climbed above the height of those last few little trees, we could see whole of Circle Valley spread out below us – whole of Eden that we knew, with thousands and thousands of lanterns shining all the way from where we stood on Peckham Hills to Dark shadow of Blue Mountains away in the distance, and from Rockies over the left, with the red glow of Mount Snellins smouldering in middle, to the deep darkness over to our right that was Alps. And above all of it the huge spiral of Starry Swirl was still shining down.

Of course, with no trees to give off light with their lanternflowers or to warm the air with their trunks, it was dark dark up there – you could only just barely make things out in the starlight and the light from the edge of forest – and it was *cold* cold, specially on our feet. But us newhairs dared each other to run up as far as the snow. The ice felt like it was burning, it was so cold, and most kids took ten twenty steps, yelled and came running down again. But I took Gerry right up to the ridge of the hill and then, ignoring Old Roger yelling at us to come back, went far enough down the other side so that the others couldn't see us.

'We've made our point now, haven't we, John?' Gerry said, shivering. We only had waistwraps on, and buckskins round our shoulders, and our feet were hurting like they'd been skinned. 'Shall we go back down to rest of them now?'

My cousin Gerry was about a wombtime younger than me – his dad was giving his mum a slip, in other words, about the time that I was born – and he was devoted to me, he thought I was wonderful, he'd do just about anything I asked.

'No, wait a minute. Wait a minute. Be quiet and listen.'

'Listen to what?'

'To the silence, you idiot.'

There was no *hmmmmmmmm* of forest, no *hmmph, hmmph, hmmph* of pumping trees, no starbirds going *hoom, hoom, hoom* in the distance, no flutterbyes flapping and flicking, no *whoosh* of diving bats. There was no sound at all except a quiet little tinkle of water all around us coming out from under the snow in hundreds of little streams. And it was *dark* dark. No tree-light up there. The only light came from Starry Swirl.

We could barely make out each other's faces. It made me think about that place called Earth where Tommy and Angela first came from, way back in the beginning with the Three Companions, and where one waking we would all return, if only we stayed in the right place and were good good good. There were no lanterntrees back there on Earth, no glittery flutterbyes or shiny flowers, but they had a big big light that we don't have at all. It came from a giant star. And it was so bright that it would burn out your eyes if you stared at it.

'When people talk about Earth,' I said to Gerry, 'they always talk about that huge bright star, don't they, and all the lovely light it must have given? But Earth turned round and round, didn't it, and half the time it wasn't facing the star at all but was dark dark, without lanterns or anything, only the light the Earth people made for themselves.'

'What are you *talking* about, John?' Gerry said, with his teeth chattering. 'And why can't we go back down again if you just want to talk?'

'I was thinking about that darkness. They called it Night, didn't they? I'm just thinking that it must have been like this. What you get up here on Snowy Dark: it's what they would have called Night.'

'Hey John!' Old Roger was calling from the far side of the ridge. 'Hey Gerry!' He was scared we'd freeze to death or get lost or something up there.

'Better go back,' Gerry said.

'Let him stew a minute first.'

'But I'm freezing *freezing*, John.'

'Just one minute.'

'Okay, one minute,' said Gerry, 'but that's it.'

He actually counted it out on his pulse, one to sixty, the silly boy, and then he jumped up and we both climbed back over the ridge. Gerry went running straight down to the others, but I stood up there for a moment, partly to show I was my own man and didn't go scurrying back for Old Roger or anyone, and partly to take in how things looked from up there on top of the ridge: the shining forest, with darkness all around it, and above everything the bright bright stars. That's our home down there, I thought, that's our whole world. It felt weird to be looking in on it from outside. And though in one way the bright forest stretching away down there seemed big big, in another way it seemed small small, that little shining place with the stars above it and darkness looking down on it from the mountains all around.

Back with the others, Gerry made a big thing about his freezing feet, asking some people to feel them and rub them, begging others to let him ride on their backs until he had warmed up, and generally hopping and skipping around like an idiot. That was how Gerry dealt with people. 'I'm just a fool, I won't hurt anyone,' that was his message. But I wasn't like that. 'I'm not a fool by any means,' was *my* message, 'and don't assume I won't hurt you either.' I acted as if I didn't feel the cold in my feet at all, and pretty soon they were so numb anyway that I really didn't. I noticed Tina watching me and smiling, and I smiled back.

On we went, just below the snow and along the top edge of forest, where there was a bit of light from the trees, Old Roger grumbling and moaning about how newhairs had no respect any more and things were different from how they used to be.

'Old fool was scared he'd have to go back to Family and tell your mums he'd lost you,' said Tina. 'He was thinking of the trouble he'd be in. No more slippy for Old Roger.'

'Like he gets it anyway,' said dark-eyed Fox, who my mum had told me once with a shrug was like as not my father. (But then another time she said it could have been Old Roger – he wasn't quite such a fool once apparently – or maybe a pretty little newhair boy from London she once slipped with. I wished I knew, but lots of people didn't know for sure who their dad was.)

We came to Cold Path, which ran down beside a stream that carried meltwater from a big snowslug. Woollybucks made this path, and we crept up to it in case there were some on it now. There weren't, but there were lots of fresh buck tracks coming down off the snow and onto the muddy ground beside the stream as it headed down to forest below. The bucks had come down already. The dip had brought them down from wherever it was up there they normally lived, and from whatever it was that they normally did up there.

'I saw a big big bunch of them in this exact spot once,' said Roger. 'Coming down the path from the snowslug there. About ten fifteen wombs ago. There were ten twelve of them, plodding down in single file from up on Snowy Dark there and . . .'

I stopped listening then. I looked up into the blackness of Snowy Dark as he talked, and wondered. No one knew anything about that place up there except that it was high high and dark dark and cold cold *cold*, and that it was the source of all the streams and the great snowslugs ('glay seers', as Oldest called them), and that it surrounded our whole world.

But then I noticed a light high up there in sky: a little far-off patch of pale white light hovering up there in darkness.

'Hey look! Up there!'

Normally when you see something that you don't know what it is, it only takes a second or two before you *do* know, or at least can have a good guess. But this I couldn't make out at all. I really had no idea what it could possibly be. I mean, there's one source of light in sky: Starry Swirl. And there's another source on the ground: living things, trees and plants and animals, plus the fires we make ourselves. But the only light I'd ever seen in between these two sources was from volcanoes like Mount Snellins, and they were red red like fire, not pale and white.

It sounds dumb but all I could think of for a moment was that it was a Landing Veekle, one of those sky-boats with lights on them that brought Tommy and Angela and the Three Companions down to Eden from the starship *Defiant*.

Well, we were always taught that it would happen sometime. The Three Companions had gone back to Earth for help. Something must have gone wrong, we knew, or the Earth people would have come long ago, but they had a thing with them called a Rayed Yo that could shout across sky, and another thing called a Computer that could remember things for itself. A waking would come when they'd find *Defiant*, or hear the Rayed Yo, and build a new starship and come for us, across Starry Swirl, through Hole-in-Sky, to take us back to the bright light of that giant giant star.

And for one sweet scary moment I thought it was finally happening now.

Then Roger spoke.

'Yeah,' he said. 'That's them. That's woollybucks alright.'

Woollybucks?

Well, of course that's all it was! It was obvious now. That pale light wasn't really in sky at all, it was up in the mountains, up on Snowy Dark, and it was just woollybucks. Michael's names, I was glad I hadn't said anything out loud. Woollybucks were the one thing we were supposed to be looking for, and I'd mistaken them for sky people from bloody Earth!

I felt a fool, but beyond that I felt *sad* sad, because for a few seconds I'd really thought that the time had finally come when we would find our way back to that place full of light and people, where they knew the answers to all the hard hard questions we had no idea how to solve, and could see things we can't see any more than blind people . . .

But no, of course not. Nothing had changed. All we still had was Eden and each other, five hundred of us in whole world, huddled up with our blackglass spears and our log boats and our bark shelters.

It was disappointing. It was sad sad. But it was *still* amazing just to think the mountains up there were so high. I mean, you could see their shadows against the stars from back in Family, and you could see they must be big big, but you couldn't see the mountains themselves, only the lower slopes where there were still trees and light, and you couldn't really tell which were the mountains and which were the clouds above them. I'd only ever been to the lower hills before and I'd imagined that Snowy Dark behind them was maybe two three times higher than that ridge of hills that Gerry and I had run up to the top of. But I could tell now that it was ten twelve times that high.

And right up there – so high up, so far away, in a place so different from where we were now that it was more like looking into a dream than at a real place in the world – a row of woollybucks were moving in single file across the slope, and the soft white lanterns on the tops of their heads were lighting up the snow around them. Just for a moment as the bucks went past, the snow shone white, and then it became grey, and then it went back into blackness again. And though woollybucks are big beasts, two three times the weight of a man, they looked so tiny and alone up there in their tiny little pool of light that they might as well have been little ants. They might as well have been those little flylets that live behind the ears of bats.

And in the back of my mind a little thought came to me that there *were* other worlds we could reach that weren't hidden away in Starry Swirl, or through Hole-in-Sky, but here on ground, in Eden. They were the places where the woollybucks went, the places they came from.

'There were about twelve thirteen bucks that time I was telling you about,' Old Roger said. 'They came down here and we did for four of them before the rest ran away back up the hill where we couldn't follow. You know old Jeffo London, the bloke with one leg that makes the boats? Well, he had two legs back then and he got a bit overexcited and went after the other seven eight bucks. He got lost up there in Dark. We waited as long as we could, but pretty soon we were freezing too, so we went down the path a bit and waited there for him. No one thought he'd make it back but, just before we were about to head back to Family with the bucks, he bloody did! He came stumbling down the path with these kind of white burns on his toes and his leg. It turned to black after a while – a black burn, though they call it gang *green* for some reason – and that's why he's only got one leg. We had to cut off the other one, saw it off with a blackglass knife. Harry's dick! You should have heard him yell. But the rest of us, well, we were pretty happy to be going back with all that buckmeat. And we were popular when we got back, I can tell you. We were happy. Slippy all round, I reckon. I know I . . .'

'Yeah alright, Roger,' David interrupted. He didn't like it when people laughed and joked about having a slip. 'Alright Roger, that's interesting I'm sure, but *that* lot's not coming down, are they?'

Old Roger peered up at Snowy Dark and pretended to look. He was at that age when folk start going blind: eighty wombtimes old or thereabouts. He didn't want us to know how bad it had got in case we decided he shouldn't be the head huntsman for our group any more – which he really *shouldn't* have been – so no way was he going to let on that all he could really see was a blur. 'No, I suppose,' he said, 'it's . . . um . . . always hard to tell with woollybucks.'

This is nuts, I thought, letting this old man lead us. Food was getting scarcer in our group and Family in general. Not *really* scarce, but we all went a bit hungry some wakings. And yet who did we send out to lead a woollybuck hunt for our group? This blind old fool!

'They're headed away from us,' David said coldly. 'So we'd better get down again and try and get the ones that came down earlier.'

'How do you know that lot up there aren't the same ones that came down?' asked Met. He was a big tall boy who wasn't all that bright, and didn't often speak. 'Maybe they've been down already and now they're going up again?'

'Look at the tracks, Met,' said David, poking Met hard in the arm. 'Look at the bloody tracks. They're all going downhill, aren't they? There's none coming up. Look at the way the toes are pointed, Einstein. So that means a bunch of them are still down there, doesn't it? And I'd say they'll stay down there too while Starry Swirl is still out.'

'Couldn't we wait here until they come back up again?' asked Met.

It was a stupid suggestion. All the wraps we had to cover ourselves with were our bitswraps round the middle and a buckskin round the shoulders, and our feet were bare and cold.

'Oh clever,' said David, and he looked at Met with his smile that wasn't really a smile, wind whistling in and out of his ugly hole of a face, with that other bit of mouth that went up where a nose should be and always seemed red and sore. 'Stay up by all means, Met, but I don't think I fancy a dose of gang green myself.'

He was always a sarcastic bastard. But that, and hitting people, was about the nearest he got to being friendly.

'Anyone want to freeze up here with Met, go ahead,' David said. 'Otherwise let's get down out of the cold to where the woollybucks actually are, eh?'

It was cold cold. Even if you put your back against a tree trunk it was cold, because they were only stumpy little trees up there and they didn't give out heat like a big redlantern or whitelantern does down in the valley. But then again, I thought to myself, Met's idea wasn't *so* dumb. If we could only find a way of staying up there for a bit longer we could spear *loads* loads more bucks, because they always did come up and down these paths down from Dark around dips. So why didn't we think about ways of keeping warm up there? Why didn't we bring some more wraps with us, or make wraps that we could tie up round us? Why hadn't we found a way of putting wraps round our feet? Why had we decided that it was too bloody cold and difficult up by Dark to even *try* and work out a way round it?

But that was how it was. We walked down beside the stream again and pretty soon tall trees were all around us again, there were lanterns wherever we looked, white and red and blue, and that little crack in the hills had widened out into Cold Path Valley. It was a small place: in an hour you could walk right across it to the narrow little gap in the hills that led back into Circle Valley where we lived.

'I wonder where the woollybucks go,' I said. 'I wonder if there's another forest they go to beyond the hills.'

'Another forest?' snorted Fox. 'Don't be daft, John. There *couldn't* be anywhere else as big as Circle Valley.'

'That's wrong! When Tommy and Angela and the Three Companions first saw Eden, they saw lights all over . . .'

'Beyond the hills the Shadow People live,' Lucy Lu interrupted me in a loud slow dreamy voice.

She was a woman with a round pale face and watery eyes who used to go round the other groups in Family and offer to talk to the shadows of their dead in exchange for bits of blackglass and old skins and scraps of food.

'That's crap,' said Tina. 'There's no such thing as Shadow People.'

I agreed with her. I'd got no time for things that people saw out of the corner of their eye, or in dreams. Harry's dick, there were enough real things to look at face on! There were enough things you could put your hands on and hold.

'You wouldn't say that if you saw them like I do,' said Lucy Lu in that dreamy voice, like she was only half in our world and half in a shadow world which only she could see.

'Some people reckon sky is a huge flat stone,' Gerry broke in suddenly, 'and Starry Swirl is rocklanterns growing underneath it, like you get in caves. This big flat stone, it sits up there with its edges on the top of Snowy Dark. Dark is really there to hold it up.'

'That is *really* crap,' said Tina with her throaty laugh. 'Boy, that *really* is. And no one else even says it either apart from you, Gerry. You made it up just now. Trying to be different like your hero John.'

'No I didn't!' Gerry laughed.

He was happy to have headed off an argument between me and Lucy Lu and Fox.

'Of course you did,' Tina told him. 'It's the most half-arsed thing I ever heard.'

'Yes, and make sure you don't say that sort of thing in front of Oldest either,' said Old Roger. 'They wouldn't like it. How could Tommy and Gela have come down from Starry Swirl with the Three Companions if it was just rocklanterns on a stone?'

'So Gerry can't have his own ideas?' I said. 'But Oldest can make up any fairy story they like and then force us all to accept that it's true?'

'You watch it, John,' said David. 'You bloody watch what you say.'

'Newhairs!' complained Old Roger. 'When I was young we showed respect to our Oldest. We'd never say the True Story was made-up.'

I didn't really think it *was* made up. I didn't doubt that Tommy and Angela and the Three Companions had come down from sky. We had the Mementoes after all, we had the Earth Models, we had old writing and pictures scratched on trees. We had all kinds of reasons for believing it was true. I just didn't like the way that some people were allowed to take that old story and keep it for themselves and make it say what they wanted it to say.

~ ~ ~

Pretty soon Old Roger divided us up into pairs and had us spread out across Cold Path Valley, looking for woollybucks. I was in a pair with Gerry. We were sent to the narrow gap called Neck, which went through into Circle Valley proper.

'Right up to Neck, mind,' Old Roger said, 'but not beyond. That way you should spot any bucks that try and run that way from the rest of us.'

We walked over to Neck, and squatted down with our spears to wait for bucks. There was a place above us that I'd visited once twice on the spur of hill that formed the right hand side of Neck as you looked back towards Family, and I pointed it out to Gerry.

'There are five six good dry caves up there,' I told him, 'with a bit of open ground in front of them so you could sit there and look out over forest. And a bit below them there's a pool, ten twelve foot across, warm warm from spiketree roots.'

Gerry glanced up where I was pointing and shrugged.

'It would be a good place for Family to live,' I told him. 'Much better than where we live now. It's got everything you need: a pool, caves. It's handy for woollybucks. Blackglass too, I dare say, if you looked hard enough.'

Gerry laughed.

'You say *weird* weird things sometimes, John. What do you mean *a good place for Family*? Family *is* a place!'

'It's a place, *and* it's a bunch of people,' I said. 'The people could move, couldn't they? Or some of them. The people and the place don't have to be the same thing. Family could move and this would be just the place to move to.'

'But we've got to stay by Circle!' Gerry protested. 'Otherwise Earth won't be able to find us when they come back for us! Come on, John, you . . .'

Then he broke off, and laughed like he'd realized I was joking, but I'd fooled him just for a moment.

I wasn't sure myself if it was a joke or not.

'Let's go out into the big forest,' I said.

Gerry shrugged. He'd do whatever I wanted. He was one of those that need other people to tell him what to do and what to be.

'We were supposed to stay in Cold Path Valley,' he pointed out.

'Yes, but we'll just go a little way.'

~ ~ ~

It was pretty soon after we went through Neck and into Circle Valley forest that we met the leopard.

We were in one of those openings you get in whitelantern forest, where an old group of trees has died and crumbled and no new ones have come up yet from Underworld. All around us were whitelanterns and spiketrees with flowers shining white and blue, with flutterbyes feeding on the lanterns, and starflowers growing beneath the trees. But right here, in this open space, there were only little tiny starflowers growing close to the ground, and Starry Swirl was plain to see high above us, with no branches and lanterns in the way.

I was just kneeling down to get a drink from a stream when I saw it.

'Look Gerry, there!' I whispered, scrambling back up to my feet.

'What?'

A group of starflowers among the trees shone out for a moment and then faded again. And then the same thing happened among another lot of trees over to the left of the first lot, flowers appearing and fading. And then the same again, a bit further on.

'Gela's tits!' Gerry says. 'Quick! Get up a tree!'

I didn't move. Another lot of flowers appeared and disappeared. Meanwhile Starry Swirl shone down and flutterbyes fluttered and sparkled, and the trees went *hmmph, hmmph, hmmph,* and forest went *hmmmmmmmm,* like always.

More flowers lit up and disappeared, and this time we could see the dark shadow of the leopard itself, almost invisible behind those shiny, shimmery starflowers on its skin that slide back towards its tail as it goes forward, so they seem to stay in one place. It was circling round us, like leopards do, circling round and round: pure silent darkness, slipping behind the bright flowers that rippled across its skin.

'We could make it to that whitelantern just there,' Gerry whispered. 'It couldn't run that fast.'

Both of us were watching that dark shadow moving through the trees, each of us slowly turning round and round so as to always be facing it. (We must have looked weird, standing there side by side and turning round together.) I glanced quickly at the tree Gerry was talking about and I saw he was right. We could easily make it, just so long as we didn't trip up on something while we ran. Of course the leopard would stop circling as soon as it saw us make a move. It would stop circling and attack, but if we chose our moment right we could be over at the tree and pulling ourselves up into the safety of its branches before it reached us. And then all we'd have to do is yell and wait and pretty soon Old Roger and David and Fox and all the rest would arrive hollering with their spears and bows and arrows, and the leopard would disappear back into forest. Grownups would tell us off for not staying in Cold Path Valley but we'd have a good story to tell, so they wouldn't really mind, specially if we spiced it up a little bit: the leopard's jaws snapping at our feet as we swung up into the branches, its cold eyes peering up at us . . . all that stuff that people always put in to make things seem more exciting than they really were.

But then again, I thought, a story like that might be fine and good but it wouldn't reflect on *us* specially, would it? People would enjoy the story for a waking or two but it wouldn't make them think better of Gerry and me. We'd only have done what anyone would have done: spot a leopard, look for a tree, run.

'You run if you want,' I whispered – both of us were still slowly turning and turning round on the spot so as to be facing that dark dark creature circling round us –'you run.'

'What? You . . .'

But Gerry was too scared to stand and argue and so he ran, belting as fast as he could go across the clear space to the tree.

Well, I saw the leopard stop. I saw it turn. I saw its eyes flicker as it steadied itself to sprint towards him.

'Here,' I yelled.'Over here!'

It turned its head back to look at me. Gerry scrambled into the lower branches of the tree and began to climb up to the top. The leopard crept slowly forwards in my direction and then stopped and watched me. Now that the beast was still, the spots down its sides stopped moving backwards and just flickered where they were like real starflowers do. Beneath them its skin was black *black*. Not black like black hair, not black like the feathers on a starbird, not black like a charred bit of wood. None of those are *really* black. But a leopard's skin has no fur or hair or feathers or scales. It doesn't catch the light. It doesn't have contours. It doesn't have different shades in it. It's black black like sky behind Starry Swirl. It's black black like a hole that goes right through to the bottom of everything, like Hole-in-Sky.

I felt like crying, I felt like yelling out that I'd made a mistake and I wanted the game to stop. I wished I'd just run like Gerry had done, like every other kid would have done, and every grownup too, unless they were in a whole gang of hunters and they had strong spears with proper blackglass heads. All I had was a kid's buck-hunting spear, with a shaft made from a redlantern sucker and a lousy spike off a spiketree shoved onto the end of it and glued there with boiled-down sap.

But there was no point in crying or yelling. There wasn't even any point in being scared. It wasn't as if I could tell the leopard I wanted to give up and not play any more, was it, like a kid playing hide and seek? It wasn't as if the leopard was going to say 'Fair enough then, mate, game over'. I'd made my choice and now I was stuck with it.

So I got myself in a good position and I readied my spear and I watched the leopard, waiting for its move. And I stopped having feelings. There was no point in feelings just then, so I made up my mind not to feel anything at all. I was quite good at that.

'Help!' Gerry began to holler from the treetop. 'Gela's sake, come and help us! It's a bloody leopard here! It's a big big leopard and it's going to eat John!'

'Shut up, Gerry, you idiot,' I hissed. 'You break my concentration and I bloody *will* get eaten.'

The leopard watched me. A leopard's eyes are round and flat and big as the palm of your hand, and they don't move in the leopard's head like our eyes do. They don't turn from side to side. But when you're up as close as I was, you can see that inside the eye there *are* things moving, little glints that shift and glitter. And it's like you're looking into the thoughts in its black head, like you can actually see them. You can see them, but you can't understand them. You can only see they're there.

The leopard began to sing.

Looking straight at my eyes with those blank glittery discs, it opened its mouth and out came that sweet sad slow song that leopards sing, in that sweet sad voice that they have, that voice that sounded just like a woman's. Everyone had heard it of course: that lonely *ooooo-eeeee-aaaaa* from far out in forest that sounded so human that you just couldn't help thinking it *was* human in some way. Everyone had woken up in middle of a sleep and heard it out there. And everyone had thought to themselves, Gela's heart, I am glad *glad* I'm here in Family with people all around me. And then they'd listened out for the friendly familiar sounds of other groups in Family with different wakings: folk cooking meat and scraping skins, folk building shelters with branches and bark, folk hacking at trees with their stone axes, folk chatting and laughing and arguing and shouting things to one another.

And that sweet sound of other people awake and busy, that gentle sound, it made the leopard off in forest seem far away, like another whole world, much too far away to think or worry about. It was just an animal after all, just an animal out there beyond the fence, hunting its prey in its own funny way, no different from a bat really, or a tree fox, or a tubeslinker. And so they sighed and rolled over, and got themselves comfortable among their sleeping skins and got themselves cosy and ready to go back to sleep. And it was almost *cosier* for them now than it was before, hearing that lonely leopard out there when they were safe and warm inside the fence, just like it was cosy cosy hearing rain on the bark roof of your shelter when you were dry and warm inside.

But for me all this *wasn't* happening out there beyond a fence. The leopard was here and I was here too. And it was singing not to some stonebuck or hopper it had cornered, but to me. It was singing me a lullaby, singing a lament for long ago, singing a song of love, a slowly fading song, slowly fading away, sinking back, peacefully fading back and back into the distance, fading and fading and fading until it was far away, not here at all any more, but lost and forgotten . . .

And suddenly the beast was coming right at me, hurtling across the few yards of space that lay between us, its jaws open wide wide, its eyes glinting, its head down ready to kill, while its peaceful song lagged and faded behind it, just like its spots. I pulled myself out of the dream. I lifted my spear. I waited for my moment, knowing that I'd only get one shot at this, only one chance to get it right. I lifted my spear, and I readied it, and I told myself to hold steady and wait. Not yet . . . Not yet . . . Not yet . . .

Now!

Michael's names, that next moment felt good! I got it just right. I shoved my spear into that leopard's mouth and it went right down its big hot throat.

Wham – the butt end of the spear caught me in the chest and sent me flying. *Splat* – a great big gout of the leopard's greeny-black blood came spurting out all over me. That big black beast crashed to the ground and began to thresh about, bubbling and gurgling and clawing at the horrible hard thing stuck in its throat that was stopping it from breathing. Quickly I rolled away from its flailing feet. *Aaaargh-aaargh-aaargh*, went the leopard, trying to knock away the spear, *aaaargh-aaargh-aaargh*. It was drowning. It was drowning in its own blood. Pretty soon it stopped making that noise and just gurgled and twitched a bit. And then it was still.

'Tom's dick, John, you've bloody killed it!'

Gerry had jumped down from the tree and was running towards me.

I scrambled to my feet. My head had gone all weird and I didn't know what to do or think or say.

'Lucy Lu reckons leopards are dead women,' was what I came out with, talking in a funny bright voice. 'You know, Shadow People. She says that's why their voices sound like that and their songs are so sad sad. Of course it's crap, like everything she says. I mean . . .'

'What are you on about, John, you bloody idiot? You did for it, look! All by yourself! Tom's neck, you did for it *all by yourself*.'

I was shaking all over. I couldn't have been shaking any more, I reckon, if I'd just spent an hour wandering around naked on Snowy Dark.

'I'll tell you a funny thing,' I said, 'when we saw those woollybucks up there on the snow, I thought for a moment they were a Landing Veekle from Earth. Hah! That was pretty dumb of me, wasn't it?'

Gerry laughed.

'Tom's dick, John! You just killed a *leopard*!'

'But I suppose one waking someone *will* come, won't they? They say the starship was damaged when Angela and Michael chased after it in their Police Veekle and tried to stop it. They say it leaked. But even if the starship broke on the way back, and even if the Three Companions died, the people on Earth would find it sooner or later, wouldn't they? I mean it had a Computer, didn't it, and a Rayed Yo? Okay it's two hundred wombtimes ago now that they left Eden. But think how long it must take to build a new starship. I mean it takes old Jeffo half a wombtime just to build one lousy log boat to fish with out on Greatpool.'

Gerry took my shoulders and shook me.

'Gela's tits, John, will you *stop* talking about bloody sky-boats! You've killed a leopard! All by yourself! With a kid's spear!'

It was weird weird. The leopard was still twitching in front of me, I was covered with its black blood, and I was shaking shaking all over. But tears came into my eyes as I thought about the Three Companions, who left Tommy and Angela on Eden to try and get back to Earth: Dixon, who had the idea to steal the starship, and Mehmet, who Angela liked best because he was kind, and gentle Michael, who named the animals and plants. I wished I knew just what happened to them when they set off back across sky to Earth in their leaky sky-boat.

And I wished we knew how long it would be before someone came for us from Earth.

2

Tina Spiketree

John was *interesting*. I mean he looked nice, and I fancied him in that way, but what fascinated me most was the way he behaved. All that hunting trip he was trying to be different, trying not to be the same as all the other newhair guys. He went right up that icy ridge. He annoyed Old Roger and David by questioning the True Story. He stayed still and quiet while Gerry was trying to get laughs with his cold feet. Yes, and I'd given him that oyster, and he'd been pleased, but he didn't make a *thing* out of it like others boys would. He didn't make a big thing about how he and I were going to have a slip. And now, while the rest of us were hunting bucks, he'd done for a leopard all by himself, which no one *ever* did, not unless they were cornered and had no choice. And his cousin Gerry was telling everyone that John *did* have a choice. He had plenty of time to run up a tree, but he'd decided to stay on the ground and try his luck.

So why had he done it? I could just about imagine some silly boy doing a thing like that for a dare, or doing it because his friends said he was a wimp, but John wouldn't go for a dare, and no one thought he was a wimp. He'd done it for some other reason. I hadn't figured out what it was, but I could see that John was like a good chess player: he didn't just do what seemed right at one moment, he thought ahead. He thought about where he was trying to get to, four five moves on.

Well, I was a bit like that too. I knew when to bide my time. So I didn't ask John why he did for the leopard, however much I wanted to know, and I didn't make a big fuss of him like most of the others did, and for most of the walk I fell behind him, leaving him to talk to the ones who wanted to go over the story of the leopard, over and over and over again. But I smiled to myself as we walked back to Lava Blob and then to Family, because I was looking forward to figuring him out.

~ ~ ~

Family was in eight groups, all bunched up together among the big old rocks that stuck up out of the ground between Greatpool and Longpool and up towards Deep Pool. Each group had its own space with bark shelters and a fireplace where embers were always set glowing. (It could take half a waking to get a new fire going with twigs or blackglass sparks, so no one liked to let a fire go out.) The outer edge of Family was formed by the pools or by rocks, or, when there wasn't any natural sort of barrier, by fences made by piling up branches and rocks to keep out leopards and other big animals. First group inside the fence on Peckhamside was Batwing, so that's the bit of the fence we came to first.

Old Roger Redlantern and big dumb Met dragged away the branches that made the Batwing gateway.

'Leopard kill!' Old Roger hollered out. 'Jade's boy killed a bloody leopard!'

'John did for it,' yelled Gerry excitedly, 'my cousin John!'

Lately the grownups in most of the groups had decided we needed more food-trees in Family to help with our problem of not enough to eat. They'd decided we'd have to get rid of trees whose fruits were no good as food, like redlanterns. And when we'd set out six wakings before, Batwing had been busy chopping down a big redlantern tree, and they'd been at it all the time we'd been away, hacking away at that tree with stone axes for four wakings. They'd finally managed to pull it down with ropes maybe two three hours before we got there, and when we came in through the fence, there was the big tree lying on the ground with bits of broken axes strewn around it. (Someone would need to go over to Blue Hills soon for more blackglass.) The ground was still warm and sticky with sap.

Some little kid had got himself in the wrong place when the hot hot sap sprayed out. He'd been badly burnt. *Burnt* burnt. If he lived he'd have the scars forever. And now he was yelling and yelling in a shelter, and his mum sobbing by his side. Everything was spoiled for him and her, everything wrecked, by one stupid moment. But the rest of Batwing were pleased pleased with their work. They were walking round that great big fallen thing, and whacking at it with sticks and talking about what a bugger it'd been to get down, and how much bark they'd get off it, and how much wood. And the kids were looking forward to eating the stumpcandy. And everyone was trying not to notice the screaming kid in the shelter.

'Boy killed a leopard!' Old Roger boomed out again. 'Young newhair. Jade's boy John.'

John and Gerry were carrying the dead thing tied onto two branches. I was walking behind them, with ugly old David and handsome shallow Fox. Four others were carrying the big woollybuck that four of us had cornered and done for about the same time as John got the leopard. A lot of eating that buck was going to give, and a lot of skin and bones too to make wraps and tools with, and normally everyone would have been impressed, but now all they were interested in was the leopard. They came running over to touch that weird black skin that was so smooth smooth that it was almost like touching nothing at all. They wanted to look into its dead dead eyes. They wanted to feel the ridges down its sides where the starflower spots had glittered and flowed when it was alive.

'Look at the big black teeth on it,' the Batwings said, reaching out to touch.

'Careful with them,' said Old Roger, though a leopard's teeth aren't exactly fragile. 'They belong to Redlantern, don't forget. We don't want good knives damaged.'

'I saw him kill it,' Gerry kept saying over and over. 'I was up in a tree and I saw it! John could have climbed a tree too but no, that's not my cousin John. He faced it all by himself with an ordinary kid's buck-spear. Imagine that! Just an ordinary spear with a spiketree tip.'

And Gerry looked around at the impressed Batwings, and the people from other groups who'd started to appear: Fishcreek, Spiketree, Brooklyn. He was thrilled, because no one had ever been so interested in what he had to say. (He wasn't a boy that was particularly funny or clever or interesting. He didn't really even have opinions of his own. I'd hardly even noticed him until now.)

'*And* he killed it cleanly in one go,' Gerry told them all. 'One single stab.'

'Well, he wouldn't be here to tell about it if he hadn't, would he?' said a Batwing boy about mine and John's age. 'It's not like a leopard's going to stand there and let you have a second go.'

The boy was called Mehmet. He was named, like a lot of people were, for Mehmet Haribey, who was one of the Three Companions. But, though the True Story said that Mehmet Haribey was friendly and kind, Mehmet Batwing didn't look all that friendly. He had a narrow clever face and a little pointy yellow beard, and he was a sarky bugger who liked to find fault with people.

Well, I can be pretty sarky myself when I want to be, and I can deal with sarky people, no trouble, but Gerry didn't know how to handle them at all. I saw him look at Mehmet and frown, but he really couldn't work out what exactly Mehmet was getting at, so he shrugged and carried on.

'A bloody great leopard,' he yelled out again excitedly, turning away from Mehmet. 'John says I can share the hearts. And it's fully grown, not just a little one. It sang at him and everything. Sang like a woman, even when it was running towards him. You should have heard it. You should have heard. Like a lovely gentle woman it was, even when it was running at him with its jaws wide open. Fully grown it is. Have you ever seen such a big one? Biggest one ever, I'd say. John says I can have one of its hearts, because I was there too when the leopard came.'

We passed on through the group and into Redlantern group area, which came before Spiketree. And Redlanterns got out some fruit beer and passed it round in dried whitefruit shells for all us to drink and celebrate the double kill.

'John, you idiot,' said John's mother Jade, with that smile of hers that was supposed to send men crazy. 'Why couldn't you climb a bloody tree like any normal person?'

I looked at her and wondered why men couldn't see the emptiness inside her. It was like she was acting being a person, she was moving her pretty body around to make it seem alive, but inside she was lost lost.

'Jade, Jade,' said her sister Sue, laughing. 'Your only son kills a leopard by himself and *that's* all you can say?'

Sue Redlantern was Gerry's mum and she was a batface, like David, and like my own sister Jane. She was as ugly ugly as John's mum was beautiful, but she was kind and giving and everyone knew it, not only in Redlantern but across whole of our side of Family.

'He's a bloody fool,' said Jade.

I looked at John. His face was still still, but Gerry was upset on his behalf.

'Your son John is *brilliant* brilliant,' he told Jade hotly. 'He's bloody brilliant. How many kids of twenty wombtimes have ever . . . ?'

'You should say *years*,' said Old Roger. 'You should say *fifteen years*, not twenty wombtimes. You know what Oldest say: the world doesn't come from a woman's belly.'

'How many kids of fifteen *years*,' Gerry said, 'have ever done for a leopard on their own?'

'He *is* a brave boy,' said Roger, 'even if he is rude to his elders.'

'He's a bloody *lucky* boy,' said sour David, pursing his ugly batlips that split open right up into where his nose ought to be.

Little kids were crowding round with toy spears cut from whitelantern twigs.

'How did you kill it, John? What was it like?'

There weren't only kids from Redlantern around us now, but from my group Spiketree and from Brooklyn and even from London and Blueside, right across the other side of Family. Grownups had come over too.

'Right down the throat, I hear,' said an old Fishcreek guy called Tom. He was another batface and he had clawfeet too, poor bugger, so he couldn't ever have been a hunter. But he was clever with making things out of wood and stone – spears, saws, axes, knives, boats – and he liked to *talk* about hunting. He liked to show that he knew about it.

'That's the best way, of course,' he said. 'A good clean kill. But it's far from easy.'

'Too damn right,' Gerry said. 'It's hard hard. John only had a . . .'

'It's not that hard,' John interrupted. 'It just *seems* hard because it's dangerous. It's like balancing on a branch at the top of a tree. Really, when you think about it, that's no harder than balancing on a branch near the ground, which anyone can do. The only difference is that you're done for if you don't get it right, and that makes it *seem* harder.'

I smiled. I liked what John had said, and I liked that he didn't say it to pretend to be modest, but because he was annoyed with the smallness of Family that got so excited about a little thing like someone killing one lousy animal. But Gerry looked at him in dismay. Why was John cross that people were making a fuss of him? Why didn't he like it that everyone said he was great? Poor

Gerry, who no one noticed much at all, he just couldn't figure it out.

'John only had a second to get it right,' he repeated. 'Too early or too late and he'd have been done for.'

After they'd cut out its two big hearts, grownups tied wavyweed ropes round the leopard's front legs and hauled it up into the meeting tree in middle of Redlantern group for everyone to see. They'd take its skin off later, and pull out its long black teeth and claws for knives, and then they'd dry its guts for string, and clean its bones for diggers and hooks and knives and spearheads (bone is better than tree spikes, though not as good as blackglass). And of course someone or other would eat its eyes: someone who was getting older and beginning to be scared of darkness coming, because people said a leopard's eyes kept the blindness back, even though they tasted foul. The rest of a leopard's meat was *bitter* bitter, enough to make you sick, so when Redlantern had taken the bones and skin and guts and everything else useful off that leopard, they'd have to take the meat itself back out of Family again and dump it a good distance off for the tree foxes and starbirds to eat up.

As to the big woollybuck that we'd done for at about the same time John and Gerry met the leopard, well, like I said, any other time people would have been pretty excited about that too. It would be good eating for many wakings, after all. It had a good big skin that would make a lot of wraps, feet you could melt down for a glue that was as good as boiled sap, and teeth you could use for seedgrinders (the best kind, which didn't leave grit in the flour like stone seedgrinders do). Most times we could all have expected a bit of praise for getting it, and a few questions about who had done what in the hunt, but this time no one cared. Redlantern just settled down without any fuss at all to skin it, and cut off the tasty lantern on its head, and slice up its body into the Redlantern group portion and the portion that we Spiketrees would take back for our share. (One leg for us, five for them: that had been the deal.) But, all the time they were stripping down the buck, they were talking talking about the leopard whose useless meat was hanging in the tree above them.

'How did you do it, John?'

'Weren't you scared?'

'What did it feel like?'

'Well done, our John,' said Bella, the Redlantern group leader, who'd just come back from a meeting right over in Starflower. 'Well done, our John. This will do us good at the next AnyVirsry, my hunter boy. This will be to the credit of Redlantern among all the other groups.'

She was a clever woman, wiry and always a little bit weary-looking, who people from right across Family came to with problems and arguments. Lots of people said she was the best group leader in whole Family. She worked away waking after waking, not a bit like our lazy old Liz Spiketree, keeping things going, sorting things out, holding all kinds of boring stuff in her head that most people couldn't be bothered to think about at all.

And John was close close to her, so I'd heard, though I'd heard other, weirder, things as well.

~ ~ ~

Then Lucy Lu spoke up.

'The shadow of John's grandmother was in that leopard,' she told everyone in her sing-song voice, as if there could be no doubt about it at all, if you only could see the world through her special special eyes. 'She wanted him to kill the leopard that she was trapped inside of and release her back to Starry Swirl.'

She never liked it when someone else was getting too much attention. She always wanted to make herself the one who knew best about whatever was going on.

'I thought you said the Shadow People lived on the far side of Snowy Dark,' John muttered.

I don't think Lucy Lu heard him, but it made me laugh, and John glanced round at me and smiled.

'And she's at peace now,' cried Lucy Lu, 'she's at peace. And she won't ever have to ...'

But then a London boy called Mike came running over from Circle Clearing.

'Hey, where's John? Oldest want to see him. Oldest have heard about the leopard.'

Poor John. I could see he wasn't going to get any time to himself for some while yet, so I drank down my drink, and picked up some of the meat to take back to Spiketree.

'Never mind, John,' I told him, before I headed off. 'It'll blow over in one two wakings, and then maybe we'll meet up Deep Pool, yes?'

3

John Redlantern

And so we hauled that bloody old leopard down from the tree again and off we went, virtually all forty-odd of Redlantern group, with more joining in from other groups as we passed through them. People who'd normally be sleeping came out of shelters to look at us. Even people in boats on Long Pool waved as we went past.

'It's my cousin!' Gerry kept calling out. 'Only fifteen years old and he killed a big leopard. I saw him do it.'

He was pleased pleased about the glory I was getting. He was *smiling* smiling and kept looking round at me to check that I was smiling too.

I didn't want to disappoint him, and I did my best to look pleased, but truth was I was getting tired tired of it, and fed up with this silly little world we lived in, where one boy doing for one animal could be the most exciting thing that happened for wakings and wakings. I mean, okay I took a risk, but it wasn't *that* big a risk really, not if you kept your nerve and concentrated on what you had to do. It wasn't such a small target, after all, a leopard's gaping mouth.

You're all of you hiding up in trees like Gerry did, I said in my head to all those friendly smiling people, and that's the trouble with bloody Family. You eat and you drink and you slip and you quarrel and you have a laugh, but you don't really *think* about where you're trying to get to or what you want to become. And when trouble comes, you just scramble up trees and wait for the leopard to go away and then afterwards giggle and prattle on for wakings and wakings about how big and scary it was and how it nearly bit off your toes, and how so-and-so chucked a bit of bark at it and whatshisname called out a rude name. Gela's tits! Just look at you!

And the thing was, the meat was starting to run out in Circle Valley. It was no good just hiding up a tree and giggling. Something was going to have to happen or a waking would come in the end when people in Family would starve. That's assuming that there wasn't another rock fall down by Exit Falls, in which case we might all drown instead.

Never mind drowning or starving from lack of food, though. I was going to starve inside my head long before that, or drown in boredom, if I couldn't make something happen in the world, something different, something more than just *this*.

That's what I was thinking about; but Gerry, who loved me so dearly, he didn't see all this going on inside me at all. He was happy happy. I put on a smile and that was enough for him. It was enough for everyone else too.

Well, nearly everyone. Tina understood, and Jade could have seen I was faking it too, not because I was close to her – I wasn't – but because I was *like* her. I was restless like she was. Restless and empty inside and hungry for something more than just ordinary things.

And there was one other person too that saw what was really going on for me. It was Gerry's little clawfoot brother Jeff, who shared a sleeping shelter with Jeff and me. He was only fourteen fifteen wombtimes old, not even a newhair, a weird little kid with a gentle face and great big eyes, like Gerry's big gentle eyes, but with something completely different going on inside them. He'd been hobbling along after us ever since I got to Redlantern area, and it was only when we reached Circle Clearing and stopped by the edge of it that he finally got close enough to speak to me.

'You're sad, aren't you, John?' he said to me.

I just shrugged, and stood there, and waited to be told when Oldest were ready to see me. And half of bloody Family stood there and waited with me.

~ ~ ~

They were sitting side by side on the edge of Circle Clearing like three empty skin bags: Gela, Mitch and Stoop. Their backs were propped up against a big old whitelantern trunk with several layers of bark and a woollybuck hide wedged in between them and it to stop them getting burnt by its heat. And, like always, women were fussing round them with food and wraps and scoops of water.

Beside Oldest was the hollow log in which they kept the Mementoes, and someone had opened it up for them and taken out the Model Sky-Boats, which Tommy Schneider, the father of all of us, is supposed to have made himself: the big starship *Defiant*, the little Landing Veekle, and the Police Veekle, in which Angela and Michael chased after *Defiant* when Tommy, Dixon and Mehmet tried to take it away from Earth. The three Models now lay at their feet, dark and shiny with the buckfat that had been rubbed into them for generations to stop the old wood from shrinking and cracking.

But Oldest had got bored of the Models, and now they were arguing between themselves, while Caroline Brooklyn, the tall grey woman who was Family Head, squatted beside them and tried to soothe things down.

'Each Any Virsry was supposed to be three hundred and sixty-five days after the last one,' old Mitch was saying.

'I *know* that, you stupid old man,' said old Gela. 'We all know that. But what I'm telling you, if you'd only bloody listen, is that you count the days all wrong.'

'I'm sure we can come to an agreement,' purred Caroline.

'I don't get them wrong, you lazy old woman,' Mitch told Gela. 'You just get behind in your count because your fat heart beats so slow and you sleep too much.'

'Yes, she's behind alright,' said bent old Stoop, 'but you're behind as well, Mitch. You're days and days behind the true time.'

'No I'm not,' said Mitch, 'your heart beats way too fast, and it always has done. And anyway I'm oldest of Oldest, and you should listen to me. I'm a hundred and twenty years old, you know, and I'm closest to the beginning, and that means my wakings are the true days like they had back on Earth.'

'Don't talk rot,' spat fat old Gela, 'you're just a muddled-up old ...'

Caroline laid her hand on Gela's arm.

'Here he is,' Caroline said in that special kind voice that people used with Oldest, half respectful, and half like they were talking to a little kid. 'Here they all are: the boy John Redlantern who did for the leopard and most of Redlantern with him by the look of it, plus a whole lot of other folk besides.'

All three Oldest peered towards us with their blind blind eyes. You don't get much past Old Roger's age without losing your sight, and our Roger was forty fifty wombs younger than any of these three.

'Hello Oldest,' I said.

Caroline gestured to me to approach.

'And the leopard too,' she instructed. 'Bring it forward. My, will you look at that!'

Reluctantly I squatted down in front of the three Oldest. They reached for me with their thin and shaky hands, and I crawled closer as I knew I was supposed to do, and guided their bony old fingers so they could feel my face and my hair and my shoulders, prodding me and pinching me like I was some bloody *thing* and not a person at all.

'John Redlantern, you say?' queried Stoop. 'Who are you, boy? Who was your grandmother?'

'Yes, come on boy, spit it out. Who are you?' complained old Mitch.

'My mother's mother is Star.'

'Never heard of her,' said Gela, who was named for the first Gela – *Angela* – the mother of us all. 'Who was *her* mother?'

'Star's mother was Helen.'

I looked at the Models that were still lying there. *Defiant* is a tube covered in long spikes. The real one was longer than Greatpool, more than a hundred fifty yards, and so wide that the LandingVeekle could hide inside it. When it set out from Earth those long spikes would start to burn with purple fire, until suddenly the Single Force would open up Hole-in-Sky and let *Defiant* fall through from one side of Starry Swirl to the other. It was like jumping across Greatpool without crossing the water in between.

'Helen Redlantern?' Stoop gave a wheezy little laugh. 'That cheeky minx. Gave me a bit of a slip once or twice way back. Gave me a *nice* little slippy slide. She still alive, is she?'

'No, Oldest. Cancer ate her, four five wombs . . . I mean four five *years* ago.'

'Four or five wombtimes is *not* the same as four or five years,' muttered old Mitch, giving me a weak slap across the face. It didn't hurt, but I dare say he intended it to, the vicious old sod. 'And you should count properly in years as befits all true children of the planet Earth. Don't you forget it, young man.'

'Where's this leopard, then?' Stoop demanded, and all three of them withdrew their hands from me and gazed greedily beyond me with their sightless eyes.

'Tell the boy to pay his respects,' they said, as if I couldn't hear them for myself. 'Tell him to pay his respects to Circle while we examine the beast.'

So I walked out by myself into middle of the clearing where Circle of Stones was laid out: thirty-six round white stones, as big as baby's heads, in a circle thirty feet across, marking where the Landing Veekle had rested when it came down to Eden, with five stones in middle of it representing Tommy and Angela, the parents of all of us, and their Three Companions who'd tried to return to Earth. You weren't supposed to go nearer to Circle than a couple of yards. Some people even said that if anyone were to touch the stones or go inside Circle, other than Oldest and Council and those they chose, then that person would surely die before their next sleep. I didn't believe that, but I knew the rules, so I stopped three yards from Circle and, as I was supposed to do, bowed my head slightly slightly towards the five stones in middle.

Those stones were the centre of everything. Everyone knew that we had to remain here in Family, in our groups packed in close around Circle, because this was where the Earth people would head when they came back to find us.

But as I finished paying my respects and turned away again from the stones, a thought came to me.

'If they had crossed sky and found their way right across Starry Swirl,' I said to myself, 'they would surely look a little more widely for us than just this one place.'

And then I felt a bit scared by what I'd just thought, like a little kid might feel if he had wandered too far out into forest and, just for a moment, wasn't sure of the way back.

~ ~ ~

We ate well in Redlantern at the end of that waking, and when I finally lay down in the shelter with Gerry and Jeff, sleep didn't come to me for a long time. The leopard's heart was heavy heavy in my belly and the leopard's life, its echo, kept prowling prowling through my mind, like a blackness slipping by behind the little steady lights of my thoughts, singing its tricksy song. Every couple of minutes it was there in front of me again, about to strike. Every couple of minutes I lunged out at it again with my spear.

4

Mitch London

When that boy John had gone away with his dead leopard, Stoop and Gela went straight off to sleep, the dozy old fools. Those two were more dead than alive. But I felt out of sorts and I couldn't settle. It was that Redlantern boy that had done it. He'd pretended to show us respect because we were Oldest, and because Caroline and the others made sure all our visitors acted polite, but he didn't like us and he made sure sure he showed it, the little slinker.

You'd have thought the young ones would be interested in us. You'd have thought they'd want to know the things that only Oldest had got to tell, but they didn't, the little fools. They didn't want to know anything that came out from our blind old wrinkly heads, even if it was the story of their own Family.

Bloody Redlantern boy. But he wasn't there for me to moan at, so I shouted at the women instead, telling them to take away the starship and the Veekles.

'Leave them lying there, and someone will trip over them and do them damage. I've told you that before.'

'Okay, Mitch dear, we'll put them away,' they went, as if they were talking to a little kid rather than the oldest one in whole Family. 'Gela and Stoop are resting now. Aren't you going to take a nap too?'

'I don't feel like it.'

'What do you want to do then, love? What are we going to do with you?'

'Get out Earth Models for me,' I told them. 'I want to make sure they're being properly looked after. Last time I checked some fool had let water get to them.'

'They're dry now. We got a nice new log, remember? A nice dry log for them. And Jeffo London made a new greased lid to cover up the end.'

'That one-legged fool. He probably broke the Models when he was shoving them back in with those clumsy hands of his.'

'Oh dear, Mitch! We *are* out of sorts, aren't we?'

They brought House over and put it into my hands so I could feel its funny square shape and its smooth sticky surface, and the door, and the little holes that Tommy called Wind Ohs. I held it up to my nose to smell the grease and sweat in it, going back to the times before anyone alive was born.

Not that I could smell anything much now. It wasn't just my eyes that had gone. It was all my bloody senses.

'Still all in one piece,' I said, holding it out for them to take it back. 'Don't bloody drop it, mind, like that silly girl did a few years back. Remember that thing was made by Tommy himself before he went blind, and show it some respect. Angela helped him cut the bark and smooth it and glue it together. It's older than me, that House. It was made before I was born.'

'Older than you, Mitch,' they chirruped, just like I was a bloody kid. 'My, that is *old* old.'

'Now give me Plane. Come on, get on with it.'

I felt the long flat wings of Plane and the two hard jets underneath.

'Be careful with those jets,' I told them as I gave Plane back. 'They've been broken off too many times by clumsy people that don't know how to look after old things properly.'

'Don't worry, Mitch dear. We'll be careful careful. Here's Car for you now. Got it safe? Holding tight?'

'Of course I've bloody got it. Michael's names, stop fussing, woman.'

I liked Car best. I'd liked it since I was a little kid, because of the wheels that turned. I liked to hold Car and press the wheels against my hand so I could feel them move. I liked to make it say *brrrm brrrm brrrm*.

'Why don't you tell us the story, Mitch? About what Tommy used to say when he played with Car and the sound he used to make?'

'I'm too old for stupid kids' games.'

'Oh go on, Mitch. You know you like telling us. Show us how Car went along the ground, why don't you? And then maybe you'll be ready for your nap?'

'Oh alright then, if it will stop you nagging. Give me House back.'

I took House from them and put it down in front of me. I put Car in front of House, with its wheels on the ground. I felt the back of Car and pushed it back and forth a little bit to feel that special way it moved so smoothly over the wheels. The wheels are made of bits of bark, which Tommy and Angela rubbed round and smooth against a stone, and glued to the ends of two straight sticks.

'Right . . .' I began, but then I got a tickle in my throat that made my body double up with coughs.

'Right . . .' I began again.

'Mitch,' one of the women said, 'the round bit's . . .'

I didn't take any notice.

'Like I was saying, Tommy himself told me about this Car. He was old and blind, like I am now, and he was sad sad, because Angela was dead and he blamed himself for it, and all his kids blamed him for it too. In the end he did for himself. But he liked talking to us littles sometimes. I suppose we were nicer to him than the grownups. And he told us . . . He told us . . .'

I had to stop and cough again.

'Mitch,' that annoying woman said again. 'I just wanted to . . .'

'Gela's tits, girl, will you *stop* interrupting me!'

That shut her up.

'What Tommy told me,' I went on, 'was that when they want to go somewhere on Earth, they don't walk like we do.'

I stopped to try and remember exactly what Tommy said, and then I remembered something else instead. I remembered I was the first kid in whole Family to have a batface, and the other kids used to tease me, but Tommy was nice about it. He said he had an auntie just like me back on Earth, and I mustn't worry about it. He said it was just a *hare lip*. I thought that was a good word for it, but when I told the other kids, they laughed, and said they didn't know what a 'hare' was, but anyone could see I looked like a bat.

It made me sad sad, thinking about that.

'Back on Earth,' I said after a while, 'they didn't just have bark shelters like we do. Their shelters had sides that went straight up like a cliff, maybe for five six times the height of a man, or more than that even.' I touched the greasy roof of House. 'And there were shelters *inside* the shelters called rooms. And some of the rooms were on top of other rooms, with hard ground in between them called floors. And they had telly vision in the rooms, which let them see moving pictures of things happening far away. And when they wanted to cook meat they didn't even have to light a fire. They had hard boxes made of white metal that were always hot inside because of lecky-trickity, so you could just put the food inside and it would be cooked.

'And if you wanted to go somewhere on Earth, you didn't walk the way we do. Once, in the old old times, Earth people used to go about on the backs of animals called Horses that let people ride them. They were as big as woollybucks, with sharp pointy teeth. But there weren't enough horses, so in Tommy's time, people mostly went in cars like this one. You got inside them, like a shelter, and they ran along by themselves on their wheels, as if they were alive.'

I felt in front of me again for House, and found the door in it. And then I made two of my fingers walk from House to Car, like Tommy had done when I was a little boy.

'One step, two step!' I sang out, like Tommy had done.

I reached for Car.

'Mitch,' that woman said again, 'that round bit . . .'

'Will you *shut up* when I'm telling a story!' I shouted at her.

I was angry angry. As I put my hand on Car, my heart was racing like it was going to burst, but straight away I could feel something was wrong. Car should roll forward smoothly, not rock from side to side.

'What's wrong with it?'

'One of those round bits have come off, Mitch. Those *wield* things. I think you may have pressed down on it too hard when you coughed.'

'What? The wheel's come off?'

'That's right. But don't worry. We can glue it back on again. We'll get some sap boiled up now and glue it on.'

'Why didn't you tell me the wheel had come off? And why didn't you take it out of my way when I coughed?'

Everything breaks doesn't it? Everything bloody breaks.

My heart was pounding pounding so much it hurt, and tears were running down my face.

5

John Redlantern

When I woke up Gerry and Jeff were still both fast asleep, and so were all the rest of group. I chucked off the woollybuck skin I slept under and crawled outside. *Hmmph, hmmph, hmmph,* went the old redlantern tree our shelter leaned against, as it pumped its sap down into hot hot Underworld, and pumped it up again. *Hmmmmmmmmmm,* went forest with all its thousands and thousands of shining trees that stretched all the way from Peckham Hills to Blue Mountains and from Rockies to Alps. No one else was awake in whole group, except for David who was on lookout, and he just grunted and walked off out of the clearing. I went to the food log in middle of our group, near the glowing embers of the fire, took the flat stone off the top of it and felt inside for a handful of dried starflowers and a bone to chew on. *Aaaah! Aaaah!,* went a starbird off in forest.

Over on Blueside, Starflower group were just starting to wake up. Meanwhile London, which was just inside of those two groups, were coming in from forest and getting their dinner on the go. Soon the smoky smell of roasting stonebuck was drifting through whole of Family.

I pulled a scrap of green fat off the woollybuck bone with my teeth and began to chew it. The air was warmer since last waking. The dip was ending. Cloud was coming back over sky like a big dark skin and only a little bit of Starry Swirl could still be clearly seen, way over by Alps. I looked round at our group's little space among our redlantern and whitelantern trees, our circle of twenty little shelters made of bark laid over branches leaning against tree trunks. I looked at the glowing embers that we never let go out, the flutterbyes flipping and flapping around the lanternflowers, and at Old Roger snuffling and snoring on that skin he slept on out in the open because he didn't believe in shelters. There were bones stacked in piles ready to be made into tools, and a little heap of blackglass (which Oldest called *obsijan*), and spears and axes and piles of logs and twigs for the fire. Over to one side was our old group boat that we sometimes used for fishing on Long Pool and Great Pool but we couldn't use just now because the skins had begun to come off from one end of it and needed gluing on again. It all seemed small and boring after what I'd seen by the light of the woollybucks' headlanterns. Whole *Family* seemed small and dreary and dull.

Redlantern grownups had decided I could have a no-work waking as a treat for doing for the leopard. The rest of the newhairs and men would go out foraging as usual but I could have whole waking to do whatever I wanted. What would I do with the time? I wondered as I chewed my breakfast off that bone. I wanted to go straight out into forest again and back to the edge of Dark. Or maybe down towards Exit Falls, that narrow gap between Blue Mountains and Rockies where Main River poured down all the water from all the streams in Circle Valley into whatever lay below. I was sort of interested in looking at it, because it was the only way out of Circle Valley apart from Snowy Dark. People of Old Roger's age could just remember when it had been wider there, so that you could have climbed down from Circle Valley and found out for yourself what was below it. But no one did when they had the chance, and then there was a big rockfall. A great flat slab came sliding down on Rockieside of it, and now tons of water poured down between two sheer cliffs, and it wasn't an exit at all.

But I'd only got one waking, and that wasn't long enough to get to Exit Falls or anywhere else at the edge of the valley. And anyway I was sore sore and bruised in my chest from when the spear butt had hit me, so in the end I just stayed inside Family Fence.

I walked through Spiketree and over to Batwing. Batwing group woke before Redlantern and they were already on the go out there around their newly fallen tree, whacking at branches with blackglass axes. Glittery flutterbyes were flitting and flapping around the opening of the stump.

'Hey John,' called that strange smart boy Mehmet Batwing, with his thin face and his pointy beard, pausing with an axe in his hand. 'Off to do for another leopard, eh?'

'Think I'll take a rest from leopard-killing for one two wakings, Mehmet. Leave a couple of them for the likes of you.'

'Good candy?' I asked a little clawfoot kid that was hanging round there.

He took a stick and banged it on the side of the stump to drive the flutterbyes away. Off they flittered, flashing their glittery wings.

'Have a bit,' he said, pleased to have a chance to give something to the big boy that did for the leopard, 'see for yourself.'

I peered down into the stump. Its pipes had emptied themselves of sap in one last convulsion, and the soft pipeflesh had shrivelled up like it does when the sap has gone, so now there was nothing inside the hollow trunk but air, hot, moist, sickly-sweet air coming up from far below. I could feel the heat of it on my face. I picked up a small stone and dropped it in, putting my ear to the opening to hear it rattling down and down and down into the fiery caves of Underworld, where all life began: all life except our own.

'Don't you want any stumpcandy?' the kid asked, banging the stump again to stop the flutterbyes from settling back down on it.

I looked back in. There were a few crystals of sugar forming inside, already smeared with flutterbye droppings and bat dung with bits of flutterbye wing in it. It wasn't much of a candyfeast, not like you get with an old tree that's fallen of its own accord. But I picked off a couple of crystals, wiped off the batcrap on my waistwrap and stuck them in my mouth to suck.

A wailing started up in one of the shelters. It was that little kid who'd got burnt when the sap spouted up. He'd been quiet for a little while – I supposed a time comes when you're so exhausted that even pain doesn't keep you awake – but now he was off again and I could feel whole Batwing group wincing around me. They were all worn out by it. They'd had enough. The little clawfoot kid beat his stick forlornly on the stump. The grownups and newhairs lowered their axes, looked up wearily, and then began hacking away even harder at the tree. The more noise they made, the less they'd have to hear that kid's screams of pain.

Me, though, I didn't have to be in Batwing at all, so I wandered off. But that screaming kid, it didn't matter where in Family I was, I could still hear him. And even way over Blueside, as far away as you could get from Batwing and still be in Family, people were talking about it:

'Boy called Paul, apparently, twelve wombs or so, burnt all down one side of his face and his chest. Sticky redlantern sap all over the place and those dumb Batwings didn't even have a pot of water on hand to douse him down. You should always have cold water ready when you take down a hot tree.'

'Yes, and wear skins all over, and keep kids out of harm's way.'

'Paul his name is. Nasty sap-burn. Batwings getting a bit careless lately, I reckon, a bit cocky and careless. They had something like that coming to them for a while, I'm sorry to say. Not that it was the kid's fault of course. I blame the grownups.'

'Tree coming down and no one keeping an eye on the kids! I ask you. But that's Batwing for you, isn't it? Not that the kid deserved it. Paul his name was, apparently.'

That was what Family was like. You couldn't get away from other people's feelings and thoughts about everything that happened. Gela's tits, *every* bloody little thing that happened, in no time everyone in Family was talking talking about it and poring over it and prodding it and poking at it and clucking their tongues over it. Everyone was deciding who to give credit to and who to feel sorry for and who to blame, like these three boring questions were the only ones there were. I wished I'd just gone out bloody scavenging with all the rest and not even taken a no-work. At least then I would have been outside Family.

Still, I made the best of it. I got given some roasted birds stuffed with candy by the youngmums over in Blueside in exchange for telling them about the leopard. I got some dried fruits to chew in Brooklyn. I had a swim in Greatpool, and some little kids came and showed me their little toy boats made of dry fruit skins greased with buckfat.

In London everyone was in their shelters in mid-sleep, except for just the lookout, a big slow boy called Pete about a womb older than me, who was leaning on a bark rest against a tree stump and chewing the end of a twig from a spiketree.

'Alright there, John?'

'Not bad.'

'Heard you did for a leopard, eh?'

'Yes, up Cold Path way.'

'Long way off then. You can't get much further than that.'

'No.'

'Only maybe Exit Falls. That's further, isn't it?'

'No, it's nearer, but of course there's also whatever's below Falls, as well. And whatever's across Dark.'

'Below Falls? I've never heard of that. Are you sure . . . ?'

Then a slow smile spread over his face.

'Below Falls! Michael's names, you're winding me up aren't you, you slinker? There's no such place as Below Falls, is there? You had me for a minute there.'

'Well, of course there's something below it, Pete. Where do you think the water goes? You could even climb down next to it once, until that big slab slid down on Rockieside, and Fall Pool filled up.'

Pete shuddered.

'Who'd want to climb down? There might be *anything* there. And we've got everything we need right here in Circle Valley.'

A woman in one of the shelters heard us speaking and stuck her head out, a plump big-breasted grownup woman two three times my age with, I guessed, five six kids sleeping there in the shelter with her.

'You're John, aren't you? The boy that did for the leopard out there?'

Out she came smiling. She didn't have her wrap on.

'I'm Martha,' she said. 'Would you like a little slide, my dear?'

Pete looked away politely and began to hum.

'We could go over there in the starflowers,' Martha said, pointing to a big bright clump growing over beside the stream.

A lot of women thought if you did a slip with a young guy who was fit and healthy, it would stop you having batface babies, or clawfeet. Us young guys didn't argue.

'Yeah, okay,' I said.

We went over to the clump of starflowers and she knelt down so I could give it to her from behind. This wasn't about pleasure for her. She didn't move or moan, only gave the odd tiny little sigh for the sake of politeness. And we could hear that kid over in Batwing all the while we did it, wailing and crying in pain.

'Kid called Paul, apparently,' she said while I was still pushing in and out of her. 'Nasty sap-burn when they got down that big old redlantern tree.'

She considered this while I kept on humping away behind her.

'Wouldn't happen here in London. We keep our kids under control. No way would a London kid be let near a tree that was about to come down. And we'd always have a pot of water ready just in case as well.'

'Keep the littles under control, eh? It's got to be the . . .' I muttered but then I came in her with a shudder, and she rolled over on her back among the flowers, lifting her knees and cupping her hand over herself to keep the juice that she hoped would make her another well-behaved London kid with straight lips and unclenched feet to live its life out in that particular little trampled clearing called London, among those particular bark shelters and that particular little group of people, who liked to think there was something different about them from everyone else in Family.

And there *were* differences, I thought, kneeling above her but looking away across Family towards Batwing on the far side, and thinking about the groups between here and there. For example, the names. Blueside just means the group that's furthest over Blueway, the side nearest Blue Mountains, Redlantern just means we've got a big bunch of Redlantern trees (which we're slowly cutting down and replacing by chucking whitelantern seeds down the stumps). But London and Brooklyn were proud proud of the fact that *their* names came from across Starry Swirl, from Earth. The Earth folk had a *big* big Family, with many many groups in it. Angela's group was called London and the people there had black faces like Angela did. Tommy's group was called Brooklyn, though some people called them the Juice. (As for the Three Companions, who took *Defiant* back across Starry Swirl, leaving Tommy and Angela in Eden, we don't know the group names of Dixon and Michael, but they say Mehmet's group was called Turkish, even though his last name was Haribey. I don't why.)

So, yes, London were different from Blueside, Blueside were different from Batwing, Batwing were different from Redlantern. Each Family group woke at a different time, slept at a different time, had its own particular way of doing things and deciding things, its own little things they were proud of about themselves (like London and Brooklyn being the names of groups on Earth), its own particular combination of strong people and weak people, kind people and selfish people, batfaces and clawfeet. But the differences were so small, I thought, and so dull dull dull. Really we were all alike. In fact, we were so on top of one another, so in each others' lives and in each others' heads, we were hardly separate from one another at all. Like Oldest always banged on and on about, we were *all one*. It was really true: one Family, all together, all cousins, all from one single womb and one single dick.

'I've got some milk if you want some,' Martha said, cupping her hands under her breasts.

'Yeah, okay,' I said, and I bent down while she held one of them for me to kneel and suck the warm sweet stuff.

'That's better,' she said after a bit. 'They were beginning to hurt.'

She stroked my hair briefly, without much interest.

'Had a new baby die on me,' she explained. 'Twenty thirty sleeps ago. Little batface baby. Really bad batface, poor little thing. His little face was practically split open from top to bottom, and he couldn't suck, no matter how hard I tried to help him. In the end he just . . .'

I felt her shaking as she began to cry. That was the reason she'd been awake. She couldn't sleep. She couldn't think of anything else but the dead baby. That was what it was like for mums when a baby died. They couldn't think of anything except the gap where the baby had been. Martha London didn't know how to fill up the time. She didn't know how to let the baby go.

'Ten kids I've had in all,' she said. 'All but two of them were batfaces. And, well, you love them anyway, but . . .'

She released the breast she was holding and scooped up the other one for me.

'Only three of my kids are still alive,' she said. 'Three girls. All the rest died. All my boys died. Last three all died as babies.'

I sat up.

'Well, maybe your luck will turn now.'

She nodded, lying there under the flickering starflowers, her face all smeary with tears. The flowers were so bright that their stems made little lines and shadows, always moving and changing, all over her body. Her hand was still cupped between her legs to hold in my lucky juice.

'If I have another boy a wombtime from now,' she said, 'I'll call him after you.'

~ ~ ~

Those slips with oldmums were funny things. When you thought about it later, you got hard all over again and you remembered your dick going in and out of her, and you wanted to do it some more. And when you heard other boys boasting to each other about the grownup women that had asked them for a slide, you worried that maybe they were getting more of it than you, or maybe that they were getting something better than you'd had. And the batface boys who oldmums never wanted to slip with, they listened to rest of us and thought to themselves, It's not fair. Why can't that happen to me? (But they didn't *say* it, because they knew us smoothfaces would just laugh at them and say, 'It's because you're *ugly*, Einstein. Ugly *ugly*. The clue's in the name. It's because you've got a face like a bloody bat.')

But straight afterwards, you felt sort of empty, like the spark had been taken out of you along with your juice, and nothing meant anything at all. That was what it *actually* felt like afterwards, but that feeling didn't last long, and seeing as that part of it wasn't fun to think about or talk about, you soon pushed it out of your mind, you forgot about it till next time, and no one ever spoke about it at all.

I didn't want to walk through Circle Clearing and maybe get tangled up with bloody Oldest, so I walked along by Dixon Stream where it flows down towards Stream's Join and the log bridge. The only trouble with going that way was there was a place down along the stream where that one-legged London bloke Jeffo made boats, and he was boring boring and hard to get away from.

'Hey! Who's that? Aren't you that John Redlantern that did for that leopard?'

Damn. I'd hoped he'd be out on the water in one of his boats but he wasn't. He was sitting on a bit of log below a whitelantern tree, working on a new one. He was a big man of about sixty wombtimes with a soft weak face, no teeth, and that one leg of his missing below the knee. He'd got a three-yard length of split trunk from a redlantern tree that he was working on. He'd already scraped the dried old tubes out of it, cut the ends straight with a blackglass saw and smoothed off them off with roughstone. He'd got a special fire place for boiling down redlantern sap into glue. There was a deep hole in middle full up with a hot sticky sludge of boiled sap, and round it a circular trench filled with redhot embers. He was scooping the sludge out with a bark spoon and smearing it onto the pieces of buckskin he'd stretched tight over the open ends of the log. The skins had dried hard hard from when he first glued them on, and now he was spreading more glue all over them, ready to stick on another layer of skins.

'How long you've been working on that one, Jeffo?'

'Oh twenty wakings at least, I'd say.'

'How many boats you reckon you've made?'

'Oh thirty, forty. They don't last that long, you know, boats. It doesn't matter how much glue you use, sooner or later the ends come off and then down they go and it's, "Jeffo! Jeffo! Can you glue the ends back on this one?". "No I can't," I tell them. "You'll need new soft skins that can be stretched, and if the wood's soaked at the ends at all, you'll need to start again with a new log." And then of course it's "Jeffo! Jeffo! Can you make us a new one then?"'

'Don't you get bored?'

'Well, if I do, I can go fishing in my own boat. That's like going for a walk for me, going out on my boat. Move as fast on the water as you can with your legs on the ground, I can. Faster, in fact. No one beats old Jeffo in a boat. And anyway I *like* making boats. It's good work. Tommy and Gela themselves taught it to us. Make boats, they said, and a waking will come some time when you'll figure out how to build a boat like the one that brought us here with the Three Companions. And then you'll get back to Earth.'

Tom's dick and Harry's,' I thought, that's the trouble with us! That's what's wrong with the way we are. We live as if Eden wasn't where we really lived at all but just a camp like hunters make when they stay out in forest for a few wakings. We're only waiting here to go back to where we really belong.

'Don't you think we'd need something a bit more than an old tree-trunk with skins glued onto it, Jeffo, to get to Earth?' was what I said aloud. 'I mean, think about it. Things that fly aren't heavy like your boats, are they? Bats and flutterbyes and birds, they hardly weigh a thing. But your boats take two or three people just to carry them down to the water.'

'Do you think the Landing Veekle was light like a flutterbye? It was as big as Circle of Stones, remember,' Jeffo snorted. 'And it was made of metal that's heavy like stone. Nah, they found a way to make heavy things fly, like heavy things can float on water.'

I guessed it was true. Somehow the Earth people must have found a way of making heavy things fly. But how? Well, I had no more idea than Jeffo or anyone else. I was no different from the rest. We knew so little, and Earth knew so so much. We might as well be blind for all we understood about things. No wonder we longed for Earth. No wonder we pined and pined for that waking when Earth would finally come. No wonder old Jeffo told himself he'd make a sky-boat one waking out of a bloody old log so we wouldn't even have to wait for them. No wonder Lucy Lu with her big weepy eyes could get blackglass and skins from all over Family with her stories about how our own shadows would fly off to bright bright Earth when our heavy old bodies had died.

'You got lost on Snowy Dark once, didn't you?' I said. 'We were up the edge there two wakings back, up on Cold Path, and Old Roger told the story of it. But what I don't get about it is how *did* you get lost?'

He looked away and I thought at first he was going to refuse to answer me.

'Bloody woollybucks led me on, didn't they?' he said after a bit. 'I kept following their headlanterns and then when I lost them, there was nothing left to see at all. I mean *nothing*. Couldn't even see my own hand if I held it up in front of my face. Tom's neck, it was cold *cold*. There was nothing to see, nothing to touch, nothing at all but coldness. It's an evil place up there, boy. They say all Eden was like that until life came up from Underworld and we came down from sky. Just darkness and ice and rock everywhere. All I can say is if that really is so then it doesn't bear thinking about. It's bad bad.'

He shook his head.

'Anyway I didn't know where I was. I didn't know why I couldn't hear the others yelling for me. Of course I yelled myself, but all I could hear was the echoes coming back from high up there above me. Echoes, and echoes of echoes, and echoes of echoes of echoes, so I could tell there was more and more of it up there, more ice and rock, colder and higher, and . . . and . . .'

Ugh. He sounded like he might start crying like a kid if he carried on like that, so I butted in quickly.

'So how could we ever hope to survive in a boat that went all the way up to Starry Swirl, Jeffo, if it's so cold and dark even just up above the edge of forest? Think how cold it must be right up out there among the stars.'

He looked at me resentfully.

'They had a way, didn't they? Tommy and Angela and the Companions, they had a way. They knew stuff that we don't know about, like metal and plastic and lecky . . .' he stumbled on the word, 'and lecky-tricktity. They knew how to fly and they knew how to keep warm. If we keep on building boats, we'll find a way too.'

So he said, but meanwhile he was angrily smearing glue onto an animal skin at the end of a log, *exactly* as he'd done with every other boat he'd ever made. He wasn't trying anything new, and he never had done, not once in all those thirty forty boats he'd made.

'How did they get your leg off?' I asked.

'Sawed it off with a blackglass knife, the bastards. Didn't Roger tell you that? You ask a lot of questions, young man, I must say. A lot of rude questions. I don't want to talk about it, alright? It's not a thing I like remembering. Would you, if you were me? You get on now, John, and leave me to finish this boat off in peace.'

Smiling a little bit to myself for my cleverness in getting away, I made my way back through Brooklyn and Spiketree and finally back to Redlantern, where the hunters and scavengers were just coming back from forest with a chewy old starbird and a couple of bags of fruit. Not enough, nothing like enough for forty-odd people. If we hadn't still had three legs of that woollybuck left over, we'd have all been hungry that sleep.

6

Tina Spiketree

At the end of a waking, two sleeps after he did for that leopard, me and John Redlantern walked up along Dixon Stream. We climbed the rocks beyond London and Blueside fence until Deep Pool was there below us, shining with wavyweed and water lanterns and bright beds of oysters.

'It's like there's another forest down there, isn't it?' I said. 'Another little Circle Valley, with the rocks around it like Snowy Dark. Only difference is that this forest is under water.'

It even had a narrow little waterfall at its lower end, where the water poured down on its way to Greatpool, just as all the water of Circle Valley poured out down that narrow gap at Exit Falls.

'Yeah,' said John, with a snort. 'And if there's ever another big rockfall over Exit Falls, whole of Circle Valley forest could end up under water too.'

People didn't come up to Deep Pool much and there was no one else there. We climbed down to the edge of the water, took off our waistwraps and dived in. The water was clear like air and warm warm as mother-milk. The stream that fills Deep Pool comes down icy cold straight off Dixon Snowslug over in Blue Mountains, but the tree roots and water lanterns heat it up.

'So that was pretty brave of you,' I said, when we'd come up to the surface by the water's edge, 'killing a leopard all by yourself.'

We grabbed hold of warm roots and faced each other, close close, with the warm warm water up to our shoulders.

'Most people tell me that,' John said, with a little laugh, 'but you make it sound like a question.'

I nodded. It *was* a question. I was trying to get the measure of him. He looked nice, no doubt about it, he looked beautiful, and it was obvious obvious why he was a favourite with oldmums looking for baby juice. Plus he was quick and clever, and other kids respected him. And he was a big name in Family too now, one of the names that everyone knew. It was all good good, but I still didn't completely get him. No one did. There was something about himself that he held back.

'Well,' I said, 'I think sometimes people just do one brave thing, and then that's it. Or sometimes people are brave in just one way.'

He shrugged.

'Yeah, it's true. One brave thing doesn't mean much. And sometimes people do brave things when they just haven't got time to think.'

'Is that what happened with you?'

He thought about this.

'It's true I didn't have much time to think when the leopard was circling round us. But I knew I had a choice, and I knew no one would blame me if I ran. So, no, I didn't just stand there because I couldn't think of anything else.'

'Why then? It was only a bloody leopard. It's not even as if we can eat the things.'

'I did it because . . . Well, I'd never really understood about those moments before and I reckon a lot of people never really do get to understand them, but what I realized then was that I wasn't just deciding what I wanted to do, I was deciding what kind of person I wanted to *be*. So I made my choice on that basis. And from now on, whenever I have a decision to make, I'm always going to make it in that same way.'

'What, you mean always doing the dangerous thing?'

He snorted.

'No, of course not. That'd be nuts. I'd be dead in no time. What I mean is I'm always going to think about where I'm trying to go and what I'm trying to be, not just about what I want right then at that moment.'

I smiled and kissed him. I liked what he said. It was how I saw things too. I'd not done for any leopards, and I had no leopard-killing plans, but when I did a thing, I was always careful to check that I wasn't just doing it because it was easier, or just doing it to avoid upsetting other people.

'Good plan,' I told him. 'And I'm the same.'

'Yeah? In what way?'

'Well, I'm a Spiketree, and I cut my hair in spikes, and I'm spiky spiky spiky. I tell people what I think and I don't let other people put me off doing what I think I should do. And if something scares me, I think, Yeah, but should I do it anyway?'

He smiled and nodded, and I kissed him quickly again, then pulled away.

'Okay, Mr Leopard Killer,' I said, 'let's see how long you can hold your breath then. I bet I can get more oysters than you.'

I plunged down into the bright blurry water, looking for the pinnacles of rock where the oysters clung onto ledges six seven feet below the surface, opening and closing their shining pink mouths. I grabbed handfuls from three different pinnacles and burst up to the surface again. I was flinging the oysters onto the rocky bank, when John bobbed up right next to me.

'Ha ha! I've got more than . . .' he gasped, but I'd already dived down again before he'd finished speaking, down through a big glittering shoal of tiny fish.

We built up a whole pile of oysters on the bank, then lay on the soft ground under droopy yellowlantern trees and tore them open. The oysters wheezed and fizzed as they died and we pulled out bits of the shining flesh, sometimes feeding them to each other, sometimes playfighting over them, sometimes stealing the juices from one another's mouths and tongues.

'Do you want some slippy, Mr Leopard Killer? Do you want a slide?' I whispered, kissing him and putting my hand down to feel his dick. 'You'll have to do it the back way, though, because I don't want a baby on my hands. I'm really not cut out for being a youngmum, stuck in Family with the blind oldies and the clawfeet and a bunch of little kids.'

I didn't think there'd be any doubt about how he'd answer me, but I was wrong.

'Let's leave that for now,' he said. 'Let's leave that for later on.'

Well, I was *surprised* surprised. Yeah and offended too. What was the matter with him? What did he think we'd come here for? There weren't many boys in Family that would turn down an offer of a slip from me, and not many men either, judging by the way they looked at me, though Family rules said grownup men shouldn't do that with newhair girls.

'You been going with too many old women, John,' I told him. 'Like that Martha London you went with on your no-work waking. Old Martha who lost her little baby not long ago. Looks like she and the others have worn you out.'

John looked surprised that I knew. More fool him. You can't do anything in Family without everyone knowing about it, and weighing it up, and picking it over, and making their bloody minds up about what they thought about it. I'd heard about John and Martha London from four five people and I wasn't too pleased about it. Okay, all the boys go with oldmums when they get the chance, but I'd let him know he could have me, hadn't I? And you'd have thought that would have been enough to keep him going a waking or two, wouldn't you? You'd have thought he'd have saved himself for me.

'It's nothing to do with that,' he said. 'That's different. That's just a Family thing. It's just . . .'

He stopped to think. In fact he ended up spending so long thinking about it that he seemed to have forgotten me entirely. Certainly, when he did speak, he didn't show much sign that he knew why it bothered me.

'Yeah,' he said. 'Maybe it's not such a good idea, going with oldmums whenever they suggest it. Maybe it's one of those things that I was talking about: the things we do because it seems easier at the time, and we don't . . .'

'Yeah, whatever, but coming back to my question . . .?'

'Well, it's . . .'

'Don't you *want* me?'

'Yes I do, but . . .'

He laughed.

'Come on, you know I want you. You've just had your hand on my dick! I could hardly keep it inside my wrap when we were walking over here. But just now I want to eat oysters and talk about things. Is that so weird? There's loads of things I want to talk about and not many people who would know what I meant. We could have a slip, but that would be the easy thing, the obvious thing, and maybe it would be more interesting if . . .'

'Talk to me then,' I said. 'Tell me something you think only I will know what you mean.'

He pulled open another oyster, ripped out the fizzing pink meat and tossed the empty shell back into the water.

'Well, you know what I said about why I did for the leopard. I've been thinking a lot about that. I've been thinking that that's what we always get wrong in Family. It's like whenever we get a choice like that, we always run to the tree, and we've been doing that so long that it's become what Family is: a thing that hides away from anything scary and waits for help to come.'

'So what would we do if we were different?'

'Well . . .' He hesitated here, like he himself was in two minds about what he was going to say next. 'Well, I don't think we'd live in a huddle round Circle of Stones, waiting for Earth to come and fetch us back.'

'Don't you think Earth will come, then?'

He looked at me sharply.

'No, I'm not saying that. Of course not. They've got to come sooner or later. I'm just saying that we shouldn't just spend our lives waiting for them in the same spot, and dreaming about going back to Earth. People say we must be good good, and make sure that Earth will like us when they come, so that they'll want to take us back. But they'd like us better, wouldn't they, if we tried to live like Earth people? Finding stuff out, trying new things, making things better. What's there to like about a Family that huddles up in one place wake-dreaming, and won't budge even if that means starving or drowning?'

I laughed at that idea.

'Not much,' I agreed.

'And anyway,' he said, 'it's not as if there's any reason to think Earth will come any time soon. Okay, we know the Three Companions went back to *Defiant*, and we reckon they'd have taken *Defiant* back through Hole-in-Sky. But there was something wrong with *Defiant*, wasn't there? It was damaged when Angela and Michael tried to catch it in the Police Veekle. And the True Story tells us that the Three Companions knew the chances were against *Defiant* getting back in one piece, or them getting back alive. I mean, that's why Tommy and Angela stayed, isn't it? So that at least some life would carry on?'

I nodded. 'And it's been two hundred wombtimes, so something *must* have gone wrong or they could have mended *Defiant* and come back long ago. But even if the Three Companions died and *Defiant* was too damaged to be mended, it still might well have got back to Earth. You know, like a boat drifts back to the shore. And . . .'

'And Earth would have found out what happened from the Rayed Yo and the Computer. Yes, I know all that. But it would take them a long time to build a new starship. They say that first one took them thousands of years.'

'*Years,*' I teased him. 'Who says "years" except oldies?'

He shrugged.

'Thousands of wombtimes, then. And that's why we shouldn't live like waiting for Earth was the purpose of everything. And we shouldn't just huddle up like this in one place and do the same things over and over and over again.'

'But the True Story says that Earth will come to Circle of Stones, and if we aren't there, they won't find us.'

'I know,' John said. 'I know.'

He thought for a long time, and twice he started to speak and then stopped again.

'But surely,' he said at last in a small quiet voice, like he almost didn't want to hear himself say it. 'Surely, if they can get a boat all the way across Starry Swirl, they'll still be able to find us if we're a few miles away from Circle? Isn't that a chance worth taking? I mean, there's not much point in us all waiting here if we're going to run out of food and starve, is there? Otherwise all Earth will find is a pile of bones.'

I kissed him.

'Now do you want a slip, John?'

'No, not now. Another time. There's too much in my head.'

I wasn't offended this second time. In fact I quite liked that he had things going on in his head that were big enough to drive out that one thought. Not many other boys in Family would have had anything but slippy in their heads. Not if they'd been up here beside me by Deep Pool, with no wraps on, and no one else there, and me telling them I was up for it. In fact I couldn't think of one that would say no. Except for the ones that preferred other boys, of course.

'It would be easier in a way,' I said, 'if we knew for sure they *weren't* coming from Earth. We're a bit like a mum whose kid's been lost in forest. She can't get on with anything until they find the bones.'

John thought about this.

'But it would be lonely lonely, if we knew that,' he said. 'It would be sad sad sad.'

7

John Redlantern

Old Lucy Lu said that every living thing had a shadow hiding away inside its body, waiting to get out. It was crap, but in a *way* it was true of a lot of people. Take Gerry: he might laugh and shout and play the bloody fool, but there was a shadow looking out of his eyes that was different from what he showed the world, a worried worried shadow peeping out that was always afraid of being left alone, or being laughed at, or even just being seen. Or take Bella: she was clever and wise, but she was *half* shadow. More than half. So much of her was shadow that it was like she hardly knew her own body at all.

But Tina had no shadow like that. Her face and her body weren't hiding places, they were *her*, and she knew it, and that was why men and boys couldn't take their eyes off her. They could tell that what was pretty pretty about Tina went all the way through her. It was *all* of her.

I had wanted to slip with her badly badly as we walked up to Deep Pool. And at the end of that waking, when I crawled into that little shelter I shared with Gerry and Jeff, I couldn't sleep for ages, thinking about how badly I wanted her again. And I wondered why I didn't have a slide with her while I had the chance, and I knew the reason was more than what I'd told her, but I didn't know what it was.

And when I did sleep, I had that dream that everyone had in Family, that dream of Earth, coming down from Starry Swirl in a shining Veekle to take everyone home. But I was far far away when the Veekle came. I saw it come down from sky in the distance and I ran and ran towards it, but things kept getting in my way, and I couldn't move forward, and I knew that pretty soon it would lift up again into sky, and return to Earth without me, and never come back.

~ ~ ~

Next waking Bella sent me out scavenging. It wasn't a proper hunt and I had to stay just outside Family Fence because I was with big Met and Gerry and Jeff, and Jeff can't walk far with his clawfeet. Of course there weren't many pickings just outside the fence because everyone scavenged there, but we were lucky, sort of, because pretty soon Met spotted the tail end of a slinker disappearing down the air-tube of a whitelantern tree.

It was the grey kind, the thickness of a man's arm and maybe two three times as long, with thirty forty pairs of little claws and glittery eyes and an ugly mouth full of vicious little spiny black teeth. That was the kind you had to watch out for if you were looking for candy in stumps and air-tubes. Littles sometimes got excited about candy and forgot to check for slinkers, and then slinkers came up and bit them in the face – there were quite a few in Family with scarred faces or missing eyes or noses – so grownups always told us to kill any slinker we found near Family. And lately we'd taken to eating the creatures too. There was a fair bit of meat on one of them, when you picked it out of the shelly bits and the bones, even though it tasted of mud and it gave some people bellyache.

Anyway when we saw it go down the tube, we backed off for a bit to give it time to turn itself round in there. Meantime we took out some wavyweed string that we had in our bag and made a loop in it. I had a club with me. It was a good one, made of a whitelantern branch with two big stones shoved into the hole at the bigger end and sealed in there with buckfoot glue. I gave it to Met, who was tall and clumsy and not too bright.

'Don't *you* want to do for it, John?' he asked, like it was my right, since I'd done for the leopard, to kill any animal I liked.

Met was one of those many people who look to others to tell him what to do and what to think.

'No, you saw it, Met, you do for it.'

The flutterbyes had fluttered off when the slinker appeared, but flutterbyes don't have much memory, and, now the slinker was out of sight, they'd all started coming back again after the candy. And pretty soon there was a bat there too, a tar bat, leopard-black, swooping and diving like a scrap of darkness in the glittery forest, snatching up the flutterbyes as they came up from the tubecandy.

Silly bat didn't know what was coming. *Snap!* Out shot the head of the slinker and got it with one crunch, along with a couple of flutterbyes. *Click click*, went its feet as it backed down the tube again.

I looked at Met. He'd have preferred me to take charge really, but he could see from my face that I was leaving it up to him.

'Er . . . You two ready with that string then, Gerry and Jeff?' he asked.

The three of them crept forward quietly and Gerry and Jeff stood each side of the tree trunk with the loop dangling over the hole. Met stood in front of them with the club ready.

Another bat came looping down. *Whoosh*, went its wings as it dived through the flutterbyes, snatching up a big fat blue one with its little hands. Then up it swooped again, up through the shining branches, up, up, up, gobbling down the flutterbye as it went. Up, up, up, then round and down it came again, right down, right next to the tube hole.

'Now!' yelled Met as the slinker's head came out. Jeff and Gerry pulled tight. Met brought his club down *smack*. The bat swerved away with a little shriek.

Three things could easily go wrong at this moment. One, the slinker pulls back too quick and you don't get him. Two, you get him with the club but not the string, so he's dead but he drops back down the tube to Underworld, to rot or be eaten up by whatever it is that lives down there. Three, you get him with the string but not the club, so he's still alive and threshing and biting like crazy and you have to hold tight and hope the string doesn't break or he'll get you with those vicious spiny teeth. This time, though, they got all of it right. The string caught the slinker round the neck, the club mashed its head so that, if that slinker wasn't dead straight off, it certainly near enough was, and Gerry and Jeff pulled it out of the hole, its body still twitching and its little claws still waving about and clicking and grabbing at the air.

'Got yer!' yelled Met delightedly, giving it another whack with the club.

Gerry ran forward to trample on it. Met hit it again.

But Jeff, he was a strange little boy. He had been part of all this up to that moment, but now suddenly he was standing back from what was going on, like he was looking in from outside.

'We're here,' he said. 'This is happening. We are really here.'

'Of course we're bloody here, you dork!' exclaimed Met, giving the quivering slinker another whack.

But Gerry regarded his brother with a concerned expression. He was protective of Jeff, and at the same time he looked up to him, even though Jeff was the younger of the two of them. He knew there was something strange and special about Jeff while he, well, he was just Gerry.

Jeff squatted down by the slinker, touched its mangled head as gently as if it was a baby, ran his fingers along its hot scaly body.

'Poor old thing. Poor old tubeslinker.'

'What are you talking about?' snorted Met, looking at me and Gerry to see if we'd have a laugh with him, but we wouldn't.

'It's just a bloody *slinker*!' Met said.

'I wonder what it's *like* to be a slinker?' Jeff said.

'What do you mean, what's it like to be a slinker?' exclaimed Met, once again looking at me and Gerry. Surely we could see *that* was funny?

'What does a slinker think about, I mean,' Jeff persisted.

I think kids like him – I mean clawfeet, batfaces, the ones who are left on the outside of things – can go in different ways. Most of them are desperate to please and to get in with the other kids. Some turn into bullies and try and control people, like David Redlantern. But a few choose just to stay outside and think their own thoughts. Jeff was one of that kind. He was smart smart, much smarter than Gerry. He had *much* much more going on in his head. And he had his own angle, his own way of seeing things that he wasn't going to set aside to please anyone else. I liked him for that. I was on the outside of things too in my own way. Not that I was a clawfoot or anything but I just felt different. *Different* different. So in a way I felt a connection with Jeff. In some ways we were alike, though in other ways gentle little Jeff wasn't like me at all.

Met rolled up the dead slinker and tied it up with string while Gerry and Jeff went to the air-tube and pulled out all the candy they could reach. When we got back to Family we found out that our old slinker was the best catch of that waking and everyone told Met what a great hunter he was. Yet time had been – not generations ago, but even just when I was a little kid – when people would kill a slinker and just leave it out in forest for the tree foxes and starbirds because they didn't think the meat was good enough to be worth carrying back.

~ ~ ~

When we'd eaten in group, and after I'd let Old Roger beat me at a game of chess, I walked across to Spiketree again and looked for Tina.

'You two *are* getting on well, aren't you?' said the Spiketree people, giving each other knowing looks, like there's something clever about being able to spot when a boy and a girl fancy each other, like it doesn't happen all the bloody time.

Tina and me went back up past Brooklyn and London and Blueside – with people in *all* those bloody groups as well looking at us and looking at one another, as if to say 'Do you see what I see?' – and we went up over the rocks to Deep Pool, shining down there in its own hiding place, with rocks and bright trees all around it, like a world inside a world inside a world. And we scrambled back down to the place on the bank where we'd been last time. A single jewel bat was swooping low over the water in a series of long runs. A couple of small ducks sat in middle of a mass of lilies and cooed and rattled to one another, smoothing down their wings with their hands and flashing their little green headlights. Far off in forest out Blueside, a female starbird called *Aaaah! Aaaah! Aaaah! . . .*

And suddenly a male starbird answered right up beside us: *Hoom! Hoom! Hoom!* It made us jump because we'd not even noticed it up in the tree there, hidden in a mass of bright whitelanterns. It rustled its golden wings and rattled its blue tail feathers so that the coloured stars glittered. It tipped its head and looked at us with one of its flat black eyes, the little lights glinting inside like secret thoughts, and its black hooked beak opened and closed, as if it was about to say something and then changed its mind. Then its scaly arms came out from under its wings and it touched the tips of its fingers together, so we could just hear the clack of its long black claws.

Tina untied her waistwrap and dived straight down into the warm water. *Whoosh!* Off went the starbird over the water and away into forest with a clatter of wings and whitelantern branches, and a series of loud cries: *Raa! Raa! Raa!* I followed Tina. We didn't bother with oysters. We'd taken the easy ones last time anyway. Instead we raced across to the far side of the pool and back again, pushing through the floating streamers of the water lanterns when we could, or diving under them when they were too thick. Down there under the surface it felt like we were flying over those pinnacles of rock that went down and down, and over shining water lanterns and wavyweed, with green and red tiger fish and tiny bluefish swimming through it in shoals. Down and down, shoals below shoals: Deep Pool wasn't like Greatpool or Longpool where you could dive and touch the bottom. In Deep Pool you couldn't make out where it ended.

'So have you thought of some more things for us to talk about?' she asked me, after we'd climbed out again.

She threw me half a bunch of water lantern nuts.

'We're *here*,' I said, after munching for a bit. 'Have you ever heard our Jeff say that? We're here. We're really here.'

Tina didn't laugh at this like Met did. She narrowed her eyes. She thought carefully about what I might mean. Then she nodded.

'Yeah,' she said. 'I've heard him. We're here. *And* . . .?'

'Most people in Family never think about it. You do your chores, you have something to eat, you have a bit of a gossip and a moan, you have something else to eat, you have a slip, you go to sleep . . . and they never think once about where they are, or where they might be.'

'I'd say they dream a lot about where they *might* be.'

'They wish they were back on Earth, you mean? They wish they were with the Shadow People. They wish a boat would come down from sky and take them away from all their sorrows. Is that what you mean?'

'Yes. All that.'

'That's the same thing as *not* thinking about where they are or where they might be,' I said. 'That way they don't even have to try.'

Tina frowned.

'But wouldn't *you* like to be on Earth? With the light in sky and everything?'

How we all longed for that bright light. How we'd always longed for it.

'Yeah, of course,' I said. 'But there's no point in going on about it, is there? I'm not *on* Earth, am I? I might never get there in my lifetime. I'm in Eden. We're in Eden. This is what we've got.'

I waved my hand at the scene in front of us: that little jewel bat leaving a sparkly trail as it skimmed the surface of the water with the tips of its fingers; that whitelantern branch hanging down over its own reflection; those tiny shimmery little fish nipping in and out of the tangle of roots round the pool's edge.

Hoom! Hoom! went the starbird off in forest.

Aaaah! Aaaah! came back the reply.

'Yeah,' said Tina, 'this is what we've got.'

She moved over near me, and looked right up close into my face.

It was different now to last time. Sometimes boys and girls did a slide together just to stop themselves having to talk, and stop themselves having to notice what was happening. Sometimes it was like going to sleep, or stuffing your face with food. Sometimes it was like hiding from the leopard up the bloody tree. That was why I hadn't wanted to do it before. But right now, if we did it, it would be different. It wouldn't be like hiding away from the leopard. It would be like facing it. I leaned forward to kiss her sweet cruel funny mouth. I leaned forward. She moved towards me. I . . .

Paaaaarp! Paaaarp! Paaaarp!

The sound came from Family and echoed round the rocks. *Paaaaarp! Paaaarp! Paaaarp!* An ugly sound on many different notes that didn't fit together. *Paaaaarp! Paaaarp! Paaaarp!* Up from Circle Clearing. *Paaaaarp! Paaaarp! Paaaarp!*

'Gela's tits!' hissed Tina, sitting back up.

We'd heard it many times before. It was the signal for whole Family to come together. It was AnyVirsry. Oldest must have finally agreed on their days and their years. They must have decided that this was the moment – this was three hundred and sixty-five days after the last AnyVirsry – and called for Caroline and the rest of

Council to get out the hollowbranch horns and get hold of all the newhairs and young men they could find to blow them.

Paaaaarp! Paaaarp! Paaaarp!

It was an ugly noise but it carried well. It carried all over the valley, querulous like Oldest themselves. If there were woollybuck hunters up by the snows at Cold Path they'd hear it. If there were people digging out blackglass out by Exit Falls they'd hear it. If there were people up by Dixon Snowslug looking for stumpcandy, they'd hear it and know what it meant.

Paaaaarp! Paaaarp! Paaaarp!

'We don't have to go straight away,' Tina said.

'We don't have to go at all,' I said.

She looked at me.

'That's true. What could they do to us?'

'Nothing really. Nothing much.'

Tina smiled ruefully.

'No. But if we don't go now, that's all we'll be thinking about, isn't it? The fact that we've been called to AnyVirsry and haven't gone.'

I nodded. Family was inside us, not just out there in the world. If we didn't do what Family asked, Family out there wouldn't need to say anything, because it would be accusing us already from inside our own skin. Kissing would be no fun, slipping would be no fun. I felt my dick shrivel just at the thought of it.

So we started climbing up the rocks away from Deep Pool and back to Family.

~ ~ ~

London was at the beginning of their waking. Blueside had been right in middle of their sleep. In Brooklyn, only the youngmums and oldies and clawfeet and little kids had been there in group, because everyone else was out on a big groundbuck hunt up Alps way. But it didn't matter whether it was your waking time or your sleeping time or whether you were inside or outside of Family Fence. Everyone was now moving towards Circle Clearing.

As we came back through Family, we saw oldies, youngmums, little kids, newhairs, people who'd been sleeping, people who'd been eating, people who'd just been starting a new waking, all already on their way. And, though we couldn't see them, we knew that, across forest, hunters and scavengers would be abandoning whatever it was they were doing too and turning back, though some would have a couple of wakings' walk ahead of them. All the people in Eden, all the people in the world, were heading for Circle Clearing. That was how it was: you could be out in forest, or up on the edges of the hills, or over by Exit Falls where the water goes roaring down into darkness, but wherever you were, and whoever you were, you were *still in Family*.

By Dixon Stream, passing through old Jeffo's place, with his logs and his gluepit and his skins, we caught up with Gerry and little Jeff.

Gerry looked at me like he always did, checking out my mood, getting ready to adjust his own.

'Bloody Any Virsry!' he said, as soon as he was sure that I was annoyed, and he slashed at a low-flying bat with a stick.

It was a lucky shot. He broke its wing. It fell to the ground, twitching and squealing and holding out its tiny naked little hands as it if was appealing to us for pity.

'Gotcher!' Gerry muttered, stamping out its life.

Jeff looked down at the little corpse for a moment – it was a silvertip, no good to eat – and he looked at his brother and at me and at Tina, then back at Gerry again.

Paaaaarp! Paaaarp! Paaaarp! went the hollowbranch horns, demanding our presence and our obedience.

8

Tina Spiketree

Soon everyone who'd been in or near Family when the horns began to blow was in Circle Clearing. Hunters and scavengers who'd been a bit further out were still coming in. Others might not be there for a waking or two.

In middle of Circle stood Caroline Brooklyn, the Family Head, and Oldest, and Oldest's helpers. The rest of us stood in the space between Circle and the edge of clearing, each group in its own little clump with its leader at the front. And one by one these leaders – fat old Liz Spiketree, thin weary Bella Redlantern, blind Tom Brooklyn – went up to Caroline to say how many in their group were here already, and how many were out hunting or scavenging and not back yet. A woman called Jane London, who was known as Secret Ree, sat just outside Circle with a bit of white bark, listening to all this and scratching the numbers down. Then we all had to wait while they added up the group counts and worked out the count for whole Family. This went on and on, like it did every AnyVirsry.

'Harry's dick,' I said to my sister (who was also called Jane), 'how hard can it *be* to add up the numbers from eight groups?'

There was a lot of muttering and a lot of going back and forth from the edge of Circle to the groups waiting around. Some babies cried. That Batwing kid with the burn was groaning and moaning. Newhairs were giving each other looks and chucking things.

Then at last all the group leaders gathered together with Caroline and Oldest in Circle, and Caroline shouted and raised up her hands to get our attention.

'There are two hundred and twenty-six women in Family,' she announced, 'one hundred and fifty-six men . . .'

Same number of boys and girls are born, they say, but loads more boys than girls die when they're still small. That's why there are always more women, even though women sometimes die having babies.

' . . . and a hundred and fifty children under fifteen years,' Caroline said. 'That makes five hundred and thirty-two people in Family, with sixteen of them still on the way here.'

'Five hundred and thirty-two,' wavered old Mitch, leaning on Caroline's arm in middle of Circle, like a skeleton covered in dry yellow skin, with wispy white hair and a thin straggly beard. Little wizened Stoop and fat Gela stood beside him. All three were held upright by a couple of those women that were always fussing round them.

'Family has never been this big,' Mitch said. 'When I was a child there were barely even thirty.'

'Imagine that,' I whispered to Jane. 'Imagine just thirty people in whole world. How could they bear it? Even five hundred and thirty-two is way too few.'

Now the count was done, we didn't have to stay in our separate groups, so I whispered 'See you later' to my sister and started to make my way through Family towards John.

'One hundred and sixty-three years it's been,' says fat Gela in her heavy wheezy voice, 'one hundred and sixty-three years since Tommy and Angela came to Eden.'

'In a boat they came,' went on little Stoop, when Mitch had poked him irritably with his bony fingers. 'First in the starship *Defiant*, a wonderful sky-boat that could travel across the stars, and then in the Landing Veekle that came down from *Defiant* to the ground.'

'Remember!' Mitch called out in his thin wavery voice. He had a batface, not the full batface split right up into his nose, but a little split in his upper lip, and 'Remember' came out more like 'Rememfer'. He was about to say something else, but then began to cough, and his eyes went even more red and watery, and he couldn't speak.

I had reached John meantime. He was standing with his cousin Gerry. I squeezed his hand. I could feel the grownups' eyes watching us. I could feel them thinking, That's no way to carry on in an Any Virsry.

'In the round Landing Veekle boat they came,' said old Gela, her blind eyes bulging as if she'd just swallowed a big fat flutterbye by mistake, 'and this Circle marks the place where they came to land.'

Their helpers led the three of them slowly round Circle of thirty-six white stones, which were supposed to mark the outline of the Landing Veekle, and guided Oldest's blind hands so they could brush each stone with a bundle of twigs.

Michael's names, it took a long, long time! There were whispers and murmurs. A little child began to wail and was hissed at to be quiet. Another little announced he wanted a piss. John's cousin Gerry farted loudly, and newhairs and children laughed. Even some of the adults had a job to stop themselves smiling. Any Virsry had only just started and everyone was already bored. Even our grandmothers and their men were bored, though they wore a mask of respect.

Round and round the thirty-six stones went Oldest, slowly slowly slowly. People whispered. People wrinkled up their faces as Gerry's fart wafted past them. People yawned. Blueside had been in middle of a sleep when the horns went, after all, and Redlantern and Spiketree were both right at the end of a waking.

Finally, Oldest returned to the centre once again and Gela poked Stoop, who looked cross at first, but then remembered what he was supposed to be doing.

'There were five people who came down in the Landing Veekle,' he went on, 'and three of them returned in it to *Defiant* to try to get back to Earth. They were the Three Companions.'

Stoop paused and gazed at us as if his brain was stuck. We waited.

'*Defiant* was damaged,' he finally said in his little high voice, 'and they knew it might break. But it had a thing inside it called the Computer, which could remember things, just like a person can, and another thing in it called the Rayed Yo, which could call out across space, so even if the Companions died, Earth could get news of us. And . . . and even now . . .'

Again he stopped, as if thoughts had suddenly stopped happening inside his shrivelled old head.

'And even now Earth may be finishing a new sky-boat like *Defiant* to come and find us. So . . . So . . .'

'So we must stay here and be a good Family and wait patiently,' said Gela impatiently, 'so that they will be pleased with us and will want to take us all back home to Earth.'

'Sky-boats take a long long time to build,' wheezed old Stoop, holding up his hand to stop Gela. '*Defiant* was as long as Greatpool, remember. And made . . .' He had to stop to cough. 'And made . . . and made not of wood but of metal, which takes a long long time to find.'

'Think how long we've been looking for metal in Eden,' wheezed Gela, 'and we still haven't found a single bit.'

'Rememfer!' gasped Mitch, before he began another fit of coughing.

A flock of jewel bats darted back and forth across the clearing. The trees had been pruned for generations to encourage them to grow more flowers and give off more light, and that meant there were lots of flutterbyes for the bats to feed on.

John looked at me, and I gave him a little oyster smile. He seemed alive alive and new new new, next to this old tired boring Any Virsry, going slowly round the same old things.

'Remember that Tommy and Angela stayed in Eden,' Mitch said

when he'd finally managed to clear his throat, 'and they made four daughters: Suzie, Clare, Lucy, Candice – and one son, Harry. But Candice was bitten by a slinker when she was a little girl and she died before she had reached six years.'

'And Harry slipped with his sisters,' said Stoop, 'and . . .'

'But Tommy said we must remember that a man should *not* slip with his sisters,' interrupted Gela, 'nor his daughters, nor even his cousins, not if there are others to slip with.'

'And Suzie gave birth to two daughters who lived: Kate and Martha. And Clare gave birth to three daughters: Tina, Candy and Jade,' said Mitch.

'And Lucy gave birth to three daughters, Little Lucy and Jane and Angela. And Harry was father to all of these, so he's our Second Father. Just like Tommy, he's the father of us all.'

I yawned, and John yawned, and Gerry yawned in imitation of John.

'And Harry had to slip with *these* girls too,' said Mitch, 'though they were his own daughters, and the children of those unions were Janny and Mary and . . . and . . .'

A look of panic came over that bitter old shrivelled batface of his . . . He'd forgotten! The long string that held his precious years together was broken! He couldn't remember the next name in his list.

And then he smiled. Of course, of *course*.

'The children of those unions were Janny and Mary and *Mitch* . . .'

Silly old fool. The child he'd forgotten was himself! The older people laughed affectionately with him. A lot of the younger people didn't laugh at all.

But for some reason I *did* suddenly laugh. It came out loud and harsh. And John looked at me in surprise and then laughed too, and then of course so did Gerry, and other newhairs also took it up as well, all round the clearing.

Old Mitch noticed the mocking bark of us newhairs and turned on us, his watery blind eyes wide with distress.

'You mock, newhairs, you mock our memories. But think of this! I'm a great-grandfather to you, and though I'm old old, one hundred and twenty years, I'm standing before you now. And listen . . .'

He coughed and spluttered and had to have his back patted by one of the helpers before he could go on.

'And listen to this,' he went on at last. 'When I was young like you, I knew an old man too. He was my father's father, and my mother's grandfather, and I saw him standing there in front of me, just as you see me. And – listen to this! – that old man, my grandfather, was Tommy who came from Earth. I *saw* him, I *touched* him, and he came from another world beyond the stars!'

Tears of frustration were running down his face. He knew that, whatever he said, whatever threats he made, the time would soon come when he was dead, and then the time when our grandparents were dead, and then our parents. And when that point came it would be up to us whether we kept the True Story alive or let it die.

'I saw and touched Tommy,' old Mitch almost sobbed. 'Think of that before you laugh, newhairs! Think of that!'

His sadness was so painful that I had to look away. Some of the younger ones around me actually wept, they felt so ashamed of laughing at him. I felt ashamed too but yet at the same time I was angry with myself for allowing the old bastard to touch my feelings like that. Gela's tits, had he or the other two ever spared *anyone else's* feelings? They spoke harshly to children. They told us we knew nothing. They prodded and poked us as if we were things.

'The children of those unions were Janny and Mary and Mitch *and* . . .' prompted Gela. She was bored and tired too, and when Mitch didn't respond, she carried on herself. 'And Stoop and Lu and Gela and . . .' She named all the rest of the twenty-four brothers and sisters in her generation. 'And Peter,' she finished with a gasp. 'And we were the ones who started the first seven groups in Family, and made the big fence. And we were the last to know Tommy who came from Earth, so you should remember us.'

And then at last Oldest were done. Their helpers settled them down on the ground with logs and buckskin to hold them up, and then the group reports began. One group leader after another gave their account of all the things that had happened over the year since the one hundred and sixty-second Any Virsry: the babies born; the people who'd died; the girls who'd got pregnant; the big hunts. It was *boring* boring. Bloody Batwing alone must have spent twenty minutes talking about that redlantern tree they'd chopped down and how they were shoving whitelantern seeds down the tubes in the hope that a whitelantern would grow up in its place.

'Well I never!' I whispered to John. 'How unusual! Whoever would have thought of *that*!'

He smiled, and, seeing him smile, Gerry smiled too.

Two hunters from London came in from forest, so then there were only fourteen left to come, fourteen from Brooklyn still on their way back from their buck hunt out Alpway.

'Now it's time to discuss the Genda for Council,' said Caroline, when the last report was done.

And now each of the group leaders came up with things they wanted to talk about: fish getting scarce in Greatpool, a leopard seen skulking half a mile from Batwing, an argument between Blueside and Starflower about some trees, a request from London for Blueside to move their group further up Blueway, so London could have a bit more space . . .

'We'll help you move the Blueside fence further out,' said London leader Julie. 'We're not expecting you to do it all on your own. But our group is getting bigger.'

'You've been helping with that, haven't you, eh, John?' I whispered to John. 'You've been helping London get bigger. You and that woman Martha.'

He pulled a face at me and stuck out his tongue. I laughed.

'We'll help you pull down the fence and move it, Blueway,' Julie repeated.

'No chance,' said Blueside leader Susan, who was round and solid and stubborn, like Lava Blob. 'We've worked hard to get our group all nice with shelters and everything. Why would we want to hand it all over to you lot?'

'Yes, but we can't help that we're in middle of Family. We haven't got any new forest to move into.'

'Maybe you should split your group into two. Start a new group beyond Blueside, like we did when Starflower started at hundred and fortieth AnyVirsry . . .'

But Caroline stopped the discussion.

'This is for Council, not for now. Right now we are just deciding on the Genda. What other things are going to be on it?'

Some little kids near to where me and John were standing started a silly playfight, chasing round and round the grownups' legs.

'Not enough meat any more,' said old blind Tom from Brooklyn. He was the only group leader that was a man. 'Not enough meat, not enough fruit and seeds and stumpcandy.'

'So what are we going to do about it?' Caroline said. 'What do you want us to discuss?'

'Last useful thing we did was back at AnyVirsry hundred forty-five,' Tom said, 'when we stopped School.'

What he was talking about was that up to hundred and forty-fifth AnyVirsry, there was School for kids between six years and twelve. Every waking, all the kids came together in Circle Clearing and a grownup called Teacher told them about writing and counting and the lost things from Earth and all that stuff. But at hundred and forty-fifth they'd decided they couldn't spare kids from hunting and scavenging. So now most kids couldn't write and Family relied on the remembering that happened at Any Virsries to pass on the old stories. There was a big argument in Council back then, apparently, when they finished with School, one of the biggest arguments ever.

'We got more food in after that,' Tom Brooklyn said, 'with the kids to help, and no grownups tied up with being Teacher. Life was easier for a bit.'

'So what should we give up now?' asked Caroline.

'That's what we need to talk about.'

And then, Harry's dick, *John* joined in the discussion!

'It's not a matter of giving something else up,' he called out.

Well, everyone looked at him, every single person in whole Family. Even the little kids mucking around the legs of the grownups stopped and stared, because every single person in Family that was old enough to talk knew that, when the Genda was being agreed, the only ones who spoke out were the group leaders. Okay, maybe once twice in the past at an Any Virsry, a group leader had asked a grownup in their group to comment on something, but there was no way a kid or a newhair would ever have said anything, no way that they'd even have been asked. And no one, newhair or grownup, had ever ever just shouted something out.

So now everyone was looking at John. But they all looked in different ways. His mum Jade was looking across at him with a funny puzzled face, like she didn't know what to feel. Gerry was looking at him like he was some kind of hero. David Redlantern, that hard batface, was glaring at him like he was a piece of buck shit. Bella Redlantern, standing out there with the other leaders by Circle, looked embarrassed but also a little bit proud.

And that, I suppose, is how I felt too. Embarrassed but a bit proud.

'It's not a matter of giving something up any more,' John went on. 'We haven't got anything else to give up now anyway. We all scavenge and hunt every waking anyway, don't we? What else are we going to do without? Sleep?'

Caroline looked at Bella Redlantern as if to tell her: 'He's one of yours. You sort him out.'

'I think what John's trying to say . . .' Bella began.

'We need to find a way of getting past Snowy Dark,' John called out, 'find new places for people to live.'

Tom's dick and Harry's, that settled it for me! John *wasn't* one of those people who only do one brave thing.

'Past Snowy Dark?' exclaimed Caroline. 'Past Snowy Dark? Oh come on, boy, *everyone* knows that's impossible.'

She looked firmly away from him.

'Anyway,' she said briskly, 'that's enough time wasted. Let's move on to . . .'

But John *still* hadn't finished!

'How do we know it's impossible?' he said. 'How do we really know? We've never tried, have we? Not for a long time anyway. You should talk in your Council about having another go at it. Trying somehow to get across Dark. Or down Exit Falls. *Or something*.'

'We certainly should *not*. For one thing you're just a newhair boy and you can't tell us what to talk about, and for another it's a stupid idea. We've just talked now about how we had to give up School to have more time for hunting and scavenging, and how the hunting has got hard again. How could we possibly spare people for trips up onto Snowy Dark when we need all the grownups and newhairs and big kids to find food? It makes no sense at all.'

'It makes no sense not to,' John said. 'There's going to be more and more people and less and less for us to eat. We've got to find more to eat somewhere else.'

Everyone was embarrassed and uncomfortable by now. Quite a few people shouted out to John to shut up.

'Leave it, boy, we need to get on with the Genda.'

'Shut up, newhair! It's not your place to talk.'

But he *still* kept on.

'Well, if we don't try and get past the mountains, then why don't we at least spread ourselves out a bit across forest? Send one group over to Cold Path Valley maybe. One up by Dixon Snowslug.'

Now Caroline lost her temper.

'Be quiet, boy!' she snapped. 'Be quiet *now*. Whole Family is here, *whole* Family, and it's not the business of one silly newhair to stand up and tell us what we should discuss.'

With a mighty effort, and the assistance of two helpers, old Mitch rose up to his feet.

'What's the newhair saying?' he demanded to know.

'He says we should send groups over to different parts of the valley,' said Bella, 'so as to make it easier to find food.'

'No!' blind Mitch cried out into the pitch darkness around himself. 'No, no, no, no!'

Stoop and Gela were also getting up now, staggering to their feet with their helpers fussing round them.

'We must stay here,' Stoop cried, and then gasped for air. 'This is where they'll come to find us! This is where they'll come! And we must remain one, one Family, that's what Angela taught us. One Family that does things together.'

'Don't worry,' Caroline said, putting a hand on Stoop's shoulder. 'No way are we going to ever break up Family. We have one mother and one father. We always have been one Family and we always will be. If we break up then things will turn bad, one group against another, that's what Angela said. But it is not going to happen and that's final. So no discussion. No argument. *We – all – stay – here*.'

David Redlantern was pushing grimly towards John through the Redlantern people.

'But Family can't go on growing and growing,' called out John, 'and . . .'

David grabbed his shoulder.

'Enough!' he hissed.

Caroline pretended she hadn't heard.

'So what other things do we have to put on the Genda?' she asked briskly.

9

John Redlantern

When Genda was set, that was the end of the first waking of Any Virsry, and everyone could go back to their groups to eat and sleep. The next waking Council would meet and talk about the Genda and then we'd all sleep again, and then there would be the final waking when we'd all be called back in and be told what Council had decided. After that Oldest would do the Earth Things, and we'd have the Show.

I was going to sneak off with Tina again, but David was still standing right behind me.

'No you don't, boy. You're coming back to group with me. Bella needs to talk to you.'

'What about?' said Tina. 'Is she going to tell him off for talking sense?'

David turned his angry red batface on her.

'You keep out of Redlantern business, Tina Spiketree.'

I shrugged and pulled a face for Tina and followed David back to Redlantern, where the grownups were stirring up the embers of our fire and feeding it branches so we could cook. Everyone looked at me as I arrived in our clearing. People stopped halfway between the woodpile and the fire with firewood in their arms.

People came out of their shelters.

'I'm ashamed of you, John,' began Old Roger. 'People will say Redlantern can't bring up their newhairs properly.'

Lucy Lu said that I hadn't just shamed the living members of our group but the ones who'd died as well.

'The Shadow People are crying,' she said, 'they're begging me to make sure that Family is never broken up.'

Bella came out of her shelter.

'You were *rude* rude there, John. Rude to Family and rude to me. What do you think other people will think if someone in my own group talks out like that without even letting me know that's what they are going to do? If you had something you wanted saying, you could have raised it with me beforehand. We all knew AnyVirsry was coming. As it is, you've made me look like a complete fool.'

Everyone watched her and watched me. How would I react? How would she follow on from what she'd said?

'I'm sorry,' I said humbly. 'I just thought it needed to be said. I hadn't thought about it before. It just came out.'

I liked Bella. I was close close to her. And I respected her too. She wasn't just our group leader, she was one of the cleverest people in whole Family.

Bella nodded. I thought I could see a tiny smile.

'Alright, John. I'm tired and hungry. We all are. So we'll eat now, and then afterwards you can come to my shelter for a proper talk about this. I want to know exactly what's on your mind and I want your reassurance that you won't show me up like that again. But we'll talk later.'

Presently Fox and Lucy Lu, who were organizing the cooking, handed round smoked fish and whitefruit and crushed starflowers and bits of muddy, chewy slinker, and we all began to eat together round our fire. And all around us, all over the camp, we could hear the sounds of other groups eating too. (People's talking sounds different when they're eating. It rises and falls in a different way. More gently, more steadily.) You never normally heard that sound coming from all over Family at the same time because one group would be sleeping, one getting up, one returning from a waking's scavenging. The only time we experienced it was when an AnyVirsry was on.

Somewhere out over Peckhamway a leopard was singing to its prey.

'What are you going to say to Bella in there?' Gerry asked. 'Are you going to tell her to stuff it, then, or what?'

I looked at him, meaning to answer him but all the time listening to the lonely deadly sound of the leopard out there, and how it sounded alongside the friendly gentle sound of Family eating and talking all around. And I was thinking, thinking, thinking, about Family and about how things were. Before I'd even begun to think of an answer to Gerry's question, I'd already forgotten it. In fact I'd completely forgotten he was there.

~ ~ ~

Bella's shelter was bigger than everyone else's, and taller too, so that people could sit in there with her and have meetings. She had a pile of sleeping skins in the far right corner opposite the entrance hole, and more skins piled all round the edges for folk to sit on when she had meetings and talks. The shelter was built up against the warm trunk of a big whitelantern tree, and one branch of the whitelantern had been pulled down and held in place with ropes and rocks, so the branch was inside the shelter, with two or three lanterns usually shining at any one time. If she didn't want light she'd cover over the lanterns with skins.

She was squatting over on the sleeping skins when I came in, thin bony Bella, with her narrow hips and tiny breasts and her clever weary shadowy face.

'You are a silly boy, John Redlantern,' she told me, 'and I'm going to have to shout at you for a bit.'

I nodded.

'Never, *never* speak out of turn at a meeting again, alright?' she yelled. 'Do you *understand* that, John? Do you understand? You've shamed *me*, you've shamed Redlantern, you've shamed yourself. And you've achieved *nothing*. Nothing at all. Do you really think Council's view will be changed by a silly little *newhair* just because he got lucky with one bloody leopard out Cold Path way? Does that make you the big man of whole Family, do you think? Does that make you more important than your group leader or your Family Head? I don't bloody think so, John. And don't think I don't know it was you and Tina Spiketree that started up that nasty laugh when Mitch forgot himself. Don't imagine I didn't notice that too.'

The funny thing was that she was yelling at me, but it was like she was acting in one of those story-plays that people put on. Like the story of *Angela's Ring*, when Angela loses the ring her mum and dad gave her, and she cries and screams and tells Tommy he's worse than shit, and how she hates him and she hates Eden and she hates the kids and she wishes she was dead. Or like *Hitler and Jesus*, where Hitler yells at Jesus he's going to kill all his group, the Juice, kill them like they were slinkers ('Over my dead body!' goes Jesus, and Hitler says, 'It *will* be over your dead body, mate, because I'm going to nail you up to a hot spiketree till your skin's all burned off.') Often when people act these things you can see they're not really in them. They might be shouting but their eyes aren't angry like their mouths are. And it was like that now. *We* were in a story-play – Bella and me – and we didn't have to pretend with our faces, only with our voices, because the play wasn't for us really at all but for the rest of group who were outside listening and couldn't see us.

'Don't speak out of turn again, John, alright?'

'I'm sorry I shamed you.'

'And if you want something said at Any Virsry, talk to me, not to whole Family without me even knowing about it, alright?'

'Yes, Bella.'

She looked at me, staring hard hard into my eyes, then she smiled her little tight smile and relaxed a little bit (as much as she ever relaxed) and nodded, as if to say: okay, the play was over now.

'So why did you do it, John?' she asked me in her normal voice, low enough so that no one outside would hear the words (not unless they came right up outside the shelter and put their ear to the bark, and no one would dare do that with whole group there to see them). 'If you wanted it said why didn't you talk to me about it?'

'I only thought of it then and that's the truth. It just came into my mind when Tom said that thing about how we'd given up School already and now we'd have to give up something else. Gela's tits, I thought, what's the point of that? Why can't we see that there just isn't enough in this valley for us?'

Bella studied my face carefully. Then she nodded.

'Actually, I agree with you, John,' she finally said. 'Something needs to give and we need to start preparing people for that. But you know there's more to it than just yelling things out at AnyVirsry. You've got to work round people, win them over, meet them halfway, do things gradually. That's what Council is all about.'

'So how many people in Council apart from you agree with me?'

She considered this.

'Not one. Not yet. But I'm working on people, John. I'm working towards the idea that we may need to spread out a little.'

'It's not just a matter of spreading out a little. We've got to get past Snowy Dark.'

Bella shook her head.

'Right over the top of Dark? I can't see it. I mean it's a few wombs now since I was up by Dark, but I do know what it's like up there. You think you've been there, John, but you haven't. Furthest you've been to is up to the top of Cold Path. That's barely the beginning of Snowy Dark. Barely the beginning. It's so cold cold and so dark dark up beyond there that I don't see any way we can ever get over it.'

'Well, we'll go down Exit Falls then.'

'Oh John! Do you have any idea what that would be like? It might have been possible before the rockfall, but now the only gap is where the water drops down from Fall Pool between massive cliffs, down, down, down into darkness. And think of the weight of all that water. All the water from Greatpool, all the water from all the snowslugs that come down into forest from Snowy Dark.'

'Suppose there's another rockfall one waking that fills up the gap completely. Whole of Circle Valley could end up as one big pool. What will we do then?'

'Well, we'll just have to hope that doesn't happen.'

'Why just hope? Why not try and find a way out?'

'No one could get across Dark.'

'So Tommy and Angela and the Three could go up into sky from Earth and cross Starry Swirl and come down to Eden, but we can't even hope to cross the lousy mountains?'

Bella laughed.

'Dearest John. You can't do everything at once. At the moment Family isn't even ready to spread itself out right here in Circle Valley, let alone try to cross Dark. Let's work on spreading out a bit first, eh?'

'How long will that take?'

'I don't know. Maybe in two three Any Virsries' time we can talk about setting up a new group down the river a bit, or over by Lava Blob. Right now it isn't even on the Genda. You've got to be patient about these things.'

'*That* patient and we'll all bloody starve.'

She smiled.

'There's a little time, I think, before that happens. You need to give people time. And you need to remember that, after all, everyone is concerned that we shouldn't go against what Mother Angela taught us: to wait here and care for each other, until Earth comes back.'

I remembered the dream I'd had – the dream that *everyone* had – where the Veekle came down from sky and I was far away.

'Yes, but she didn't want us to starve, did she?' I said stubbornly, driving my own fear away.

'John, my dear, I do love you. And it might sound strange to say after I've told you off, but I'm proud of you too. Come over and sit with me.'

I moved over to sit next to her on her sleeping skin, tense tense because I knew what was coming next. She kissed my cheek. She ran her hands over me. She took my own hand and placed it between her legs. Older women would ask young guys for a slide and no one thought anything about it. But Bella didn't do it like, say, that Martha London did it. She'd never had a baby and she wasn't looking for one now. That wasn't what it was about. In fact she didn't really go for whole slip thing much at all, just a rub with fingers.

And the other thing that was different about what she did was that she only did it with me, a boy in her own group. That wasn't the usual thing, not women with boys that they'd cared for since they were little. Women were *allowed* to do it with whoever they liked, of course, but that wasn't the usual way it happened. Women did the mum thing with boys and they did the slip thing with boys, but they did them with *different* boys.

'I'm tired and I'm tense, darling,' she said, 'and there's such a hard waking ahead of me tomorrow in Council.'

Well, I loved Bella. She was good to me. Of all the grownups in Family, she was the one that really knew me. And I admired her too. She was clever, one of the cleverest in whole Family. But I didn't like doing this and I wanted to stop. I just didn't know how to get out of it. So I did what she asked of me while she held my arm and pressed my hand down exactly where she wanted it, so hard sometimes that it hurt me, shutting her eyes and screwing up her face as if it was hard hard work she was doing and not pleasure at all.

And I'll tell you something: it was hard work for me, not just this time but every time. It was like her body was shut away in some tiny little place in middle of her shadow – her live happy body, long-lost, hidden under all her cares – and she needed me to let it out for her just for a moment, to release the tension for a moment of being squeezed away in there so she could relax and go to sleep. It *was* hard work. But at last she gave a little gasp, pressed my hand down extra hard and then released it and I knew she was done.

'Thankyou, John, and now I need to sleep.'

I wasn't happy. I wasn't at ease. But I gave her a kiss on the cheek and emerged out of her shelter into group. People who'd been listening outside when she was shouting at me had moved onto other things now, like fixing shelters, or scraping skins, or playing chess. It was like they were doing the opposite of listening, like they were trying their best to notice everything else but the fact that my telling-off had taken a funny turn into something else. No one said anything. Jade, my mother, busied herself with scraping a skin so hard that it was like she was angry with it. Only my aunt Sue and her boys Gerry and Jeff looked at me kindly. Gerry got up and came towards me with a worried worried face but I signalled to him I wanted to be on my own.

And David glared over at me, his eyes like cold fire in his raw batface. He was refastening a new blackglass head onto the end of his best hunting spear, using resin glue and buck sinews. He thought he knew perfectly well what had happened with Bella in there and he hated me for it. He glared at me and then looked away and spat onto the ground beside him. I'd humiliated Bella and the entire group in front of Family but she'd still taken me into her shelter and slipped with me (or so he thought). *He* did whatever she asked of him and she left him outside, and didn't seem to want to get close to him at all. It would be no good me telling him that I didn't like what Bella did with me. No good at all. He was a batface, and batfaces always hated the way that oldmums would slip with the rest of us but not with them.

~ ~ ~

I went over to Spiketree but I didn't get a welcome in Spiketree either. You wouldn't believe that only a few wakings previously everyone was fussing over me and telling my how great I was for killing that leopard. Now it was 'Here comes trouble' and 'Don't think Tina's coming out to play, John, because she's in there talking to Liz.' (Liz was the Spiketree leader: a fat, tetchy, self-important woman, not a patch on our Bella.) 'Liz wants all our newhairs to stay in group till AnyVirsry ends.'

So I went round the edge of Brooklyn towards Stream's Join, trying to keep out of the way of other people. A bat looked down at me from a branch, a little jewel bat with its trembling wings spread out to cool, rubbing its wrinkly face with its little black hands.

Sometimes I hated Eden. Eden was all I knew, all my mother knew, all my grandmother knew, but sometimes I longed and longed for the bright light that shines on Earth – as bright everywhere as the inside of a whitelantern flower – and for the creatures that lived there, with red blood and four limbs and a single heart like us, and not the green-black blood and two hearts and six limbs of bats and leopards and birds and woollybucks. And sometimes I felt that if I ate another mouthful of greenish Eden meat I would vomit out my guts. And yet I'd never tried anything else, never would try anything else, unless I ate the meat of another human being. And no one in Eden had ever done that.

I crossed over the log bridge by Stream's Join – in my head I was begging the shadows of Tommy and Angela to fix it for me that boring bloody old one-legged Jeffo wouldn't be there on the path by Dixon Stream – and I headed up to Deep Pool, clambering down the rocks and diving straight into its warm warm water, down among those bright canyons of wavyweed with all those little shining fish darting away from me.

They said men shouldn't slip with their sisters, or their mothers, or their daughters – they said that was bad bad slip – but then they told you that Harry did just that, slipping with his sisters, and then with their children, and how it was a good job he did, and that we should honour him for it, because if he hadn't we wouldn't be here. Yes, and really we were all brothers and sisters anyway. All of us, every one us, had the same mother and father, Tommy and Angela, so whenever *any* of us slipped together it was *always* bad slip in a way. And Bella might not be my mother, but she was my cousin, like everyone else in whole Family. And in a way she *was* my mother too because she looked out for me when I was little. She told me things. She listened to me. She was more of a mother to me than Jade, because Jade never wanted to be a mum. (She didn't fancy staying behind in group with the littles and oldies and clawfeet.) So it was *double* bad slip me doing it with Bella, or letting her do it with me. It was bad bad, even if we didn't do the full slip.

That's what I was thinking while I swam up and down Deep Pool, swimming really hard, to wear myself down and to make the water wash over me and clean my skin. 'It's bad, it's bad, it's bad. I'm bad, I'm bad, I'm bad.' Then I pulled myself out of the water onto the bank where Tina and I had sat. I pulled a whitelantern flower from a tree and turned it round in my hand: a shining sphere of whiteness, with just a little opening in it for the flutterbyes to go in and out. I held it up close to my eye and looked inside. A tiny flylet was crawling in there, surrounded on all sides by beautiful bright white light. There was no darkness in there. That little flylet didn't have to see a black sky above, or dark trunks of trees. All it could see was light. Just thinking about it brought tears up into my eyes.

And then a strange feeling came over me, a feeling that this same thing had happened here before, long ago, but in this exact same place. Someone else had sat here beside Deep Pool and looked into a lanternflower and cried. And that someone, well, it was Gela herself. I don't mean bloody old Gela Oldest. I mean *first* Gela. I mean Angela Young, my great-great-grandmother, the mother of us all. She'd come here and sat in this exact place all on her own, so as to be where Tommy and the children wouldn't find her. And she'd plucked a lanternflower and looked inside it, remembering her far-off world full of light and all the people in it. She'd cried and cried and cried until she had no tears left, and then she'd scrumpled the lanternflower and tossed it into the pool.

They say that Angela and Tommy didn't get on so well. It's said he got angry when he didn't get his way. It's said she was full of bitterness for what he'd done to her, because it was his fault she'd come to Eden, his fault and the fault of his friends Mehmet and Dixon. She'd never have come here at all of her own choice, and she'd never have been with a man like him either.

'No wonder she cried,' I said to myself.

But then I thought, Tom's neck, what *is* this crap? I'm starting to talk like bloody Lucy Lu. Muttering to shadows. Communicating with the dead. How could *I* know what Angela felt? How could I know that she came to this same place? I'm just doing what everyone else does, wake-dreaming, playing with silly stories and pretending they're true, grieving over bloody Earth, feeling sorry for myself because I can't have everything given to me that I want.'

I scrumpled up the lanternflower and tossed it into the pool, just like she had.

'Tom's dick and Harry's!' I said out loud, after I'd splashed water on my face. 'We're in *Eden*. Maybe no one will ever come to take us back to Earth. And anyway that *isn't* "back", it wouldn't be *going back*, because none of us has *ever been there*.'

'You talking to yourself now, John?' said Tina.

She'd crept down the rocks, quiet quiet as a tree fox. I didn't know how long she'd been there or what she'd seen.

'Shall we see if we can find some more oysters?'

'Yeah okay, but don't think we're going to carry on with that slide we started, because we're not. I'm not in the mood, okay?'

'Because . . . ?'

'I don't feel like that now.'

'I went looking for you in Redlantern, and Gerry told me that Bella had you in her shelter and that everyone reckoned that . . .'

'Just leave it, alright?'

For a moment she looked like she was going to get angry, but she saw something in my face that stopped her. She nodded and shrugged and gave me a little strained smile.

10

Gerry Redlantern

I felt sad sad. I felt scared. I felt sorry sorry for John. I felt sort of sorry for Bella too, sorry and angry all at once.

I liked things best when everyone was getting on with each other. I liked it when everyone thought that John was great. I liked it when I met people from other groups and they said John was brave brave or Bella was the best group leader in whole Family. And I hated it that John and Bella had upset people and made them angry. I think I hated it worse than I would have done if they were angry and upset with me. But I didn't *blame* John or Bella for that. I knew that people who were stronger than me didn't mind so much what other people thought. I knew they sometimes had other reasons for doing things that seemed important to them, even more important than being liked, even more important than being kind. In fact that was *why* I admired them: because they had something I didn't have – a will of their own, I suppose. So I didn't blame them, but I wished wished that everyone would go on liking John as much as I did, and go on saying what a great great group leader Bella was, and not whisper and hiss any more.

Secrets were another thing I hated; secrets and people not saying what they meant. Gela's heart, it was hard enough to make sense of anything without all that!

'Why's no one talking?' I whispered to Fox when John was in Bella's shelter and everyone around had gone quiet quiet.

He winked and ruffled my hair like I was a little kid, then got up and moved away from me.

I went to my mum.

'Is John's slipping in there with Bella?' I asked her. 'Why is everyone so quiet?'

Sue squeezed my hand, but wouldn't say anything.

Even Jeff wouldn't talk about it.

And when at last he came out of Bella's shelter, John didn't want to talk to me either. He waved me away, walked off out of group, and didn't come back until four five hours later when we were all sleeping or trying to sleep.

'You okay, John?' I whispered as he crawled into the shelter he shared with me and Jeff.

But he didn't answer me, just crawled between his sleeping skins and lay still.

I didn't sleep hardly at all before the next waking. It was always hard anyway when an Any Virsry put your sleeping and waking times back to front, but it was harder still when the world was all turned upside down. There was so much weird weird stuff going on. Everyone had thought John was great, but now whole Family was angry with him. Everyone in Family said Bella was the best group leader, but now even her own group were thinking thoughts about her so bad bad that they wouldn't speak them aloud.

Yet both John and Bella seemed to have *chosen* this. They'd done things on purpose that they knew would cause upset. They were like smart smart people playing chess who suddenly throw away a queen and you can't see the reason, but you know they must have done it on purpose, for some reason they've spotted three four moves away.

'Are you going to try and speak out again, John?' I whispered. 'When Family comes back together in Circle Clearing, are you going to do it again?'

John didn't answer, but Jeff whispered across to me from his side of shelter.

'Let him sleep, Gerry. Let him sleep.'

~ ~ ~

Paaaaarp! Paaaarp! Paaaarp!

I was wide awake when they blew the horns for second waking of AnyVirsry.

Paaaaarp! Paaaarp! Paaaarp!

I hated that noise all of a sudden. It was like everything that is bad about Family, like watching eyes, like tongues telling secrets and spreading stories in that way that people have, using words they don't really mean so you have to try and guess.

Paaaaarp! Paaaarp! Paaaarp!

John sat up and rubbed his little beard with both hands, and yawned. He looked tired tired.

Paaaaarp! Paaaarp! Paaaarp!

Jeff was sitting up too now, rubbing his twisty feet and watching John with his eyes slightly narrowed. My little brother was another one like John, who played his own particular game and didn't care what other people thought, and I guess that meant he could understand John in a way that I couldn't. They were like chess players, and people like me were more like pieces on the board.

Paaaaarp! Paaaarp! Paaaarp!

We didn't have to go to Circle Clearing, because Council always spent second waking of AnyVirsry going through the Genda by itself, but the horns were to tell whole Family it had to get up and get on with doing stuff, and not fall back into our own group waking and sleeping times until AnyVirsry was over.

We crawled outside our shelter, John first, then me, then Jeff. Old Roger and Bella and my mum Sue were toasting starflower stems and dried fish for everyone to eat.

'Hello John,' Bella called out, and I could see her trying to catch his eye so she could try and find out what was going on in his head.

But John took the food she gave him without looking at her face.

'Hello, Gerry darling,' said my mum Sue, giving me my food. 'You look tired, my dear. All you newhairs are to go scavenging today. Don't go more than an hour's distance from here, okay? You're going with John and Met again, plus Candice and Janny. Jeff will need to rest his feet this waking, so we'll find him jobs to do back here in group.'

Paaaaarp! Paaaarp! Paaaarp!

~ ~ ~

Me, John, Met, Candice and Janny headed out Lava Blob way with spears, ropes, bags and a stone-headed club, looking for stuff to eat. All the time I was watching watching John to try and figure out what was going on inside him, but it was no good: his face was still still like a mask.

Of course, with everyone staying near Family for Any Virsry, and everyone awake at the same time, we ran into other people much more than normal: grownups and newhairs and little kids from different groups, all scavenging together and disturbing each other's prey. That's one reason why groups don't usually all keep the same wakings: so as not to get under each other's feet all the time. But they were all out there now, Blueside, Batwing, London, Starflower . . . all the groups together, even the ones whose sleeps and wakings were the other way round to ours. And, when they saw John, a lot of them had things to say.

'Rude little slinker,' said a man about forty fifty wombs called Tom Fishcreek (poor bloke had clawfeet *and* a batface). 'What you think you're doing spoiling Any Virsry for everyone?'

Him and a couple of other Fishcreek men had hung up an old torn fishing net made of wavyweed string. The other two were up in a whitelantern tree and they'd tied threads to the legs of flutterbyes and were jerking them up and down to try and lure bats into the net.

'Yeah,' called down one of the others in the tree. 'If you want to be rude to grownups, John Redlantern, stick to the ones in your own bloody group next time, alright? Leave the rest of us out of it.'

And he leaned out right over a whitelantern flower, so that its light shone up into his face, and then he spat down from the tree. John had to step out of the way to stop it from landing on his head.

I was angry angry.

'Tom's dick! You'd better . . .'

But John put his hand on my arm at once and shook his head to tell me to leave it, he didn't want any fuss.

'I'll give you one thing, John,' Janny said, as we moved on through the trees. 'You're a bloody idiot and you pissed Caroline off something rotten, but you really couldn't have made Any Virsry any worse than it already is.'

She laughed. She was a batface like my mum and ugly as anything, but she was always cheerful cheerful.

Up ahead of us, two Blueside oldmums were kneeling in front of a small pond, their bony bums sticking up as they picked out pondsnails.

'Carry on like that, John Redlantern, and you'll break Oldest's hearts,' said one of them, called Lucy.

'Worry too much about breaking old Mitch's heart, and we'll all starve,' John told her. 'Which would probably break his heart too, don't you think?'

'What do you know about things like that, you silly newhair?' Lucy Blueside said. 'You should hear yourself. You should hear what rubbish it sounds.'

'He's not talking rubbish,' I said hotly. 'This is my cousin John you're talking about, the one that did for that leopard by himself. He's *smart* smart, way way cleverer than you.'

The other woman, Mary, laughed angrily at that.

'Harry's dick, boy, look at him!' she said. 'Your precious cousin's just a newhair kid that hasn't even managed to grow a proper beard yet. Do you really think that doing for one old leopard means that he knows better than Caroline and all of Council, with all their wombs of experience?'

Our Janny laughed.

'You're wasting your breath, girls,' she told the Blueside women. 'John could say up was down and black was white and Gerry'd still stand up for him.'

'More fool him,' said Mary Blueside. 'And by the way, what's this I hear about young John there and B . . .'

'So what is your suggestion as to how we're going to feed ourselves when there are two three times as many of us?' John interrupted her.

'Like I said,' said Mary Blueside stubbornly, 'that's for Caroline and Council to sort out, not the likes of you. Now if you'll excuse us, some of us are trying to find some food for our group right now.'

'Yeah, I can see that,' John sneered. 'Pondsnails. So tell me honestly, did you ever think of eating pondsnails when you were kids?'

'What I did when I was a kid is none of your business, newhair!'

'Yes,' I broke in, 'but John means that . . .'

'Leave it, Gerry, leave it,' said John in a tired tired voice, and he walked on again, leaving the rest of us to catch up with him.

'So are we actually going to do some scavenging ourselves?' asked Candice. She was *pretty* pretty, but she was always finding fault with everything, and I was a bit scared of her sharp tongue. 'Or are we just going to wait around while John has his own personal AnyVirsry out here?'

'Yeah,' said big slow Met. 'I don't like having all these people moan at us. It wasn't *us* that spoke out in Circle. It's not *our* fault.'

~ ~ ~

I felt sorry for John, with everyone complaining about him. And I kept remembering how he'd looked when he came out from Bella's shelter last night: lonely lonely, and waving me away so he could stay alone.

But not *everyone* moaned at him. Once we came upon a group of newhairs from Brooklyn – Mike, Dixon, Gela and Clare – and they were full of praise for him.

'Good for you, John. Why shouldn't we newhairs have a say if we want one?' Mike Brooklyn said. 'We have to scavenge and hunt like grownups, we have to help look after littles and oldies, so why can't we have a say as well?'

'Yeah, what you said was right, John,' Dix Brooklyn said. 'It's all fine fine for Oldest to say we should keep everything like it's always been but they'll be dead soon. We've got to think about how it's going to be when we're grownups and Family's bigger.'

'So how big *will* Family be when we're old then, John?' asked Gela Brooklyn, and it wasn't in a sneering way to make fun of John, but because she really wanted him to explain.

That made me pleased pleased for John.

'You mean when we've had kids and our kids have had kids?' John said. 'Well, it'll be thousands, won't it? Think about it. There were just two people here once, one hundred and sixty-three years ago, and now we're five hundred and thirty-two. That's – what? – more than two hundred times what it was. And in another hundred and sixty years . . .'

'What? Will it be two hundred times what it is now?' Gela laughed nervously. 'Tom's neck, I don't even know the name of that number.'

'It would be,' said John. 'Except that most people would starve before then.'

He was about the only newhair I knew who ever thought about

anything except what was happening for them now. And that was what was good about John, and why I stuck by him, but it was also what was scary about him, and about people like him. He would take risks and he would do things that would make people turn against him, if he thought that would work out best in the long run. I just didn't have that in me.

But I did have it in me to follow someone no matter what.

11

John Redlantern

After we'd spoken to those Brooklyn newhairs, we spread out a bit and started looking properly for stuff to eat. There wasn't much to find, what with all of Family milling around, and all we got was a few lousy little bats and some dirty scraps of stumpcandy – but after about four five hours Candice spotted a little stonebuck grazing in a clump of starflowers. She knew better than to go straight in after it because, once it spotted us, it could run two three times as fast as any of us – we've only got two legs, it has six – but she crept back to rest of us and signed to us with her hands where it was so we could spread out around it. I was crawling slowly through the flickering starflowers when I put my hand on what I thought was a funny shaped stone. But when I glanced down at it I could see straight away that it wasn't a stone at all. It was a ring, like the rings some people carve out of wood and polish up with buckfat to put on their fingers.

But this one wasn't made of wood, it was hard and smooth, and it reflected the light of the flowers like water does. I knew then it was made of *metal*, that hard smooth shiny stuff that comes from Earth. (It was said you could find it in Eden too, hidden in the rocks, *mixed up* with the rock in some way, but no one knew where to look.) And if it was made of metal, it must have belonged to one of the First Five, to Angela or Tommy or one of the Three Companions.

And then I had a thought that sent a chill going right through me and made my head spin.

Tom's dick! This could be *the* ring, the Lost Ring, Angela's ring that they sometimes do that play about! It could be that actual one.

Anyway, whether it was that ring or another one, it was a Memento, and if I told anyone about it, they'd make me hand it over to Oldest to keep with the other Mementoes – the Boots, the Belt, the Backpack, the Sky-Boat Models, the Earth Models, the plastic Kee Board with its rows of squares with letters, and the blank square that once showed pictures that could move and talk . . .

Bam! The stonebuck bowled straight into me, knocking all the wind out of me and sending me flying, back onto a big ant's nest.

All the others laughed.

'He kills a bloody leopard,' Janny teased me, 'and then he doesn't notice a stonebuck when it comes right at him.'

'You idiot, John,' said Candice. 'That would have been a good waking's kill for us. What in Harry's name did you think you were doing?'

I stood up, hastily brushing off angry ants with their bodies flashing red in warning that they planned to sting. I felt a fool, but I could have completely explained myself and satisfied all of them – even miserable Candice – if I'd only shown them the ring. It was a find that Family would value more highly than *ten* stonebucks, and any one of the others would have admitted straight away that they'd have been just as distracted from the hunt as I'd been if they'd been the one that found it.

I would have *liked* to show it to them too. I didn't want them to think of me as a wake-dreamer, or as someone that didn't pay attention in a hunt: it wasn't the idea of me I wanted people to have, and it wasn't true either. But you've got to think about where you are trying to *get* to in the future, that was my rule, that was my leopard rule, not just try and make things easy and comfortable right now, and I decided in that moment that it would be better not to show the ring to anyone just now. So I closed my hand around it – it had a lovely smooth cool feeling – and I smiled and shrugged and said nothing. I had sewed a little pocket on the edge of my waistwrap as a place to put small useful things like bits of blackglass and stumpcandy and whitelantern seeds, and I slipped the ring in there when no one was watching me, and kept quiet, and we carried on hunting and scavenging.

'You've gone all weird since that leopard, I reckon,' Candice said. 'I mean, speaking out in AnyVirsry, talking about going across Snowy Dark, what was that really all about? Don't give me all that about not enough food, and Exit Falls and all that. That's not for us to sort out, and you know it. I reckon you just like the attention.'

'He's been weird since he's been slipping that Tina Spiketree, you ask me,' Janny said.

Met looked at me. Gerry looked at me. Was I really going to let these two girls take the piss out of me like this? But I didn't say anything. We walked on. Pretty soon we came across David, who was out with Fox. He had just killed a stonebuck with his long blackglass-tipped spear and was looking mighty pleased about it.

'Hey, that was my buck!' exclaimed Candice. 'I spotted that and we would have killed it too if John had just been paying attention.'

David gave a bark of laughter and repeated the old saying: 'It's not your buck unless your spear's in it.'

He looked at me.

'Not paying attention, eh, John? Too much slip if you ask me. Slip with Martha London, slip with Tina Spiketree, slip with bloody Bella Redlantern herself. This boy must think that's all he's here for, making juice for women. Juicy John, that's what we should call him. Juice is all he's bloody good for.'

There was so much hate and envy in his ugly bitter batface. I remembered how he'd looked when I crawled out of Bella's shelter and I thought to myself that, if he could have driven his spear into me now as he'd just driven it into that stonebuck, if he could have done it without being blamed for it, well, he could have done. He would have done it gladly.

On Earth that had sometimes happened, the stories said. One human being would sometimes do for another like we did for bucks and slinkers. In fact sometimes whole groups would turn on one another like when Hitler and the Jar Men turned on the Juice. It was said it had happened there because Family on Earth had split apart, with groups moving away from one another and acting like each one was a Family on its own. It was even said that the White people had once taken the London people – whose skins were black like Angela's – and tied them up with ropes and traded with them like we in Family traded blackglass and buckskins and leopards' teeth between the groups. (That was *history*, and it was one of the things that kids used to learn when we had a School.)

And when I saw that look on David's face and saw what it was that he would like to do to me, I had a glimpse of what would happen to us if Family was broken apart. I had an image come into my mind of a big old tree being pulled down, a big old tree that gave warmth and light and fruit and bark for shelters, and I saw the deadly scalding sap that comes spurting up from Underworld when the trunk first breaks.

'Making juice for women that should know better than go with a silly boy who's got nothing to him but a pretty face,' David said. 'That, and trying to break up Family, that's all John here is good for. Oh, and getting big ideas just because he was lucky enough to have some leopard run right onto his spear.'

He gave me a horrible smile.

'Tell the truth, Johnny boy. You didn't plan that at all, did you? You didn't plan to do for the leopard. You were just so bloody scared you were frozen to the spot.'

Gerry stood up for me at once.

'That's crap, David. He could easily have run like I did, but he . . .'

Paaaaarp! Paaaarp! Paaaarp!

David broke off. We all broke off the ugly little play we were acting out to listen to the horns from over Circle Clearing. They weren't calling us back to Circle, just telling us that the Council had finished the Genda and that we should finish what we were doing soon and go back to our groups and eat and sleep.

'I'll be watching you, John,' David told me, 'when AnyVirsry starts again, so don't try any more of your tricks.'

His speech was always a bit spluttery, like all batfaces' speech, but his anger and his hate made it even more so. He was spitting his words out like they were poison. I had to wipe them off my face.

'And don't think you can get away with whatever you want just because you're Bella's little darling and her little slip-buddy, because you won't. She may be group leader but that doesn't mean the rest of group will go along with whatever she wants, nor the rest of Family. And anyway a waking will come soon when she sees through you too. Slippy might make people go silly and lovey-dovey, but lovey-dovey doesn't last forever, Johnny boy. It doesn't last long at all.'

Met had his stupid mouth wide open. Gerry had tears in his eyes. Candice looked sour. Janny looked like she was trying to see the funny side but couldn't.

David pulled his spear out of the dead buck and transferred it to his left hand. Then with his right he took the animal's back feet and slung the warm carcase over his muscly shoulder in one single move.

'Anyway,' he said, 'if you'll excuse me, I must be going. *I've* got some food to take back.'

'Looks like you've met your match, Mr Leopard Killer!' said Janny when he was out of hearing.

I shrugged. David scared me, it's true, and I was scared by the thought of whole Family turning against me, with Bella no longer able to protect me. But David hadn't told me anything I didn't already know.

'We'll see about that,' I said. 'The play's not finished yet.'

~ ~ ~

We went back to Redlantern with our scraps of food, and we accepted our small share of David's buck. He smirked at us as we laid out our sorry little haul of bats and grubby stumpcandy.

Bella looked strained and distant. She wasn't supposed to tell us what she'd been talking about in Council until we were all together again in AnyVirsry, but there was more to her distantness than that. She avoided my eye and slipped off early to her shelter, after ordering us all to stay in group for that sleep and not go wandering.

But I went to the group latrines that we'd dug in middle of a clump of starflowers and I took out the ring from the pocket at the edge of my wrap and I held it up close to a flower.

It felt smooth smooth, but it wasn't just smooth. On the outside was a little wavy line that ran right round it where the metal was a different colour, and on the inside, Gela's heart, there was tiny tiny writing. Not many newhairs could read, but Bella had taught me the letter sounds and I knew how to put them together to make words. I could read a lot of the old names and words that were carved onto the trees round Family. And I could certainly read the name inside the ring, written in tiny tiny letters with a neatness no one in Eden, scratching on trees or stones or bits of bark, could ever hope to equal, and no one over about thirty forty wombs, with their fading eyes, could ever hope to read. It was just about the best-known name in all of Family.

'To Angela,' it said, 'with love from Mum and Dad.'

Well, there have been lots of Angelas – or Gelas or Angies as they usually get called – but this could only be the Angela that came here at the beginning. This *was* her ring. It really *was* the same one they told the story about, the ring her mother and father gave her back on Earth, the one she lost in forest when she was looking for stumpcandy and could never find again.

Another shiver went through me, right through my body and my mind, almost like when you're having a slip and you come. It was one of those moments when you wonder whether there is some kind of big misunderstanding and really this is all just a dream or a made-up story, and not the real world like you thought it was. It was *strange* strange to hold that same ring in my hand, and to know for certain that one part of the True Story really really *was* true. It was weird weird to be connected to that story myself, to be the ending of it in a way, to be the one in Family who finally found Angela's ring for her. It was even stranger that it happened so soon after that weird feeling I'd had when I was by myself up by Deep Pool, and I'd felt that our mother Angela had been there too.

Michael's names! Lucy Lu would have *loved* this if it had happened to her. We'd never have heard the last of it! It was like Angela's shadow really was here somehow, following me around. It was like she wouldn't let me go.

Squatting down there among the starflowers, pretending to be taking a crap, I went through the story in my head. How Gela lost the ring. How she screamed out to Tommy and the kids for help. There were no other people in the world then but Tommy and Gela and their kids. She screamed at them to come and help her, she screamed and screamed like she hated them all, demanding that they crawl round on forest floor for hours and hours, waking after waking, looking for the missing ring that her mum and her dad had given her.

'It's only a ring,' Tommy says to her. 'It's just a *thing*, really, isn't it? Like a stone or a bit of wood. You've still got us, honey. You've still got me and the kids.'

'I don't want your bloody kids,' she says, 'and I *certainly* don't want you, you selfish shallow worthless man. I want my mum. I want my dad. I want my home that *you* stole from me.'

And then she cried and cried and cried, it's said for nine whole sleeps and nine whole wakings, while the kids blocked their ears and made silly noises with their mouths to shut out the cruel things she said, and the sad sad thoughts in their heads. Until that waking, the story says, the mother of us all had been warm and kind and a source of strength. But after it, she didn't smile for a whole womb and she never again spoke to Tommy with any love in her voice: never ever again.

I heard someone coming over to use the latrine. It was Old Roger – he'd be grunting and spluttering and stinking there for half an hour – so I slipped the ring back in its pocket and moved away.

12

Tina Spiketree

So third waking of AnyVirsry came, and we were all back together in Circle Clearing. Everyone in the world was squeezed into the space between Circle and trees (*really* everyone this time because all the hunters had returned by now), with jewel bats diving back and forth above us and forest humming all around. I stood with my sister Jane – bloody group leader Liz had made me stay with Spiketrees this time – and John stayed over with the Redlanterns, so I could only wave to him. He looked tired tired. I guess we all did, but he did more than most.

Council got ready out there in middle of Circle and Oldest were propped up there on their padded logs by six seven of their helpers, and then AnyVirsry started off again with the Mementoes being brought out to remind us yet again that we were all one Family and that we came here from Earth. Out came the Boots, the Belt, the Backpack, the Kee Board, and the helpers took them round all the groups so people could reach out and touch them and feel the weird stuff they're made of that no one knows where to find or how to make (except maybe Boots, which seem to be made of some kind of skin). Kids were excited excited. All the littles wanted to touch Kee Board, and push down those little squares with letters on them.

Oldest were allowed to take these things out of their hollow log whenever they wanted, but they were only shown to whole Family once every year at Any Virsries, and for little kids, seeing something from that long ago was like seeing something from a dream. They couldn't quite believe that it was all really there again.

And it wasn't just kids that got excited either. Some grownups cried when they saw the Mementoes, and when they reached out to touch them, some had trembling hands, full of hope and longing, for many people thought that when you touched the things from Earth it made aches and pains go away, or brought dreams into your head of that bright bright world, bright as the inside of a lanternflower. And as for that horrible Redlantern woman, Lucy Lu, she went into a bloody trance.

'I feel them!' she cried out, the lying slinker. 'I feel their presence all around us!'

But pretty soon helpers gathered the Mementoes all together again, shoved them back into the log and closed them inside with a greased lid, and then Family Head Caroline went pacing round in front of Council and Oldest, going through the Genda and telling us what Council had agreed, with little Jane London, the Secret Ree, hurrying behind her with the notes she'd scratched at the meeting on pieces of bark.

Behind the two of them were lined up all the group leaders: our Liz (that fat, ugly, bossy old thing), and old blind Tom Brooklyn, and silly gushing Flower Batwing, who thinks she is young and pretty when she's really old and wrinkled and dried up, and Mary Starflower, who likes to draw in breath when someone else speaks, like they've said such a terrible, stupid thoughtless thing that she wonders whether it can ever ever be undone, and Julie London with her hard, sharp, pushy face, and Candy Fishcreek, who always whispers so that everyone has to be quiet quiet to hear her, and Susan Blueside, who doesn't seem smart enough to be a group leader but is stubborn like a lump of rock. Susan Blueside didn't look too happy, so I guessed she'd lost the battle over London group's move. But the one that stood out from the rest was Bella Redlantern. She was right at the end of the line, next to Liz, but the space between her and Liz was fully twice the space that was left between any other two of them.

'London is to be allowed to move ten yards Blueway,' Caroline announced, 'as long as they rebuild Blueside fence ten yards further out and help Blueside build new shelters.'

Secret Ree winced and pointed at the writing on one of her pieces of bark. Caroline frowned for a moment, but then corrected herself.

'London is to be allowed to move *twelve* yards, as long as they rebuild Blueside fence *twelve* yards further out,' she said.

She studied the bark writing for a moment to remind herself what was next.

'Each group,' she went on, 'is only going to be allowed to fish on Greatpool during their normal group waking, and each group is only allowed one boat and one net out there at at a time. And no net used on Greatpool can be more than four yards long. This is to stop taking too many fish.'

There were some grumbling sounds from people in Family who liked to think of themselves as fishers. (Silly buggers. Would they rather catch *all* the fish and then have no fishing to do at all?) Caroline glanced across at the notes again.

'Youngmums,' she said, 'will have to scavenge and hunt like everyone else when their babies are three periods old. Clawfeet and oldies can look after the littles.'

There were grumbles from youngmums and clawfeet, but on Caroline went.

I waited. I didn't *really* expect anything but I wondered if there'd be anything to suggest that they'd even considered John's idea about Family moving out wider and not going on forever huddling round the old Circle of Stones. But no, nothing. And when they'd been through all the stuff that had been decided, Caroline said this:

'We have only discussed the properly agreed Genda. We have

not discussed things that were not properly raised. And we've all agreed that Family must stay together, here, side by side, around these stones that mark the spot where Tommy and Angela and the Three Companions came down from Starry Swirl, and from where the Companions set off on their way back to Earth. Family must not be broken. We must remain one, and we must remain in the place where our sisters and brothers from Earth will come to find us, as we all know one waking they will. And we must work together and live peacefully so as to try and be worthy to be taken back to our true home, even though we've forgotten so much, and fallen so far from what we once were.'

She looked out towards where Redlanterns were standing. She searched the faces until she found John's. She looked straight at him.

'I hope that's understood,' she said. 'It's Council's decision and it's mine, and it must be accepted by whole Family. And that means everyone here.'

I saw John look across at Bella Redlantern, but she was staring straight down at the ground, like there was something really interesting going on down there.

I could see John was *angry* angry. I could see him struggling inside himself.

Caroline looked round at us all, letting her words sink in.

'And that's the end of the . . .' she began.

But then John broke in. It was like sap bursting from a cut tree.

'Think about it, Caroline,' he called out. 'Work it out. It doesn't take an Einstein.'

All round Clearing, people groaned. Not this *again*. Not this rude little newhair once more. Ugly David Redlantern was pushing towards John through Redlantern group.

'If we were two once and now we're five hundred and thirty-two,' John went on, 'how big will Family be in another . . .?'

Whack! David slapped him hard across the back of his head with his big hard hand.

'Leave him be!' I yelled out.

'Get off him, David!' I heard John's faithful Gerry shouting, and I saw him pushing and shoving at David. But David swatted Gerry away like he was an ant, grabbed John by the hair and stood there solid as a tree.

Meanwhile, all round Circle people reacted, each one in their own way. Some laughed, some gasped, a few cheered, and many many called out in angry disapproval, not at what David had done, but at John for causing trouble.

I could see David lean forward and hiss out a warning, and then he gripped John's hair more tightly, lifting him up a little so he was hanging by his own hair roots.

'And that's the end of the Genda,' Caroline went on, with that particular rock-like stubbornness that she did so well, as if nothing had happened at all and she was just carrying on with what she had to say, 'and now it's time for me to go through the Laws that Harry, our second father, and his three sisters, carved on these Circle Clearing trees.'

Secret Ree passed her some pieces of bark with the Laws copied onto them, and then walked to the edge of the clearing through London group, so that while Caroline walked round inside Circle, she could walk round the trees and point to each carving, as Caroline read out from the bark what it said.

'*You mustn't kill anything except animals to eat and animals that are dangerous,*' read Caroline. '*You mustn't do anything to harm the family.*'

She paused and looked round at us all.

'That means you must not do anything to break Family up,' she said.

'*You mustn't slip with a child or with anyone that doesn't want to do it,*' she went on, '*and grown men mustn't slip with young girls.*

'*You mustn't steal things.*

'*You must come to Any Virsries and to Strornry Meetings.*

'*You must respect the Old.*

'And that,' said Caroline, frowning round at us, 'means not just Oldest, but group leaders, and Family Head, and *all* grownups.'

She glanced in John's direction for a moment, and then went on reading.

'You must look after clawfeet.

'You mustn't foul streams or pools.

'You must wait for Earth to come, and keep the customs of Earth, so Earth will take you home.'

John had a point, I thought, he really did. Of course we wanted to go back to Earth, but could we really wait in this one place forever, just in case they came?

And was that really the custom of Earth, anyway, to wait in one place? They were the ones who built a boat that could travel through the stars.

13

John Redlantern

'I'm watching you, John, so keep your mouth shut,' growled David, shoving me forward suddenly so I nearly fell.

I wanted to rub the back of my head where he'd been pulling my hair, but of course I didn't. I acted like it hadn't hurt at all. And I ignored Gerry too, standing beside me, looking anxiously into my face. Gela's tits, there was no way I was going to admit to him, or to David, or to anyone else that David had hurt or upset me. I stood up straight and watched what was going on in Circle, like nothing had happened. That was Caroline's game and I could play it too.

Helpers were lifting Mitch and Stoop and Gela to their wobbly feet. We'd got to the bit of Any Virsry called Earth Things, where we had to listen to three old blind people tell us about things that they'd never seen and didn't understand.

Scrawny old Mitch told how Earth spun round and round like a top so half of it is all lighted up by the star and half of it is dark, and saggy grey Gela told how the people there found metal in the ground that could be used to make knives that wouldn't smash like blackglass does.

'And they found a thing called the Single Force,' she said, 'that could carry them between the stars.'

'They found another kind of force that was even better than that,' broke in little Stoop excitedly, with his blind eyes rolling around in his soft fat head, 'a force that could be made to run along strings for miles and miles, and could be used for light and heat and for machines called telly visions that could make pictures that could move and speak. It was called Li . . .' He stumbled on the word, just like old one-legged Jeffo had done, over by Dixon Stream. 'It was called Li . . . Leck . . . Lecky-trickity . . .'

'Li . . . Leck . . . Lecky-trickity . . .' Gerry mimicked under his breath, looking at me to see if I was pleased.

'It's important to remember the Single Force,' Gela came back, not happy with Stoop's interruption. Her blind eyes bulged at us. 'That's what got us here, and that's what will take us home. And not only that,' she carried on hastily before the others could break in, 'but they had animals called horses too that could carry them about. Imagine that! Animals!'

'And cars,' Mitch said, and began to cough and cough while his helpers whacked him on the back.

The helpers got out the Earth Models, and then, with a lot of coughing and wheezing, Oldest told us about *houses*, which were shelters as big as hills, and *roads*, which were paths made with hard shiny metal, and *trains* and *planes* and *drains*.

'Drains were like streams underneath every shelter,' Stoop said. 'They'd wash all your piss and shit away, into a pool as big as Greatpool, covered with a roof of stone.'

'Planes were a kind of bird made of metal,' Mitch said.

'Trains were long thin shelters that slid along a smooth metal path,' said Gela, 'so you could go to sleep in one bit of a forest and wake up in another.'

They were flagging now, and the group leaders began to prompt them with other things to say.

'What about hosples where they made you well?' whispered Mary Starflower.

'What about those clones with their big feet and their red noses?' murmured Susan Blueside.

'What about money?' prompted Tom Brooklyn.

'Ah,' said old Gela, 'money was numbers you held in your head.'

'You could trade them for things you wanted,' said Mitch.

Trade things for numbers in other people's heads? Nobody'd ever understood what that meant, but Oldest spoke about it at every Any Virsry, as if a waking would come when someone would jump up and yell out, 'Yes of course! Of course! I've figured it out now! I know how that worked!'

What was the point of saying words if we didn't know what they meant? We were like blind people pretending to see.

But they say that even Tommy and Angela themselves didn't understand how Lecky-trickity worked or how you made the Single Force. They didn't even know where metal was to be found, or how to get it out of the stone it was mixed with, except that you had to heat it with fire.

~ ~ ~

Littles got hungry and started to grizzle and cry. Newhairs giggled and whispered and pinched each other, and Oldest themselves, who'd started off so excited that they couldn't bear to let each other finish what they had to say, got too tired to carry on. In fact they were so drained and pale and wobbly all of a sudden that they looked like they might die right there in front of us in their precious Circle of Stones. They had to be helped to step back and sit down and wrap up with skins and be given stuff to drink. And then Caroline and Council and Oldest and helpers got out of the way, and in came Big Sky-Boat, and everyone cheered and clapped and laughed.

It was time for the Show, and it was Brooklyn's turn to do it. A whole bunch of them were carrying that great silly wooden thing that was supposed to be the starship *Defiant*. It was three times the length of a normal boat, and not quite straight. It had poles sticking up from it to hold up a wobbly bark roof like the roof of a shelter, and long branches sticking out of its sides for people to carry it with. It even had another little boat inside it, which was supposed to be the Landing Veekle. And crammed in, at the front and back, were the Three Disobedient Men, laughing and waving to us.

Of course Big Sky-Boat was *tiny* tiny compared with the real *Defiant*. The real starship was longer than Greatpool, and so big that if it ever came down to the ground it would never get back up again into sky. (Even the real Landing Veekle was the size of Circle of Stones, and it was carried *inside* of *Defiant*.) But all the same our silly little Big Sky-Boat still looked stupidly big compared to the little log boats that we used to fish on Greatpool and Longpool, and it had so much stuff on top of it that anyone could see that it would have toppled over straight away if you actually put it in water. Plus, with that curve in middle of it, there was no way you could have paddled it straight.

But of course Big Sky-Boat never *did* get put in water. It was carried every Any Virsry by a bunch of people holding the ends of three strong branches that were stuck through holes in its sides. Those three grinning Brooklyn men inside it were supposed to be Tommy Schneider, our first father, from whose dick came every one of us, and his two friends Dixon Thorleye and Mehmet Haribey. They were setting out from Earth into Starry Swirl, as calmly and cheerfully as if they were just going fishing out on Greatpool. Tommy's face had white wood-ash mixed with buckfat smeared over it, to show that he had white skin.

'Let's go further out,' says Dixon, when they're getting near the edge of Circle of Stones.

'No, we shouldn't,' says Tommy. 'Earth Family doesn't want us to do that, do they?'

'Yeah,' says Mehmet, 'and this Sky-Boat belongs to everyone, remember, not just to us.'

It was said that it took thousands of hundreds of people to build *Defiant*, and take it up to sky in pieces, and to put it together up there. It took thousands of people all across Earth to find the metal and plastic and everything else they needed in the rocks, and thousands more to get it out and carry it to where it was needed. All Earth was part of the work, which took hundreds or thousands of wombtimes.

'I mean,' says Mehmet, 'it's not like we made it ourselves.'

'True,' says Tommy, looking serious serious. But then he smiles and looks out at the people all around the clearing: in front of him, behind, left, right.

'Should we do it, kids?' he calls out. 'Should we go further out?'

'No! No! Don't do it!' yell all the kids in Family, laughing and squealing with delight.

'Yeah but why not?' says Dixon. 'It won't hurt anyone. And anyway, I feel that it's what Jesus wants us to do. To cross over Starry Swirl and find new worlds. Let's just do it!'

'No! No!' yells everyone.

But Tommy laughs, and cups his hand over his ear, and shrugs, like he can't hear us any more.

'Okay,' he says. 'You've persuaded me. Let's give it a go, eh?'

'Well,' says Mehmet, 'I suppose so. But I feel bad bad about Earth Family.'

'They'll get over it,' says Dixon, and off they move in their giant boat right up to the edge of Circle of Stones.

It felt kind of shocking to see that silly thing there next to Circle, where none of us were allowed to go.

But then in comes President, the Family Head of Earth, wearing a special President's wrap with four five big white stars on it done in ash on a square stained blue with starflower juice.

'Hey! Come back!' she yells up to them. 'We don't want you to do that now. Things are hard hard for us on Earth just now. Every time you take one of those sky-boats out across the stars, we all have to work extra hard to give you the stuff you need to make the Single Force. We haven't got the time for that now. We've got better things to do.'

Mehmet looks at Tommy. Tommy looks at Dixon.

'Just this once?' Dixon pleads with the other two. 'I promise you, it's what Jesus wants.'

Tommy and Mehmet look at each other.

'Yeah, just this once,' they agree, and they carry on right up to Circle, ignoring the President, who shouts up 'Stop! Stop! Stop!' in a silly high voice that makes littles laugh.

In comes Small Sky-Boat, which is meant to be Police Veekle. It also has a bark roof and is carried on another set of branches, but it looks even more wobbly and silly than Big Sky-Boat, because it is made to come apart. The real Police Veekle was as big as Landing Veekle, apparently, and it went round and round sky of Earth, looking for problems and trouble. (Sky there was more full of boats than a hundred Greatpools, and in some of them people were doing bad things, like dropping things onto Earth.)

Sitting in the Small Sky-Boat are Angela our mother and Michael Name-Giver. They were called Orbit Police. Angela has her face darkened with clay and buckfat to look like the real Angela.

'Go after those silly buggers, you two,' says President, 'and get them back before they go and lose our boat in Starry Swirl. They really don't know what they're doing, and anyway, they're not doing what Earth Family wants.'

Being Orbit Police meant that Angela and Michael had the job of stopping people who didn't do what the President and Family wanted. Their boat hurried after the Big Sky-Boat *Defiant*, with Angela and Michael both yelling and shouting out:

'Hey! Come back! Stop! That's not your boat to take away!'

Angela looks out at us standing all round the clearing. She looks left, she looks right, she looks in front of her and behind, and then she raises her eyebrows and holds out her hands, palms upwards, as if to say, 'Are you guys not even going to help?'

The kids know quite well this is their invitation to join in.

'Stop! Don't do it!' they yell out excitedly to those three naughty men in Big Sky-Boat. Lots of the little kids have fierce angry faces as if they're really cross, and really think they can change the story.

'Stop!' they yell. 'Go back!'

But the men in Big Sky-Boat take no notice at all of them, or of Angela and Michael either, until Small Sky-Boat is really close. Then finally Dixon looks back at them.

'Back off, you two, or you'll get hurt!' he yells out. 'We've got the Single Force here. We've already started it going. We've made Hole-in-Sky and we're going through. You can't stop us! So back off!'

'No, we won't back off,' says Angela. 'We won't back off and we *will* stop you – or sink trying. You come back here, mate! We're not going to let you go!'

~ ~ ~

If only the men in Big Sky-Boat had listened, was what we were all supposed to think. If only they'd listened and followed the Laws of Earth and respected President, then we wouldn't be here in Eden, standing around in our buckskin wraps and wondering how you find metal and what lecky-trickity is and how you make a sky-boat. We'd be there on Earth with that big star above us and the light all around us, the sweet white light, pure and bright like the inside of a whitelantern flower, and we'd *know* about metal and lecky-trickity and all of that. Telly vision, computers, we'd know it all, without even trying.

But then it wouldn't have been *us*, though, would it? I thought to myself. Tommy and Angela would never have got together, would they? No way would she have slipped with him if she had all the men on Earth to choose from. And that means that none of us five hundred and thirty-two people would ever have lived on Earth, or on Eden, or anywhere else.

It was a strange strange thought. All this time we'd been grieving about how things were, but if things weren't this way, there wouldn't be an 'us' to grieve anything.

~ ~ ~

Well anyway, pretty soon, that *Defiant* starts to spin round and round like a log in the water at the top of Exit Falls.

'Oh, oh, oh!' yell Dixon and Mehmet and Tommy together as they whirl round.

Purple fire is flashing along the long metal spikes that stick out from the huge starship's shiny metal sides, each spike as tall as a full grown tree. It's tipping tipping on the edge of Hole-in-Sky, just like a log on the edge of Exit Falls. Single Force is pushing it closer, the Single Force that made the Hole itself. It's tipping over, it's tipping, it's about to fall . . .

Small Sky-Boat comes nearer and nearer till it's right alongside, and then *it* starts to go round and round too, and it starts to tip over as well, pulled towards Hole-in-Sky.

'No! No!' yell Angela and Michael, the two orbit police.

'Back off, you idiots!' yells Mehmet from *Defiant*. 'Back off or you'll get dragged through as well!'

'Back off!' yell Dixon and Tommy.

'It's too late,' yells Michael back, 'the bloody resin's gone. The skin's come off the end of our boat. The water's coming in. We're sinking. We can't paddle any more. You've got to help us!'

'Yeah! Help us!' yells Angela. 'We're sinking.'

'And whose fault is that?' ask Tommy, Dixon and Mehmet all together, looking at Family round the edge of the clearing, like they expect us to say it's Michael's and Angela's for being foolish enough to chase after them.

'Yours! Yours! Yours!' yell out the kids, and the newhairs, and most of the grownups too.

'Come on! Hurry up! Help us!' Michael and Angela scream and yell, like they haven't got time for all this discussion.

Tommy and Mehmet and Dixon look at each other.

'Quick! Quick! Help them!' yells out whole Family under the whitelantern trees.

'Yes,' says Mehmet, 'I suppose it is our stupid fault really, and we've got to save them. Quick, Dixon. We'll try and get them into Big Sky-Boat before we drop through Hole.'

This bit is tricky for the people holding the branches, who have to move round each other, and duck under each other's branches, but, as it tips over, the Police Veekle presses up against the starship *Defiant*, and Dixon and Mehmet and Tommy reach out and pull Angela and Michael across into their boat, and then Big Sky-Boat, with all five of them inside, moves between the stones and out into the forbidden Circle to show that it has fallen through Hole-in-Sky.

Just in time. Only just in time. The people carrying Small Sky-Boat let it fall into pieces and throw them away in different directions, to show that Police Veekle has been destroyed by Single Force and its purple fire.

Meanwhile the great starship *Defiant* goes right out into darkness beyond Starry Swirl until Earth and Sun are hidden completely among all those stars. And there they find Eden, a world on its own, far from any stars, which isn't like Earth at all.

'There's no Sun here like we have on Earth,' says Angela, looking out. 'But look, everywhere is shining shining, as far as you can see.'

And the others look out, each one in a different direction.

'Shining everywhere,' they say. They are amazed amazed, because they didn't have shining forests on Earth, and they thought light only came from stars and Sun.

'Let's get down and look at it,' says Tommy.

They have that other little Boat inside the Big Sky-Boat, the Landing Veekle, and they take it out and all get into it, helped by the people from Brooklyn that were carrying the Police Veekle until it fell apart. (The real Landing Veekle was round, but we don't know how to make boats that way, so ours is long and thin.) It carries them down from sky, right into middle of Circle of Stones.

Out get Tommy and Dixon and Mehmet, out gets Angela. But Michael is sick sick and they have to help him down.

'You bloody idiots,' Angela tells the three men. 'Look what you've done to Michael. Look what you did to our boat. Look where you've brought us. Take us back to Earth now. I want to see my group again. I want to see my mum and my friends. I didn't want to come here to this dark dark place.'

Tommy looks ashamed, so do Dixon and Mehmet. The Three Disobedient Men all stand in a row with their heads hanging down like naughty kids.

Some of the real kids laugh.

'Bad boys!' they shout out. 'Bad bad boys!'

'Our boat's damaged too, I'm afraid,' says Mehmet. 'We're sorry sorry. It's cracked. It might leak. We'll try and mend it, but we may sink and drown on the way back.'

'You bloody idiots,' says Angela again.

Then Tommy and Dixon and Mehmet get back in the Landing Veekle and go up to the Big Sky-Boat *Defiant* and squat down by it with pots of glue and skins to try and fix it. And while they work up there, Angela and Michael (who's started to feel better again) wander about and explore Eden.

But of course really they are wandering around among us, through the crowd, round the edge of the clearing and back again into Circle.

~ ~ ~

This part of the story is called *Michael and His Names*, and it's the bit that kids love the best.

'Where is this place anyway?' Angela asks. 'What do you think it's called?'

'I don't know,' says Michael. 'Let me think. Perhaps we could call it . . .'

He pauses.

'It's Eden!' yell out all the kids round Circle, because of course any fool knows that!

Michael frowns, like he thinks he's heard something but he's not sure. He holds his hand to his ear.

'Perhaps,' he says, 'we could call it . . .'

'*Eden!*' the kids yell again even louder.

'I don't know,' he says, 'it's on tip of my tongue, but I can't quite think of the name.'

'*Ed-en!*' the kids bellow.

Michael smiles.

'E-den,' he says slowly, 'I think we could call it Eden.'

The kids all cheer.

'Look at this,' says Angela. 'What's this?'

She's pointing to a whitelantern tree.

'*It's a tree!*' the kids yell out, laughing. How could anyone be so dumb as to not know what a tree is?

I guess it made everyone feel good to see Angela and all of them not knowing these things we knew so well, after we'd had to listen for so long to that big big list of wonderful things they had on Earth, which we didn't understand at all. It was kind of reassuring to know that they didn't even know what a tree was, when we were feeling useless useless for not knowing about metal and telly vision and horses and the Single Force.

'We'll call it . . .'

Michael hesitated. The kids laughed. They *loved* all this. I suppose I did too. I loved it but at the same time I hated it for trapping us and making us feel so helpless and babyish and small.

'We'll call it . . .'

'*A tree!*' yell out the kids.

The grownups are smiling and laughing too, and a lot of them are joining in with the kids. Everyone is tired tired, what with the wakings being changed, and the long weary list of Earth Things, and the Laws and the Genda and all, but now everyone is brightening up again.

'We'll call it ... a ... *tree!*' goes Michael, who is really a skinny little guy of forty wombs or so called Luke Brooklyn who's mainly known in Family for being clever with blackglass.

Everyone cheers.

'And what's *this?*' asks Tommy, looking over from Big Sky-Boat, which he's trying to fix, and pointing at a little jewel bat swooping overhead. (He was supposed to be up in sky at this point, but no one seemed to mind!)

'What's *what?*' goes Michael, looking where Tommy pointed. The bat has gone.

'This!' says Tommy, pointing to another bat.

'What's *what?*' goes Michael again.

'*This here!*' says Tommy, showing him another bat again.

'Oh *that,*' says Michael. 'Well, I don't know about that. I've no idea. I've never seen anything like it. I don't know *what* to say.'

'It's a *bat!*' yell the kids.

Michael frowns and screws up his face. He can almost hear them but not quite.

'It's a *bat!*' they yell again.

He holds his hand to his ear.

'*It's a bat!*' the kids bellow again.

He frowns like he still can't hear, and he scratches his head.

Michael was called the Name-Giver because he gave us the words that we still use for all the animals and plants that live in Eden, and found out things about them like how they came up from Underworld when everything was ice, and how dry starflowers could feed our skin like Sun did on Earth. But in the Show he was also the name-*hearer*, because he didn't actually *choose* the names. He only heard us, faintly faintly, shouting them back to him from the future. And then he took them, and gave them to the things in the world, and sent them out again to us the slow way, through the five six long generations between us and him.

'It – is – a – BAT!' the kids yell even louder.

He nods. He smiles.

'I think we'll call it a bat!' he says, and everybody cheers.

And then the same thing happens with flutterbyes and birds and anything else that Luke Brooklyn happens to see, until Dixon brings the game to a stop by calling down from sky.

'Michael? Gela? We've done all we can without metal and lecky-trickity to help us,' he says. 'It doesn't look that good to be honest. Do you want to chance it, or do you want to stay here?'

'I'm going back,' says Michael. 'I miss Earth, and I've already given names to everything that's here, so my job's done.'

The other three men come back from *Defiant* (they don't bother with the Landing Veekle this time: they just walk). And Michael walks over to stand with them, leaving Angela facing them all by herself.

'I miss Earth too,' says Angela, 'I miss it so much. I miss Sun and I miss all the people I love. But I'd still rather live in this place than die in sky. If one of you blokes will stay here with me, then if no one comes back for us quickly, we could have kids and start a new Family here in Eden, and wait for however long it takes for Earth to come and find us.'

Of course, it wasn't Angela really, that woman standing there with her face smeared with fat and clay, it was a plump little red-headed woman called Suzie Brooklyn. And she wasn't much good at acting. She didn't know how to say the words like she really meant them, and you could hear she was just repeating things that someone else had taught her. But even so it was sad sad, seeing Angela there all alone, facing those four men, making up her mind not to go back to Earth.

'Go on! Give her a slip!' some man yells out from over in Starflower group, and quite a few people laugh, including Angela, who has to put her hand over her mouth to stop herself.

'I'll stop with you, Angela,' says Tommy. 'We took you here against your will. We should let you have what you want now. We owe you that.'

It's said that of those four men, it was Mehmet that she fancied most, and Tommy that most got on her nerves. But Mehmet didn't offer to stay with her, and Tommy did.

'You owe her a damn good slipping, mate!' that bloke yells out again.

Not so many people find it funny the second time, but Tommy is really a bloke called John Brooklyn (a tall thin dark bloke with curly black hair, who reckoned to know all the best fishing places in Longpool) and he *does* find it funny. He sort of grins and gives the bloke a thumbs up, forgetting that he is supposed to be playing a part. And that makes Angela giggle too, and she has to compose her face and make it sad again.

'You owe me more than that, mate,' she says, but she holds out her hand anyway, and he leaves the other three, and walks over to her, and takes it. And then the other three say goodbye and they get into the Landing Veekle and go up to Big Sky-Boat *Defiant* in sky. With a lot of difficulty, whole of the Landing Veekle is put back into *Defiant* with the men still inside it, and then it's carried out of Circle.

Those three, Michael, Mehmet and Dixon, the three that went back up to the starship, were the Three Companions. (They weren't the same three as the Three Disobedient Men, because Michael was with them, and Tommy wasn't.) And of course, we didn't know what happened to them. Did they get back to Earth? Did they drown? And if they drowned, did the starship get back without them, like an empty boat drifts to the bank? We all thought it must have done, or at least got near enough to Earth to shout out with its Rayed Yo. How could a huge great thing like that be completely lost?

'This sky-boat is so busted up,' yells down Mehmet as *Defiant* moves out of the clearing,'that they'll probably need to build a whole new sky-boat to come and fetch you.'

'Yeah,' says Dixon. 'It could take a long time getting together all that metal and plastic from under the ground. You're going to have to be patient patient.'

'But we won't forget you,' calls out Michael as they disappear into the trees. 'And Earth won't forget you either.'

~ ~ ~

'I wish you'd never brought me here,' says plump red-headed Suzie Brooklyn.

She knows this is an important moment, and she tries her best to put Angela's anger and sadness into her voice.

'I wish I hadn't too,' says John Brooklyn.

'I wish I could go home to Earth,' she says.

'A waking will come sooner or later when they come back for us,' he says, saying the words all in a rush, without any feeling at all. 'Or someone else will come in their place. You'll see. We belong on Earth. Our eyes nod . . .'

He pulls a face at his mistake, and corrects himself.

'Our eyes need the bright light. So do our hearts. We won't be . . . We won't be here forever. If they could make Hole-in-Sky once, they can do it again.'

Suzie Brooklyn nods.

'We'll make a Circle of Stones here to show where Landing Veekle stood,' she says. 'That way we'll always remember the place and know to stay here. And we'll hunt in forest round it and fish in the pools. And we'll tell our children, and our children's children, they must always stay here, and wait, and be patient, and one waking Earth will come.'

'Yes, Gela, my dear,' says John Brooklyn. 'But don't you worry.

Earth *will* come, it really will. One waking they'll come and take us home.'

One waking they'll come and take us home.

Tom's dick and Harry's, there were tears all round the clearing.

14

Caroline Brooklyn

So that was another Any Virsry done. While everyone left Clearing to go and eat and sleep, I made sure Oldest were alright, and said thankyou to the group leaders: Liz, Flower, Candy, Susan, Tom, Mary, Julie, Bella. (There was something weird going on with Bella but that was for another waking.) A few of the older people in Family came over to say thankyou for my work, but most people just hurried away as quick as they could back to their group fires and their shelters. They'd had more than enough of me these last few wakings: me and the Laws and everything.

Well, I didn't mind that. I'd had enough of them too, to be honest. I felt tired tired. The characters in the Show had to play a part for less than an hour, but I'd had to play a part for three whole wakings, and play it like it was really me. No giggling, no winking, no forgetting my words. Rest of Family had no idea how tiring that was, except maybe some of the group leaders, the really good ones I mean, the ones who understood there was more to it than just enjoying the feeling of being someone big. Not that I minded playing the part of Family Head, of course I didn't. I'd played it so long that in a way it seemed more real than ordinary Caroline Brooklyn. After all, even to be an ordinary person you have to play parts. It's just that you don't have to stick to one; you can be a strong person one minute, and the next be weak. I liked the discipline of sticking to one thing. And I liked being the centre of things too, and that always kept me going when AnyVirsry was happening, knowing that I was at the centre of it all, but afterwards the tiredness always hit me.

'Yes, you go back to group, Tom,' I told Tom Brooklyn. 'I'll be along shortly when Clearing has emptied out. That was a pretty good Show that Brooklyn group put on there. No boats dropped like last time, no one forgetting what they were supposed to say. I felt proud of you all.'

'Shame Suzie didn't put herself into being Angela a bit more. She was better in practice.'

'Don't worry, Tom, she did alright. You off now too, Mary? Good AnyVirsry, I thought, though it's left us with a lot of work to do. You going too, Susan? Sorry you didn't get what you wanted about the London move, but I'll make sure sure they do the work they promised to do to get you lot sorted out again.'

'We said ten yards in Council meeting. Not twelve like Secret Ree wrote down.'

'She was right there with us when she wrote it down, Susan. I'm sure she wouldn't have made a mistake. But don't worry, like I say, we'll make sure London helps you get sorted. A few wakings and you'll be fine.'

It was a hard hard job too, keeping Family together. There was always someone that wasn't happy, always someone that needed soothing down. That was what that silly kid John Redlantern didn't understand. Any fool can break a thing. In two minutes, you could take one of Jeffo's boats out on Greatpool, knock the ends off it with a stone and let it sink, but building a new one took wakings and wakings, and keeping one going meant work every time it was used: greasing it, checking the skins are tight, making sure the glue isn't getting wet or coming loose.

Of course sometimes you've got to make changes. Did the

Redlantern boy really think he was the only one who'd even noticed that? Of course you have. We had to give London a bit more space, didn't we? We had to change the fishing rules out on Greatpool. But what he didn't understand was the work work work that goes into just keeping things going waking after waking after waking. Silly little slinker.

'Yes, you head back to Batwing now, Flower. I'm going in just a minute myself. Good AnyVirsry, I thought, though we'll need to talk more about that Redlantern boy.'

He was still in Clearing, I noticed. All of Redlantern was filing out, but John Redlantern was standing there by himself, like he was another Family Head who had to wait, like me, for everyone else to go first. I thought of going to talk to him, or maybe of telling him to leave, but I reckoned that would just make him feel even more important than he already did. He'd go in his own time. I'd think about how to manage him when I'd had some sleep; how to manage him, and how to manage Redlantern group. I noticed that Bella had slipped off without even saying goodbye.

'Think I'll head off now, Caroline,' said Liz Spiketree, 'get back to group and make sure they're all settled.'

'Yes, you go, Liz. Thanks for your work in Council. I'll follow you in just a minute.'

'Okay if I put the barks away now?' asked little Jane London.

'Yes, go on, Jane. I'm done with them now. You go back to London and get some rest.'

Jane got on my nerves to tell the truth, with the way she kept correcting me and pointing to the bark all the time, and I was sure that she sometimes wrote down what she thought we ought to have said, and not what we actually said at all. Susan Blueside was right, it *was* ten yards Blueway that we said London could move, and not twelve like Jane wrote down. I'd need to speak to her about that. She could *not* be allowed to use her position as Secret Ree to help her own London group. One *more* problem for another waking.

'I'm off, Caroline,' said Tom Brooklyn. 'See you back in group in a minute?'

'Yes, I'll be along soon.'

I looked up and saw that John Redlantern was *still* standing there. A couple of his friends had stopped to talk to him, but now they headed off and left him on his own again, stretching and scratching and looking round, like he was in no hurry at all.

I had a bad feeling. I always felt tired after an Any Virsry, and I always felt a bit sad too. (Like the people in Show feel sad, I suppose, when they have to stop being Michael Name-Giver or Tommy Schneider and have to go back to being themselves.) But I had a different feeling this time, like something new had crept into the world that wouldn't ever go away again.

'He's only one silly newhair,' I told myself. 'Don't fret about it. Just a silly newhair trying to get himself noticed. It's not such a big thing. It just feels that way because I'm tired.'

A Starflower oldmum called Clare came over.

'Good Any Virsry, Caroline, thanks. Can't have been easy handling that cheeky Redlantern boy.'

She glared over at John. He had his back turned to me now, but he was still standing there.

'Honestly,' she said. 'Newhairs these wakings! He does for one leopard, and he thinks he's more important than Council and Family Head.'

'I know, newhairs eh? But I suppose we were all young once.'

'Well, we weren't like him and his sort, that's for sure. But anyway, thanks again, Caroline. I'm off back to make sure our whingy littles get settled down nice and quick.'

As she walked off, John glanced over towards me, then looked quickly away.

However much I told myself it was just because I was tired, I had a *strong* strong feeling that there was trouble stirring in Family that was different from any trouble we'd had before. And more than that,

I felt it was something I'd been warned about. I just couldn't think when.

And then suddenly I did remember. It was in the Secret Story.

~ ~ ~

The True Story we remembered at AnyVirsries was only part of what had been handed down to us from the beginning. There were some things that Angela told to just two of her daughters, Susie and Clare, the ones she thought most sensible and grown up, and told them to pass on only to girls that they knew they could trust. That first Clare was the one who started Brooklyn group, and she was my mum's grandmother. Angela's words came down from her, through my mum, to me.

And one of the secret things from Angela she told me – one of the many – was this.

'Watch out for men who want to turn everything into a story that's all about them. There will always be a few of them, and once one of them starts, another one of them will want to fight with him.'

My mother told me that Tommy Schneider, the father of all of us, was one of those men. And, out of the Three Companions, Dixon Thorleye was one too. 'Dixon liked to think he did what Jesus told him,' Angela said, 'but Jesus always seemed to tell Dixon to do the one thing that would make him the hero of the story.' That's why Dixon couldn't bear to just go back down to Earth when the President told him to, and nor could Tommy either. They had to take *Defiant*, and go charging off across Starry Swirl, like they knew better than whole Family of Earth.

Yes, I thought, John Redlantern was trouble in *just* that way. He might think he was worried about us not having enough food, or about Exit Falls getting blocked up, or whatever, but that wasn't *really* what his shouting at AnyVirsry was all about. What it was really about was him being the hero of the story, and no one else. I'd never had a challenge like that at AnyVirsry before, never, but I could see now that, once John had started it, David Redlantern had picked it up. He was another of those men that Angela warned about. I'd need to watch him too. I'd need to find a way, somehow, of heading off this whole thing.

I sighed. Every AnyVirsry brought me and Council a whole lot of new hard work but, Gela's heart, this time it was going to be hard hard hard.

I looked across at John again. Thanks be to Mother Gela, he was finally moving. About time! Nearly everyone else had already left Clearing, and now he was going too, heading off by himself towards Stream's Join.

I really hadn't wanted to leave while he was still here, but now at last I felt I could go. Back to Brooklyn, and a bit of meat, and a long long sleep.

Next waking I'd have a no-work waking, and rest up, and Brooklyn group would look after me. And then, who knows, maybe things would seem more manageable again?

15

John Redlantern

I kept thinking about Michael naming everything, and the children shouting back to him what to say. I'd seen that same story acted out so many times, but now I couldn't stop it going round and round inside my head. Whole Family was busting to leave the clearing, but I just stood there and stood there, trying to take it in, and trying to decide on what I'd do next.

First Oldest were led away to sleep in their shelters on the edge of London, all grey and wobbly and worn out. Then everyone else started to go, each group gathering together its littles and clawfeet and oldies and heading off back to their own fires and shelters. And, while the clearing was emptying, Council left, one by one, all except Caroline, with Secret Ree tucking her writing-barks under her arm and rushing off to hide them in a secret place she had somewhere that no one but Council was supposed to know about.

But I stayed where I was, and over in middle of Circle, Caroline stayed where she was as well, nodding and smiling to anyone that came up to her, or looked in her direction. Sometimes, when she wasn't dealing with anyone else, she glanced over towards me, and I thought maybe she was going to speak to me about what I'd done, but when I caught her eye she quickly looked away. She tended not to deal with troublesome newhairs in Family – that was a job for group leaders – so I guessed she was just waiting for me to go.

Well, I'd go in my own good time. I had things to think about.

~ ~ ~

When Michael named the plants and the animals, did he hear us calling back to him? Was that possible? Because if he did, then I should be able to hear voices from *our* future too, voices calling back to me, telling me what I needed to do, because I'd had an idea. And it was a big idea, a big *big* idea. It was big like Dixon refusing to obey the President, big like Tommy and Angela lying down together to bring us all into the world. And if I went through with it, it would be a story like those stories that would be remembered, and talked about, not just for a period or two, but for generations and generations.

But what was it that those future people would call out to me when the story was acted out? That was what I was trying to figure out. Were they shouting 'Go ahead! Do it! You'll save us from starving and drowning!' or were they telling me 'No, you'll ruin everything! You'll lose us Earth forever!'?

The clearing emptied quickly. Everyone was anxious to get away from that cramped space between the trees and Circle of Stones. Some people wanted to eat, or to settle down their littles, but most just wanted to crawl under the bark roofs of their shelters and sleep. I wouldn't have minded sleeping myself. I was so tired and felt so battered. And I was *dreading* dreading the things that might soon be coming my way if I stayed awake, *really* awake I mean, like I was awake when I stood and faced that leopard.

'Hey John? What you doing?' Gerry asked.

Little Jeff stood behind him, watching me with his big clever eyes, as if he already knew what was in my mind.

I looked round for David, but he had already gone. I guessed he thought I couldn't do much harm now Any Virsry was over. That made me smile. There was a *lot* of harm I could still do.

'Go on back,' I said to them. 'I might go see Tina for a bit. I'll join you later.'

Then Tina herself came over.

'Tom's dick, John, you don't let go, do you?' she said, and laughed. It seemed she'd enjoyed my boldness earlier that waking. 'Shall we go up Deep Pool for a bit before we sleep? Swim in the water. Clear our heads of all this?'

I nodded.

'Good idea,' I said, 'but I've got something I need to do first, though. I'll come to Deep Pool a bit later, if you're willing to wait for me.'

'What have you got to do?'

'I'll . . . I'll tell you later.'

'Does it involve Bella by any chance, or Martha London?'

'No, no. Nothing like that. You'll understand when I tell you.'

She examined me closely with her eyes narrowed. Then, reluctantly, she shrugged and nodded and headed off.

I noticed Caroline looking at me again. All of Council had gone, and nearly all of Family, but she was still standing there. I made a pretence of leaving myself, heading in the general direction of Stream's Join, but walking slowly and letting people pass me. When there was no one left behind me, I doubled back to Circle Clearing.

Sure enough, Caroline had gone, and so had everyone else. There was no one there but me.

~ ~ ~

Nothing looks more lovely than something that's about to end, and that's true even if you yourself are going to be the cause of its ending.

That clearing was beautiful *beautiful* with the bright whitelanterns all round, extra bright and shiny as they were from being pruned for all those wombtimes since the beginning, and with shiny bright

Main Stream running past one edge of it. But of course there were other pretty clearings in forest, and what made Circle Clearing special were the white stones in middle. They were what made it different from every single one of all the other gaps and openings in forest between Alps and Rockies, and between Blue Mountains and Peckham Hills. That white Circle gave it a mystery and a story. And they made it ours.

So I hesitated, feeling in the little pocket at the edge of my waistwrap for Angela's ring, as if I thought she might help me decide what to do. But she was silent. All I heard was, far off in the future, voices calling back to me across time.

'No, no, don't do it!' some of them were saying. 'Angela said we must stay together by Circle, John. You know she did. She made Circle herself! Her and Tommy. They made it to show us where we must wait until Earth comes back for us at last!'

'Do it, John, do it!' other voices were saying. 'Angela wanted us to make a life on Eden. If she hadn't wanted that she'd never have stayed and never have laid down with Tommy.'

They couldn't settle it for me. They were no use at all. I'd have to make up my own mind. My mouth was dry, my hands clammy with sweat, but I looked around one more time to make sure no one was watching, then walked over to one of the stones and picked it up.

No one had ever picked up one of those stones before, not that I'd heard of, not since they were first laid there by Tommy and Angela themselves. It was just a stone, cold to the touch like other stones, heavy like other stones, but I felt like the thing might burst into flames in my hand and sear off my skin. I feared it would shriek out loud, like a living creature, screaming for Oldest and Council and Family to come and save it. I even feared, a little tiny bit, that I would simply drop down dead.

But of course none of that happened. It was just a stone, wasn't it? It wasn't alive. It wasn't even dead. It was just a stone. And once I'd taken it over to Main Stream and chucked it in, I couldn't even tell it apart from the other stones that lay on the bottom there, lit by the shining weed. It was just another stone, and the fishes swam over it like they swam over the other stones, trailing their spindly boneless hands. So I went back for another, and then another. Then I took two at once, then another two. I'd gone completely numb by then. I wasn't feeling anything. I wasn't thinking about where this would lead to. I wasn't noticing anything around me. It was like with the leopard. I was doing the job I'd set myself.

Then a voice called out to me, a real human voice, as I was halfway between the remains of Circle and the stream, and I felt like my heart had stopped in my body.

'Hey, John! You're breaking Circle!'

It wasn't David or Caroline, not a grownup at all, just little Jeff hobbling into the clearing.

'Go away, Jeff. Don't get involved in this.'

'What will this do to Oldest, John? Think what it will do to them!'

I'd been shutting all my feelings out of my mind, like I did when I was facing that leopard, but now, just for one moment, they all came pouring in. I imagined old Mitch's feelings about this special place, made by his grandmother and grandfather, which had been here for all his long long life, and I knew that I'd ruined all that. I'd ruined the peaceful centre of Family. Even if I stopped now, I'd already ruined it. It was all broken to pieces forever.

I looked at Jeff. He could see the horror in my eyes and his own eyes reflected it.

'Don't you believe that Angela told us to wait here for Earth?' he asked me. 'Or do you just think that she was wrong?'

Not many people in Family could have asked those questions without letting you know what they thought you ought to reply, but Jeff really wanted to know. He watched my face and waited for me to answer.

'I think Angela knew a whole lot of things,' I said at last, 'but I don't think she knew just how *long* long this wait for Earth would be.'

He didn't say anything. He just stood looking up at me, studying my face.

'It needs to be done, Jeff,' I said. 'I don't like it, but it needs to be done. We need to break away.'

Even now he didn't speak, but after a few more seconds he slowly reached out and touched one of the stones in my hands, like he was making himself part of what I was doing. He nodded.

'I'll go back to Redlantern, then,' he said.

'Yeah,' I said. 'That's best.'

I waited until he'd gone before I went to the stream and dropped in the stones I was holding. Then I went back for two more, and two more after that. I finished off with the five stones in middle. It didn't take me long. There was no more Circle in Circle Clearing. It was empty and blank. It was sort of . . . dead.

And I felt dead too. Empty. I couldn't find any feelings inside me about anything. I knew I must have destroyed Circle for a reason, but I could barely remember what that reason was. I knew that big big things would happen now as a result, but I couldn't make myself care what they would be. It was like I'd turned to stone myself.

But I walked up Dixon Stream by myself – even old Jeffo was asleep in his shelter – and I climbed the rocks round Deep Pool to where Tina was waiting for me.

She'd been squatting on the bank, eating nuts. She stood up as I came scrambling towards her.

'You took your time, John. What have you been . . . ?'

When she looked into my face her expression changed completely.

'Gela's heart, John! What's up with you? What have you done?'

I didn't say anything at all. I pushed her back down on the ground again, I pulled off her wrap, I pressed my mouth against hers . . .

'Hey John, careful. I don't want a baby . . .'

I pushed into her and into her and into her until I was ready to come, which was pretty soon. And then, when I'd spurted out my juice over her belly, I didn't even speak to her, just dived into the pool and swam a long way under the warm bright water before I surfaced, as if I could wash away everything just by letting the water rinse the sweat from my skin, as if this would make Circle whole again, or make it alright with everyone that it had gone.

Tina didn't swim. She waited for me on the bank and when I tried to climb out, she kicked me back in again. And she didn't do it in play. She really kicked me.

'Just tell me what you did, John.'

I didn't want to hear my voice say it, but I knew I had to.

'I destroyed it, Tina. I destroyed Circle of Stones.'

'You . . . You *what*? You're bloody joking, aren't you, John? Tell me you're joking.'

But of course she could see by my face, and by everything that had happened so far, that I wasn't.

'Tom's neck, John! You *idiot*. You bloody idiot. Who do you think you are?'

She grabbed her wrap and started climbing up the rocks away from me.

'Hey Tina, wait . . .'

'Keep away from me, John. You did it on your own. You can take what's coming to you on your own. I'm not part of it, alright? I'm going back to Spiketree. Don't come after me. I mean that, John, I really mean it.'

Well, I could *see* she meant it and I really hadn't expected this. I'd thought that she'd be of the same sort of mind as me. In fact I'd thought she'd be impressed by what I'd done, like she was impressed with the way I spoke out at AnyVirsry. I'd thought it would make me seem brave and strong in her eyes.

I listened to her climbing up the rocks, heading back to sleeping Family where some time soon, maybe in an hour, maybe in two or three or four, someone or other would wake up and pass through Circle Clearing and see what I'd done.

And I knew I was alone in whole world. I was lonelier even than

Angela was, all those wombs ago, when she came up here by herself and cried.

I took Angela's ring out of the pocket in my wrap. Of course I didn't really believe Angela would come to me or anything. I wasn't like Lucy Lu. But I sort of hoped I would be able to see her in my mind as I'd seen her before.

It didn't happen, though. Why should it? And why would Angela want to help me out anyway, when she and Tommy made Circle and started Any Virsries? They didn't want those things ended, did they? Whole point of those things was to last and last. And Angela had specifically told all of us to stay by the stones and wait for Earth.

I put the ring away again. For a bit I just sat there rocking back and forth on my haunches, like I've seen mothers do when they've lost a child and they don't know how to get through it, just rocking and rocking and rocking themselves to make a rhythm and make the time go past.

~ ~ ~

After a bit I made up my mind to get back in control of myself.

'It's not like I've made some kind of blunder,' I told myself. 'This wasn't a mistake. I thought about it. I knew what I was doing. I knew it would be horrible, for everyone else and for me. But I was trying to make something happen that needed to happen.'

I couldn't see Angela or feel her presence, but I could sort of feel the voices of people in the future watching this scene that I was in. *John All Alone*, they'd call it. The scene that came after *John Destroys Circle* and *Tina Dumps John*.

I imagined them standing round me, those future people, looking in, calling things out. I couldn't hear what they were saying. Maybe they were thanking me for what I'd done. Maybe they were shouting out to me that I'd done wrong. But in a way it didn't matter, the same as it didn't really matter whether Tommy and Mehmet and Dixon, the Disobedient Three, did wrong that time they refused to listen to President and carried on instead towards Hole-in-Sky.

'No. Don't do it!' we yelled out to them, every Any Virsry. But the fact is that if they hadn't made that choice, we wouldn't have existed. We wouldn't even have been there to yell back to them. Most probably no human being would ever even have heard of this dark world called Eden.

So we couldn't really mean it, could we, when we called that out to them? Or at least we could only really mean it in those dark dark moments that no one ever talks about when life itself seems to have no worth at all.

~ ~ ~

Then I heard a shout coming from Family way. It was quite faint. I couldn't hear the words.

Soon there was another shout, and another, and then the horns started up. It wasn't long slow blasts this time but the quick *Parp! Parp! Parp! Parp! Parp!* that means a Strornry Meeting. All over Family people would be waking up, afraid. What could it be? What dreadful thing could have happened? They'd look round anxiously at each other, to see if anyone else had a clue. What could it mean? What terrible event could justify another meeting so soon, when they hadn't even had half a sleep to let them recover from the three wakings of the last one?

I stood up. A couple of jewel bats were zipping along just above the surface of Deep Pool: dark shadows, fast and smooth across the smooth bright water, one just a little in front and to the side of the other. Their little arms were hanging down and their fingertips were trailing over the surface as they swerved and darted around the lilies looking for fish. If they saw one – *grab!* – they'd have it in a flash and then, all in one smooth smooth movement, they'd curve off up to the rocks and the trees to find a place where they could divide the fish up between them with their sharp little teeth and their nifty little hands. If I'd left the stones alone I could have been out here now watching those bats with Tina, with nothing at all to worry about. Life would have been easy for me. Family wasn't going to starve yet, after all. Not for a long time. Not for another generation maybe.

But it was like with the leopard. I'd made a decision that I knew could turn out badly, I'd taken a chance on it and now it was too late to go back. The leopard had to be faced.

I started up the rocks, heading back towards Family.

16

Tina Spiketree

The thing with John was that everyone thought he was so brave, and *he* thought he was too. I'm not saying he boasted about it because he didn't, but that's how he saw himself: someone who faced things, someone who never flinched or turned away.

And in one way he was *brave* brave. He did things that no one else would do, like facing that leopard, and throwing the stones in the stream. No one else in whole Family would have done either of those things. Well, okay, some would face a leopard, but not on their own and not without a strong blackglass spear, and not when they were only twenty wombtimes old. But definitely no one *no one* else would have done what he did with the stones. No one else would have even dared to *think* about it.

So he *was* brave in those ways, but there were other things, things that most people did every waking and didn't think anything of, that John just couldn't bring himself to do. People didn't think of it as him being scared. And he didn't see it that way either. But all the same he was.

He didn't really have any close friends was one thing. I mean, he was a good-looking bloke and he was smart smart and strong and a fighter and a leader – and no one had any complaints if he wanted to hang out with them, no complaints at all. So if you asked him to name his friends he could give a long list, and if you asked them, they'd say, 'Yeah, sure, we're friends with John Redlantern, he's alright.' But he didn't have any particular kids he hung out with, except only his cousin Gerry. And Gerry, well, he was more like John's shadow. John could handle Gerry up close to him because Gerry didn't ask anything of him at all. Gerry wasn't his equal.

And then there's the way he didn't want to slide with me that first time up at Deep Pool. I reckon that was because he was scared too. I mean he was okay doing it with the mums around Family, like that Martha London, so why not with me? Well, it was that equal thing again, wasn't it? I was equal to him, and that scared him.

I don't mean he didn't *want* equals. I'm just saying it scared him. I mean those oldmums, they didn't ask anything of him, did they, only his juice. He could say yes, he could say no, it made no odds. Either way he could just walk away. But it scared him if he couldn't be in control of things. It really scared him.

In that respect, not just some people but *most* people were braver than John was. I mean, *I* liked to get my own way too, of course. Everybody knew that about me. I liked to get what I wanted. But the thing was, if I didn't get it, well, I just tried something else. It didn't *scare* me. I didn't have that fear that he had, which he didn't even know was there, that fear which made him hold everyone at a distance, that fear of not controlling things.

And now, all on his own, he'd decided to change the history of Eden forever. He hadn't told me about it. He hadn't told *anyone* about it. He chucked the stones in the stream all by himself, while I waited for him like a bloody idiot, not knowing what he was doing or why he was taking so long, and then he came up to Deep Pool and expected me just to accept what he'd done. He expected me to trust him. He expected me to support him and line up with him, even though he hadn't trusted *me* enough even to tell me what he was planning. It's that *equal* thing again. He just didn't quite get it.

He didn't quite get that other people apart from him had their own thoughts and their own plans and their own things in their heads.

I was *so* angry with him about that. I mean, Michael's names, I hated AnyVirsries like he did. I hated Oldest and their remembering. I wouldn't have cared if I never heard them go on about Angela and Tommy and lecky-trickity and that bloody Big Sky-Boat *Defiant* ever again, and I agreed with John that there was no point in going on and on about Earth all the time. So, if he'd discussed his idea with me, maybe I'd even have come round to it. But, Gela's heart, just to decide on his own to bust Family apart, and then to come to me and expect me just to accept it and carry on with him and be beside him when Family found out? To expect me to share the shame and blame for something that I'd never even been told about? I don't bloody think so.

I went back to Spiketree, trying not to catch the eye of the lookout for that sleeping, who was a bloke called Rog that was always trying to get me to slip with him, and I crawled into my shelter.

My sister Jane said, 'Everyone's been talking about you, Tina. They've been saying that . . .'

'Just shut up, Jane, alright?'

Pretty soon after that, the horn started. *Parp! Parp! Parp!*

~ ~ ~

A woman in Blueside had had a heart attack and she and her daughters didn't come to Strornry. A couple of blokes in Brooklyn couldn't sleep. They'd set off hunting and didn't get back until most of it was over. A few newhairs had gone out for a little bit of slip, like I thought was the plan for me and John when I went up to Deep Pool. But everyone else in the world was there, back in Circle Clearing, like AnyVirsry all over again.

But the thing was that it wasn't Circle Clearing any more, because there was no Circle. And that was really horrible. It was like you saw someone you knew in forest and you called out to them, but when they turned round towards you, you found out that their teeth and their tongue had fallen out, and their face had a big empty hole in middle of it. And the weird thing was that nobody wanted to go near that gap where Circle had been. People had always stayed round the edge of the clearing in any meeting, whether AnyVirsry or Strornry, and always kept well back from the stones, but now they squeezed even *further* back, pressing up tight together right under the lantern trees to be as far as possible from where the stones had been. And that made the hole in middle look even bigger and emptier and more horrible.

Yes, and it was what we called a *fug* that waking. The cloud had come down low in the last few hours, right down into the treetops, making the highest lanterns into fuzzy blobs of light. And a fine rain was falling, not like the soaking rain you get in the hills round valley's edge, but fine valley rain, like wet mist. And it was hot and stuffy. Everyone's skin was shiny with rain and with sweat. It was like there was no sky, no forest even, and this sad lonely little scene, this clearing with a hole in middle, was all on its own in the world, a stuffy little cave with no air in it, surrounded by nothingness. There weren't even any flutterbyes or bats coming in and out of the clearing, because they don't fly when there's a fug, they hide up and keep their wings dry, and wait for the cloud to lift.

People's faces were grey and exhausted. They hadn't left Any Virsry feeling happy, but they'd thought that at least they could get some sleep. And now this! Lots of women were crying, some men as well. Little kids and babies saw their mums crying and they cried too. Other grownups, instead of crying, had stone-hard faces. They were waiting for someone to shout at, someone to blame.

Oldest weren't out in middle like they had been in AnyVirsry. They couldn't hack it. Their helpers had sorted out a little space for them on one side of the clearing, with their padded logs to rest their backs against. Old Stoop looked like he was about to die any minute.

But Caroline and Council were out there, far away from us all in middle of that empty space. And Caroline, that cold grey woman, was full full of rage. Her rage was like boiling sap inside a tree that's about to fall, just waiting for someone to give it that last push when the sap would come spraying out to scald and maim anyone standing near. Jane the creepy little Secret Ree and Council were all around her and they all looked pretty much as angry as she was, except for Bella Redlantern, who just looked terrible, like she was about to be sick.

~ ~ ~

And then John came, poor old John, all by himself, coming from Londonside. There was a sort of gasp from all round the clearing and people standing on Londonside pulled hastily aside to let him past, like they were afraid of even touching him, like they were afraid of catching something from him if they stood too near to him.

A dreadful silence fell. Even the babies seemed to know to shut up crying. And he walked right out into middle, walking *stiff* stiff and straight straight with his head held up, as if to say he was ready to take whatever they were going to do to him. But his face was white, and he wasn't looking anywhere but straight in front of him. (I bet he looked like that when he faced the leopard.) When he was three four yards in front of Caroline, he stopped.

He was only twenty wombs old. Only fifteen years in the old time.

'You did this, didn't you, John Redlantern?' Caroline said.

And there were three four seconds of total silence.

'Yes I did,' he said then in a small quiet voice. 'I did it because . . .'

'I don't wish to hear why you did it.'

'I did it because . . .'

'I don't wish to hear, do you understand?'

'I did it because I . . .'

Well, Caroline stepped right up to him and slapped him across the face so hard that he nearly fell over. You could see that she'd hurt her hand as well.

'Those stones were laid here by your great-great-grandparents,' she hissed into his face, 'laid here to mark the special place where our Family arrived in this world, and the place we're to wait for Earth to return. We've honoured them and kept them safe and clean for six generations, the special stones that Tommy and Angela chose and touched with their own hands and laid out in the exact spots where they've been ever since. And you, at twenty wombs old, you arrogant sneaky little tubeslinker' (her voice went all ugly and twisted and choked up when she said that), 'you think you know better than everyone else alive or everyone who's ever lived.'

'Don't be too hard on him, Caroline,' muttered Bella behind her. 'Remember he's only a kid.'

'Only a kid?' called out David Redlantern, striding out from the crowd into the clearing.

Oh boy, what an ugly, evil brute he was with his thick short limbs and his red batface always oozing, always quivering. Not that all batfaces are like him. My own sister Jane was a batface, and she was as sweet-natured as anyone could be, but David, he was cruel and cold and hard, and his batface just made him seem crueller and colder and harder still.

'Only a kid, you say, Bella,' he sneered in his spluttery voice, 'but that didn't stop you from getting him to slip with you in your shelter, did it? It didn't stop you having a little slide with him on the exact same waking he insulted Council here in front of whole Family. We thought you were calling him in to tell him off, but no, you got him in and slipped with him, with whole group awake all around you. We knew what was going on. We heard the silence. We heard your breathing getting fast. We heard you gasp. What kind of group leader is that?'

'Is this true, Bella?' demanded Caroline, turning round.

Bella's head was hanging down.

'We didn't slip but we did, well, *touch*. I did tell him off but I wanted him to know also that he was valued and that his concern was . . .'

'What nonsense,' Caroline said, and we'd never in our lives heard Head of Family talking to a group leader like that. 'I've never heard such total garbage. We'll need to reconsider the leadership of Redlantern, because you obviously aren't fit to lead anything. But we'll sort *that* out later. For the moment . . .' She turned back to John. 'For the moment the business of Strornry is this. How do we deal with this selfish, stupid, arrogant little slinker of a boy, who has defiled the memory of Mother Angela and of Father Tommy and of the Three Companions? How do we deal with a silly boy who has deliberately broken something that was precious to every single one of us?'

'Hang him up from a spiketree like we hang a buckskin out to dry,' said David. 'Spike him up to burn, like Hitler did to Jesus.'

He gave a hard laugh.

'They say Jesus was the leader of the Juice,' he said. 'Which sort of fits when you think about it, because juice is about the only thing old Juicy Johnny here has ever been good for.'

There were a few cold little titters of laughter, but Caroline told him off.

'This isn't a time for jokes,' she said.

'I'm not joking,' David said. 'Spike him up.'

And he stayed there, out in the open space on his own, standing with his muscly arms folded and his thick stumpy legs apart. He wasn't a group leader. He didn't really have any more right to speak out than John did, other than the fact that he was a grownup. But he didn't go back to the edge of the clearing with everyone else, and Caroline didn't tell him to. She just turned her attention away from him, like she couldn't face another fight.

And the thought came to me – well, I didn't properly *think* it through, but I sort of glimpsed it in my head – the thought came to me that up to now it had been the women in Eden that ran things and decided how things would be, but now a time was coming when it would be the men. Some of them might be good men and some would be bad like David. But it would be men rather than women for the next bit. Something had changed, and it would never be how it was before.

'We need to discuss this,' Caroline said. 'Let's decide who ought to speak first.'

'How about his mother?' murmured Candy Fishcreek.

'Yes,' agreed Caroline, scanning the crowd surrounding her, out round the edge of this stuffy little cave of cloud. 'His mother. Jade Redlantern. Where are you, Jade?'

A rustling came from the place where most of the Redlantern people were standing, and you could see which one was Jade because hers was the only face that was still looking forward.

'I'm here,' she said in a small wavery voice.

And it was an odd thing. Jade wasn't just pretty, she was a great beauty. She knew how to stand and how to hold herself and how to move herself, so as to command envy and desire and love. If men spoke or came up to her – and women too – she could dismiss them, or tease them, or give them their heart's desire just by the way she moved her face and her body. But now she was lost, she had no idea how to speak or to compose herself. It sounds harsh but what she reminded me of was a whitelantern fruit that looks all ripe and lovely till you turn it round and you see the hole where the ants have got into and hollowed it out inside.

'Well, um, he's not all bad, John isn't . . .' she began.

It was like she was talking about someone she didn't even know that well.

I looked at John. He was watching her. You couldn't read the expression on his face, but his eyes were sort of hard and shiny. Not shiny with tears but with something like the *opposite* of tears, I thought, though I suppose it didn't make a lot of sense.

' . . . but it's a bad thing he's done,' Jade said lamely, and she sort of made a face, like it really wasn't all that much to do with her, and didn't say anything else.

'Can I speak, Caroline?' said Bella Redlantern.

Caroline turned round to her.

'Go on,' she said coldly.

'I didn't know what he was going to do, and I haven't talked to him about it,' she said, 'but he's a boy who feels passionately about things, feels passionately about the future of Family especially. I don't really understand why he did this, but he will have done it because he thought it would help.'

'Help?' asked Caroline. '*Help?*'

She looked around at us all, making an incredulous face, trying to get a reaction out of us. Some people tittered, some shouted out 'Shame on you Bella! Shame!', which was just what Caroline wanted.

'I may be getting too old for this,' Caroline said, 'I may be missing something obvious. But if you take something that is dear and precious to other people and calmly destroy it, how can you call that *helping* them?'

She didn't wait for an answer.

'Who else wants to comment?'

'Make him put Circle back again!' called out a fat dim woman called Gela Blueside.

'But it can never be what it was!' Caroline said. 'Think about it. We could make another circle. We could use a rope to measure it out and make something that looked pretty much the same. And I daresay that *is* what we'll do. But it'll never again be the stones that Angela and Tommy chose, never the stones they laid in place with their own hands.'

Gela Blueside began to cry like she'd been scolded.

'And I'll tell you something,' Caroline went on. 'If and when we do restore that Circle, no way will this wicked boy have the honour of coming anywhere near it.'

'Do like David said,' called a big dark gloomy Starflower man called Harry. 'Spike him up. Like Hitler did to Jesus. That will repay Mother Angela for the hurt that's been done her. Otherwise we'll all bear the burden of it, on and on and on.'

'Yeah, that's right,' called out a sharp little woman called Lucy Fishcreek. 'If he doesn't pay the price for it, we all will. Us and our children and our children's children too.'

'That's true,' said Julie the London leader, with the authority of Council in her voice, 'that's *true* true. He's shamed all of us, not just himself.'

'Angela is crying,' wailed that horrible wet-eyed Lucy Lu from Redlantern. 'Angela is *crying out* for our help.'

Harry's dick, I thought, it could really happen. They really *could* spike John up like Jesus.

But Candy, the Fishcreek group leader, whispered: 'Remember the Laws, remember the Laws on the trees. We mustn't kill.'

Caroline nodded.

'Who else that knows him wants to speak? He's got no brothers or sisters, has he? How about his cousins?'

Gerry stood up. Poor kid. He was white white as anything but he wanted desperately to do right by his hero John.

'John's brave, don't forget. He does stuff no one dares to do. Remember how he did for that leopard!'

Tears came from his eyes. How brilliant everything had seemed to him back then, when he'd been the one to witness John do for the leopard. How happy he'd been for John when whole Family praised him.

'He's braver than just about everyone in Family,' Gerry said. 'Maybe the bravest one of all.'

He looked round at his little brother, weird little clawfooted Jeff, who was younger than him, yet in a way much older. I think Gerry was hoping Jeff would think of better arguments than he could. And Jeff did speak, but all he would say was that weird phrase he came up with at the weirdest times, for no obvious reason at all.

'We are here,' he said. 'We really are here.'

Some people laughed, some yelled out that if he wasn't going to talk sense, he should shut up his bloody gob.

'He means this isn't a dream,' Gerry tried to explain. 'He means that this isn't just some kind of story.'

'You don't say!' someone called out sarcastically. 'I *never* would have known that.'

But it *was* like a dream, in that gaping space, with the mist shutting us away from forest and from sky. It was like an evil dream. Either that, or everything *else* had turned out to be a dream and the only true thing in the world was *this*: Family, our miserable, bitter, lonely Family, full of stupid people, full of hateful, disappointed people, full of sour people, full of ignorant people who never thought anything through for themselves.

'Why don't you let *John* speak!' I called out.

David turned on me. He was still out in front there, like he was another centre, separate and apart from Caroline and Council. Hateful hateful man, I'd often seen him secretly looking at me, longingly, knowing quite well that I'd never let him near me. But now he felt power on his side.

'Oh-ho! I wondered when his little slippy girl would speak!'

'Bella is right,' I said. 'He did it for a reason and you ought to hear what he has to say.'

Caroline frowned.

'Why should we let him tell us his silly ideas, just because he's done something wrong?'

But she was wavering and several people in the crowd called out.

'Yeah, let him have his say.'

'It's only fair.'

Caroline nodded.

'Alright then, John. You have two minutes.'

And she turned and looked at Secret Ree, who nodded and laid down the bark that she'd been scribbling on, and put her finger on her own wrist to count out one hundred and twenty pulses.

'You said I've offended Mother Angela,' John said. 'But I don't think I have. She wanted the best for all of us, it's true. But we all know that she sometimes felt trapped and stifled here and longed to break out. Remember the story of Angela and the Ring? Remember how she cried for nine whole sleeps and nine whole wakings? Remember how she said she hated Eden, and even hated her own . . . ?'

'You're calling Angela to your defence?' interrupted Caroline, furious. 'How *dare* you? If Angela cried for nine wakings when she lost a ring, *think* how she'd be crying now!'

'She *is* crying,' wailed Lucy Lu, in that fake dreamy voice of hers. 'She's crying like she's never cried before.'

'You said you'd give him two minutes,' I yelled.

'What I mean is this,' said John. 'Angela told us to wait by the stones because she didn't know how long it would be before Earth came back. But she wouldn't have wanted Family to stay huddled up in this little place for all this time, using up all the food, getting tired and bored, starting to hate one another. She'd have wanted us to find new places, new air, spread out, explore, make the best of things. That's why . . .'

'Two minutes is up!' snapped Caroline briskly, though I could see that Secret Ree was still counting. 'You've had your say and Council has heard enough evidence. Council will consider its decision. Except you, Bella, you can go back to your people over there.'

So Bella had the shame of crossing the clearing to where the Redlantern people were, and squatting down among them as an ordinary person, while Council huddled together without her and conferred in whispers. It was like we were watching some kind of play, bunched up together under the trees. There was Council in the centre; there was John standing just out from the centre on his own, his face pale and blank, not looking at anyone; and then, to one side, and a bit further out, there was David, arms still crossed, legs still apart, scanning the crowd with hard hard eyes, as if he was checking each one of us out to see who was with him and who wasn't.

Pretty soon the huddle broke up. Caroline stepped away from the rest of Council.

'We've made our decision,' she said. 'We're all agreed. John Redlantern can't stay in Family. He must leave within two hours. After that he won't be part of Family any more. The Laws won't apply to him, and if he's found near here, he can be treated as we'd treat a troublesome animal. Like a tree fox or a slinker.'

Then she looked around the crowd, searching for people that she knew had a connection with John – Gerry, Jeff, Bella, Jade, me.

'And listen carefully to this. Redlantern group can give him whatever it wants to let him take with him, but after he's left, no one is to give him anything any more – no food, no blackglass, no buckskins, nothing – and no one is to talk to him or look for him or spend time with him, or they too will be thrown out of Family.'

She gave a firm little nod and a little sideways glance at John.

'That's our decision about John Redlantern. And that's the end of Strornry.'

17

Sue Redlantern

We made our way back through the fug to Redlantern clearing. It was a dreadful time, a time that was neither waking nor sleeping, neither real nor a dream, and it seemed as if it could never reach an end, but only sink downwards deeper and deeper into itself, until it swallowed up all memory of happiness, or fun, or anything else except this fuggy nothingness. We were exhausted and hopeless. Sweat and rain ran down our faces and we were too tired to wipe it off. Out of all of Redlantern group, only David seemed untouched by the misery, just as he'd been untouched by fun and happiness in the past. While we crept back with our shoulders hunched, he strode along beside us with a satisfied look that was almost a smile. But even David knew to keep his mouth shut, and hardly anyone else spoke at all, though many wept silently, including me. Even the littlest of littles must have understood that our safe familiar world had been torn in two. And some of them cried, and some were beyond crying.

We had no leader to guide us. Bella normally got hold of any problem that faced our group and helped us see what we had to do – 'This is the thing we need to concentrate on; this is what we need to do first; these are the questions we need to answer . . .' – but now she walked silently among us, looking at no one. Old Roger wrung his hands together. Fox and the other young men and women trudged along in a little group of their own.

John himself was in a daze. Jade, my sister, trailed along on one side of him and a little behind, but as ever she had no idea what to say to him, or how to approach the business of being his mum. My Gerry walked on his other side, weeping and pestering him with questions.

'What are you going to do, John? Where are you going to go? I don't want you to go. Haven't you got a plan?'

And my boy Jeff, the sharpest and gentlest of us all, walked silently next to me, watching everything.

~ ~ ~

We ran into our shelters and felt inside our skin bags and storage logs for things for John to take with him: blackglass, spearheads, rope, skins, a net, some dried meat. There was no one else taking charge so I did my best to organize things, keeping an eye on Gerry all the time to make sure he left John alone and didn't pester him when he needed to be able to think.

'Let him be, Gerry. He knows you love him, but he can't look after you as well as himself just now . . . Come on, Roger, you can spare him a couple of decent spearheads, for Gela's sake . . . Tom, can you see if there's some more string over there that he could take? Janny dear, I know you're sad, but can you just wrap up that meat in a clean bit of skin?'

Meanwhile my pretty sister Jade stood helplessly and watched as we brought things to her son and he bundled them up together, as if she was waiting for instructions on how a mother should behave.

We said goodbye to him. Gerry hugged him. Jeff hugged him. Old Roger hugged him. I hugged him and told him to take care and be patient and not do anything else that would cause upset to Family.

And meanwhile, I said, we'd work on Council to change its ruling, and let him come back again. After all, Council were the ones who kept telling us we had to keep whole Family together.

'It won't go on forever, John,' I told him. 'You've upset everyone *badly* badly, but when people have calmed down a bit, we can look at it all again, and try and find another way through.'

He didn't anwer me. He didn't speak at all. He shouldered his bundle, picked up the fire-bark with its smouldering embers, turned and and nodded to us, and then set off along a little path that went between Batwing and Fishcreek clearings and out into forest. (He didn't want to have to walk through someone else's group area.)

'Take care, John,' I called after him. 'And don't give up. We'll sort something out.'

He stopped, turned one more time and raised one hand in a little half-wave, and then carried on.

Suddenly Bella screamed.

She'd been hiding in her shelter all this time while we'd been getting things ready for him, and no one had noticed her come out.

'John!' she cried out, 'John! Wait for me!'

She ran after him, sobbing, and grabbed hold of his arm, begging him to let her go with him.

'Don't leave me, my sweet boy! Don't leave me!'

No one had ever seen her like that, her of all people. For not only in Redlantern but all across Family, we relied on her to be one of those that keep calm and sensible and in control when other folk were getting upset.

'I don't want to lose you, John, my darling,' she wailed, with tears pouring down her face. 'I want to go on caring for you, my baby. This is all my fault.'

John didn't say anything. He was pale, he was sunk into himself and, though he submitted himself to her clinging kisses, his face was turned away from her to the path ahead, as if he was simply waiting for the moment when this distraction was removed from him and he could continue on his way.

'John, my sweetheart,' Bella tried again, pawing at him, running her hand down his chest and his belly, like she was his lover and they were about to have a slip, 'John, my dear sweet darling. I love you. I love you better than if you were my own child. I love you better than if you were my man. Let me come and look after you, my darling. Let me come with you and hold you and keep you warm.'

None of us really knew what to do, or what to think. She never talked like that. She was always sensible sensible. She was always reasonable and restrained. But when I went after her, and took her hands and tried gently to release her grip on John, she just shook me angrily away.

'Let me come and look after you,' she pleaded with him. '*Please*, John. Please, my pretty darling. *Please!*'

She kissed him again, and then rubbed her hand against the front of his wrap, like she was trying to make him hard.

He flinched and pushed her hand away.

'No, Bella,' I said, 'that's not fair. That's not helping. Try and think of John and the position he's in.'

'I *am* thinking of John. No one thinks of him more than me. He knows that. I love him better than his own mum. What has Jade ever done for this boy of hers, that cold leopard-woman with her sweet empty song?'

'Leave me alone, Bella, alright?' muttered John. 'I don't need this. Just leave me alone.'

He said it two three times, and I backed him up as best I could.

'He needs to go, Bella,' I told her. 'Let him be. He knows you love him. He does know.'

'Let the lad deal with this, Bella my dear,' said Old Roger, who'd come after me to help.

'Let him be, Bella,' called out Jade who'd come up behind Roger.

'I don't want this, Bella,' John repeated, glancing down at her, and then looking away from all of us again at the path through the lanterntrees up ahead.

'You don't . . .?'

Suddenly Bella understood. She let go of him. She stood back. For a moment she looked like she'd seen one of the Shadow People. Then she let fly a dreadful scream that they must have heard all over Family right up to Blueside, and flung herself to the ground, which was sodden wet from all that fuggy rain like it was soaked in tears, and writhed about in the mud till she was covered all over with it.

No one in Redlantern knew what to do about her. But we did know that, right at that moment, John was the one we needed to concentrate on because he was the one that had to go. So all of us just sort of moved away from our old leader, and carried on with the business of saying goodbye to John.

'Go on, John. We'll sort this out. You get on your way, and remember that we'll be working to get you back here as soon as we can.'

John nodded, gripped his bark of embers against his chest and walked on without another word to anyone.

But Jade, who of all people you'd think would want to concentrate on John, went over to Bella and squatted down beside her and comforted her. She'd finally found something useful she could do.

~ ~ ~

When John was out of sight, all of us except Jade and Bella walked back into the space round the fire between our shelters, where David was sitting on a log, fixing a leopard tooth spearhead on a shaft with strips of dried buck gut, and making a big show of being busy. I noticed that Met, that lump of a boy, went over and sat by him. And near them, with her eyes rolled upwards to the grey-black fuggy sky, sat Lucy Lu.

'We'll need a new leader, I suppose,' I said. 'A new leader to help sort out this mess.'

David snorted.

'And preferably one that doesn't slip with her own newhairs.'

'I want to go after him, mum,' sobbed Gerry. 'He's not just my cousin. He's my best friend. They can't expect him to be all alone forever.'

'It won't help him if you do,' I said. 'That will just confirm that he's a bad influence on newhairs. Leave him be, and maybe we'll be able to find a way of persuading Family to let him back, once things have calmed down.'

David looked up.

'What? Have him back? Are you nuts? Do you really think we're going to let him destroy our Circle, hurt whole Family, shame his own group, and then let him back in again with nothing but a telling off?'

'Mother Angela herself is telling me he had to go,' cried Lucy Lu suddenly in that hollow voice she put on, like she was talking in a cave far away. 'He had to go, but now that he's gone, she'll help us put Circle back, and make things how they were. Oh sweet sweet Angela, our dear good mother. She's telling me that if Council wants me to, she'll guide my hand to find the stones that bad John threw in the stream, and put them back exactly where they were.'

18

John Redlantern

I walked and walked and walked, straight past Lava Blob with its funny shy hoppers waving their mouth feelers at me and wringing their hands, past the little pool where Tina first gave me that pink oyster. The bundle that Redlantern group had given me was heavy heavy, the fire-bark was hot, and the going was hard hard in that sticky fuggy air, but even so it was much easier to keep walking than to stop, however weary I was, because while I walked there was a rhythm, but when I stopped there would be nothing to do but think about what I'd done, and what I was going to do next.

I walked without a rest for the time of a whole waking and a whole sleep, all the way to that place up the slope by Neck of Cold Path Valley, with the caves and the warm pool. I climbed up the slope, crawled into one of those caves, spread out sleeping skins under the little shiny rocklanterns, lay down and fell asleep at once. I'd worn myself down so much with that long long walk that even my worries couldn't keep me awake, so sleeping took up a bit *more* time before I had to think about what I was going to do next.

But when it did come, waking up was *hard* hard. It was like having a cold stone pressed down on my chest. I was completely alone. Everyone in the world was more than a waking's walk away from me and forbidden to talk to me forever. I was cut off from Family like Family was cut off from Earth.

What if Earth comes now? I thought. What if that Landing Veekle finally comes down from sky after all this time and I'm not there?

It was *scary* scary thinking of being left in a world with no one else there at all. I'd always been the kind of person that tries not to rely on anyone. I'd always kept myself separate. You didn't need to be chitter-chattering to other people all the time, was what I always thought. You don't need to take all your problems to other people to fix, or tell other people every single little thought that comes into your head. But now I could see, *easily* easily, that everyone needs other people. People needed other people like they needed air. And for a while I felt so lonely I could barely breathe.

And all the scary scary things that had happened came back and filled up my head, so that it almost felt that they were all still happening. Over and over again I was standing by myself in front of whole Family. Over and over I was telling Tina what I'd done and seeing the icy anger on her face. Over and over I was walking away from Redlantern and hearing Bella wailing while the rest of them tried to make things seem okay. Over and over I heard her final dreadful scream.

It wasn't even as if I was a proper grownup yet. I was only a newhair of twenty wombs. And I could easily have cried like a kid. But then I thought, No, this is one of those leopard moments if there ever was one.

I began to talk to myself out loud. It calmed me down and helped me concentrate.

'Get a bloody grip, John Redlantern,' I said. 'What are the odds of Earth coming right now when they haven't come for a hundred and sixty-three years? And even if they *did* come, I'd see the Landing Veekle from here, wouldn't I, with all those lights on it? Yes, and anyway they wouldn't go without me. Sue wouldn't let them. Gerry wouldn't, nor would Jeff, or Bella or Old Roger or Janny or Tina . . .'

It helped a lot, saying the names of people that wouldn't agree to go back to Earth without me.

'Or Jade,' I added, as an afterthought.

Then I reached into that little pocket sewn on the bottom edge of my wrap, and took out the metal ring, and I turned it over in my hand, and slipped it on and off my finger, and held it near a whitelantern so I could see the tiny words: *To Angela with love from Mum and Dad.* I thought about Angela Young all on her own by the edge of Deep Pool, scrumpling up that lanternflower and throwing it into the water: kind, strong, lonely Angela, the mother of us all, who'd never wanted to come to Eden.

I pressed the ring to my lips and tears came into my eyes. I wiped them quickly away.

'Tom's dick, pull yourself together,' I said. 'If push came to shove, I could even trade my way back into Family with this ring. I could tell them I'd just found it and it was a present for all of them, to make up for Circle. They'd all think I was great.'

I squeezed the ring in my hand.

'But I'm not that bloody desperate, am I? Not even close to it. Things won't go on like this forever. I won't always be on my own. One way or another, I'll have people around me again, and I'll bloody make things change, just like I planned.'

I nodded firmly to myself and slipped the ring back into its little pocket.

'So what's the plan?' I asked myself.

I noticed that I sounded like Caroline Brooklyn running a Council meeting, and that made me smile.

'What's happening next?' I said. 'What's on the Genda?'

I stood up and stretched myself. Sky was still grey-black and starless. Down to my left was the narrow opening of Cold Path Valley, with the hills rising up again on the other side. In front of me whole of Circle forest stretched out, half-buried in fug, but still shining shining all the way to Blue Mountains, and still, as ever, going *hmmmmmmmm*.

'I'll have a dip in that little pool first,' I decided, 'and then I'll hide away my stuff, and then I'll have a hunt and a scavenge, and get some fruit and some starflowers and maybe some fresh meat. I'll concentrate on all that for a bit, and then I'll eat, and then I'll start thinking about the next step. How to get across Dark. How to make wraps warm enough. What I'll do for light. How to find my way through.'

19

Tina Spiketree

Horrible Lucy Lu Redlantern went from group to group with her weepy eyes and her fake echoey voice, saying that she'd heard from Angela herself, the mother of all of us, and Angela had promised to help her pick out the stones at the bottom of the stream that came from Circle and put them back exactly where they were before. Council pretended to think about it carefully, and pretty soon the groups heard from their leaders that they'd all decided to accept Lucy Lu's proposal and let her do it. Oldest had agreed as well, apparently, though how Council got any sense out of them I don't know, what with them quivering and whimpering and weeping over by Circle Clearing, and old Stoop gulping and gasping to get enough air to breathe.

So then Council got a bunch of newhairs together, one from each group, and a length of rope to make a circle, and Lucy Lu made a big thing out of reaching down into the water, and touching this stone and that stone, and shaking her head again and again, and then trembling and rolling her eyes and moaning when she sensed which stone was the 'right' one for each position in Circle. Afterwards everyone pretended they thought Circle was all mended and back to how it was before, but no one really believed it. It didn't look the same, and I could tell for certain they weren't the same stones, because when I was a kid I'd noticed that one of the stones on Blueside of Circle had a black line going right through it, like it was made of two halves, but now there wasn't one stone there that wasn't a pure white.

It was a fake Circle and everything in Family felt fake. We went scavenging, we ate our meals round our fires, we pretended life was going on just like it normally did, but each of us secretly knew it would never go back to how it was, no matter how many times Lucy Lu came round rolling her eyes and speaking in that fake dreamy voice.

'Mother Angela says we've done well. We've driven evil out of Family and made it whole whole again! Better even than it was before.'

John *evil*? I could have hit that lying tubeslinker Lucy Lu. John was stupid and selfish, yes. But he'd done a braver thing than she had ever done in her life. In fact the braveness of what he'd done was so far beyond her reach, that she couldn't even begin to *see* how brave it was. All she could see was an advantage to her in ganging up on him with the likes of Caroline and Council and David, and in helping them out by bringing precious dead Mother Angela in on their side. A lot of people are like that. They don't think about what's really true at all, only about what it would suit them best to say.

'I thought Angela was the mother of *all* of us,' I said to her. 'I thought she was John's mother as much as yours.'

'Oh Tina, Tina, Tina Spiketree,' she cried, rolling those bulgy weepy eyes, 'you want to watch your ways, our sweet Mother says, or you'll be the next to go. Bad John has filled you up with his juice and his poison, and Mother Angela weeps and weeps for the harm he's done you, my darling, harm that you can't even see.'

She didn't look at me whole time she was saying this. She was looking up at sky, to make us think she could see Angela looking down at her, but she kept peeping round at leader Liz and at the other people round the Spiketree fire, trying to work out if what she was saying was going down alright, or if she needed to swap it for something else.

I spat on the ground and walked away. I missed John and I worried about him too. I didn't like to think of him all alone out there. I wondered what that would be doing to his proud proud heart and, in a way, I felt bad that I hadn't gone with him, like I'd let him down. But at the same time I was annoyed with myself for feeling that, because he was there by his own choice, and it was his own choice too that I hadn't been a part of it.

My little batface sister Jane came running after me. She took my hand and we walked together to Greatpool, and sat there side by side on the bank.

'Don't worry, Tina,' she said, 'none of us believes what Lucy Lu says.'

Out on the water log boats were moving slowly through the shining fug, trailing their nets behind them.

'No one believes it, but everyone *half* believes it, or she'd have shut up long ago.'

Swish. One little jewel bat had come out on its own in spite of the fug, and it swooped down over the water, trailing its right hand across the surface. But it didn't catch anything and, after one more run, it gave up and turned back into forest.

'Bloody John Redlantern, why *should* I feel bad about him?' I said. 'He didn't consult me about what he was going to do. He didn't tell me a bloody thing. So why should I feel bad that I'm not out there with him, tossed out by Family, sharing the punishment for what he did?'

But then we heard a wail from Blueside across the water. It was that long low sound that people made when someone died.

'Gela's heart,' I cried, jumping to my feet. 'Not John. Surely not John?'

~ ~ ~

A bunch of Starflower grownups had had a nasty surprise out on a hunting trip. They'd found a dead body hanging from a tree by a rope, already half-eaten by starbirds. It wasn't John, though. It was Bella Redlantern. She'd killed herself in the same way that Tommy did, the father of all of us, when he was old old and blind and couldn't bear living with it all any more.

But we hadn't even got all the stones ready to bury her when there was *another* death. Little old Stoop finally couldn't get the air inside him quick enough any more and he keeled over and died with his skin turned blue and his eyes bulging out of his head like a frogbird's. So they wrapped him in buckskins and laid him along with Bella, over in Burial Grounds, out in forest on the far side of Long Pool. And whole Family filed past each of them and each of us laid down the stones we had brought, first around them and then over them, until they were quite covered up. And then Caroline took two big flat stones that Secret Ree had scratched their names on, and laid on top of these two new heaps, squeezed in among all those hundreds of other heaps, with 'Tommy Schneider, Astronaut' and 'Angela Young, Orbit Police' side by side right in middle.

'Bella Redlantern, Group Leader', Secret Ree had written, 'Stoop London, Oldest', and now she beat slowly slowly on the big funeral drum – it was the other special duty of Secret Ree – while four five people blew on hollowbranch horns to make that special lonely funeral sound that begins loud and falls away.

PAAAAAaaaaaaaaaaaarrp! PAAAAAaaaaaaaaaaaarrp!

BOOM BOOM BOOM, went the tiny Secret Ree on her great big drum, and then she stopped and put her hands on the tight buckskin to silence it, and Caroline stood up and did the Funeral Speech about what fine people they both had been in spite of their faults, and how

Bella's and Stoop's bones would now rest here peacefully until Earth finally came.

'And then at last they will be taken home to Earth,' she said, 'and buried there to rest peacefully under the bright bright Sun in the world where human beings were meant to be.'

She paused, and looked around at all of us. The fug was still pressing in on us, and the sweat was pouring down our faces.

'And let us *all* remember,' she said, 'that even if we die here on Eden before Earth comes, we will all still return, just so long as we do what we were asked to do, and stay here together in Family, next to Circle of Stones.'

That was the end of the funeral, and we all picked our way through the heaps of stones and hurried away from that horrible place with that stale and musty smell of death that crept out through the gaps between the stones.

~ ~ ~

On the way back to Family I caught up with Gerry Redlantern and his weird little brother Jeff. Gerry was in a bad bad state. He'd barely slept or eaten since John went away.

'I can't stand this,' he muttered. 'I'm going to go out and find him. I know where he'll be. He'll have gone out Cold Path way. There's a place just inside main valley, Alpway from Cold Path Neck, near where he did for that leopard. He said it would be a good place to live. And he's been on about Cold Path since we went up there. He's been on about how the woollybucks get up and out of the valley that way, and over Dark, and how if they can do it so could we.'

'If you go you'll be chucked out of Family, same as he was,' I said.

'I don't bloody care,' he began, 'I'll . . .'

Then he broke off because we heard a familiar sound coming from Peckhamway: a sound like women singing, like beautiful

beautiful women's voices singing a sad sad song. It was leopards of course, and not just one leopard this time, but two three of them, singing in harmony. They don't often hunt together, but once in a while they do, usually when there's a specially good catch. And of course Peckhamway is the direction of Cold Path Neck.

David Redlantern came by with a couple of newhairs trailing behind him. All three of them had blackglass spears.

'Sounds like those leopards have found something yummy to eat,' said David, grinning his horrible cold batfaced grin at us. 'What can it be, I wonder? Not by any chance our old friend Juicy John, do you think? What do you reckon? He did for one leopard, alright – credit where it's due – but how would he cope if three of them came at him at once?'

The boys with him laughed loudly.

'I reckon that'd be a bit much even for John, Dave,' said one of them. 'Looks like poor old Juicy John might have ended up as a leopard's dinner.'

It was Met Redlantern, a stupid big empty-headed kid I'd often seen out with John and the other Redlantern newhairs, scavenging or hunting in forest.

'You piece of shit, Met!' Gerry hissed at him. 'John was your friend. Only a few wakings ago he let you get the glory for that slinker when he could have had the glory himself!'

Met looked sort of uncomfortable but he laughed that same loud laugh that he'd done before.

'Glory for a slinker?' he said. 'I don't think so, Gerry. What glory does anyone get for a lousy slinker?'

'He'd have let you be the one to do for it even if it had been a buck,' said Gerry hotly. 'You know he would.'

'What? Like he shared that leopard glory with you?' said Met.

'He let me have one of the hearts!'

'Well, who wants to eat two?'

'You three are arseholes,' I told David and his little friends. 'John is better than all of you put together, and what's more you know that yourselves, if only you had the guts to admit it.'

They laughed again, that horrible laugh. And all this time those leopards were singing that beautiful dreamy song. And of course for all we knew it really *could* be John out there, trapped between them, not knowing which one of them to face while they circled round him.

'Arseholes, eh?' said David, still grinning, and he looked straight at me. 'That's *good* good, coming from a silly little girlie who likes it up the arse as everyone knows. You're going to have to change your tune one of these wakings, Tina Spiketree, and it won't be so long now. It won't be so long at all.'

I looked into his eyes and I could see the rest of his thoughts as surely as if he spoke them aloud. A time was soon coming, he was thinking, when I would have to call him whatever he told me to call him, and treat him however he wanted to be treated: a time when he would do to me *whatever* he pleased and whenever he felt like it, with whichever bit of my body he chose.

The time of men was coming, I could see. Women had run things so far, when there was just one Family, but that was over now, and in this new broken-up world it would be the men that would get ahead.

And right there and then I finally made up my mind. I didn't want to be in Family any more, not this Family, not with the likes of David rising up to the top.

'Let's go out and find John,' I said to Gerry, when David and his two little shadows had moved away.

I said it to Gerry and not to his little brother Jeff. Jeff had always made me feel uneasy, and anyway he was a clawfoot and I didn't reckon he could walk that far.

Gerry looked at me like I'd saved his life. He'd been longing to go after John ever since John left, and talking about going after him too, but he was one of those people that just can't do a thing all on their own, but need someone to follow, someone to give them permission, someone to show the way. His whole face changed and he laughed out loud.

'Harry's dick,' he said, 'I *so* want to do that.'

Then he glanced guiltily at his little brother.

'You'll have to tell mum,' he said. 'Tell her I love her and that, and that I'll be alright.'

Jeff looked up at him with his big naked eyes.

'But I'm coming too.'

~ ~ ~

Probably me and Gerry could have done the walk in one long long waking, but with his little brother hobbling along with us, we took three wakings and had to stop every hour to let him rest. Towards the end of each waking, we carried him between us, Jeff holding on with an arm round each of our necks, or me or Gerry would take a turn carrying him on our backs.

We didn't have any proper hunting stuff, no bags or string or bows or anything, only the simple spiketip spears we'd had with us when we went to Stoop and Bella's funeral, so all we could get to eat were a few bits of fruit and stumpcandy and one grey old groundrat. (It had made a tunnel into an ant's nest, and I got Gerry to dig with his hands on the opposite side to where it had gone in until it panicked and scuttled back out of its hole, all covered in flashing red ants. Then I did for it with my spear.) We couldn't even cook the rat properly, only scorch it in a hollow in a spiketree, like hunters do when they don't want to take fire with them on a trip.

Most of the time the fug stayed down. Sometimes it moved away a bit, and we could see twenty thirty yards of space under the trees. Sometimes it was like we were stuck in a tiny world a few yards wide, with nothing in it but us and a few trees and the odd starflower, and nothing beyond but white shining fug. And then it was sticky and hot, and it was hard hard to walk and carry Jeff.

Once, we heard the hollowbranch horns back in the camp, like the sound of another world: *parp parp paaaaarp, parp parp paaaaarp.* Two short one long: it was the special sound for getting wanderers to return, when there wasn't a Strornry or an Any Virsry. They were ordering the three of us to come back. We heard it again at the end of that waking when we were trying to get some sleep. And a couple of times we heard hunters in forest around us, talking and grumbling as they looked for us.

'Bloody newhairs. Why can't we just let them go?'

'Leopards might have done for them already for all we know.'

But we kept still and quiet and waited, and they passed on.

Third waking, the fug lifted and, quite unusually, there was a dip again straight away. Starry Swirl was bright in a black black sky, the air was cold and sharp, and ahead of us we saw the lights of forest rising up into Peckham Hills, the great black shadow of Snowy Dark looming up against the stars behind them.

'Do you two realize what we've done?' I said. 'Have you actually got it through your heads? We've left behind our mums and our sisters and our brothers. We've left our friends and our aunties and our uncles, maybe for good.'

I stopped and looked back into forest we'd come through, though all there was to see was branches and lanterns and starflowers and flutterbyes.

'And we've left the warm fires in our groups,' I said, 'and the old blokes playing chess, and the kids kicking footballs, and the grownups acting out the old stories like *Hitler and Jesus* and *Angela's Ring* and *The Big Row*, and boats fishing out on Great Pool, and one-legged Jeffo boiling up redlantern glue, down there by Dixon Stream. We've left behind Family, maybe forever. Think of that. Maybe we'll never lie in our shelters again and hear other groups getting up and coming home. Maybe we'll never eat with our groupmates again around the fire.'

Jeff stopped. His twisted feet were all cut up with walking and, even now the dip had come and the air was cool, his face was still pouring with sweat. It was from pain as much as anything, I reckoned, but there was a bit of fever in there too.

He stood there looking round, taking it all in. Starry Swirl shone down above us, so bright bright that it gave a faint light of its own on the branches and the forest floor, over and above the light from the flowers. All round us birds were squawking and squeaking and peeping and pooting like they do when a fug ends, and flutterbyes were everywhere, and bats were coming down from the hills in big flocks, swooping and diving to catch the feast. And it was like Starry Swirl had called them all out of their hiding places, like Starry Swirl ruled over us all.

'We're here!' he said. 'This is happening. We really are here!'

'You're a nutter, aren't you, Jeff?' I said, and I swiped him across the head, not hard enough to hurt, but hard enough to show he was annoying me. 'Why do you have to keep saying that all the time? Don't you know how weird it sounds?'

He shrugged and rubbed his head.

'I say it to remind myself,' he said, and started to hobble forward again. 'Otherwise I'd forget.'

On we went with our slow slow walk. Two three hours later we came to Neck of Cold Path Valley, where Cold Path Stream comes out between two spurs of the mountains into Circle Valley.

Gerry and me were supporting Jeff between us, but now Gerry released himself from Jeff's arm and began to run ahead, leading the way to the bottom of left hand spur of Cold Path Neck.

'John!' he called out. 'Hey John! John! It's me. It's Gerry. It's Gerry and Tina and Jeff!'

Tom's dick, Gerry,' I told him, 'come back here and help me with Jeff. I can't carry him up there all by myself.'

20

John Redlantern

'It really wouldn't be hard to make wraps that could keep our bodies and arms and legs warm up there,' I said to myself.

Everyone knew you could wrap up in woollybuck skins, even in a deep deep dip, and they'd keep you warm, but you can't keep loose skins from slipping and coming off if you're walking. So I just needed to find a way of fixing them on around people's arms and legs and bodies so they held tight and didn't slip. Skins can be cut and sewed together with wavyweed string or dried gut, after all, and old pictures on trees round Circle Clearing showed Tommy and Angela in wraps that must have been cut just like that because they fitted tightly round them.

I scratched some shapes on a bit of bark. You could cut two T-shaped bits of skin for the front and back of the body, I figured out, and then sew them together, leaving a hole at the top for the head. Or you could cut two square shapes, sew them up with holes left for arms and legs, and then make separate tubes for arms. And to keep heads warm you could make something like those masks that grownups sometimes used when they acted out animal stories to kids: a skin wrap with little holes for eyes and mouth. You could even sew it onto the neck hole of a bodywrap to make things extra warm.

The hard thing, though, was figuring out how to make wraps for feet. You couldn't just sew skins together round feet because they'd get soaking wet in the snow. And anyway, walking on them would wear them down and pull them apart. So you'd need to make them so they'd keep the water out and, at the same time, you'd need to make them extra strong and hard on the bottom.

The water part wasn't such a problem, I thought. When people made lids to go on the end of storage logs, they rubbed them all over with buckfat. It was smelly smelly, but if it rained, the water just ran off. They did the same with the ends of boats, smearing buckfat on the hardened skins to keep water from getting into the glue.

'We could use woolly buckskins with the fur inside and the outside greased and greased,' I said to myself. 'Or even two layers of greased skins. And as well as sewing the wraps into shape we could make them stronger by wrapping greased string round and round them, like you wind gutstring round the back end of a spearhead to hold it in place on the shaft.'

But how could we make that hard bit on the bottom? I remembered the Boots that were brought out with the other Mementoes at Any Virsries. Everyone agreed that the tops of them looked like they were made out of some sort of skin (though it wasn't like buckskin at all) but on the bottom they had a thick flat layer of plastic to make them stronger to walk on. I thought about cutting a shape from bark and fixing it on, but I reckoned bark would crack after a while, or crumble when it got wet and soft from the snow. Then I thought about how old Jeffo made the ends of boats, by covering smooth stonebuck skins with glue made from redlantern sap, and sticking them together in layers, before putting a layer of grease on the outside. When they dried they were hard hard, so you could rap your knuckles on them, just the same as you could rap your knuckles on the log part of the boat.

'Perhaps we could make the footwrap and grease it all over on the top,' I muttered, 'but on the bottom stick on layers and layers of buckskin and redlantern glue until it's as hard hard as the ends of one of Jeffo's boats, and then cover the glue with more grease.'

I thought and thought about this. I thought so hard about it that really and truly I forgot all about where I was, or what had happened, or the fact that I was alone. All I cared about was figuring out how to make a hard bottom on a footwrap.

In my mind I felt the skin ends of a log boat. They were hard hard, but after a time they did come off, and once they were off they were too stiff to be stretched over the end and glued on again, so they just got thrown away. I remembered playing with one of those thrown-away boat ends when I was a little kid. It was hard but it was brittle too: not hard and brittle in the way that blackglass was, because you could bend it a little bit, but if you bent it too far it would snap.

'Harry's dick,' I muttered. 'That's no good.'

You didn't want something brittle on the bottom of someone's foot, did you? I walked up and down a bit, watching my feet. I could see that my feet bent and moved as I walked to fit the ground. It would be uncomfortable walking on something that didn't bend like that, and anyway a thing that didn't bend would surely snap after a while. I remembered how the hard bit at the bottom of the Boots was hard *and* bendy, which was exactly what was needed. But the hard bit of Boots was made of plastic, which came from under the ground on Earth. What could I use that would be like that?

I wondered about using buckfoot glue instead of redlantern sap, because buckfoot glue isn't quite so brittle, which is why they used it on the ends of the best spears to hold the gutstring bindings in place: it didn't crack away from the blackglass in the way that redlantern glue would do, if the spear hit something hard like a tree. But buckfoot glue isn't so easy to get, because you have to melt a lot of hard bucks' toes to get even a little bit of glue, whereas to get redlantern sap all you needed to do was look for dribbles of dried sap down the sides of trees, or hack a little hole in the side of a tree and let it run out. (Tom's neck, I realized, *whatever* kind of glue I used,

I'd need to make a pit to melt it in, like the one that Jeffo had down by Dixon Stream.) Yes, and even buckfoot glue was a bit brittle, and even good spears did fall apart.

I got up and paced around my little camp. I was thinking thinking. The fug had lifted and there was a dip straight after it. Sky over Circle Valley was opening up to Starry Swirl, birds were cheeping and screeching, bats were pouring down the hillside in flocks, but I hardly noticed the change coming on at all, just threw a woollybuck wrap over my shoulders to keep warm without really thinking about it. I'd got a set of chess pieces that Redlantern had given me – the dark pieces were blackglass and the white made of dry spiketree wood – and I'd marked out a board for myself on the dirt. I squatted down and played against myself for a few moves, then jumped up again and began to pace around, thinking thinking.

I thought about those scraps of buckskin that lay around when people had been cutting out shapes, and how after a while they became dry and hard, and I remembered how you could make them soft and bendy again by wetting them, or by rubbing grease into them. I wondered if you could mix grease with glue to make something that was hard *and* bendy like the plastic at the bottom of the Boots.

'I need a glue pit. I need a load of redlantern sap. I need some buckfeet. I need some more skins. I need some grease.'

That was ten twenty wakings' work for me right there, just getting all that stuff together.

'I'll dig a pit first,' I decided. 'Make a deep pit, line it with clay, and dig a fire trench round it in a circle.'

Then I thought maybe I should look for another buck first. That way I'd get skins, grease, feet and something to eat.

It suddenly struck me that there was a dip going on, and that Starry Swirl was shining down from most of sky. I'd been so busy thinking that I hadn't noticed before that moment that the air was growing colder.

'Yeah, another buck,' I went on, 'that makes sense. There'll be woollybucks coming down now in the dip. I'll go down into Cold Path Valley and look for them.'

I went to get my spears, the good spear that Redlantern group had given me, and a spare. It was strange. Now I'd paused from all that thinking thinking, I remembered something else that I hadn't noticed at the time. It was a sound I'd heard when I was down in forest getting in some starflowers: a drum and horns that started loud and faded, the sound of a funeral. And then I remembered hearing the hollowbranch horns two three other times too: two short blasts and a long. Family had been calling back wanderers. I'd let it all go past me. I'd shrugged it off. I'd not even wondered who it was that had died, or who was being called back and why.

'What does that mean?' I wondered. '*Why* didn't I notice? Why didn't it worry me?'

And yet it *still* didn't seem to worry me. I just felt restless restless, pacing up and down, slapping the shaft of my spear against my hand, trying to think what else I should look for while I was out hunting bucks, down in forest in Cold Path Valley. No, I didn't feel worried, but I wasn't at peace either. There was no peace in me at all.

'Some clay,' I muttered. 'Some soft clay for the glue pit. And maybe some . . .'

But then I heard a voice call my name.

'John! Hey John! John! It's me.'

It was Gerry, I could tell that pretty much straight away, and it was weird weird, because at first I wasn't pleased.

Oh Harry's dick, not Gerry, that was my first thought. I'm way too busy to bother with him.

'Hey John! It's Gerry and Tina and Jeff!'

I had shut all my feelings away inside me these last wakings, I suppose, shut them down so they didn't get in the way. But now a little glimmer stirred inside me of being pleased and grateful. I was about to go down and meet them but then I changed my mind.

'No,' I muttered, 'no. That's not the right way to start things off.'

It needed to be *them* coming to *me*, not me going to them. I didn't want to have to owe them anything, not when I had so many plans.

I cupped my hands round my mouth and called down to them.

'Hi there, I'm just up here by the caves.'

I put my spears back in their place, and squatted down to wait for them in front of my game of chess.

21

Tina Spiketree

John had made himself his own little camp up the slope of that rocky spur to left of Cold Path Neck. He'd got a couple of spears neatly propped up beside the mouth of a cave, one of them a real blackglass hunting spear that Redlantern had given him, plus wraps and skins and bags piled up neatly inside, and four stonebuck legs hanging on strings. He'd got a little fire going and had marked out a chessboard on the ground and – Gela's tits! – when we got up to him he was calmly sitting there, playing chess against himself.

Tom's dick, I thought, what a poser. He'd been alone all those wakings and as far as he'd known, he was going to stay that way. Surely *anyone* would feel relieved to have friendly visitors in that situation? And anyone else would have come to meet us. Anyone else, for that matter, would have thought that maybe we'd need a hand with Jeff. But no, not John. He'd thought it all out carefully and he'd chosen to wait and be found there like that, playing chess by himself as if he was resting after a good waking's work.

Jeff stopped where he was, taking this all in, but Gerry disentangled himself from his little brother and went running straight up to John, giving him a big hug and kisses with tears running down his face. As for me, though I released myself from Jeff as well, I hung back, waiting for John, waiting to be given some attention. But it didn't come. Considering all that we'd given up to be here with him, all that we'd quite possibly lost, John was so distant distant that it was just weird.

'I thought I heard a funeral a couple of wakings ago,' were his first words. 'Is that right? Who was it that died,?'

Gerry looked round at me to see if I was going to answer, but I gave a little shrug to let him know that he should do it. John might want to make me do all the hard work, but I wasn't about to let Gerry do the same thing.

'It was old Stoop,' said Gerry. 'Old Stoop finally bought it. But . . .' He looked back round at me like I had the power to take the sting out of the news somehow. 'But it wasn't just Stoop, John, it was . . . well, it was Bella too.'

At once John looked away from all three of us, out over Circle Valley. He kept his face still still, but his whole body tensed up tight.

'Bella? You don't mean *our* Bella? Not Bella Redlantern?'

'Yes, ours,' Gerry said, looking round at me yet again, hoping I'd help him out.

'Did for herself, John,' I said. 'Hanged herself from a tree like Tommy did.'

'Yes, but . . .'

He squatted down again by his chessboard and looked at the little carved pieces for a long time like he was considering his next move.

'It wouldn't have happened if I'd let her come with me, would it?' he said after a time.

'No, John,' said Gerry, 'but . . .'

'It wouldn't have happened if I'd not spoken out or destroyed Circle,' he said. 'She'd still be group leader then, wouldn't she? Still leader, still best leader of the bunch.'

'It wouldn't have happened either, John,' I said, 'if she'd kept her hands off you. She might have been a good leader but no other leader in whole Family would ask a boy to slip with her that she'd helped to raise. Not even the worst of them.'

'I didn't slip with her,' John began. 'She just . . .'

But then he broke off.

'They write something on a stone for her?' he asked after a moment.

'Yes. It said: "Bella Redlantern: group leader",' Gerry told him.

John nodded and swept his hand over his chessboard, ending the game he'd been playing against himself.

'You three hungry? I did for a little stonebuck the other waking, and I've still got a couple of legs. I'll get this fire going a bit and you can eat.'

So we ate, and then Gerry and Jeff went off to sleep in a cave about twenty yards off and John and I went into the cave where he'd been sleeping and kept his things. The walls and ceiling of all of these caves were covered in rocklanterns that glowed red, blue, green and yellow, so it was bright bright in there, brighter than outside in forest, and in all that light I saw his face in a different kind of way. I'd been intending to have a go at him for the way he treated me, but he looked so *weary* weary, and so worn down and wretched that I just didn't have the heart for anything like that, though most probably I looked nearly as weary and worn down as he did.

He didn't seem to have the same problem with having a go at *me*, though.

'You shouldn't have brought Jeff,' he said. 'How can we cross Dark with him?'

'What do you mean I shouldn't have *brought* Jeff? According to whose plan? According to what agreement?'

He looked up at me. He passed his hands over his face. I could see that we could go on and on with this or we could let it go, and I didn't have the energy to go on and on. So, as a way of stopping things, I took his hand. Immediately he pulled me up against him and we were kissing and running our hands over each other, and ripping off each other's bitswraps and pulling each other down onto the sleeping skins he'd got down there on the sandy floor. And then we were sticking our tongues and things into each other, and licking each other, and he was pushing into me like he'd die if he didn't get in there quick enough, and I was pulling him up inside like he was still taking far too long. And we rolled over each other and pulled each other this way and that way into every possible angle and every possible way of tangling our bodies together we could think of. And it was *sort of* a way of getting close, but at the same time it was a way of keeping apart and not having to be close at all. And it was sort of a way of feeling we were alive and in the world, and at the same time a way of shutting the world away completely.

I didn't want babies and he didn't want them either, but he needed so badly to have someone he could be inside and not be alone, and I needed so badly to have someone fill up my emptiness, that we forgot all about that. He came inside me two times, the first time with a soft little groan and the second time with a big loud lonely cry, like a cry of pain. Pretty soon after that he was fast fast asleep. I guessed that he hadn't slept much since he was chucked out of Family, however calm calm he'd pretended to be when we arrived, however cool cool.

Come to that I hadn't slept much either, but I *still* couldn't sleep now. I lay there for a long time looking up at the little shiny lumps of squishy rocklanterns on the roof of the cave with the little cave flutterbyes bumping and flapping around them, and I listened to John breathing and making little whimpering sounds in his sleep, and I wondered what would happen next.

Gela's eyes, I thought. Family might have been bad – it was too small, it made me feel like I couldn't breathe – but look at me now! I'd got myself into a world with just three other people in it, a world consisting of me and three boys: one of them cold and distant, one with no will of his own, and one who was just weird. You try to get away from something bad, and things just get worse and worse.

Well, they do get worse if you don't think straight, I told myself. Look what you've bloody done. As if there wasn't enough trouble to deal with already, you've come over here to the one person that's made an enemy of everyone, and caused all the trouble in the first place. And he'll cause more and more, you know he will, because he can't leave a thing alone, he can't bear anything that hasn't got his personal mark on it.

And then I thought of cruel cruel David back in Family, and cold Caroline, who refused even to consider whether John had a point, and bloody old stupid bossy Liz Spiketree and the creepy Secret Ree, and I thought, I hate this whole world. I hate Eden, this miserable dark place we're all trapped in for bloody ever. We shouldn't *be* here, that's the real problem: it wasn't the world we were made for. We were meant to live in light.'

Pretty soon John started to snore and I couldn't stand it in that lousy cave for a minute more.

~ ~ ~

There was more air outside, but of course not the bright light of Earth. It was dark like Eden always is, darker even than in the cave: dark except for the lanterns and the stars. In fact, I thought, it was *still* a cave really out there, still a cave, only with stars instead of rocklanterns. That was what Eden was like. We were trapped inside a dark little cave with no way out of it. And even though I'd never known anything else, and probably never *would* do, I longed and longed for that different world that was full of light. I don't mean just longed for it in a sad wistful way. I longed for it like a blind person must long to see. I longed for it like you'd long for air if you couldn't breathe. I had to stop myself from screaming out.

'What's keeping you, Earth?' I muttered. 'When are you going to bloody come for us?'

'Hello Tina, are you alright?'

Weird Jeff was out there, sitting on a rock. He'd been looking out over forest of Cold Path Valley with the dark shadows of mountains all around it. A couple of starbirds were calling out to each other across it. *Hoom! Hoom! Hoom!* came from some way off and then, quite near, *Aaaah! Aaaah! Aaaah!* Two three monkeys were chasing through the trees below us, making their funny clicking noises, and flashing their bright blotchy skins.

'Why are *you* up?' I asked him, and it came out almost like I thought he'd done something wrong.

He looked at me with his big round eyes.

'My feet hurt,' he said. 'They hurt too much for me to sleep.'

He wasn't crying or anything – that wasn't what Jeff was like – but he lifted up one of his twisted old feet to show me. It was all bloody and raw.

'Michael's names! That must hurt.'

I looked around to find some water. Streams in the hills could be really cold because they came fresh down from Snowy Dark, but I found a small pool just a bit below the caves that was warmed by hot spiketree roots. Water came into one side of it cold cold from Dark, and trickled out the other side warm warm, as it made its way down to Cold Path Stream. I led Jeff down there and helped him bathe and get all the dirt off. Then I mashed up some starflowers, which they say help a bit with raw wounds like that, and smeared the mixture onto his twisted old clawfeet.

I'm not someone who likes to look after people all that much. I never played mummies when I was a kid. I never wanted to help look after the littles back in group like some young girls do. I never looked forward to the time when I'd have kids of my own. But it felt good to have something to do. And after I had dried his feet off as best I could, I put my arm round him and we lay down by the pool there and pretty soon, what with the trickling trickling water and everything, we both went off to sleep.

~ ~ ~

'What are you doing?'

I was really scared for a moment. Someone was standing over us with a spear.

Then I saw it was John.

'Oh, it's you.'

Jeff was still asleep but I released my arm from around him, rubbed it a bit because it had gone numb, and sat up. I don't know how long we'd been there, but the dip had passed and sky was grey-black again like it normally was, with Starry Swirl hidden away again until the next dip. I didn't want to wake up. I'd been having that lovely dream that everyone has, the dream about Earth, where there isn't darkness behind everything but only light, light, light.

'I don't want women slipping with young boys in my new family.'

What? Gela's *eyes*, there were so *many* different things wrong with that single statement that it was hard to know where to start!

'I'm *not* slipping with him, you idiot. He's a little kid, for Gela's sake! His feet were hurting, I came down here with him to help him wash them, and we fell asleep . . . And another thing, *I'm* a kid too. I'm a newhair, like you are, not a woman. And *another* thing, what do you mean *your new family*? A new family? Yours?'

He opened his mouth to answer but I hadn't finished.

'Yes, and what business is it of yours who I slip with anyway? You didn't ask me when you went with Martha London or with . . .'

I was going to say Bella, but I stopped in time.

'We should have new rules,' he said. 'New family rules about who slips with who. It was different on Earth. It hasn't always been like how it is now in Family.'

'We can talk about it,' I said.

He nodded.

'And as to building up a new family,' he said, 'well, we've got to, haven't we? We can't go back to the old one.'

He relaxed a bit and squatted down.

'You shouldn't sleep out here like this. There were three leopards near here only a couple of wakings past.'

'Yeah. We heard them back in Family. David said they'd probably done for you.'

'He should be so lucky.'

He examined the tip of his blackglass spear the way grownup hunters do, checking to see that the edge was still good.

'We need to build up a new family and we need to find out how to get across Snowy Dark and find a new place for ourselves,' he said.

I thought about this.

'Well, we can probably find a few more kids who'll come and join us. We could go back through forest, meet up with newhairs when they're out alone, see if we can talk them into coming over.'

He nodded.

'Yes, that's what we'll do. There'll be enough of them wanting to, I'm sure. Trouble is, the more that come over, the sooner we're going to make Council so angry that they'll want to stamp us out.'

'How could they, though? In the end, how could they?'

'They could kill us.'

'Kill? I know people would *like* to kill us, but no one's ever done for another person, have they, never even once on Eden.'

'Things are different now,' said John, the one who'd *made* things different whether we wanted him to or not. 'Everything's different and always will be from now on.'

Back up at the caves Gerry had woken up.

'Jeff?' he called out. 'Tina? John?'

'Down here!' John called back.

He turned back to me.

'I've started to think about how to cross Dark,' he told me. 'We need to begin building up a big supply of skins, and buckfeet. We won't keep them all here, though. We'll hide them in different places. People are going to come over here from Family sooner or later looking for us, and we don't want them taking all our stuff. We'll need a lot of skins and we'll need to find ways of covering ourselves like they did on Earth, so as to keep warm. It can't be that hard. The hardest bit is covering up our feet in a way that will keep out the snow. I've been thinking about how to make footwraps, with buckgrease to keep out the water and something hard on the bottom to stop them wearing through.'

He broke off, looking down at Jeff.

'*He* won't be able to manage it, though, will he? I wish you hadn't brought him. It won't work with clawfeet.'

Jeff opened his big innocent eyes.

'What about a horse?' he said.

He must have been awake for a little while.

John snorted.

'Horse? What are you talking about?'

'Back on Earth they had animals called horses, remember? They were animals that could carry them anywhere they wanted to go.'

'Yes, Jeff,' I said, like a grownup talking to an annoying little child, 'we know that, dear, but this isn't Earth, is it? There aren't horses in Eden.'

Jeff sat up.

'I don't think horses were a special kind of animal,' he said. 'I think they took baby animals and then raised them up so as to make them *into* horses. We could use woollybucks.'

'Yes, Jeff,' John said, 'but the Earth animals weren't like Eden ones, were they? They had eyes like our eyes, eyes that you could look into and see what they were feeling. They *had* feelings. They had one heart like us, and red blood, and four limbs. They were almost *like* people. You could understand them. You could teach them things.'

We none of us said anything for a bit after that. It was funny. I'd just assumed at first that it was Jeff being crazy as normal, but when

I thought about it, it struck me that maybe this idea of his wasn't as mad mad as it first seemed.

'I suppose we could *try* and catch a baby woollybuck,' I said. 'Yeah. Why not? It's worth a go.'

'We could ride on their backs and then we'd have their headlanterns to light our way,' Jeff said.

'And they *know* the way, don't they?' I said. 'Remember those ones we saw when we were here before, John? With Old Roger? High up on Dark? They were going somewhere, weren't they? They weren't just hanging around. And their lanterns were lighting up the snow.'

I looked at John.

'Come to think of it, John, how else exactly did you think we *were* going to see our way? You couldn't keep torches burning long up there, could you? And if you break a branch of lanterns from a tree, they only last half an hour tops before the light fades.'

John didn't say anything to this.

'What was your plan, then?' I demanded. 'Were you thinking we'd just *feel* our way across Dark?'

'I haven't bloody worked it all out yet, alright?' he said.

I smiled because, for a moment there, after all his grownup plans, he was just a kid again, all bristly and red because someone had criticized him.

Gerry came up to us. He had his spike-headed spear in his hand.

'What's going on? What are you talking about?'

'Jeff was saying we could catch a baby woollybuck, a little buckling, and make it into a horse to lead us through Dark,' I said.

Gerry nodded. He knelt by the stream and scooped up some water to drink with cupped hands, then squatted down beside us.

'A horse. You've often thought about that, haven't you, Jeff? An animal that would be a helper.'

He looked proudly at me.

'He's got all kinds of ideas, my brother. He's *smart* smart.'

I laughed and felt a bit fonder of these two weird boys than I had done before.

'Good,' I said. 'We'll bloody need them. Tom's dick, we'll need all the ideas we can get.'

I looked round at John, but he'd forgotten all about us and was sunk deep down inside himself.

'Our Eden animals *do* have feelings,' Jeff said. 'A leopard has feelings, a woollybuck does, a bat does, a slinker does. They all do.'

'He's *always* said that,' Gerry said, as if his little brother's word was enough to make things true.

John stirred beside us.

'Okay,' he said, 'we've got lots to sort out. We need to get all the skins we can as well as meat to eat. We need to try and catch a baby woollybuck alive . . .'

'We could make a fence that would stop it running away,' Jeff said.

'Okay, you start making your fence then, Jeff, or thinking about how you're going to do it. You couldn't do a long hunting trip, anyway, even if your feet weren't all done in like they are now. Gerry can stay and help you. Me and Tina will go towards Cold Path and see if there are any woollybucks still down there. We won't be away more than a waking this time. In another waking or two we'll go the other way, towards Family, and see who we can find.'

There was no choice about it, no asking us what we wanted. And though I really wasn't scared of him, and I really could stand my ground against him when I felt I had to, and even get the better of him, it was just too much hard work to argue every time.

'And some time soon,' John said, 'we'll decide about new family rules.'

New family! Look at us! Three newhairs and one little clawfoot kid, sitting by a small pool below a few caves. But in John's mind we were a new family already.

Come to think of it, that's what gave him the power he had. He thought he could bring things into being just by believing in them, and he was so sure of it that it sometimes turned out to be true.

'So that was our first family meeting, was it?' I said. 'Our first strornry?'

Gerry giggled and pointed up at two silvertip bats sitting on a branch watching us, gently fanning their wings, with their skinny little arms folded across their chests and their little wrinkly batfaces looking like they were frowning with concentration.

22

John Redlantern

There was some stuff that Bella had done that wasn't good, but she'd been the best grownup in Family all the same. And she'd looked after me, she'd *made* me, and I loved her. But it was me that caused her death.

I couldn't get round it. If I hadn't done what I did, she wouldn't have lost her place in Family and she wouldn't have done a Tommy. Her place in Family and in Redlantern group was everything to her, which is how it should be for a leader in a family. She gave up her whole self to being a group leader and member of Council and she couldn't go on without her job, because all it left of her was a shadow.

The first few wakings after they told me, *I* felt like doing a Tommy a lot of the time. I'd never really have done it of course. That really *would* have been following my own feelings and not thinking about the future, and I'd made up my mind I'd never make decisions like that. But still, whenever I wasn't busy dealing with something else, whenever there was a gap to be filled, it came back into my mind. *Wham!* Bella was dead, Bella did for herself, and it was all down to me.

I made sure not to let the others see this, of course, and I made sure it didn't stop me from getting on with what I needed to do.

In fact what I decided was that Bella's death made it even *more* important to carry on with my plan and see it through. The fact that my idea had done for her meant that I *had* to make it work or her death would have been for no purpose at all.

I felt Gela's ring in its little pocket on the edge of my wrap. It helped to remind me that bad things were bound to happen. People died, people lost things and couldn't get them back, however much they wanted to. It happened to Gela, it happened to Tommy, it happened to everyone, not just to me. I mean, Angela didn't just lose Earth, and her mum and dad and her friends. She didn't just lose the ring. A couple of wombs after the ring, she lost her daughter Candice. A slinker bit the little girl on the lip when she was reaching for stumpcandy, and the bite turned bad and she died.

And then Tommy lost *Gela*, and then . . . Well, it goes on. That's just how it is.

~ ~ ~

Me and Tina went up Cold Path Valley and towards the place where Cold Path itself comes down from Dark. I had my blackglass spear and my spiketip one, Tina had two spiketips, and we had a skin bag with us that I'd brought from Redlantern, plus a roll of thick wavyweed rope. I liked her being there. She was strong and quick and she wouldn't let anything defeat her, not even me.

I thought maybe we'd be too late for any woollybucks, seeing as the dip had been short short and had passed over while we were asleep. (Never do *that* again, I thought to myself: what's the point of living up Cold Path way if you don't go after woollybuck in a dip?) But bucks do sometimes stay down in forest for a waking or two after a dip and, sure enough, after we'd got a couple of little birds and bats, we found three good bucks by some rocks along the stream. I stayed in front of them, lying low, while Tina went in a big circle out round the rocky bit and back again behind them. There were three of them, two fully grown and one about three-quarters size. They weren't just having a drink, they were eating wavyweed from the water, like bucks sometimes do. They were standing with their back legs on the bank and their middle legs splayed out at the edge of the stream, and they were using their front legs like arms, reaching into the water and yanking up the shiny weed. They were in no hurry to move on and the soft lanterns on their heads weren't shining bright like they do up on Dark, but just softly glowing.

Well, it couldn't have been a better time to find them because the strong muddy smell of the fresh weed would prevent them from getting wind of us. They lifted their big heavy heads from time to time and stared out into forest with those round flat Eden eyes, but I kept myself down, just peeping over the edge of a ridge, and they didn't see me.

When she was ready behind them, Tina made a sound like a starbird: *Aaaah! Aaaah! Aaaah!* The bucks lifted their heads again and looked round, but after a few seconds they carried on gorging at the weed. I crept forward. I'd left the bag and the rope behind on a rock so that all I was carrying was my good spear ready in my right hand and the other spear in my left.

I was about ten yards from the stream when they all looked up again. They knew something was up now, and they dropped the weed they were holding back into the water, so as to have all six legs ready for running.

I made a starbird noise – *Hoom! Hoom! Hoom!* – to tell Tina to close up behind them. The bucks were sampling the air with those four feelers they had round their mouths, at the end of their long bendy snouts. One of them growled softly, and the lanterns on the heads of all three of them started to shine more brightly. Then they began to move off to the left.

Tina jumped up behind them and ran towards them yelling.

They turned and ran straight towards me. I kept down low until they were nearly on top of me, then threw the blackglass spear straight at the first one. I got it right in the shoulder, right in deep so I knew it wouldn't need another spear to finish it, then turned and chucked my second spear at the second buck, the newhair. The spear got it in the face. It didn't badly injure it, but the creature was scared and turned round again, which meant that Tina, jumping across the stream, could get it smack in the side with one of *her* spears.

The other buck ran off. We ran up to the two injured ones threshing about on the ground there, and Tina did for them both with her remaining spear. Then she knelt and dipped her fingers in its greeny-black blood.

Gela's tits, that was enough meat for two whole groups and there were only four of us here to feed.

'Michael's names!' I said laughing. 'How are we expected to get this lot back to the caves?'

Tina stood up, licking the blood from her fingers and laughing too. It felt great. It felt, for the first time since I'd been out of Family, like everything might work out well.

'One of us can stay here and guard them to keep off the tree foxes and starbirds. The other can go back to get Gerry. Then we can take them back one at a time. Look at all this meat, look at all this woolly skin! And we've only been hunting a couple of hours!'

'Didn't get a live baby, though,' I said.

'No. Do you really think that would work?'

'Worth a try, I reckon, like you said. And, think about it, if there had been a baby one here, we *could* have got it, couldn't we? If one of us had done for its mother the other could have jumped the baby and held it down, and we could have tied its feet with rope so it couldn't run. Those little bucklings can't be *that* strong.'

She bent and ran her fingers through the wool on the big old buck.

'Enough skin here to try and make some warm wraps for us, and even some of those greased footwraps you were talking about.'

'Easily. If it's enough to keep two big bucks warm, it should do for all of us.'

'Taste the blood,' she said. 'You should taste the blood when you make a kill.'

She got some more on her fingers and offered them to me to lick. All round her mouth was stained dark with buck blood.

'You should see your face,' I said, laughing as I took the thick sweet stuff.

'You should see *yours*!'

She reached out to pull me towards her for a kiss.

And I wanted to kiss her too, but at the moment our lips touched Bella came back into my head. I thought about her tying a wavyweed rope to a branch and round her neck, all alone, all alone in forest, thinking I didn't care about her. I thought of her testing the rope to make sure it was firm and then getting ready to jump, knowing that in the next second there'd be a horrible scary choking time and then nothing, nothing, nothing ever again.

I froze up inside. Kissing me must have been like kissing a stone.

'What's the matter, John?'

I didn't tell her. I didn't like to talk about things like that. I didn't want people to think things like that were a problem for me.

'We shouldn't hang about,' I said, trying to move away in my head from that cold cold stone inside me, which was how it felt to know that Bella was dead, a big icy lump of stone filling me up. 'We've got two dead bucks here, look, and foxes and starbirds will soon want their share. I'll mind these bucks, and you run back and get Gerry. You won't need to run all the way. You should be able to call him not far from here, if you just get above the trees a bit.'

Tina looked at me, and shrugged.

'We need to get some clay,' I reminded myself out loud, as she walked off. 'Clay to line the glue pit with.'

23

Tina Spiketree

Six seven wakings after we did for those bucks, me and Gerry went over Lava Blob way, hoping to meet people from Family. John was busy trying to figure out how to make wraps that could keep a person warm up on Snowy Dark, sitting surrounded by woollybuck skins, and a leopard tooth knife, and string made with dried wavyweed, and more string made of buck sinews and dried buck guts. He'd been absorbed in this for several wakings, absorbed like only John could be, cold and distant and sunk down inside himself, not caring or noticing anything else at all, and it was good to get away from him.

Jeff stayed and helped him. He was good with his fingers, and good at thinking of new ideas, and his feet weren't up for another long walk.

Gerry and me had done for a few bats on the way to Blob, and picked a bit of fruit. We'd brought some embers with us on a piece of bark and now we lit up a little fire to cook the bats and soften the fruit. Hoppers came out of forest and looked at us, funny yellow hoppers, wringing their four hands together like they wanted to say something but were too shy. They waved the long feelers around their mouths in our direction, and went *Peep peep, peep peep.* Gerry chucked them a few fruit rinds and they hopped forward, snatched them up and darted back again to a safe distance to munch them up, watching us all the time with their big flat eyes.

'Are you glad you followed John?' I asked him.

He looked at me and I noticed that his eyes were every bit as big and round as his brother's. For some reason it just wasn't something you noticed as much with Gerry as you did with Jeff, I suppose because Gerry's eyes didn't have Jeff's weird clever mind looking out of them, only the mind of an ordinary young newhair, who didn't really know what he thought about anything.

'Of course I am,' he said. 'John's the best. He always knows what to do.'

'But aren't you missing your group, and your friends? And your ...?'

'Yeah, but John's plan is important, isn't it?' he interrupted me quickly, before I could name his mum. 'We had to give up on Family for that.'

His lip was trembling. He was having a job not to cry.

'Why do you think John's plan is important?'

'Well ... it's ...'

He looked uncomfortable. He wasn't used to having to think about the reasons for things himself. He relied on other people to do that for him.

'Well, there won't be enough food in Family, will there, pretty soon,' he finally remembered, 'if Family keeps on growing. That's what John reckons anyway.'

I laughed.

'I reckon if John told you to walk up onto Snowy Dark stark naked you'd do it, whatever reason he gave.'

'Yeah I would!' Gerry said hotly, 'I'd do anything for him.'

'Except maybe harm your brother Jeff.'

'Well, I wouldn't harm Jeff, no, but ...'

He broke off. We'd both heard voices in the distance. So had the hoppers. They didn't turn their heads because we were nearer to them than these new arrivals and they wanted to keep an eye on us, but the feelers round their mouths were reaching sideways, quivering. I don't know whether they smell with those things or what, but you could see they were trying to figure out what it was that was making these other sounds.

It was men's voices, heading in our direction.

'Quick!' I told Gerry.

There was a big patch of starflowers nearby and we crawled into middle of it.

'I can smell a fire,' said a man's deep voice.

I recognized the voice as a big fat bloke called Dixon Blueside. I'd never spoken more than a few words to him myself, but he was one of those people that are around a lot, and talk loudly, and always have an opinion on everything. Blueside people I knew said he was greedy with food and always took more than his share.

'Yeah, look. Over there. A fire. Who would have come out here and lit that?' he said.

'Maybe it's John Redlantern,' one of his companions said.

'Michael's names!' muttered another nervously.

'Michael's names *what*?' scoffed Dixon. 'You scared of one newhair boy and his three little friends?'

'No, but . . .'

'*John Redlantern!*' bellowed Dixon. 'If it's you round here, piss off out of our valley before we come after you with ropes and clubs like a bloody slinker! You say you want to cross Snowy Dark? Well, don't let us stop you, mate! Don't hold back on our account. Or swim down Exit Falls, why don't you? And you too, Tina Spiketree! You too! Don't think your spiky hair and your pretty little tits will help you!'

Only a few wakings ago we'd been part of one Family with these men. If we'd met them in Forest back then they'd have stopped to chat, told us where we might find some stumpcandy, asked how things were in our groups. We might not have liked each other but that would have made no difference. We were all Family then.

'Put the fire out,' Dixon said to his companions. 'Any luck they've got no spare embers and they'll have to eat their meat raw from now on.'

We heard the rustling as they swept the fire over the ground with branches. There was a yelp when one of them trod on a hot bit.

'I heard Redlantern group gave John skins and ropes and blackglass when he was chucked out,' said one of the others. 'Maybe he's left them somewhere around here and we can nick them.'

I realized I recognized this voice too. Harry Blueside was the boy's name: a slender young guy with nervous, restless eyes, who always seemed to be moving on to the next thing when he was talking, like he couldn't stand to be in one place. He was only three four wombs older than me and John. He'd once asked me if I'd slip with him. He'd said he couldn't stop thinking about me.

'Yeah, go on, have a look,' said Dixon Blueside. 'See what you can find.'

He raised his voice again.

'*Gerry and Jeff Redlantern!* You out there, you little idiots? Your mum's half frantic worrying about you! We passed her not long back looking for you. Get back to Family now and you might still be forgiven!'

I glanced at Gerry. His face was pale in the light of the starflowers, but he kept still and didn't look back at me.

'Nope. Can't see anything round here,' said Harry Blueside.

'Let's go on then,' Dixon grunted. 'There won't be much hunting where a fire's been.'

We lay in the flowers until we couldn't hear their voices at all, and we heard the *thud, thud, thud* of the hoppers coming back. Then we lifted our heads cautiously, and stood up.

Peep peep! went the hoppers.

Hmmph, hmmph, hmmph, went the trees all around us, pumping up hot sap from Underworld, like they always do, whether we're laughing or crying or slipping or dying or what. And whether we love or hate each other.

'So *there* you are!' growled Dixon Blueside.

They were just a little way off, squatted down and waiting for us to emerge, Dixon, Harry and a couple of other young Blueside men. Tom's dick! They'd tricked us. Dixon must have been signing to them with his hands when he talked about moving on.

We ran and ran, jumping over streams, diving under low branches. Hoppers scattered out of our way. *PEEP! PEEP!* Two tree foxes, tearing at a rotten old buck corpse, darted up a tree with a screech.

I reckon that Harry could have run as fast as me and Gerry, and probably the other young blokes could too. But maybe they weren't sure what they'd do if they did catch up with us, and maybe they didn't want to find out, because they stayed close to big fat Dixon and he soon got out of breath. We left them behind us pretty quickly, but we kept on running a bit longer to be sure. We were just running past Rat Rocks when – blam! – we were face to face with a bunch of women.

'Gerry!'

They were all from Redlantern. It was Gerry's mum Sue, and John's mum Jade, and their sister Angie, and two Redlantern newhair girls, Janny and Candice.

Well, Sue Redlantern just burst into tears. She didn't know whether to scold Gerry or hug him and she ended up doing both.

'Are you alright, my darling?' she asked when she'd finally managed to control her sobs and speak. 'Where's Jeff? Is he alright? What about his poor feet? I've been so worried about you. How *could* you do this to me? How could you hurt me like this, you selfish boy? Are you sure you're alright, baby? How could you go without even saying goodbye . . . ?'

On and on. Angie stood back smiling, and Jade stood further back looking uncomfortable, and me and the two newhairs sort of backed away. I liked Janny Redlantern. She was a cheerful, funny, short little batfaced kid, who knew she couldn't get by on looks, so got by on being fun and nice instead. Candice was *sort* of alright but she expected everyone to run around her and attend to her all the time and got grumpy if they didn't. And when it came to keeping things going between people, keeping things happy, she didn't do her share at all. She left it to the likes of Janny to do that work.

'I hope you're proud of yourself, Tina,' she now said, 'because you've *really* messed things up for us. You know that? You've made our lives a bloody misery!'

Janny nodded.

'I don't know why I'm even talking to you,' she said. 'It's bloody terrible back in Family now thanks to John and you three. They still don't let newhairs out on their own, only with grownups. They're watching us all the time, in case we run off too. And *you'd* better be careful careful. David – our David Redlantern, I mean – he's going round all the groups saying we should be much harder on you four than we've been up to now, we should come after John and you three and teach you a lesson so that no one else will ever dare copy you.'

Candice had sort of drifted away from us while Janny was talking, and moved towards Angie and Jade.

'What kind of a lesson?' I scoffed. 'What can David do? Spike us up to a tree like Jesus, like he said at Strornry? I don't really think so, do you?'

I didn't really mean that as a serious question, but Janny took it as one.

'I don't know,' she said, after a bit of thought. 'He doesn't say exactly. He's careful what he says. Caroline said John would be outside of the Laws, didn't she, but she hasn't said that about you three yet. And even John, well, a lot of people still say he's barely more than a kid, and he did well to do for that leopard, and if he asked to come back, we ought to let him. So I'm not sure, but . . .'

She looked round at the others. Gerry was crying now. Sue was begging him to fetch Jeff and come back to her. Angie was backing her up. Jade was sort of half-hearted chipping in. Candice was standing near Jade and looking bored.

Janny came a bit closer to me.

'But it's horrible in Family, Tina, it's horrible. I never thought of it before as a place where I was *stuck*. I never thought of it as a place I was only in because I wasn't allowed to go. But now that's exactly what it feels like, and the funny thing is, I don't *really* blame John and you for it – Candice does, but deep down I don't – because I reckon it's always been like that. We just didn't notice it. We just didn't know anything else. Do you know what I mean?'

She glanced back again. Candice was watching us, but she was far enough away so as not to be able to hear.

'David Redlantern is all over Family now,' Janny said. 'And so's bloody Lucy Lu with the Shadow People whispering in her ear, and Father Tommy and Mother Gela themselves telling her what's right and what's wrong. Funny how they always tell her we should do whatever David says!'

'Come and join us,' I said. 'Don't tell anyone this unless you really trust them, but we're just by Neck of Cold Path Valley, just up the slope on the left side as you go in. Come and find us. Bring more people if you can. Not clawfeet, though, if you can help it. It's going to be hard enough with bloody Jeff . . .'

Behind us Sue started to shout at Gerry.

'You're a silly selfish boy! If you want to go and kill yourself up on Snowy Dark that's your look out, but not my Jeff. How could he manage up there with his feet? How *could* he? You can't let him go! You can't! I want to see my little boy. I want to see him!'

Gerry's hands were pressed against his face. He was shaking and sobbing. It was too much for him. He loved his mum, he loved John, he loved Jeff. Those were the three big things in his life, and now they were all clashing with each other and he couldn't be true to one of them without betraying the others.

'Come on, Gerry,' I told him firmly, starting to move back into forest. 'We've got to go.'

That's how he is. He needs someone to take charge of him.

He turned towards me. He turned back towards his mum. She grabbed his arm. Gerry looked at me imploringly, but I wouldn't release him from my command. So at last he pulled free of his mum, and we started running off through forest.

'Gerry!' Sue screamed. 'Gerry! You piss off if you want to, but make sure you bring my little boy back to me!'

'Don't, mum,' murmured Gerry, not loud enough for her to hear, but just for himself. 'Please don't.'

'Gerry!' Sue yelled again. 'Please come back! You're my boy! I love you! Please come back to us!'

'I love you too, mum,' muttered Gerry, slowing down and half-turning towards her, like he was thinking of going back.

'Gela's sake, just keep going, Gerry!' I told him. 'Don't even think about going back.'

I might sound harsh, but after all I had a mum too that I was fond of, and sisters and aunties and brothers, and I'd left them all behind as well.

~ ~ ~

But we had a laugh when we got back to John and Jeff because they'd made a whole set of wraps to cover up John's legs and arms and body and feet, and even a wrap to go over his head with little holes for eyes and mouth. And they'd greased it all up to keep it dry in the snow, and they'd stuck layers of smooth stonebuck skin onto the bottom of the footwraps with a special bendy glue they'd made by mixing up melted buckfeet and hot grease.

'It's boiling hot when you've got it all on,' John said, peeping out of the little eye holes of the headwrap. 'And Jeff chucked water all over it lots of times and it doesn't get wet at all.'

He pulled it off again. I'd hardly ever seen his face look so happy and excited.

'Try it, Tina. You won't believe how warm it is.'

Jeff squatted behind him, at the entrance to the cave. He was watching us but he was mainly looking at Gerry. It was as if Gerry's troubled face was a bit of writing that Jeff only had to read to know exactly what had happened down there with his mum, without Gerry or me saying anything at all.

'Mind you, it took hours for Jeff and me to get it all tied on,' John said. 'But I reckon we could do it quicker and better next time we make one. We could make it all so it comes off easily, like this headwrap.'

I put the thing on, looked out of the eye holes, peered at each one of the three of them.

'It bloody stinks, John. It stinks like a woollybuck's arse.'

John laughed. Gerry laughed. Jeff looked at me like he was trying to read me too, though all he could see of my face was my two eyes. Then he began to laugh too, really merrily, like a little child.

~ ~ ~

It was only a couple of wakings later that Janny Redlantern came to join us from Family, along with a friend of hers called Lucy Batwing, and Mehmet Batwing, who was a cousin of Lucy's. (He was a funny bloke, that thin-faced Mehmet with his little pointy beard. He was friendly but always holding something back, and he had eyes that seemed to be waiting for you to make a fool of yourself.) And as for Lucy, Gela's tits, she talked and talked and talked, and I thought she'd never shut up: I suppose it was because she was scared. But Janny was good to have there.

'Thought you could do with a normal person for company, Tina,' she told me, with a sideways look at John, all covered in glue and bits of string.

She'd cheer the place up, I thought.

And then, only a waking later, four Brooklyn kids came over: Mike, Dixon (we usually called him Dix) and Gela and Clare. They were all friends of mine back in Family, specially big tall grownup Gela, who I could really trust, and have a good laugh with too. And Dix, her younger brother, was a sweet pretty gentle boy that I'd had a little kiss and cuddle with once or twice.

And then, only a few hours later on, when everyone was asleep and it was my turn to keep watch, my own little batface sister Jane came over with my big slowhead brother Harry. I heard them calling down below in Valley Neck, 'Tina! Tina! It's us!'

I was pleased pleased to have Jane there, but Harry was a worry. He wasn't good at thinking, and he got easily confused and upset like a kid, but because he had the strength of a big man, it could be a real job to calm him down.

'It's bad back in Family, Tina,' Jane said, 'it's *bad* bad. Everyone's arguing and blaming each other, and there's all sorts of scary scary talk. Fat old Liz is even grimmer than usual and she's always fretting that someone is going to try and push her out as group leader like Bella Redlantern got pushed out. Mum is frantic. Bloody David Redlantern and his lot are going round like they're the real heads of Family instead of Caroline and Council. And the way people talk! Well, all I can say is you lot want to watch out. Some of them back there talk about coming over and forcing you lot to come back, some of them talk about driving you away forever, but I haven't heard many say they should just leave you alone.'

'What do you mean "you"?' I said. 'You're here too now. You're one of the ones they're talking about.'

Jane shrugged and pursed up her nice ugly batface.

'I know. I must be bloody nuts.'

John and me got people organized. We set up hunting parties. We had people look for clay to make pots for us, and look for blackglass, and gather wavyweed for ropes and string.

We knew that where we were was a secret that was spreading round Family, and pretty soon someone who didn't like us would get to know about it, if they hadn't done already. We had no idea what they'd try but John had the idea of hiding things that were valuable to us, like woollybuck skins, in lots of different places, so no one from Family could just walk over here and nick the lot. And he insisted we have lookouts all the time above and below our camp. We even dug fire holes in three different places and kept them full of glowing embers, so that even if they came over and stamped out our fire, we'd still be able to make another. No one wants to spend half a waking just trying to get a fire to start.

24

John Redlantern

Janny, Lucy, Mehmet, Mike, Dixon, Gela, Clare, Harry, Jane, Tina, Gerry, Jeff and me. There were thirteen of us now, and yet it was only a few few wakings since I'd been all on my own. (We could have done without Harry, but there wasn't anything I could do about that.) All the new people settled in quickly in their new living place above Valley Neck, chattering and laughing and squeaking and squealing and fooling about, just like newhairs did back in Family. Sometimes I felt a bit left out of all of that, like I did back in Family too, because I'm not often one for squeaking and fooling around. But when I felt that way, I would remind myself who brought them here.

'They might think they came here to be with Tina or with one another,' I said to myself. 'But if it wasn't for me, there wouldn't be one of them here. Not one. They'd all still be in Family, and Circle would still be as it was, and nothing would be different from how it was for wombs and wombs and wombs. And it wouldn't have occurred to anyone to live anywhere else but there, squeezed in around Circle Clearing between Greatpool and Longpool and the rocks.'

It helped to remind myself of that. It helped me with pushing away that cold stone of Bella's death and pulling myself out from underneath it, and it helped me to remember that I still needed to make things go forward. If I left it to the others, no plans would get made. They'd just eat and sleep and play and slip, until something happened to stop them. They wouldn't try and figure out in advance what that something would be, or how to get round it when it came.

Well, to be fair, maybe Tina would have done, and perhaps Gela Brooklyn, and maybe even Jeff if he thought anyone would listen to a little clawfoot kid whose new hairs hadn't even properly started to grow, but none of the others.

We felt another little dip coming on at the end of a waking, and I got seven of us together to miss sleep and go straight over to the bottom of Cold Path to look for woollybucks. We took spears and ropes and I took all the wraps me and Jeff had made, while Gerry and Tina took another two sets of wraps they'd made since with Jeff's help. The way I arranged it, me and Gerry and Tina would go up the path towards the edge of the ice. Jane, Mehmet, Lucy and Mike, who just had bitswraps and shoulder wraps and bare feet, would wait at the bottom of the path for us to drive bucks down to them.

The four of them laughed at me and Tina and Gerry when we pulled on those stinky wraps, specially when we put on the headwraps that covered up our faces, but they were impressed too, I could see. It was *new* new: new like nothing in Family had been since before any of us were born. There must have been a time when people figured out how to make blackglass spears and wavyweed rope and how to stick skins to the ends of logs to make boats, but for a long time it had been like we'd forgotten that there was any possibility that things could be different to what they already were.

With our wraps on, looking like some strange new kind of creature, me and Tina and Gerry walked up the path. This wasn't just a buck hunt to me, it was a first step to getting ourselves right up on Snowy Dark. There's a faint picture, scratched on a tree near Circle Clearing, called 'The Astronaut' made by Tommy or Gela or one of the Three Companions. It's a man in a strange Sky Wrap that lets him live in places so high up in sky that there's no air left to breathe. It's one of the people who found a way of getting outside of Earth. And I felt pretty much like an Astronaut now, walking up the path with Gerry and Tina in those stiff hot fuggy wraps. I felt like an Astronaut taking his first steps up into sky.

And the wraps pretty much worked! They got a bit wet in places, specially round our feet, so that still needed working on. But even right up there by the ice, our bodies stayed warm warm, and even though our feet got a bit wet, they weren't cold like they'd have been if our feet had been bare. They weren't hurting like they did when we came up with Old Roger.

Five bucks came down from Dark with their headlanterns shining bright bright: four big ones and a little baby one trailing along at the end. We scrambled up the hillside off the path and waited until they'd gone right past us – I reckoned the wraps helped here too, because they made us smell of woollybuck and not of human being – then we crept down behind them, making starbird noises to signal to the others below to be ready for them. The bucks trudged slowly on with us behind them, their headlanterns fading to a soft glow as they left Snowy Dark behind them and got down into the light and warmth of the trees.

An hour later, near the bottom of the path, we did another starbird cry. *Hoom! Hoom!*

Aaaah! Aaaah! the others answered.

We found a place where the path went through a narrow gap in the rocks and hid up above there.

Aaaah! Aaaah! the other four called again, and then suddenly they all stopped trying to sound like starbirds and began to yell like excited newhairs so we knew that the bucks must have spotted them and would now be running back towards us again up the path.

Gerry got the first one with his spiketip spear as it came up to the gap: a good shot straight up and under its neck into its chest. The spearhead went directly into one of its hearts and Gerry was covered in thick black blood.

Now the other bucks didn't know what to do. The slopes to the side were stony and steep steep. With six legs each the bucks could still easily climb them, but they couldn't climb quickly, and they knew it, and that made them hesitate, like they thought there might be another option. And meanwhile we were coming at them from above and below. Two of them did manage to get away up the slope but we did for another of the big ones while it was stumbling on the stones. (Mehmet said the glory of it was his, but it was hard to know for sure who'd got it first, because it had spears sticking out of it all over when it went down.)

We were *pleased* pleased.

'We'd never have got these bucks if we hadn't set up over here,' I told the others later. 'That was my point to Caroline, remember? In these short dips, bucks would have been down and up again before any one from back in Family could have made it over here.'

But doing for the grownup bucks was only part of it. The best part, the strangest part, and the thing that none of us had seen or heard of being done before, was that I'd dived onto the baby buck while Gerry was doing for its mother and I'd managed to hold it down on the ground.

Eeeeeek! Eeeeeek! Eeeeeek! The little thing was threshing about like crazy, kicking with its clawed feet and squealing and squealing and shrieking enough to make your ears feel like they were going to burst. Its headlantern was flashing flashing flashing, its feelers were waving frantically, and its big round mouth opened wide and closed and opened wide again like it couldn't get enough air to breathe. It had nearly thrown me off when Tina jumped on it too, and then so did Jane and Mehmet. Lucy and Mike got the rope we'd brought with us and made a knot round its neck, tight but not so tight as to choke it, and another tied round one of its back legs, and I had the idea of taking the wrap off my head and sticking it over the head of the little buck so it couldn't see. And then Lucy and Mike and Mehmet held it, squealing and pulling and threshing, while me and Tina and Gerry got our own sweltering wraps off. Mine were all ripped open by the buckling's kicking legs and I had a big bloody gash across my arm, which I hadn't even noticed in the excitement.

We took it in turns to carry back the two dead bucks, lashed by the feet to branches, and to drag along the little living one, stumbling over the stones with the wrap over its head. And the creature made such a racket on the way back, shrieking and squealing and scrabbling away with its feet, that we never heard the yelling and shouting of the others back at camp. The first time we knew that something bad had happened back there was when two of the others came running down the rocks: big tall sensible Gela and her clever little sister Clare.

~ ~ ~

We'd left six of them back by the caves, but Dix had gone up the hill with a bow and some arrows, looking for monkeys, so there were only five there when they came from Family: David Redlantern and big stupid Met, who used to be friends with Gerry and me, and fat old Dixon Blueside and three other newhair boys. They'd kicked out our fire, taken whatever skins and meat they could find and tried to drag Janny back with them to Family and Redlantern group.

'Harry went crazy,' said Tina's friend Gela in her deep voice. 'You should have seen that brother of yours, Tina. He just went at those men with a big club. He went straight at them, bellowing and yelling, so the two who'd got hold of Janny had to let go and back off because they could see he'd mash them like a slinker.'

'So then Janny ran back to us,' Clare went on. She was a small girl, quite quiet normally, who'd make a little sharp comment and then back off again, like a groundcreeper into its hole, but she was shaking shaking now, too scared and upset about what had happened to worry about anything else.' So then we all grabbed sticks and spears and started screaming and yelling, all together, like we do when a leopard gets too near back in Family. Only it wasn't really like that, because it wasn't one leopard and a whole big lot of us, it was *six* of them, all blokes and two of them grownup men, and only five of us. *Our* Dix – Dix Brooklyn – he was up the hill somewhere, looking for bats or something, so aside from little Jeff, Harry was the only bloke we had. I'll tell you, we were scared *scared*.'

'Yeah,' Gela said. 'Harry worried them for a short time when he came at them with his club, so we followed that up as best we could by screaming and waving spears, but pretty soon they worked out it was still them that had the advantage. You could see them starting to figure that out. You could see the fear fading and the ugly grins starting to appear again on their faces. They were just beginning to come at us again when Dix came charging down the hill, yelling and waving his spear.'

'I reckon they thought it was all of you lot coming back,' Clare said, 'because they took one look at him, grabbed the skins and stuff that they'd nicked, and *ran*. I don't think they realized it was just one bloke on his own. But little Jeff was standing off to the side and one of those Blueside boys shoved him over on the ground and kicked him before he ran off . . .'

'What?' Gerry cried out once. 'Is he . . .?'

'It's okay, Gerry,' Clare told him quickly. 'Jeff's not badly hurt or anything, and . . .'

She broke off, because for the first time she noticed the woollybuck with the wrap over its head.

'Michael's names! What is *that*?'

'It's a woollybuck,' Gerry said. 'It's a live woollybuck. Hold its rope for a bit, will you, Clare? I'd better run up and see Jeff.'

It was strange. All this time the buckling had been shrieking and screaming – for its mum, I suppose, though she was dead and dangling from a branch right beside it – but neither Clare or Gela had even noticed it until that moment, just like we hadn't noticed *them* screaming and yelling up ahead. Something that I'd begun to notice was that people often don't see things they aren't expecting to be there, even if it's right in front of their faces. It was a useful thing to know. It meant there were always more possibilities in a situation than people realized.

But now Tina's brother Harry came thumping down the path. He was all red and sweaty, his breathing was heavy and his eyes were big and rolling around in his head. My heart sank. I'd seen him like this back in Family once twice.

'Gela's tits,' muttered Tina. 'He'll stay that way for hours and hours.'

'Hey Tina and John!' shouted Harry in his baby way. 'Harry drove them away with his club, Harry did. They tried to take Janny, Tina, but I drove them away.'

'That's good Harry,' soothed Tina. 'Well done! That's *good* good.'

Gerry was already dabbing at Jeff with a wet buckskin when we got up to the caves. My little cousin had some bruised ribs and a black eye, but that didn't stop him jumping up and hobbling over as soon as he saw the little buckling. From then on he was like its new mum. He never left it. He even pulled his own sleeping skin out of the cave where he slept with Gerry and laid it down for the buckling in the cave that the two of them had fenced off for a horse.

25

Tina Spiketree

Dix went off for some hot embers from one of our back-up fire holes and got our main fire going again. He felt badly that he'd not been there when David Redlantern's lot arrived, and he kept apologizing to us all. Personally, I reckoned it was lucky that he *hadn't* been there. If he hadn't come running down the hill when David's lot weren't expecting it, he wouldn't have been scary enough. He was a nice boy, a lovely boy, and nicely built too, but he really wasn't that big or scary. If he'd been there all along, maybe they'd never have let themselves be driven away.

We took John's leopard tooth knife and hacked off a leg from the little buckling's dead mum, then we cooked it up with whitelantern fruit that the others had gathered while we'd been away. Janny cried a bit. She had some nasty bruises too from where the men had grabbed her. Gela and Clare cried a bit as well, and that made Gela's brother Dix start up again about how sorry he was for not being there.

'Tom's dick and Harry's, Dix,' I told him, 'will you give it a bloody rest? You weren't on lookout or anything, were you? So you didn't do *anything* wrong going up the hill looking for stuff to eat, no more than we did anything wrong looking for bucks.'

'Lookout?' Dix said. 'Why don't I go on lookout now? It was supposed to be Janny now but I reckon she could do with a rest. I'll do the first watch and let you lot get some sleep.'

(Of course we didn't have groups of people sleeping and waking at different times in our camp like in Family. We were just one group and we all slept and woke up more or less together.)

'Yeah, alright,' I said. 'Harry can be lookout with you, can't you, Harry? I mean there's no way you're going to calm down, is there, Harry mate, for several hours at least? I reckon you could do with walking up and down a bit on lookout, to work off some of that tension.'

Pretty soon all the rest of us except for Jeff lay down and tried to rest. Not that it was easy to rest with everything that had happened going through our heads and that bloody little buckling screaming and screaming in its cave.

After a couple of hours Dix and Harry came to get me and John to take over their watch. John went down the hill to keep an eye on the path up to our camp from forest. I went up the hill, above the caves, to look out over the main valley, and to make sure no one came sneaking down from above.

I was so tired tired, what with the hunt and everything, that I had to keep moving around to stop myself from falling off to sleep. Even so I *did* nod off for a bit, right there on my feet. It wasn't for long, I don't think, but when I woke up I could tell straight off that there was something different. Something had changed.

Well, then I *really* woke up. It's a bad bad lookout that goes to sleep and misses some new thing until after it's already started happening. Like the saying goes, 'It's too late to yell leopard if it's already inside the fence.'

But what *was* it that was different? I listened and listened until I felt as if my ears were sticking out of my head on stalks like a buck's feelers. The world sounded different in some way and yet when I listened to each separate sound on its own, I could only hear ordinary things, things you heard all the time: bird calls and the little gabbling cries of bats, streams trickling over stones as they came down from Snowy Dark, *hmmph, hmmph, hmmph* from nearby trees, the stready *hmmmmm* of forest . . . Just ordinary familiar Eden things, things that were there all the time, like the lanterns shining away below.

'John?' I called softly. 'John?'

I wanted to ask him if he'd noticed anything or if he could figure out what was different, but he was too far off to hear me and I didn't want to shout too loudly. And anyway just then I finally realized what the difference was. It *wasn't* a new sound at all. It was a sound missing. The buckling had gone quiet. It had finally stopped its screaming. Maybe it's died, I thought, though I can't say I cared that much. My main thought was thank Gela it wasn't some new attack that I'd missed! And I looked forward to going back down to my sleeping skin and getting off to sleep without that bloody noise going on and on.

All the same, when my watch was done and I went down to wake Jane to take over from me, I passed by the buckling's cave to see what had happened. Jeff wasn't lying outside on his skin any more so I guessed he must have gone back to sleep with Gerry like he normally did, and I looked over the fence to see what had happened to the buck. The little animal wasn't dead. It was lying asleep on the ground with its headlantern softly glowing. But the big surprise was Jeff. He was in there too, lying there with it, with one arm draped over its woolly back, just like it was Gerry, just like him and Gerry usually lay together on their sleeping skins.

Two brothers on a skin was one thing, though. A woollybuck and a human being was something else. A little clawfoot boy and a creature with flat glinting eyes that never shut, lying down together! Well, it just seemed so weird *weird* that I had to get John just to show him. I was so amazed *amazed*, it was almost like I needed John to tell me that what I saw was really there.

'Looks like he's got his horse then,' John whispered.

'I'd honestly never never have thought such a thing could happen,' I whispered back to him. 'Mind you, I'd never have thought that someone would destroy Circle of Stones either or break up Family into two pieces.'

I put my arm round John's waist, feeling sort of proud of what he'd managed to make happen, admiring the strength that made it possible. But he didn't respond. He had never once reached out for me, this bloke I'd given up my Family for, not once since that time when me and Jeff and Gerry first came over.

But at least now I had some good friends with me apart from him and weird Jeff and empty Gerry.

'I'll tell you what,' he said after a time, 'it's a good job we hid our stuff when we did. They only got a few old stonebuck skins, and none of the good woollyskins at all. We need every bit of woollyskin we can get.'

Then we heard voices coming up from below.

'John? Tina? Gerry?'

It was three more kids come from Family to join us, three Fishcreek kids, a sister and brothers: Suzie, Johnny and Dave. They were friends of mine too, specially little Suzie with her clever sharp tongue.

~ ~ ~

That little buck, it might have shut up for a few hours, but that wasn't the end of the noise. It woke up a bit later, found Jeff lying beside it and began to scream and thresh about as much as ever. He tried to calm it down even though it was scratching and kicking him, but in the end he had to scramble out over the fence and let it do what it wanted, which was to go on yelling and kicking away in its fence, on and off, for waking after sleeping after waking.

Eeeeeek! Eeeeeek! Eeeeeek!

'Gela's tits!' said Suzie Fishcreek. 'Can't we put it out of its misery and eat it? It'd be doing *everyone* a favour.'

But of course John wasn't having that, and nor was Jeff, though he was covered in cuts and bruises that the creature had given him with its hard claws and its bony head. John had kids go down to the pool to fetch back fresh wavyweed for it, and fill up its bowl with water. He had more kids go and find fruit. But it didn't eat a thing. It sipped a bit of water and that was all, and you could see it getting thinner and weaker.

'Face it, Jeff, it's going to die anyway,' said Mehmet Batwing. 'Why not eat it while there's still a bit of meat left on it?'

But he may as well have been talking to a stone.

~ ~ ~

Paaaaarp! Paaaarp! Paaaarp!

I woke up to the sound two three wakings after Dixon Blueside and David's attack. It was one of the times when the buckling was quiet and a lot of us had gone to sleep. I was lying in the cave, with John on his own sleeping skin on the far side of it.

Not *now*, I thought, not *another* bloody Strornry! And then of course I remembered – and we all remembered, I suppose – that we weren't in Family. The hollowbranch horn was coming from far away, from a place where we didn't belong any more, and the meeting wasn't for us but for them.

And it was funny because we always hated Strornries and Any Virsries, and we always groaned and moaned about having to go, but now that we couldn't go to Strornry, we sort of missed it. It felt sad to be left out.

'What do you reckon they're talking about back there?' I asked John, when I saw that he'd been woken too. 'What are they deciding?'

'That's easy,' he said, his frowning face all blotchy with the different colours of the glowing rocklanterns. 'They're talking about *us*. They're trying to decide what to do about us.'

He shrugged.

229

'They'll spend a waking talking,' John said, 'and then, if they decide to come over, they'll spend at least a waking and a sleep getting here. So I reckon we needn't worry about them for a bit.'

Paaaaarp! Paaaarp! Paaaarp!

'But what then?' I asked. 'We know that David's going to say we should all be spiked up like Jesus. And, okay, we know Caroline and Council won't agree to anything like that. But what *will* they decide? After all, even Caroline said when they chucked you out that it was okay to hunt you like an animal. And how much longer will she be in charge anyway? How long before David calls all the shots?'

John stood up.

'A while yet, I should have thought. And no one has ever done for another human being, not since the Beginning. Even David is scared to be the one that changes that. After all he's got to live among our mums and aunties and uncles and groupmates.'

He pulled his bitswrap round his waist, picked up a pile of snow-wraps, and went out, without giving any explanation as to where he was going or what he was doing, like he wasn't connected to me at all.

Paaaaarp! Paaaarp! Paaaarp!

I couldn't sleep then, not with those hollowbranch horns going, and not in that lonely cave that John and me were supposed to share but didn't. After a bit I got up too and went outside. Mehmet Batwing, that wiry little guy with the little pointy yellow beard, was sitting by the fire hole, sharpening his spear-spike with a stone.

'Did you see where John went?' I asked him.

He shrugged. 'Off into forest that way. After bucks, perhaps.'

Mike Brooklyn was humming to himself on lookout on the shelf above the caves. Lucy Batwing was on the path below.

'Yeah, John went up into forest with a bundle of those snow-wraps of his and his blackglass spear and some embers on a bark,' Lucy told me. 'Did you two have a fight or something?'

She watched me with narrowed eyes. She was a great one for

wheedling secrets out of people and then passing them on.

But I didn't say anything. I went back up the slope. Along from the cave where John and me slept, Jeff was inside the fence in the buckling's cave. It was taking wavyweed from his hand.

'Jeff! It's finally eating!'

He was totally absorbed with the animal and he jumped slightly when I spoke to him. Then he looked round at me with his big eyes and smiled.

'This is really happening,' he whispered. 'We really are here!'

In another little cave a bit further on, Dix slept with Mike Brooklyn.

'Hey Dix,' I whispered, 'are you awake?'

Paaaaarp! Paaaarp! Paaaarp! came the horn again, from over by the fake Circle in Circle Clearing.

Dix came out and I put my arms straight round him. I wanted to be with someone for a bit: someone that was kind.

26

John Redlantern

I was torn torn all the time. We weren't going to be safe where we were forever. We had to move as soon as we could, and that meant finding a way over Dark. So I was desperate desperate all the time to get up there, and I was working working all the time on how to do it, how to make better wraps, how to light our way. But at the same time, and for the same reason, we had to watch out for attack from Family. We had to make sure that all of us were protected, and none of us were left alone. So I needed to be up on Dark as much as I could, and yet I also needed to be keeping an eye as much as I could on our little group at Valley Neck.

So of course as soon as I knew it would be three wakings at least before anyone came over from Family again, I went straight off to Snowy Dark. I didn't have time to talk to Tina about it. As soon as I knew, I was hurrying hurrying up to the ice. And then I put on new footwraps stuck together with a new mixture of glue, and I lit up the new light I'd made, with a wet hollow branch packed with buckgrease – my idea was that the grease would burn but the branch would stay in one piece – and I walked up into Dark, until all I could see was the orange circle of snow around my light, and the steam from my breath, and all I could hear were the sounds I made myself echoing from walls of rock that I couldn't see but only hear.

But then the flame began to sputter, and I had to turn round. By the time I'd got back off the ice my footwraps were getting wet again, and the wood of the hollow branch had dried out and was starting to burn. And what I wanted to do was put another set of footwraps on that I'd made with a different glue mixture, and light up another torch, this time lined with wet clay, and try again. We had so little time to get this sorted.

But I knew I needed to get back to Neck to be ready for whatever it was that Family had decided to do.

~ ~ ~

As it turned out, I didn't need to hurry back so fast. I'd been back at the caves for a whole waking and a sleep after that and then half a waking again, before we heard a thing from Family.

Most of our lot were out hunting, and I was with Tina, Jeff, Gela and Clare in front of our caves, grinding seeds and sewing up buckskin wraps, when Mike called down from top lookout that six seven people were coming. He'd glimpsed them out there crossing a gap in the trees. Pretty soon, Dix called up from lower lookout that he'd just seen them too.

Well, it could have been kids coming over to us like before, but we'd never had that many come all in one go, so it sounded more like David and his lot were coming back with their clubs and spears. We hid our buckskins and all our other things in our various hiding places, then me, Tina and Gela grabbed our own spears and clubs and went down the path, leaving Mike, Dix and Jeff by the caves, while Clare went after the others to let them know what was happening.

The visitors from Family had heard us calling out to each other and had stopped and waited at the opening in the trees just past

Neck where Cold Path Stream leaves Cold Path Valley and flows out into Circle Valley forest. It wasn't David's lot, though. Caroline herself, the Family Head, was sitting on a rock, with blind Tom Brooklyn and Candy Fishcreek on each side of her. Jane London, the Secret Ree, was squatting at her feet, and three young London guys with glass-tipped spears were standing around them. *Hmmmmmmm*, went forest. The stream splished and splashed over the stones. Above them, a little hazy but still quite bright, Starry Swirl shone down.

We knew our part of forest much better than they did. We lay low in a starflower patch under the trees to watch them, just like we did when we were hunting buck. They couldn't see us but they knew we were watching them and we could see they were playing up to that. Caroline and the two group leaders were chatting away like they were just having a little rest on a gentle walk through forest. Secret Ree was chipping in from time to time in her little fluty voice. The three young blokes looked bored and fiddled with their spears.

'Clever,' whispered Tina, 'making us come to them.'

'No way will we go to them, Tina.'

'No. You're right. But how about we just walk out like we happened to be out here hunting in forest?'

That seemed a good plan to me, so that's what we did. We came strolling out from the trees, and we acted, not surprised (because that would be like admitting we didn't have a proper lookout system), but like it didn't matter much to us whether they were there or not.

'Hi there, Caroline,' I called out.

And then we sat down by the stream, some way short of where they were sitting, and put our feet in the water, like hunters after a long waking.

Of course they knew we were playacting, just like we knew they were. And we knew they knew, and they knew we knew. Really and truly this was a *big* big thing for them that was happening, just as much as it was a big big thing for us. Us and Family were big problems for one another and both sides badly needed to talk. But the pretending, the pretending on both sides that this *wasn't* a big thing at all: that was *part* of that talk. It was an important part of it. It was a way of feeling our way forward.

But that didn't change the fact that this really *was* a big thing, this was one of those moments that people would remember and act out far off in the future, like *Angela's Ring* and *Death of Tommy*, and the departure of the Three Companions and me destroying Circle. It was one of those *big* big moments, and all of us – me, Tina, Caroline, Secret Ree – we were all in it together, we all had a responsibility together to try to make the story as good as it could be.

'We've one or two things we wouldn't mind talking to you about,' Caroline called out.

'Sure,' Tina called back. 'Just need to cool our feet a bit, though. Why don't you come over?'

She looked sideways at me, and gave me a secret slippy smile, like she might have given back there in Family, the first time we met up over by Deep Pool. And that made me sad sad for a moment because I could see how much all this other stuff – Circle, Bella, all of it – had put distance between how things were then and how they were now. It was as if when I destroyed Circle, I'd stopped just being John Redlantern and put on a kind of mask. Like I said, in the future people would tell stories about this time. Some woman would pretend to be Caroline, some girl would pretend to be Tina, some young guy would act me, just like John Brooklyn had acted Tommy Schneider at AnyVirsry back when Circle still lay in place. But what I saw now was that it wasn't just in the *future* that this meeting would become a story to be acted out. Even now, even when it was happening for the first time round, it had already become a story in a way, with me as an actor in it, playing a part, and not just being myself. *I* was acting me.

Still, there was no time to think about that now.

'No improvement in your manners then, newhairs,' called out Caroline, glancing at the others with her with a tired look on her face. 'No sign of you growing up yet.'

They got up and came over to us in a weary, grownup way, like we were naughty littles refusing to settle down to sleep. And the three young men with their glass spears followed behind them. I knew them all: Harry, Ned, Ricky.

'Nice move there, Caroline,' muttered Tina, like we were watching a game of chess, 'nice move: making us look like kids.'

We pulled our feet out of the stream, shook the water off them and stood up.

'We've decided to make an offer to you,' Caroline said. 'We've decided you can be a group on your own – Cold Path group – with your own group leader, and you can have your group over here apart from the rest of Family. But you will still be part of Family. You must still come to Any Virsries and Strornries, and you must still abide by Family decisions, and Family laws.'

'How about David Redlantern and his friends,' I said, 'were they happy with that?'

Caroline didn't let any expression appear on her face.

'They're part of Family and they'll abide by it,' she said.

'We'll make sure of it,' added blind old Tom Brooklyn with his eyes rolling about in no particular direction.

'Good for you, mate,' I said. 'But we're not a group. We're another family. A separate family on our own.'

Caroline snorted.

'Don't be ridiculous, John, you *can't* be another family! There is only one. We all come from the same mother and the same father. That's just a fact.'

'Tom's dick and Harry's, Caroline!' Tina burst in. 'That's a bit much coming from you! You told John *yourself* he wasn't part of Family any more. The Laws wouldn't apply to him, you said. He could be treated like an animal. Like a tree fox or a slinker, you said.'

I put my hand on Tina's to stop her. I appreciated her standing up for me but I needed her to be quiet because she was missing the point. This meeting wasn't really about the rights and wrongs of things. I mean, I didn't like Caroline and she didn't like me, but this wasn't about our personal feelings. Funnily enough, me and Caroline both understood that, and we were the only ones there that really did. We both knew we were there to try and build a shape out of words that her lot and my lot could both live with. It wasn't personal. It wasn't even a fight between us really, more like a job we were working on together, not so different from Old Roger sitting down with a bit of blackglass to make a spearhead, or one-legged Jeffo London starting to cut open a log to make it into a new boat.

'We'll follow the Laws,' I said, 'because we need laws the same as you do. But we won't come to your meetings and we won't do what you tell us.'

'We can't have you newhairs doing as you like,' murmured Candy Fishcreek in her soft voice. 'Otherwise any time anyone is told off back in Family, they'll just run over here to you, or run off somewhere else and set up *another* family on their own.'

'Well, who cares . . .?' Clare started to say, but I interrupted her.

'No, Caroline,' I said. 'We're with you on that. We don't want things breaking up either.'

Caroline snorted.

'Well, for goodness' sake . . .'

'So let's make an agreement,' I said, 'an agreement between two families, just like we'd sometimes make an agreement between two groups back in Family, when there was a problem between them.'

Caroline glanced at her two group leaders, checking that she had their support.

'An agreement, yes,' she said, 'but an agreement between rest of Family and Cold Path group.'

'Harry's dick!' our Gela broke in. 'You can't expect to come to an agreement if . . .'

But again I interrupted.

'You can call us what you like, Caroline,' I said. 'But it's got to be in our agreement that we don't come to Any Virsries or Strornries.'

Caroline looked at the others again. Candy Fishcreek shrugged. Tom nodded.

'Okay,' Caroline said, 'but you mustn't come near us then. Not past Lava Blob.'

'That's not . . .' Tina began, but again I put my hand on hers to tell her to be quiet. I knew we needed to have some separation from Family, and them from us, if things were going to work out, so I agreed straight away.

'Alright. We won't come past Lava Blob, as long as your lot don't come past it either from your side.'

Caroline glanced at the others. There was no disagreement. She nodded.

'And you must stop taking our newhairs,' Caroline said. 'Stop asking them to come over to you, and send them back if . . .'

Eeeeeek! Eeeeeek! Eeeeeek!

They all jumped. Caroline and Tom and Candy and Secret Ree and the three young London blokes, they all jumped together. It was the little buckling starting off on one again, behind us up on the hill. They were all fascinated, we could see, but they didn't want to show it. The four of us couldn't help smiling at each other.

'This is that baby buck we've heard about, is it?' Caroline asked stiffly.

One of our lot must have met someone from Family out in forest and told them about it.

'You caught it alive, apparently. You're keeping it in a cave behind a fence,' Caroline said.

She wanted to look like she didn't care but she couldn't completely contain her curiosity.

'*Why?*' she asked, with a cold puzzled smile.

Well, she'd let her mask slip a little here, and I let mine slip too, because I felt angry angry with her for even having to ask the question.

'Gela's *heart*, Caroline! What's the point of going on and on every AnyVirsry about remembering the Earth Things if we don't try and *learn* anything from them? We're making a horse, like they did back on Earth. I should have thought that would be obvious obvious.'

She gave a contemptuous snort.

'A horse! Gela's sake, John, the animals on Earth weren't like ours! Everyone knows that. They were more like people. Their eyes were . . .'

'Well, we'll see, won't we? We thought it was worth a try. But anyway, you were saying you wanted us not to take any more newhairs?'

'John, we *can't* agree to that!' Tina broke in.

I touched her again to show I knew what I was doing.

'I'll tell you what, Caroline,' I said, 'let's say that for next five wakings, just five wakings, any newhairs that want to come over to us can come. That way you'll get rid of the ones that will just make trouble for you if they stay. After that, okay, no more. We'll send them back.'

I purposely didn't look at Tina.

Caroline nodded.

'Another thing,' she said. 'If you're going to be doing all the hunting this side of Lava Blob, then we'll miss out on bucks. You'll have to give us some.'

'You've got whole of the rest of forest!' Gela objected. 'We'll miss out on bucks there.'

But I had my own idea.

'Okay, Caroline, but there are things we need too. Let's say we give you one skinned buck every period – we do have to keep the skins for ourselves – and you'll have to give us something in exchange. Two fists of blackglass, or two buckskins.'

'Oh that's far too much!' Caroline said.

But it was the deal we got in the end. One skinned buck to be handed over at Lava Blob each period, and skins or glass in exchange.

'That's until we leave you,' I told her, 'until we go over Snowy Dark and find our own forest.'

'Go over Snowy Dark and freeze to death, you mean,' Caroline said, with a grim chuckle.

Then she looked sharply at Gela, who was after all her own Brooklyn groupmate.

'I'm surprised at you, though, Gela. I always thought you were a sensible girl. In fact, I had you down for Brooklyn group leader in twenty thirty wombs' time. Are you and your sister and your brother *really* going to waste your lives up on Dark?'

Gela had always seemed like a grownup, even when she was little, but now she hung her head like a little kid.

'I think John is right about needing to find more space,' she mumbled quietly quietly, so we could barely hear what she said.

Caroline shrugged.

'Well, suit yourself, but I'm disappointed in you, and your mum will never get over it.'

All this while Secret Ree had been writing down everything we agreed, scratching it on a piece of bark with a leopard's tooth, her tongue sticking out with concentration.

THEY STICK TO LAWS
THEY NO A.V. OR STRORN
NOT PAST BLOB
5 WAKES THEN NO MORE JOIN
1 SKND BUCK EACH PRD
WE 2 GLSS OR 2 SKNS

'You scratch your name on that, John,' Caroline said, 'to show you agree.'

I didn't look at Tina. I knew she wasn't going to like me agreeing to things like this without talking to her and to everyone else first, and I didn't want to give her a chance to make little angry signs at me that Caroline's lot would be bound to notice. She might not like me taking charge but this was just how it was going to have to be.

And that was why I didn't go down to meet her and Jeff and Gerry when they first came over. I wanted to be quite clear that *they* were joining *me*. And it was the same for all the rest over here at Neck. None of the others would be here if it wasn't for me.

'Okay,' I said, 'but Secret Ree'll have to write another bark out for us with *your* name on it.'

'Oh *honestly*, John!' Caroline said.

But all the same she didn't refuse. I'd won that one easily and I thought to myself, now was the moment to act like we were the *big* ones.

'Why don't you come up and see our buckling?' I said. 'We can give you some meat and fruit to eat before you walk back. You'd be welcome. Gela, could you run up and get the fire going?'

And that was the agreement made between us and Family. I could imagine the story already: *John and Caroline Agree.*

27

Tina Spiketree

'That'll never last,' I told John. 'She won't be able to control David and his lot that long. I'm not sure she even means to keep the deal herself.'

'Of course it won't last,' he said shortly, 'but it'll hold for a bit, and that'll give us some time.'

He looked tired. He looked tired *tired*.

'And we *need* time,' he said. 'We need all the time we can get, if we're going to get ourselves ready for Snowy Dark.'

I took his hand, sort of expecting that he'd shake me off again, but funnily enough he didn't. He squeezed my hand back and later on, when we went to lie down on our skins under the cavelanterns, we reached out to one another and had a little slide together, not like we'd done before, all panting and sweating and grabbing, not like newhairs normally do at all, but slow and quiet like you sometimes see grownups doing in the starflowers, grownups who've known each other and been friends for a long time, having a little slip and a little chat and a little cuddle before going back to their groups again.

~ ~ ~

John was right about that agreement. We stuck to our side of it – we even sent a few kids back that tried to come over to us after those first five wakings – and it did give us some time. In fact it lasted ten periods or so, more than a whole wombtime, and in that time we got two more little bucklings, and the first one grew big, and we made all three of them into horses that would let us put things on their backs, and would come when we called them and would nuzzle up against us with their cool dry feelers when they wanted us to feed them.

And we got more skins, and we made wraps for all of us (there were twenty-one of us now, including five more girls who came over in those five wakings after the agreement: Martha and Lucy London, Julie, Angie and Candy Blueside). And some of the girls got pregnant, and Janny and Clare had babies, the first born outside Family. And John went up many times to Snowy Dark, usually with Gerry, sometimes with me, sometimes with others, and stayed up there often for a whole waking and a whole sleeping above the line of the ice and snow, figuring out how to keep alive up there, how to make the footwraps better, how to use spears point down in the snow to stop from slipping over, and how to tie people together with ropes so if one began to slip the others could hold them back. In fact he'd often hardly got down to where there were warm trees and bright lanternflowers and people to talk to, before he started busying about again, looking for dry wraps and rope and spears to take up once more to icy Dark.

It was like things were back to front with John, I sometimes thought. It was like he felt more comfortable and safe with cold and dark and lonely than he did with ordinary and friendly and warm. Ordinary waking-by-waking stuff seemed to make him restless and uneasy: the chit-chat, the joking about, the little arguments, the kids, the chores. (They do say Tommy was like that too. The first Tommy,

I mean, the father of us all. They say he was afraid of his own family, though he'd been happy happy to spend his time in sky, where there was nothing to breathe outside the thin metal of the starship, and nothing to touch, and nothing that was kind or warm at all.)

So John kept himself busy going up to Dark. But for the rest of us, things went on pretty much like they had done back in Family, except for the fact that there were fewer of us, and that we were all young, and that we were living up on the slopes by Neck of Cold Path Valley, and that when we lay down to sleep we only heard the streams and forest, and not the sound of other groups coming and going around us.

Then one waking it all completely changed.

~ ~ ~

It happened when a bunch of us were out in forest, just outside of Valley Neck. There was me and John and Gerry and Dix and Harry and Jeff, along with the first and biggest of our three little bucklings. John had given Snowy Dark a rest that waking because we'd all agreed Jeff would try and ride whole of this trip on the buck's back. He'd never ridden any of them for more than a short time before – he'd certainly never tried to ride one to really *get* anywhere – and John wanted to know how it would work out if Jeff rode a buck for a whole waking. He wanted to know it *badly* badly, because he was starting to realize that there was really no chance of us getting up and across Snowy Dark unless we could use woollybucks like Jeff had suggested, to guide us, to light our way, and to carry stuff for us.

Anyway, this little trip was meant to be more of a scavenge than a hunt, but when we'd been walking for a bit we saw a whole bunch of stonebucks off through forest, four or five of them at least. It was too good a chance of meat for us to miss, but me and Jeff and the little woollybuck weren't up to running and spearing. My arm was in a buckskin sling because I'd fallen on the ice a few wakings back and twisted it, Jeff couldn't run at all, and the buck had never been asked before to do anything but slowly walk with him on its back. So all the others went off Rockiesway after that little herd of stonebucks, leaving me and Jeff and the little buck behind.

I didn't mind. I felt like taking it easy. I walked along next to the buck with Jeff on its back, and we looked for stumpcandy and low hanging fruits that could be picked without climbing. Jeff had a name for the animal. He called it Brownhorse, and he said 'he', not 'it', when he spoke about it. And now as we wandered along, he made woollybuck sounds from time to time as if he was trying to talk to it. But I felt kind of awkward with the creatures still. I didn't like their flat flat eyes with those green glints inside them. Nor those feelers round their mouths. So I just walked along beside it, not saying much and just thinking my own thoughts. Truth be told I didn't feel that comfortable with Jeff either, though his eyes were big and deep deep and not flat at all.

For himself, Jeff didn't seem to need me there. He just sat quietly on the woollybuck's back – him on the little buck was not much higher than I was walking on my own feet – and stared around him with those big big eyes, holding onto its wool with his hands and sometimes leaning forward and patting the soft warm lantern on its head.

Hrum, hrum, went the animal softly when he did that, and Jeff would repeat the same sound back to it. *Hrum, hrum.*

And then suddenly a glass-tip spear came flying through the air and landed – *thunk* – deep in the buck's flesh, just in front of Jeff's leg. It must have gone straight into one of its hearts because the green-black blood came spraying out like hot sap out of a cut tree. The animal sank down in a trembling heap and Jeff fell tumbling off it.

'Good shot, Met,' said a big deep voice from the trees. 'Good *good* shot.'

It was big fat Dixon Blueside, and here he was, right up by Valley Neck, way way past Lava Blob where he and everyone else from Family were supposed to stop. With him were David Redlantern's little buddy Met, and another silly brainless newhair boy called John Blueside. They all three came running over, laughing, to finish off the little buck that was shivering and threshing about on the ground.

'What are you *doing*?' I yelled at them. 'This is our buck and you aren't even supposed to be here.'

'Leave him alone!' Jeff screamed at them. 'Leave my Brownhorse alone!'

I'd never seen him angry like that. He's normally so calm, like he's looking down on Eden from some faraway place from where everything can be clearly seen and everything can be forgiven and understood.

'Brownhorse?' mocked Dixon, driving his spear deep into the animal's quivering side, pulling it out, driving it back in. 'Brownhorse? Since when has a woollybuck got a bloody name?'

His two followers laughed.

'Get off him!' Jeff shouted. He had got up to his feet, and was trying to pull Dixon away from the buck.

Dixon's face darkened.

'You'll get off *me* if you know what's good for you, you little clawfoot creep.'

But Jeff wouldn't let go until the two boys took hold of him and threw him to the ground. Even so he made three big bloody scratches with his nails down Dixon's hairy back.

'We've got an agreement,' I told them. 'You'd better leave us now and clear off to far side of Lava Blob. That was the deal we made with your Family Head. That was the deal that was written down.'

'I'll come to you in a minute, my little darling,' Dixon said. 'But right now we're talking to clawfoot Jeff.'

He hit Jeff hard with the butt end of his spear as he said this, and his little friends laughed and began to join in.

'This is *really* happening, Jeff!' Met mocked. 'You *really* are here!'

'Gela's eyes, Dixon! Stop this!' I shouted. 'You'll do for Jeff if you carry on like that!'

Jeff was curled up on the ground with his arm over his face, all bloody.

'Who says we don't want to do for him, my darling?'

And now it was my turn to try and drag them back, pulling at Dixon's shoulder with my one good arm and my one hurt one.

He turned to me.

'Looks like we're going to have to teach you a lesson too,' he said, and he looked at me like David Redlantern sometimes did, like I was a juicy piece of meat and he was hungry hungry hungry. He gave me a cruel smile.

'Come on, lads,' he said. 'Creepy clawfoot's going nowhere. Let's deal with the pretty one first.'

So now they threw me onto the ground and straight away Dixon was on top of me, straddling me with his big fat thighs.

'Pretty pretty Tina,' he hissed. 'Pretty, pretty, pretty. All that power it gives you, eh? All that power. You can get boys to do anything you want just by smiling at them. You can pick them up and put them down again just as you please. Slip one waking, cold shoulder the next. However the fancy takes you. However it suits you best. Isn't that right?'

'Get off me!' I screamed.

'So how do you like it when the power is the other way round, eh, Tina? How do you like it when fat old Dixon Blueside has the power?'

He looked at the boys.

'Slip or no slip, eh? Slip or no slip with pretty pretty Tina? Which is it going to be, eh, my mates, now *we're* the ones who've got the choice? Pretty Tina, who isn't even in Family any more so the Laws don't apply. Slip or no slip? Hmmm, let me see. Let me see. What's it going to be?'

Michael's names, I could feel his fat dick hardening under his wrap.

'Slip her one, Dixie,' said Met.

'Yeah, slip her,' said John Blueside, with his nasty little eyes all shiny with hate.

Dixon started to pull at my wrap. Well, I screamed and screamed and screamed and suddenly – *blam!* – *my* boys were back: John, Gerry, my Dix, my Harry, bursting out from the trees, yelling and shouting and waving spears and clubs.

'Gela's tits!' went Met and John Blueside and off they ran, back towards Family as fast as they could, while Dixon was still clambering to his feet.

Dixon's mouth was hanging open. He wasn't smiling any more. He could see he was all alone against three angry boys and one *big* big angry man that was my brother Harry. (And Harry *was* a big man when it came to a fight, even if he was a kid in other ways.) Dixon gave me one look, one weird blank look – it was as if, just for a moment there, he was actually wondering if he could ask me for my help – and then he was off too, running through forest on his big fat heavy legs.

'No you bloody don't!' said John, and he and Gerry and Harry were straight off after him.

But my Dix stopped, my gentle Dix, and he squatted down between me and Jeff.

'Tina? Jeff? Are you okay?'

Jeff was sitting up. He was all bruised and bloody and trembling, but not badly hurt. He crawled to his Brownhorse.

'Poor old Brownhorse,' he murmured, and he made a soft little buck noise in his mouth. 'Poor old Brownhorse.'

The creature was pretty much dead already. It wasn't moving its limbs, just trembling a bit all over, but Jeff gently stroked its wool and went on talking to it like maybe its mother would have talked to it: *Hrum, hrum, hrum.*

And while Jeff stroked Brownhorse, Dix put his arm round my shoulder and gently stroked *me*. I really wasn't badly hurt at all, just had a few scratches and bruises, and my hurt arm aching badly again like it had done when I first fell: nothing more than that. But something horrible had nearly happened to me, something that we didn't even have a name for. I was shaking shaking all over, my teeth rattling together. And I leant my head on Dix's shoulder and let him comfort me, while little Jeff tried to comfort the dying animal.

And pretty soon, back came John and Gerry and Harry.

~ ~ ~

As soon as we saw them we knew something big had happened. They'd *changed*. They'd changed completely. They were trembling worse than me, they were shaking all over, and their faces were all blotchy and twisted and puffed up, so you couldn't tell if they were scared or angry or excited or ashamed or what, but you could see that whatever it was, it was *big* big big.

'What?' I demanded. 'What? Gela's heart, what have you done?'

'Yeah, what's happened?' Dix asked, gently releasing me, and jumping to his feet.

John stared at him, like he was having difficulty seeing he was there.

'We . . . er . . .' he began, and then stopped.

'You . . . er . . . what? Gela's heart, John, *tell* us?'

'We . . . we . . . did for them,' he said.

He turned to me, then to Jeff, then to me again with weird wide staring eyes that he couldn't keep still.

'You what? You *did* for them? No, no, you couldn't have. That wouldn't . . . What? You *did* for them? You mean . . . What? . . . Like animals, you mean? All three? Like animals?'

We were the fifth generation of Eden, the fifth generation after Father Tommy and Mother Angela. But no one had ever killed another human being. No one, not ever.

'Yeah, all three,' said John. 'I did for Dixon with my spear while he ran.'

His voice came out all jerky and strange.

'Then . . . Then Harry did John Blueside. He turned to try and face us with his spear, but . . . Harry . . . Harry was on top of him with his club before he could throw it, and he did for him too. He cracked his head open. And . . . and . . . Met . . . well, Gerry did for him, didn't you, Gerry? He did for him with his spear, like I did Dixon.'

John held up his own blackglass spear with his shaking hand, like it would do the rest of the talking for him. He touched the tip with his finger and held it out to show me the blood. Not greeny-black Eden blood, not blood born down in Underworld, not the blood you see when a spear comes out of a buck or a starbird or a bat, but real red blood that came down from sky. Real red blood from Earth.

'We *are* here,' said Jeff, like he'd been thinking carefully all this time about what dead Met had jeered at him, and was finally agreeing with him. 'Yes, we really are here.'

28

John Redlantern

We didn't have hollowbranch horns like they had in Family, but we'd made ourselves a drum out of a length of trunk and a bit of stonebuck skin. As soon as we'd got back to our camp – Gerry and Dix carrying Jeff between them to speed things up, and Harry and me carrying the dead buck Brownhorse – we got out the drum and Harry began to beat it, as hard and fast as he could.

BANGBANGBANGBANGBANGBANGBANGBANGBANG . . .

He was *frantic* frantic. His eyes were staring, he was panting like he couldn't get enough air, his face was pouring with sweat, and he banged that drum so hard he nearly broke through the skin.

'Easy, Harry. That's enough, that's enough,' I told him. 'We don't want them guessing back in Family that something bad's up.'

I didn't feel much different from Harry myself, though. Every few seconds I heard the squelchy thud of my spear in Dixon Blueside's back, the hissing noise of the air coming out from his lungs, the way he rolled over when I pulled it out, the choking gurgle when I shoved it right back again into his belly. But unlike Harry, I knew I had to get back in control of myself, or we'd all be done for.

'They won't miss Dixon and the others for another waking or two,' I told everyone back at the caves.

Tall, grownup Gela Brooklyn was there, and her small little sister Clare with her baby on her hip, and Mike, and Suzie Fishcreek, and batfaced Janny, and Tina's sister Jane, and Dave Fishcreek and Julie Blueside.

'Not for another waking or two,' I said. 'And even then, they won't know what's happened. That's why we had to do for all three of them, otherwise they'd have run straight back to David, and he'd have sent a whole lot more of them after us at once. We really had no choice. We really didn't.'

I looked round at their shocked faces – Gela, Suzie, Janny, Dave, all of them – daring anyone to disagree.

'As it is,' I said, 'we've got two wakings before anyone starts to worry, and by then a leopard or a fox will have got to the bodies, and then starbirds after that, so they won't be able to tell any more that it was spears and a club that did for them. They'll just be scattered bones.'

'Yes, but their mates will guess, won't they?' Dix said. 'David Redlantern and all of them.'

He had his arm round Tina. She was shaking shaking. I was shaking too.

'Yeah, they will. They'll know it was to do with us, because they'll know that Dixon and Met and John Blueside came over this way and that the three of them came past Lava Blob on purpose to make trouble. David planned it with them, I'm sure. Maybe he hoped to get us to chase back after them into their part of forest. He'll have been wanting to make trouble for a long time. He'll have been wanting to be able to go to Caroline and Family and say the agreement wasn't working.'

'So if they know it was to do with us,' said Gela in her slow deep voice, 'they'll still come after us when the three of them don't come back. Even if they pretend to Family that they're just trying to find out what happened.'

'Yes of course. So we haven't got much time. We need to get ourselves together and go.'

'Go *where*?' Dix asked.

Gela's tits, where had he *been* all this time? What did he think this whole business was all *about*?

'Over the top, of course. Over Snowy Dark. Like we've been planning, yeah? Like we've been planning *ever since we came here*.' I looked round at their faces, and I realized that it wasn't just Dix. Tom's dick and Harry's! None of them had really believed this was ever going to happen. Not one. It was always going to be somewhen off in the future, never ever now.

Still, it was too late for talking and explaining. They were just going to have to get it through their heads by themselves.

I started going through all the things we'd need to get together.

'Gela, you sort out wraps for everyone. Mike, get all our spare skins and blackglass and rope. Dave, we need all our meat and stumpcandy and seedcakes. Clare, can you sort out some embers . . .'

~ ~ ~

In a couple of hours, the drum had called everyone back. All twenty-one of us were there, plus Janny and Clare's babies, and we had the meeting, a sort of Strornry, our last in Circle Valley. It was a dark dark time. No one had ever argued with me about whether we would really go over the mountains, not once, but I suppose they'd all privately hoped that it would never really get to that. We had the agreement with Family written on bark after all, and for ten periods it had seemed to work. Family had handed over blackglass and skins to us as they'd agreed. We'd had plenty of meat to spare to keep our side of the deal. I suppose they'd all persuaded themselves that things would just go on in the same way forever with our own little family at Cold Path Neck, Old Family going its own way on the far side of Lava Blob and a bit of toing and froing going on between us here and our mums and friends and groupmates over there. Most of them seemed to have decided that going across Snowy Dark was nothing more than a weird dream of mine. Some of them had never even given it any thought.

'How do we know there even *is* another side?' said Lucy Batwing. 'Dark might go on and on. And then we'd die, wouldn't we? We'd die of cold.'

'We know it doesn't go on forever,' I told her. 'When Tommy and Gela and the Companions first saw Eden from their sky-boat, the thing they noticed was that it was all covered in light. Remember that? All covered in light, not just one patch of light and the rest dark. That was weird to them because Earth got its light from a star, and didn't have lights of its own. So they noticed it, and it stuck in their minds. That's why they talked about it to their kids, and why we still remember the story.'

'Okay, so there's more forest beyond Dark,' said Clare Brooklyn, who was nursing her baby boy, 'but we still might not reach it. Even with your wraps and woolly horses and all, we're not going to be able to keep going more than a few wakings, are we? Not in freezing cold and pitch darkness. Not even us newhairs, let alone my little Fox and Janny's Flower.'

The twenty of them were ranged around in a circle, most sitting, some standing. I was pacing around in middle. I couldn't keep still, that was too much to ask of myself, only one two hours after I'd done for Dixon Blueside with my spear.

'It's dangerous but we've got to try it,' I said. 'In a couple of wakings they'll come after us. David Redlantern and all his friends in Family. Caroline and Council won't be able to control them any more. They'll be over here with clubs and spears. Look what they did to Jeff, look what they tried to do to Tina. And that was *before* we did for David and the others.'

'Well, *we* didn't do it actually, John,' said Mehmet Batwing with an angry laugh. 'That was you. *You* did it. You and Harry and Gerry. The first killings in Eden. Smart move, John. Smart smart move.'

His thin little face was hard and cold and there was suddenly a dark ugly feeling out in whole group that each person had been keeping hidden inside until then. Two or three people muttered in agreement with what Mehmet had said, including Angie Blueside, a cousin of John Blueside who was lying dead in forest right at that moment, with Gerry's spearhole in his belly and starbirds and tree foxes feeding on his flesh. Why should we all freeze on Snowy Dark, was what a lot of them were thinking, just because John and Harry and Gerry lost their heads and did for three people who were already running away?

'I think you're forgetting, Mehmet,' said Tina in her iciest voice. She was *angry* angry. 'I think you're forgetting what Dixon Blueside and his mates did to Jeff and what they tried to do to me. Do you think they'd have left us all in peace if we'd just . . . ?'

I put my hand on her arm to tell her to leave it; I didn't need her to defend me.

'No, you're quite right, Mehmet,' I said, as calmly as I could with my tight tight throat. 'And you're welcome to stay here or to go back to Family, Mehmet. *All* of you are welcome to stay or go back. Take what's yours, if you like, and walk back to Family. Tell them it was John and Harry and Gerry who did for Dixon and his mates, and that it was nothing at all to do with you. Which is true. It's perfectly true. So go on if you want to. Go on. No one's stopping any of you. You all came to me, remember, all of you, every single one, out of your own choice. I didn't force you to come and I certainly won't force you to stay.'

I folded my arms and stood and waited. Mehmet looked around awkwardly, but all his support seemed to have disappeared.

'No,' he said, 'I just meant . . .'

'You just meant what?'

'Oh nothing. It doesn't matter.'

He was sort of smiling but under the smile he was ashamed, and under the shame he was angry angry. He was going to be trouble, I could see, and it would actually be better if he left. But if I tried to *make* him go, that would have been trouble too. That would have been even *more* trouble. It might have made whole plan fall apart.

'I'm not making anyone do anything,' I repeated. 'Do you all understand?'

There was silence for a bit.

Then Lucy London spoke. She was a short plump girl with bulgy anxious eyes.

'But if we go over Dark we won't ever see our mums again, or our sisters and brothers. I mean, it's okay not seeing them every waking like now, when we *can* still see them if we want to, up by Blob. But if we go over Dark that won't happen any more. We'll *never* see them, never never, and we won't even get a chance to say goodbye.'

'No, you won't,' I said.

'But that's not fair!' said Lucy London, and several people murmured crossly in agreement.

'I'm not making you do anything,' I repeated, as patiently as I could. 'You can go back to Family if you want. Or you can stay here at Cold Path Neck if you think you can make a go of it. It's up to you.'

'Yes, but Family is horrible now,' complained Lucy London. 'And staying here would be no good if there were only a few of us. We'd be lonely, wouldn't we? It wouldn't be any good at all.'

'Mother Angela would say it was wrong to go over Dark,' said Julie Blueside. 'Okay we came over here, and didn't stay right next to Circle, but we're still in Circle Valley, aren't we, and we'd still be able to see if a Veekle from Earth came down from sky. Plus our friends in Family would tell Earth where we were.'

'Yeah,' said her younger sister Candy. 'And my mum told me that First Angela and First Tommy and First Harry all came to Lucy Lu in a dream and told her that if we go across Dark we'll be lost forever.

We won't have the Shadow People to watch over us any more, and even after we die, we'll never go back to Earth.'

'Oh yeah?' sneered Tina's sister Jane. 'So how come Lucy Lu used to say that beyond Snowy Dark was where the Shadow People *lived*?'

'Don't bother, Jane,' said Tina. 'Once people start talking about messages from Mother Gela and the Shadow People, black can be white and white black and a thing can be true and its opposite true all at the same time.'

'Well, you've got that wrong, Tina,' shouted Julie. 'You just don't understand. Yes, in a *way* the Shadow People live beyond Dark, but not in *that* way . . .'

But then Harry started up again.

'They did for Brownhorse!' he yelled, sweating, redfaced, spit flying out of his mouth, and banging hard hard on the drum with every word. 'They were *bad* bad. They did for Brownhorse! They nearly did for Harry's sister too!'

'Leave it, Harry!' screamed Gerry. He was shaking shaking all over. 'Just bloody leave it, alright?'

And now six seven people were all shouting at once.

'Shut up, Harry!'

'Brownhorse was just a woollybuck!'

'Just because you don't know anything about the Shadow People, Tina, doesn't mean they don't exist. I'll talk about what I bloody want . . .'

'Leave Harry alone. They did for Brownhorse, Jeff's Brownhorse.'

'Shut *up*, Harry!'

'It matters to some of us what the Shadow People think, Tina, even if it doesn't matter to you.'

'Gela's tits, can't you see we haven't got *time* for all that crap!'

'They did for Brownhorse . . .'

'Don't you tell *me* what we've got time for!'

~ ~ ~

It was like a chess game when it gets stuck and won't move forward.
I needed to bring a new piece into play.

'Everybody be quiet,' I hollered. 'Shut up now and I'll show you
something!'

29

Tina Spiketree

We were in terrible danger. Three people were dead. Harry and Gerry and John were killers, and they were all three shaking shaking all the time because of their heads trying to get hold of what they'd done. And there was going to be *more* killing, and any one of us could easily end up dead in only a waking or two. This was one of the most important meetings that anyone on Eden had ever had, but it looked as if it was going to become a pointless shouting match, not about what we needed to do but about the Shadow People, or about Harry being too noisy, or about how a woollybuck had died. We were facing death yet we were fighting about nothing at all.

But then John silenced everyone. He absolutely silenced us. He took away our breath.

'Angela has come to *me*,' he said. 'She came to me over by Deep Pool. She told me she wants her children to spread out over Eden and not stay in one place pining for Earth. She wants us to be at home here in Eden, not just in this valley but at home all *over* Eden, just like people are at home all over Earth. She says Earth would expect that of us, and will come looking for us wherever we are. She says Earth will be disappointed with us if we stay only in one place.'

He looked round our dumbstruck faces. No one would have

thought it possible. He was just about the last person in Eden that you'd expect to say a thing like that. I was scared scared someone was going to laugh and it would all fall apart. And I think someone would have done too if he hadn't said something else that was even *more* weird and even *more* unexpected.

'If you don't believe me, have a look at this. Gela has given me a sign.'

He reached down, took something from the little pocket at the edge of his waistwrap and held it up between his finger and thumb. It was small small and at first I couldn't think what it was.

'You know the story of *Gela's Ring*? You remember it? Angela's lost ring? Well, this *is* the ring. I found it, soon after she first came to me.'

I started shivering all over. Some of the others cried or laughed, like Angela herself might have done if someone had found the ring for her, long after she had given it up for lost. Some of them swore. Michael's names! Harry's dick! Tom's neck! Even the two little babies picked up the strange feelings all around them and began to yell, first Clare's little Fox and then Janny's baby Flower. And after that, would you believe it, the two remaining horsebucks in their cave – Def and Whitehorse, Jeff called them – *they* started as well, like they could pick up the excitement too, and that made everyone laugh, even the ones who were crying, and even the ones who'd done for other human beings only a few hours before.

But as John moved round everyone showing them the ring, and how tiny and smooth it was, and how it was really made out of metal, and how it had tiny writing inside with Angela's name, tiny writing that could only have been done on Earth, I started to feel angry.

John had done it *again*! He'd behaved again like he was the only one in the world that needed to know or decide anything! He'd destroyed Circle without asking anyone, and kept the ring for himself without telling anyone. He'd expected us to follow him and trust him, but he hadn't trusted any of *us* at all.

I was so angry I didn't even care about the ring any more. All I wanted to do was scream and yell at John. But I couldn't do that then, could I? Angry as I was, I knew that we were all in danger. And I knew that everyone here needed to be able to believe in John and trust him, because what he said was right. We *did* have to go. We *did* have to take the risk of going over Snowy Dark.

But then an idea came to me. I realized there was something I could do to stop John having it all his own way, without messing up the things we needed to do.

'I know,' I said, 'let's do the story now. Let's do the story of *Gela's Lost Ring*. You can be the teller, Dix. I'll be Angela. Harry, you can be the first Harry. Suzie Fishcreek and Lucy Batwing, you can be the first Suzie and Lucy. Clare, you can be the first Clare, Candy can be Candice. John can be Tommy.'

Everyone was puzzled by this at first. It was too sudden, I suppose, and they couldn't see the point of it, and it sort of interrupted them in middle of looking at the wonderful perfect ring. But at the same time everyone could see it was, in a way, a suitable thing to do, to remember the story of this famous thing that had just been put in front of them. That was how we'd been brought up. Every Any Virsry we'd been told to remember things, to join the present up with the past.

As for John, when I peeked at him sideways, I could see that he was feeling just like I'd been feeling a few moments before. He was angry angry, he felt set up, he really didn't want this at all, but at the same time he knew he had to go along with it. I hadn't given him a choice, just like he hadn't given me one.

Good! Serve him right. Let him see what it felt like.

'So this is the story of Angela's ring and how she lost it,' began Dix, that kind pretty boy who had stopped to care for me and Jeff while John and the others went belting off to kill.

'Gela never wanted to come to Eden. She and Michael were made to come here against their will by Tommy and Dixon and Mehmet.

She decided to stay and start Family here with Tommy, because she thought it was better to live and see what the future would bring until Earth came back than to go into sky where it was pretty certain that she'd drown. But she was sad. She missed her mum. She missed her father. She missed her group, which was called London, like our first group here in Eden. She missed the great star – Sun – that filled up Earth with light. She missed being with people that she loved and knew. She was sad *sad* inside. But she didn't show that to people. She made the best of things. She cared for her kids and did all she could to make their life happy. She even thought about us in the future and . . . and . . .'

He hesitated here, because he was about to say that Gela made Circle of Stones, which is what the story normally said, but he could see that it wouldn't be right to say that any more (even though everyone knew quite well what it was that he was missing out), and that it was a part of the story that was now going to have to change.

' . . . and she made traditions and laws,' he said, 'that we still keep. She even made herself love Tommy, though he wasn't the kind of man she normally liked, and even though he often got angry and sulky, and once twice he even hit her.'

He looked round at John and held out his hand for the ring. I could see John didn't want to hand it over one bit, but once again he had no choice, not without spoiling the story. Clever Dix. Kind, pretty *and* clever.

'Angela had a ring . . .' Dix stumbled a bit in his words there, because of all the weird feelings that came with telling a story about the ring while the ring itself was right there in his hand, and his voice came out all thick and wobbly, like he was about to cry. 'Gela had a ring, which was given to her as a present by her mum and her father. (They knew who their fathers were on Earth: they weren't like we are here.) And the ring . . . the ring had writing inside it, tiny writing that said *"To Angela with love from Mum and Dad"*.'

He passed the ring to me and I could see that, although he was

CHRIS BECKETT

doing it for the story, he was doing it for my sake too, because he'd seen how I felt about John springing this on us like this, and he wanted to help me feel better. After all, we didn't need an actual ring to tell the story. Normally when people do the story of *Angela's Ring*, they don't have a ring at all.

'Then one waking, when she was out in forest scavenging, Gela lost her ring. It slipped off her finger somehow and she couldn't find it. And then . . .'

And now it was my turn. I was Angela. I dropped the ring on the ground (out of the corner of my eye I could see John wince) and began running back and forth, back and forth, kneeling down, standing up again, moaning, muttering, beginning to cry.

'Tommy! Tommy!' I shouted into John's face. 'I've lost it! I've lost my ring!'

John screwed up his face. He *really* didn't want to play. This was just timewasting to him, timewasting and unnecessary complication, and anyway he didn't like the ring to be out of his hands.

'I'm sure it'll turn up,' he said, without even trying to pretend to be Tommy.

'What do you mean, you bloody idiot? What do you mean *it'll turn up*, you useless lump? Help me look for it! Get it back for me. I'm not going to go on without it.'

I glared round at Harry and Suzie and Lucy and Clare and Candy.

'What are you idiots staring at? Michael's names! Find the bloody ring for me, can't you? Do something useful for once in your whole life!'

So they began to look, some getting on their knees, some walking about. Clare and Candy began to cry. Harry was shaking all over and running about like he really did think it was lost.

'I'll find it for you, Gela, I'll find it,' he bellowed. 'I'll find it!'

'Stop that racket, you snivelling kids,' I yelled at them, 'shut it now. I never wanted you, you know. I never wanted to be with him. I never wanted to touch him, never mind slip with him and have his kids . . . It's my mum and dad and my friends on Earth I love, not any of you, not you stupid lot in this stupid dark dark Eden. And that ring, that ring was the only . . .'

'Mum, please,' went Clare, and she was really crying now.

'Piss off, Clare. I can't stand the sight of you. Do you know that? I can't stand the sight of *any* of you . . .'

Whew! I *really* let rip, I can tell you. I screamed and yelled till my face was red and the tears were pouring down, and I was sweating and shaking all over. All five of my so-called kids were crying – even though one of them was actually my big brother – and a lot of the people watching were crying too. And the babies were yelling, and the bucks were going *eeeek! eeeek! eeeek!* in their cave. Even John looked scared.

It must have been scary scary that first time for those five kids, all those wombs and wombs ago, watching their mum fall apart like that and turn on them, when she and Tommy were all they had in the world. It must have been scary scary. Otherwise that story would never have kept going for so long, would it? Not when so many other things have been forgotten and lost, spreading out and out over the generations like the ripples from a stone chucked into a pool, getting smaller and fading away. And the weird weird thing about this story of *Angela's Ring* was that it didn't even have a point to it, no happy ending, no lesson to be learnt. It was like one person's cry of pain, echoing out on and on and on through the generations, even after that person was long long dead.

So why *did* we keep doing it? I'd wondered that sometimes, but now I found out. It was because doing it felt *great*!

'As for you, Tommy,' I said, turning on John. 'As for you, you selfish arrogant bastard. You took me from my mum and dad, you took me from my friends, you took me from my lovely Earth, without letting me in on your plans, without giving me a choice, without thinking about my feelings. And now you can't even find my ring. I hate you, I hate you, I hate you and I always always will.'

But John just knelt down, picked up the ring and held it out to me.

'Here it is, Gela, I've found it. I've found your ring for you after all this time.'

That threw me, I must admit. I wasn't expecting that move at all.

'What do you mean? You never found the ring, Tommy. You never did anything that useful in your whole life.'

'No,' said John. 'I'm not Tommy. I'm John. I'm John Redlantern. I'm your great-great-grandson and these are your great-great-grandchildren, trying to make our home in dark Eden, just like you did. I've found your ring, Gela. I've ended that story. You don't need to tell that story any more.'

'Give it back then. Give it back to me now.'

But he had his answer to that as well.

'No, Gela. You're dead now. You're dead and buried under a pile of stones, remember? The ring's no good to you any more, is it? But I'll look after it. We'll look after it. We'll take it with us over Dark and right to the other side, just where you want us to go.'

And he put the ring back in the pocket in his wrap and came and put his arms round me. Tom's dick and Harry's, you'd got to hand it to him! He knew how to stay in control.

My eyes were full of tears and I didn't know if they were my tears really or Angela's, just like I didn't know if I felt comfort in his arms in spite of everything, or whether I hated him more than ever.

And then the story was over, and the decision was made and we were all busying about getting things ready to go up Cold Path into Dark and leave this place for good.

30

John Redlantern

People tried to have things every which way, even smart honest people like Tina. They wanted the good bits and then they complained about the bad bits that had to go with the good bits. Well, the good bit about me was that I could make things happen, and that I stuck to a thing and didn't ever give up or let go. That was the good thing that people got from me, along with all those other things people didn't like.

When we had that meeting, I'd just done for a man. I'd killed a man I'd seen around Family ever since I was a little kid. I didn't feel guilty about it exactly because I knew he'd happily have done the same to me, and to Tina and probably to the others too. But, Gela's eyes, I was shaken *shaken* by it. All that meeting it was running through my mind over and over, my spear sticking out of Dixon's back, my spear stabbing back again into his belly, the squelch of it going in, the hiss of air, the blood bubbling out of his mouth. I hadn't stopped to look at him longer than the time it took to pull my spear out of him, and for him to roll over to look up at me, and for me to shove the spear in again to finish him off – his two friends were still running from us, and Gerry and Harry might have needed my help – but those couple of seconds were so fixed in my mind that it was like they kept happening – really happening – over and over again.

So I had that in my head, and I had all the practical things to remember, and at the same time I somehow had to make people *believe* in me, so that they'd accept being organized and they'd stay that way, and we'd have a chance of surviving. I had *all* that to think about – and there's only so much a person can hold onto at one time – and then bloody Tina drops her little game with the Ring story on me, and – Tom's dick! – I had to think about how to deal with *that* as well.

She'd say that was my fault for keeping the ring a secret, but I did that for a reason. I did it because I always knew from the beginning that when I showed it to people, it would give me power over them, but I also knew that the power wouldn't last. So I saved it up for the moment when that power was most needed, not just by me but by all of us. It was like when the leopard came at me. I knew I only had one shot at it, so I waited till the best moment and didn't just chuck my spear at it the first chance I got. And I got that right. I got it exactly right, whatever Tina thinks. I took out the ring just when we really needed it most – and it *worked*!

A couple of hours after I'd taken the ring back from Tina we were starting up Cold Path. There were twenty-one of us, plus two babies. The larger of the two bucks, Def, was in front with Jeff riding on it. After that came me and Tina, and then all the others, one by one, with the other buck, Whitehorse, at the end. Every one of us was covered up, except for our mouths and eyes, with buckskin wraps, so we didn't really look like *people*, more like a herd of weird two-legged bucks. Every one of us had the greased buckskin footwraps that I'd been working and working on even before anyone came from Family to join me, with hard layers of skin and greasy glue on the bottom. Apart from Jeff on his buck, the two girls with babies (Clare and Janny) and the three girls carrying babies inside their wombs (Suzie, Gela and Julie), all of us were carrying things on our backs: rolls of rope, spare footwraps, bags of blackglass, bundles of buckskin, things that I'd thought about and organized over the past ten periods. And we were taking it in turns to carry some big flat pieces of bark, smoothed and greased, which I called snow-boats, each one loaded with useful stuff like meat and skins and spare wraps, except for one, which was holding a pile of embers on a big flat stone. They were hard work to carry over dry ground, but once we were up on snow they'd slide easy easy over the surface, and it would only take one person to pull them along. *They* were my idea too.

'None of this would have happened but for you, would it?' Tina said to me, looking back at all this.

'No,' I said crossly. 'It bloody wouldn't. *I* brought you all to Cold Path Valley. *I* sorted out the agreement with Caroline so as to give us time. *I* worked out how to make the wraps to cover our bodies. *I* had the idea of the snow-boats and organized people to cut the bark and make the ropes to pull them. *I* went up Snowy Dark over and over again to work out how to live up there and what we'd need, even when you moaned at me for going away by myself all the time. And you all chose to come with me because you all know quite well that you wouldn't have made this happen without me. None of you would, not even *you*, Tina, and certainly not your precious Dix down there. So how come *I* get to be Tommy in the story and you get to be Gela? I'm the Gela here. I'm the one holding it all together.'

She shrugged.

'It was how I felt, that's all. It needed to come out somehow or I would've burst. Most people are like that, John. They just have to let things out sometimes, whether it's right or wrong. Not many people can keep it all secret inside like you do. And, Gela's eyes, it would be lonely lonely if we did.'

We came to the place where all that time ago we'd come with Old Roger and seen those shining woollybucks, so high up in Dark that I'd thought at first they were a sky-boat from Earth. Then we went past it, and that was the end of being in Cold Path Valley and in Circle Valley where we were born. And for one moment I had the thought that perhaps I'd made a terrible mistake, perhaps we really did need to stay by Circle of Stones, perhaps Earth would come down from sky and Family would tell them that we'd all disappeared on Snowy Dark, and they'd return to Earth without us. But I pushed that thought out of my mind. There's got to be a point where you choose your path and stick to it no matter what.

Walking on snow now, and hoping that our footwraps would stay dry and not fall apart, we followed Cold Path Stream until we came to the snowslug that the stream flows out of (not a *big* big snowslug like Dixon Snowslug over at Blue Mountains, which comes right down into the top of forest, but big enough, the height of four men or more). Then we tied ourselves together with ropes, and got our spears ready, pointed end down, to hold us steady, and we scrambled up the slippery buck path that led along one side of the snowslug.

Harry tried to run up it and slipped. People laughed at him, of course, because they badly needed a laugh, but he *hated* hated being laughed at.

'I'm stopping here, then,' he said. 'You go on if you bloody want. Harry's not going with you lot if you're just going to laugh at him.'

He began to cry. He was the oldest one of us, the only one of us you could really say was a grownup, but he cried like a little kid. It was embarrassing and frustrating but people should have made more allowances. They should have remembered that he'd done for someone too that waking, he'd killed John Blueside. And if *I* had a job getting all that through my head, it must have been much worse for Harry. *He* had a job getting anything through his head at all.

Tina went back to calm him down and coax him up the path and Gerry came up to walk beside me. He wanted to talk about the killings too. Poor kid, he'd really had the worst of it out of the three of us. I didn't know Dixon Blueside personally and Harry didn't know John Blueside hardly at all. But Gerry had done for a boy from his own group who he'd grown up with since he was a baby. Now he kept going over and over it, and I had to keep telling him over and over that we had no choice and that they'd have gone ahead and killed Jeff if we hadn't got to them in time. They *would* have killed Jeff too, they really would, and they'd have done a cruel thing to Tina that didn't even have a name.

'And if they'd got away with that,' I kept telling Gerry, 'then it would have been the rest of us who'd have been next, one by one, or all together. There were only twenty-one of us at Valley Neck, remember, and five hundred-plus in Old Family.'

'Yes, but I used to play with Met,' Gerry would say. 'He once swapped me a bit of blackglass he found for a big lump of stumpcandy.'

Or: 'We got that slinker with him once, remember? That slinker you let him kill, remember? That time Jeff said he wondered what it felt like to be a slinker. We were friends with Met then, weren't we? We were friends in the same group.'

'Yes, Gerry,' I'd say, 'but he broke our friendship when he killed Brownhorse and did Jeff over, and stood and laughed while Dixon tried to slip Tina there in forest.'

'That's right,' Gerry would say. 'It was him that broke the friendship.'

And he'd think about it for a bit, looking relieved, and then suddenly he'd frown and come up with something else.

'He was with us that first time we came up here with Old Roger, remember? He was our friend back then.'

And we'd have to go round the whole thing again.

Meanwhile the lights of forest disappeared behind us and we were truly up in Dark. All we could see was what was lit up by the headlantern of the buckhorse Def, up ahead of us with Jeff riding on its back. Rocks, snow, ice loomed up out of the blackness in the area close around us, and then disappeared again back into blackness again at the other end of the line, behind the second buck, Whitehorse.

Jeff had named his buck Def after the sky-boat *Defiant* that brought Angela and Tommy and the Three Companions from Earth and actually it was a good choice of name. When I saw that group of woollybucks up on Dark all that time ago, I thought for moment I was seeing a sky-boat up there, and Def and Whitehorse were pretty much like sky-boats for us. They might not be taking us across Starry Swirl but they were taking us across Dark and we couldn't have done it without them. I had thought before of maybe finding some way of lighting our way with lights made of hollow branches or torches made of dry wavyweed dipped in grease, like people sometimes used back in Family when they wanted a bit of extra light. But the bucks were doing much more for us than just lighting our way. They *knew* the way. It was woollybucks that made Cold Path – it was them that made it a path at all – and now they found a new path for us, even when it was hidden by snow.

And I had to admit it: *that* part of the plan wasn't down to me at all, it was down to Jeff, that weird little clawfoot kid riding out in front, a young boy whose new hairs had hardly begun to grow.

~ ~ ~

We walked for the length of a whole waking and then for another waking straight after that, because there was nowhere to sleep, and the only way of not freezing was to keep on going. Once in a while we did have to stop to get out some smoked meat or seedcakes to eat, or for Janny or Clare to give their babies a feed, or to fix new footwraps for someone whose own footwraps had got wet or fallen apart. (I didn't want anyone getting the black burn up here like old one-legged Jeffo had done.) But whenever we stopped, everyone started getting cold and scared, and Tina and me had to go up and down the line to nip off any talk about us being lost, or us dying, or us never getting anywhere. It was specially bad around Mehmet Batwing and Angie and Julie and Candy Blueside, who all walked together, and all fell silent whenever me or Tina came near.

'So where are we then, John?' Mehmet finally asked me.

'We're following the buck path, Mehmet. *You* know that. That's what we all agreed to do, remember? Remember how I gave you a choice and you chose this?'

'Yeah, but where's it leading us? We're just going up and up all the time.'

That was true. We *were* going up and it got colder the higher we went. And there was some weird thing too about the air because you had to work harder and harder to get enough of it. I couldn't help thinking about some of the old stories about Tommy and Gela and the Three Companions, and how they said there was no air at all up in Starry Swirl, and that air was like water, it stayed near the ground. Maybe the air sat in Circle Valley like water in a giant pool, and the buck Def was leading us up to a place where the air stopped and we wouldn't be able to breathe?

But then I thought that bucks themselves must need air. You could hear them breathing, you could see the steam around their mouths the same as you could see the steam around ours.

'We're going up, yes,' I said to Mehmet, 'but we are going up between two mountains, not over the top.'

'How do you figure that out?'

'Well, you can see the slope of the mountain on our left, can't you? You can see it sloping up in the lanternlight. And you can *hear* the mountain on the right.'

I lifted the front of my headwrap to give him a demonstration.

'*Mehmet!*' I yelled.

'*Mehmet!*' came back an echo from high high above us and to the right. It was far far higher than I'd imagined it would be, my own voice bouncing down from a rock somewhere up there in total darkness that quite probably no human being and no living thing would ever ever reach.

And then there were some fainter echoes, and the sound of

stones rattling down bare rock.

'See what I mean?' I said, pulling the front of my wrap down again, my beard already full of ice.

'Well, *what* a lot you know about Snowy Dark,' Mehmet said bitterly.

I couldn't win with him. If I said something wrong, that proved I was a fool. If I said something right, that meant I was trying to be clever.

Then Suzie Fishcreek cried out that she felt funny and she thought her baby was on the way. It wasn't true luckily, but we had to give her some attention and calm her down before we could get going again, and meanwhile everyone got colder and wearier and more scared, and everyone looked round for someone to blame for their feeling like this, and I guess pretty well all of them chose me.

And then, when we'd gone on for another four hours or so and even *I* was starting to think it was no good, we found we'd reached the top of a ridge. And there, below us, was *something*, something other than just more blackness and more snow. There was a source of light.

~ ~ ~

It wasn't the other side of Snowy Dark, though. It was a single tree, growing up out of a hole in the snow down there that its hot trunk had melted, just like the first tree must have done, coming up to the cold surface of Eden from the hot caves of Underworld when everywhere in Eden was like Snowy Dark. It was a huge tree, with a long straight smooth trunk, high wide branches, and white lanterns that shone out over the snowy ground all around it. Clouds of steam, lit up by the lanterns, came out from the airholes in its sides in short rhythmic puffs, and streamed upwards round the trunk. We could even hear it faintly. *Hmmph, hmmph, hmmph*: that old familiar sound.

Everyone started to talk at once, and to hurry down the snowy slope towards it to get to the heat of its trunk. Harry rushed out in front and sank in snow right up to his neck. Lucy Batwing sank to her armpits, Dave Fishcreek to his waist. All the excited chattering and shouting turned to screams of fear and I had to yell to everyone to stop and wait and calm down while we threw a rope to each of the three of them and hauled them out.

'Now keep following Def, alright?' I yelled to everyone. 'It knows the way across this stuff. We don't.'

I just hoped that Def was planning to go down to the tree and not stay on top of the ridge, because I wasn't sure how I would manage to persuade all these tired scared people that it was okay to walk back into Dark without first getting the warmth and light and comfort of a tree.

Luckily the horsebuck *did* go down to the tree. It led us along the ridge to the right a bit, round the edge of the soft snow, and then down into the valley of snow where the tree grew. And as we went towards the tree we began to see that it was even bigger, and the valley much deeper, than we had first thought, because it took much much longer to reach it than we'd expected. That tree was *tall* tall, fifteen twenty times the height of a man. But just as we were getting near enough to get a sense of the real size of it, another strange thing happened that threw us out again, so we once more doubted whether we were seeing it right.

A bat dropped down from sky and landed at the top of the tree. It stood there like bats do, gently fanning its wings, rubbing its face with its hands and staring down at us with its head tipped slightly over to one side like it was weighing us up, with steam from an airhole ten feet below billowing up around it. But it was *much* bigger than any bat we'd ever seen before. The biggest bats you ever found in forest were redbats and they were maybe a foot and a half from head to toe. But this one must have been the height of a child of fifteen wombs or so, and the distance between the tips of its pale wings must have been six feet at least. And it was a weird thing because, even though it had wings, and knees that bent backwards, and claws for feet, and a bat's face that was all twists and wrinkles, and no nose, it felt to me almost like it was a *person* up there looking down at us.

And then we all saw something that the bat didn't see. Out of an airhole came the head of a slinker. It swayed from side to side for a moment, as slinkers' heads do when they're looking for bats and birds and flutterbyes. And then, pressing itself up close to the trunk, it began to creep up the tree, not straight up, but slowly winding round and round the trunk towards the bat. Harry's dick, it was a *long* long slinker. It must have been fifteen foot long at least, I reckon, with dozens of little clawed feet all along it.

But the bat was still rubbing its face and watching us. We'd all stopped to stare at it except only for Jeff on the back of Def, which kept plodding along regardless. And the bat seemed to notice the fact that we weren't moving any more and to wonder why that was, because it stopped rubbing its face, and lifted its head, and half-lowered its hands, like we'd got it worried, or puzzled, or maybe just interested. But it still hadn't seen the slinker, whose head by now was only a yard beneath it.

I don't know why, but suddenly I yelled out.

'Watch out!' I shouted. 'Watch out!'

The people behind me laughed. Who ever heard of someone yelling a warning to an animal as if it was a person like us? But all the same a few of the others began to yell too, 'Watch out, bat, that slinker's going to get you!'

And the bat stiffened, and looked around itself, and passed its right hand once over its face, and stretched its wings out a bit, but didn't move. And the slinker crept closer.

'Watch out!' I yelled again.

And finally, in the last second that it had left, the bat seemed to get the message. It leapt up into the air just as the slinker struck. Those spiny slinker jaws snapped, only missing the bat by a couple of feet, but the bat was safe, soaring up into the freezing air.

The slinker's head, sticking up above the top of the tree, swayed from side to side, watching the bat, then twisting round to look down at us. And then the creature went backwards down the tree, spiralling down as it had spiralled up, and disappeared back into its steaming airhole.

Meanwhile the bat climbed up and up, still looking down at us, until it was just a little black shadow on the bright face of Starry Swirl. Finally it stopped climbing, turned and flew off with big slow wingbeats away over Snowy Dark.

'John! John!' people were calling me.

'John,' muttered Tina, who'd come up from middle of the line, 'get yourself together and wipe your eyes.'

I looked round. I saw their faces in the light of the treelanterns, some smiling, some laughing, some looking scared.

I put my hands quickly up to my face and wiped away my tears.

31

Tina Spiketree

How could he let himself cry like that then, when everyone needed him to be strong? Michael's names! So many other times, when he could have shown his feelings a bit more and it would have helped, he hadn't. But now, in this moment when we really didn't need it at all, he'd let himself go. And what had *made* him cry anyway? He'd been like someone watching a story, like the ones who cried when I did *Gela's Ring*. And people never just cried because of a story, did they? They always cried because it reminded them of real things. It reminded them of things they'd lost or never had, or times when they'd been found wanting, or times when other people let them down. So what did the story of the bat and the slinker do for John? What did it remind him of? The bat was him, I suppose, lonely and cold and proud up there. But what was the slinker?

~ ~ ~

The tree stood in a hole it had melted in the ice. I guess the hole was about ten yards across and three yards deep. The sides of it were steeply sloping smooth ice, glowing greeny blue in the light of the tree. But in one place they'd been trampled down by woollybucks into a sort of ramp of rough snow that we could climb down. At the bottom there was mud and big stones and trampled buck dung and puddles of water that drained into a little stream that trickled down into a hole under the ice and came out Gela knows where. The tree in middle was huge *huge* when you saw it close up. It'd take three people to get their arms right round it, and the trunk went up and up and up so high that it had reached four five times the height of a man before it had even started to put out branches.

It wasn't going to do our footwraps any good trampling round in that mud, and John and me tried to tell everyone to step on the dry bits, but no one cared about that. Everyone was rushing forward to get the heat of the tree and drink the water from the puddles and the little stream. The woollybucks were snuffling and croaking with excitement. The human beings were fighting and squabbling for the warm bits of the tree. The babies, who'd been completely quiet while we walked and walked, like they'd sunk down with us into a sort of dream, now both began to scream and yell.

Hmmph, hmmph, hmmph, went the tree, meanwhile, puffing out steam from the six seven airholes up and down its trunk, just like it must have been doing for wombtimes and wombtimes when it was all alone and there was nothing around it but ice and snow and stars.

'Hey, everyone!' I yelled. 'Don't push and fight over the tree. We'll take it in turns, alright?'

I picked out people to go and take a turn with their backs to the tree, and got ten of them in there shoulder to shoulder in a circle against its warm trunk. They squatted down on their heels, and closed their eyes, and the warmth of the tree and the steady pulse of it against their backs was more than enough, after that long long walk, to send most of them straight off to sleep. Gerry was one of the ones I picked for the first turn. He said he wanted to stay awake with John, but I told him he'd help John better if he got some rest. Another I picked out was sweet Dix.

'You come and rest too, Tina,' he said, 'you come in beside me. You're tired *tired*.'

But I told him no, though I gave him a little secret thankyou smile.

John got Jane and Mike to be first lookouts. Jane to watch the tree, Mike to walk round the top of the ice, watching the snowy slopes around us. It wasn't hard to imagine that a slinker of that size might decide to come down the tree to grab a human being if couldn't catch a bat. (It couldn't be that fussy about what it ate up here, not unless there was some other source of food for it down in Underworld.) And if there were giant bats and giant slinkers up here, how could we know what else there might be up here too?

The others that couldn't get their backs to the tree used the embers we'd been carrying with us from Cold Path Valley to start two small fires – there were fallen twigs and buckdung to use as fuel – and they huddled around those until it was their turn against the trunk, using the time to mend footwraps with the spare skins we'd brought with us. Mehmet Batwing, Angie Blueside and Dave Fishcreek grouped round one fire, Gela Brooklyn, Harry and me by the other. Bucks don't like flames, so Jeff stayed with Def and Whitehorse as far from the fires as possible, cuddled up between them. John moved restlessly about the little space around the tree, sometimes going up onto the ice with Mike, sometimes coming over to me.

'It's going well so far,' he said at one point, squatting down beside me, Gela and Harry. 'It really wasn't so hard at all, was it?'

Not everyone else was so pleased, though.

'Nice new place John's found for us,' Mehmet Batwing said to Angie and Dave as he got up to drop a bit more dung onto his fire. 'Bit small maybe, bit damp, but well worth leaving Circle Valley for, don't you reckon? Only thing is, I wonder what we're going to do for food?'

He glanced over towards us. I looked at John. He looked back at me, then shrugged, stood up and went up onto the ice, without saying anything at all.

'He's in a right state!' said Mehmet. 'Talking to bats, crying . . . and this is the bloke who's leading us into the unknown!'

'You lead us then, Mehmet,' said Gela stoutly in her strong deep voice. 'Go on, Mehmet, *you* lead us. You seem to know better than John what to do. So you take over. You make the decisions from now on. Go on. Tell us now what your next move is going to be.'

For a moment there, Mehmet looked afraid. Then he smiled.

'Oh no, *oh* no. You don't get me *that* way, Gela. John got us into this. He can get us out of it.'

'Oh I see,' Gela said, 'so you *do* trust him to see us alright, do you?'

'John? No. He's lost it. He doesn't know what he's doing.'

'But you'd still rather follow him than decide things for yourself, just like you did before back at Cold Path Valley when John gave you the choice. That doesn't make sense, Mehmet, and you know it.'

'Why are you poking your nose in, Gela?' demanded Angie Blueside.

Harry, beside me, gave a sort of groan. He was rocking on his heels and breathing hard, like he did when he was getting wound up and was going to start yelling. I stood up to try and calm things.

Then John came to the edge of the ice above Mehmet, looking down at all of us in our muddy hole. I thought he was going to join in the argument, but he didn't say a word about it. He didn't even seem to notice that it was going on.

'Take over from Mike, Mehmet,' he simply said. 'Mike's footwraps are all wet. He needs to sort that out.'

Mehmet gave Angie a look, but he obeyed.

Hmmph, hmmph, hmmph, went the tree, sending out its puffs of steam into the frozen air.

One of the babies woke up and began to cry.

~ ~ ~

Four five hours later, when the second lot of people had taken their turn round the tree and we'd all eaten a little bit of meat, we put on all our wraps again – we made ourselves back into weird, shapeless animals – and got back up on the ice again, Jeff in front on the back of Def, then John, then the whole line of us with Whitehorse at the back being led on a rope by Jane. I walked in middle with Dix.

Gela's tits, it was *so* cold when we went back out there again. And our wraps were damp, and we were tired, and both the babies were screaming, and we had no idea where we were going. But Def seemed to know, plodding along ahead of us down the snowy valley. We looked back at the tree sometimes, longingly, and for a short time its light shone on the snow around us and made it sparkle and glitter. It was strange strange how that lonely tree in its muddy hole, a tree that we knew had a horrible giant slinker hiding inside it, could still look welcoming and safe compared to where we were going now.

But pretty soon the valley turned, and we lost the tree and its light, and we were in complete darkness – even Starry Swirl was covered up again by cloud – with only the light from the woollybucks' heads to guide us. Big fluffy flakes of snow began to fall into that pool of light from the dark sky, crowding in on us in their hundreds and thousands, settling all over us and over the bucks and over those heavy bark snow-boats that we were still dragging along behind us.

When you are really tired and miserable, I've noticed, one thing that comes to help you is rhythm. If you can only get into a rhythm then you can keep going, because it's like a kind of sleep. But if someone talks, or someone stops, or something happens, and the rhythm's broken, that's when it becomes hard to bear. And so we trudged and trudged, and we didn't say anything for a long long time.

We'd been going for one two hours, the babies quiet, no one talking, our feet scrunch-scrunch-scrunching in the snow, when Dix suddenly spoke.

'What's that sound?'

Oh shut up, was what I thought. I don't care about any bloody sound. I just want to concentrate on the scrunch, scrunch, scrunch of my cold cold feet. But other people along the line had heard it too, and stopped, and some were talking and some were telling each other to shhhhhh so we could hear. The bucks stopped too. They both stopped dead, listening.

It was like a faint cry – *aaaaaaaah!* – from some dark rocks we could just make out in the bucklight up to our left.

Def and Whitehorse both started to snuffle and groan.

'The Shadow People! Lucy Lu was right, it must be the Shadow People,' someone muttered.

And there was a sort of moan up and down the line.

'No, it's not,' called out John, 'it's some kind of leopard. Get your spears ready. Hold onto the bucks.'

Gerry and Gela ran forward to hold onto the buck that Jeff was riding on. Suzie and Dave grabbed hold of Whitehorse at the back. Both animals were tugging and straining to get free, and giving little thin squeaks of fear: *Eeeeeek! Eeeeeek! Eeeeeek!*

Aaaaaaaah! came the cry again, high and lonely.

We all stood in a row, straining to see the thing in the faint light.

Then suddenly Mehmet called out.

'No! It's behind us! Turn!'

Wham! It was on top of us. While we were looking the wrong way, a great white furry beast had been rushing silently towards us across the surface of the snow. Now it grabbed Whitehorse with its jaws and front claws, snatching the buck away from Suzie and Dave and dragging it and its light away across the snow, leaving a thin black trail of blood. Suzie and Dave tried to follow it, but off the path that Def had found for us the snow was soft and deep and they were in above their knees straight away. They couldn't run over the top of snow like the leopard could.

So now the back end of the line no longer had its own light. Standing in the near darkness, we watched the snow leopard out there in the pool of light from Whitehorse's head, ripping out Whitehorse's throat. It was bigger than a forest leopard and covered with shaggy white fur like a woollybuck. Its four back feet were great flat things splayed out over the snow and, as well as two flat black eyes, it seemed to have a huge third eye on the top of its head, much bigger than the other two and kind of hollow, like a bowl. Seeing us watching it, it lifted its head from its meal and tipped it back slightly, like it was looking up at the mountainside. And then we heard a cry again – *Aaaaaaaah!* – and all of us looked round, because the cry didn't seem to come from the leopard at all but from far away above and behind us.

Crunch! While our backs were turned, it bit the lantern off the top of the dead buck's half-severed head, swallowed it, and so hid itself in darkness. And at that same moment, out at the front end of the line, Def gave a loud loud screech and pulled free of Gerry and Gela to belt off along the snowy valley with Jeff still clinging onto its back.

And that was the last of our light. It had been all we had left, that little pool of light moving through the falling snow, and now it was vanishing into the distance with the small shadow of Jeff's back in middle of it, leaving us in total darkness.

Aaaaaaaah! went the snow leopard's voice again, remote and dreamy and far away behind us. And in the same moment the leopard itself – not remote and dreamy at all but huge and strong with deadly claws and teeth – was upon us again. A forest leopard kills just once, but I suppose it makes sense for a snow leopard to kill again and again, quickly biting off the headlanterns of bucks and then coming back for more until they've got a stash of frozen meat to keep them going till the next herd comes by.

For a moment, we felt it among us. We heard a girl scream, and then, a few yards off, we heard her give a choking sound and fall silent, and we knew that the leopard had dragged her out of the line and had done for her in dark there as it had done for Whitehorse.

No one was sure who it was. Everyone was calling out for sisters and friends.

'Tina, are you okay?' went Dix, feeling for me with his hands.

'Jane,' I called out for my sister. 'Jane, are you there?'

'Lucy? Clare? Candy?' other voices were calling, and other voices answering in the darkness, until someone called 'Suzie!' and no answer came from Suzie Fishcreek, that sharp clever girl, and we knew that if we could have seen anything at all out there it would have been her blood that would have been red on the snow, hers and the baby's still inside her, and her lolling head hanging loose from her neck.

Then John's voice came bellowing out over all the crying and wailing:

'Group together, now! Group together with your spears pointing out! Do you want the thing to get us all one by one? Together in a group with your spears out! Now! Do it! Quick!'

32

Jeff Redlantern

Def ran and ran and I couldn't hold him back. All I could do was hang on tightly tightly to his fur, lying down flat against his body. I knew that if I fell off in the dark and the snow, that would have been that, that would have been the end of me. The world would still have had lots of other eyes to see through, but not mine.

Def ran on and on down that long dark snowy valley. His headlantern was pulsing and bright bright with fear, and he kept giving out a strange cry I'd never heard him make before: *Ayeeee! Ayeeee!* I heard the echoes come back from the rocks and mountains. Big snowflakes crowded towards me and rushed past. I got glimpses of huge rocks and cliffs and giant greenish hunks of ice jutting out from under the snow.

When we'd been running for some time flat out, he slowed down a little bit. I could see that the snowy ground ahead of us was breaking up and tipping down, and there were more and more of those big twisted hunks of ice sticking up, and icy cracks opening up in the snow. It was a big snowslug we'd been on all this time, I realized. Up to now it had been covered up by packed-down snow, but here the ice was cracking and bending and sticking out through the snow, like splintered bones sticking out through a broken leg.

Ayeeee! Ayeeee! went Def. He paused for a moment and then called out again: *Ayeee! Ayeee!* Suddenly he swerved to the left, and started climbing the rocky slopes above the snowslug, up up, until he came to the top of a ridge, and we could look down at the other side.

There was light below us! There were thousands of lights, white and greeny-yellow. There was a little round valley full of shining trees, surrounded by Snowy Dark.

Ayeee! Ayeee!, went Def.

I put my hand on the soft lantern on his head and tried to make him turn round again so we could go back to tell the others. He had always let me guide him that way before. It was him that found the paths, but when we came to a choice of paths, he would pause and lift his head and snuffle and sniff at the air, and wave his feelers, and then I chose for him, by putting my hand on his lantern and turning his head in the direction I wanted him to go. Woollybucks could stay up on Snowy Dark for wakings and wakings, I figured, but we needed to get down the other side. So I made sure, as best I could, that we kept heading *across* Peckham Hills, and not along them.

But now, on the top of the ridge, Def refused to do what I asked of him. I could turn his head all I liked but he wasn't going to go back. I guess the leopard was still not far enough behind.

He wasn't going to stay still either. *Ayeeee!* he cried out again, and started straight down towards the lights of the valley. I pulled back on his headlantern to try and get him to at least stop still, but he took no notice at all. There was nothing I could do to make him change his mind, nothing I could do at all really, right then, except just to remind myself to keep my eyes open and to notice the world that I was in.

'We are here,' I whispered to myself, 'we are really here.'

I might never see the others again, I thought. I might die on my own, and no one would ever know what I'd seen. But that didn't change the fact that right now I *was* seeing it. I was alive and seeing it, and it was really there.

We came down into a strange forest, where the trees were as tall as that tree up in the snow with the bat and the slinker, and had trunks that went way way up before they even put out a single branch. It made me feel small small as we passed underneath them, even sitting up there on Def's back, when their branches were so far above us. But their lanternflowers were as bright as any whitelantern back in Circle Valley, even if they were high over our heads, and the tree trunks were warm and made that same familiar sound that we'd all heard around us every waking and sleeping all our lives until we first went up onto Snowy Dark. *Hmmph, hmmph, hmmph,* they went. And whole forest went *hmmmmmmmmmmm*.

A tree fox came running down one of the trunks, and peeked at us around the side of it with its flat blank eyes, sniffling with its long bendy snout. A bright coloured bird flew past, with its hands held out in front of it. And a monkey with six long arms gazed down at me from a high high branch, bigger than the monkeys we had in Circle Valley, and with loose flaps of skin hanging down between its arms.

Everything seemed clear clear in my mind and I stared and stared, because the only thing I could do just then was to see and see and see, so I might as well do that as well as I possibly could. I felt myself grow calmer, and I could feel Def getting calmer too. His hearts weren't beating so fast and his lantern had stopped pulsing and was settling into a steady glow. I pulled gently back on it to see if he would stop, and he stopped at once, without any fuss or trouble. I got off him, and led him to a stream, and rested my back against a tree while he gathered wavyweed into his mouth feelers, using his front legs as arms.

Presently he lay down on the ground beside me and slept.

~ ~ ~

'In a way *I* was the leader, not John,' I said to myself, stroking Def's woolly back and thinking about how it had been me that made the horses and chose the paths.

'I was the real leader,' I said. It made me laugh.

Of course I wasn't a leader in the way John was. I couldn't be, and I wouldn't want to be either, not at all, not even one little bit. My life was different different from John's because I was a clawfoot, and no one expected me to become a man. Other boys ran and fought and kicked balls (even batfaces, however much they got teased), but if you were a clawfoot they left you out of all that. Other boys became men by putting on the masks of men, and shutting out of their heads all the things that didn't fit with their masks, but if you were a clawfoot no one expected you to wear that mask, or to shut those things out of your head. That was why I *saw* things that other people didn't see.

'That's why it was me that worked out how to make horses,' I said to myself sleepily, running my hands through Def's fur. 'Because there was something about animals I saw but no one else did.'

What I'd seen was that it didn't make any difference whether you were an Earth animal or a human being or an Eden animal. You still had the same thing inside you looking out of your eyes, the same awakeness. It was knowing that about woollybucks that kept me going when I was teaching them to be horses. It was knowing that they weren't really so different from us. Most boys couldn't have had that thought because they were too busy being tough hunters.

I felt peaceful peaceful, and I felt warm and safe between Def's body and the tree trunk.

Not that I'd ever worried in the way most people did, about whether I lived or died. I knew quite well that, even when someone died, the secret awakeness that had been looking out of their eyes would always still be there.

Pretty soon I was fast asleep too.

33

Gerry Redlantern

I'd always loved my cousin John and I'd always trusted him to know what to do, even if I couldn't always understand his reasons for thinking what he did. But this was where he'd led us: my brother Jeff lost all on his own out in the snow, and the rest of us bunched up in a circle, in a place so dark that it was the same as being completely blind, waiting for that leopard to strike and kill again.

It was dark dark dark. But out in that darkness that made us blind, near near, with nothing between us and it, was an animal that wasn't blind at all, and could run silently over the surface of the snow. We all had our spears pointing outwards and were waving them from side to side to try and stop it sneaking in between. But spears are only bits of wood, and most of ours didn't even have proper blackglass heads. That huge white leopard could knock them aside like twigs.

'Remember it's never met humans before,' John called out. 'It doesn't know what we are. It can't possibly know that we can't see it. Let's try and scare it. Shout! Scream! Yell as loud as you can!'

Well, we didn't want to do that at *all*. If you can't see, you certainly don't want to stop being able to hear as well. What we wanted was perfect perfect silence, so we could listen, listen, listen.

But John started yelling, and then Tina. So I joined in, and then more and more people began screaming and yelling and shouting. And of course that made the babies yell too, and the echoes from all of us came back from the rocks on both sides of us, so it soon felt like the biggest thing in whole world was that screaming and screaming and screaming all around us. And the weird thing was that once we'd started, we didn't want to stop. The screaming said how we felt. The screaming filled up the world with our feelings. And even though those feelings might be ones of fear and misery, they were so big big that they pushed away the ice and darkness, and made them seem far away.

But even all that screaming couldn't completely blot out our own thoughts. We all knew the leopard was only the beginning of our troubles. Even if we drove it away, what was going to happen next? How could we ever get ourselves out of this when we had no light to guide us and no idea where we were or where we were trying to get to?

'What are we going to do?' yelled some people in middle of our screaming. 'What are we bloody going to do?'

And some just cried, 'Mummy! Mummy! Mummy!'

But no one's mum was going to come, were they? Nobody's mum could put this right.

'Alright!' yelled John. 'It's gone! It's gone! Shut up now and listen!'

So the crying and yelling stopped, but slowly slowly, because now we'd started we were just as afraid to face the silence again as we had been afraid in the first place to cover the silence up. We'd found a sort of comfort in all that noise.

'How do we know it's gone?' came Clare's voice in the darkness, when we'd finally quietened down.

'Because it would have attacked by now if it was still here,' John said. 'We've scared it off. We've showed it we're not like bucks, we're not like anything it knows.'

'So what will we do now?'

'Where are the snow-boats?' John asked. 'Who's got the fire? I've got strings dipped in buckgrease we can light up to show us the way. We can follow Def's tracks over the snow.'

So people lowered their spears and began groping around in Dark. The ones pulling snow-boats had let go of them when the leopard struck, and no one knew where they were. Someone ran into someone else's spear and cursed. Someone knocked someone else over. But we found a bark snow-boat with a pile of skins on it, and another one with smoked meat and cakes, and then . . . and then we heard Gela Brooklyn give a sort of low wail.

'It's turned over, John. Must have been when the leopard came at us. It's turned over and the fire stone's gone. We haven't got any fire.'

It was so bad now that no one said anything, not even Mehmet. There was a long silence. And when John finally spoke you could hear the fear in his voice, however hard he tried not to let it show.

'Okay . . . Well . . . we'll . . . we'll have to . . . to feel our way forward, then. I'll go in front and feel for Def's tracks. The snow's stopped falling, hasn't it, so at least the tracks won't fill in. It'll be slow, but we'll manage.'

Well, there wasn't any other choice, was there? We left the snow-boats behind and John went in front, feeling with his wrapped fingers for the dents in the snow where Def's six feet had trod. He had to do it slowly slowly – Def's wide feet didn't make big holes like a human's feet – and we had to hope that it wouldn't start snowing anytime soon and fill them in. Slowly slowly we moved forward in a line, tied together by ropes, but most of the time holding hands with each other as well to make sure. Shuffle forward – wait – shuffle forward – wait – shuffle forward – wait. We were *cold* cold. You couldn't get warmed up going so slowly. We knew it was only matter of time before we started getting the black burn and then the gang green like old Jeffo London did. We knew that most probably in another waking's time we'd all be lying out here as dead as poor Suzie Fishcreek, meat for leopards just like she'd been. Tom's dick, we didn't even know that Def's tracks were leading us anywhere we'd want to go. He might have taken Jeff right up to the top of one of the mountains, for all we knew. Woollybucks weren't like people, were they? They were *meant* to live in Dark.

Shuffle forward – wait – shuffle forward – wait – shuffle forward – wait – shuffle forward – wait.

From near the back of the line Gela Brooklyn started to sing, an old song that they say was brought from Earth by Tommy and Gela and the Three Companions.

'Row, row, row the boat, gently down the stream,' she sang in her deep voice, 'merrily, merrily, merrily, merrily, life is but a dream . . .'

And gradually everyone joined in, not loudly, not like we were singing round a fire, but like we were all muttering the song to ourselves inside our own heads.

'Row, row, row the boat' – shuffle forward, stop – 'gently down the stream' – shuffle forward, stop – 'merrily, merrily, merrily, merrily' – shuffle forward, stop – 'life is but a dream.'

That went on for one two three hours. One time someone in middle – it was Dave Fishcreek – slipped sideways into some sort of hole or crack in the ice, and we would have lost him if he hadn't been tied on with ropes to the people in front and behind him. But they just hauled him back out, and muttered to the people following them to go a bit to the left, and shuffled forward again, taking up the song like nothing much had happened.

Another time, we heard the cry of a snow leopard, and it sounded far off – though how can you tell with snow leopards how near or far they are, or which direction? – but we just lifted up our spears a bit, and raised up our voices a bit more and kept on singing.

'Row, row, row the boat . . .' –shuffle forward, stop . . .

And then, some time later, John suddenly yelled out from the front.

'Stop! Don't come forward! Don't push!'

So we all stopped and the song died out.

'I think there's an ice crack across our path,' John called back. 'I think I nearly fell down it. Let me just test.'

We waited. Some of us heard a faint splash.

'Yes,' called John, and, no matter how he tried to cover it up, his voice was all wobbly and scared. 'It's a . . . It's quite a big crack. I just made a ball of snow and chucked it down. It's a big crack there, with a stream down at the bottom of it. Five yards down, maybe. We can't cross over it.'

Everyone waited.

'I think,' John said, 'I think I must have taken a wrong turn a bit back there. I must have mistaken some other dent in the snow for Def's tracks. I think we need to go back a bit and . . . I'll try and find the place where I went wrong.'

Go back over snow that twenty people had trampled over and find where the shallow footprints of a woollybuck had branched off? In darkness? Who was he kidding?

But we all stood there, waiting.

'Unless someone has a better idea?' John said.

Lie down on the snow and sleep, I thought. Sink down into a dream and never wake up.

I knew if I lay down I'd soon be quite numb, and then I wouldn't feel cold any more and I could dream I was back with Jeff and Sue all my other brothers and sisters and friends back in Family, cuddled by a warm fire.

'No suggestions?' John tried again. Normally he'd ask a question like that to shut up any complainers, but this time you could hear he was hoping that someone would say yes.

But no one said anything. Not Tina. Not Mehmet. Not anyone.

It was *cold* cold.

'I'll . . . I'll walk back to the other end of the line,' John said. 'The rest of you just turn round, and then you can follow me the other way . . .'

No one said anything. No one moved. John walked down the line.

Poor John, I thought. He's failed us all and he knows it. I touched his arm as he went past. I felt disappointed in him – bitter bitter disappointment – but I felt sad sad for him too. *He* couldn't just sink down into a dream and fade away. Not when it was him that had brought us to this. He'd have to struggle and struggle right up to the end.

And anyway he wasn't like the rest of us: he had no one back in Family he could cuddle up with in his dreams. He never had any choice but to keep going.

'Okay,' he called when he'd reached the far end. 'Now this is going to be a lot slower because I'm going to try to . . .'

He broke off. There was a cry from above and to our left.

Another leopard, we thought, and a moan went up and down the line. We knew we were just meat now. The leopard didn't even have to take the trouble of killing us. Give us a bit of time and we'd have done that for ourselves.

But the cry came again, and this time we could hear it had muffled words in it.

'Hey! Is that you down there? John? Gerry? Tina? Is that you?'

We looked up. There was a light high up on the snowy mountainside above us. In the centre of the light there was a buck, and on the buck's back there was a strange shining being, its mask face lit up from below by the lantern on the buck's head.

Candy cried out in fear – she thought it was one of the Shadow People come for us before we were even dead – but I laughed.

'Jeff!' I called out. 'Jeff!'

It was my brother, of course, my clever brother. He hadn't got lost at all!

'I can see you now,' he called down, while Def picked a way down the slope towards us. 'I can just barely see you. Don't go on any further, whatever you do.'

His voice echoed from rocks over the far side of the valley. We all strained to hear him.

'The snowslug is all broken up down there,' he called down.

'Don't go on that way. This is the way. Up here.'

He came weaving and zigzagging down the snowy slope.

'There's trees just over the far side of the ridge, and streams and lots of bucks. You're walking right past them and you don't know it.'

And some people started to laugh, and some to cry, and everybody to talk and talk.

'Wait there, and I'll come down to you,' Jeff called.

'Harry's dick, Jeff,' John said, as Jeff came up close, 'are we glad *glad* to see you, mate. I thought we'd had it there, I must say. I thought we'd finally run out of luck.'

Jeff laughed.

'Well, you haven't. I've got a safe place to take you and it's not far away. I'd have come sooner, but Def was too scared of the leopard and he refused to turn back. I had to let him rest and calm down and get a bit of sleep, and I needed to calm myself down too so that he'd feel safe with me, and let me lead him.'

I'd never seen Jeff like that. I'd always known he was smart smart, way more smart than me, but all the same he was just my little clawfoot brother, who stayed on the outside of everything and sometimes said weird things. But right now he was a leader, almost like John. He was barely even a newhair, but he'd become like a grownup man. And I saw that it wasn't just his cleverness that was special about him, and not just those sharp sharp eyes of his that could see things other people missed: it was also that he was strong. He was *strong* strong, far far stronger than I'd ever be, and in a way even stronger than John.

'Jeff!' I yelled, rushing towards him.

I'd forgotten the ropes that still tied me, on one side to Janny Redlantern, on the other to Martha London. As I pulled out of the line, I fell. And then they fell, and then whole line fell toppling over into the snow in front of my brother on his horse.

Jeff laughed.

'We are here,' he said. 'We really are here!'

34

John Redlantern

We followed Jeff to the top of the ridge and looked down into a little forest at the bottom of a bowl. It was tiny tiny compared to Circle Valley forest, and it didn't spread up the slopes like forest did back there. All the trees were down at the bottom, except for a few giant trees that stuck up out of the snow on their own, breathing out puffs of steam, and making little pools of light here and there on the steep snowy slopes around the little valley.

People cheered when they saw the lights of trees down there, and a few people shouted out thanks to Jeff, but we were too weary weary, and too sad, to talk much on the way down, and we stopped pretty much as soon as we were past the outside edge of forest. Tom's neck, it was good to hear the sound of trees all round us and to have light to see by, but those tall straight trunks, and the lanterns, far out of our reach, high high above our heads, gave the place a lonely feeling. And there was no coloured light, no red or blue – all the lanterns were snow white or pale greeny-yellow – and it wasn't warm in Tall Tree Valley. Even down at valley bottom where there were trees with warm trunks, you still needed to wear bodywraps.

But still, there was dry ground to stand on, and it wasn't so cold that you had to cover up your head, so we pulled the wet wraps off our feet and heads, and we had faces again, and not just buckskin masks. People looked at each other and saw friends they'd known all their lives, and, like children do when they see a friendly face again after they've been lost on their own, most of them started to cry. Angie cried. Gerry cried. Tina cried. Big strong Gela Brooklyn cried. Even Mehmet cried. Harry bawled like a baby in his big man's voice.

'Harry's sad, Harry's sad sad,' he sobbed, while Tina cuddled him to try and keep him calm.

And in middle of all of this, Dave and Johnny Fishcreek, in each other's arms, began to wail out their grief for their sister Suzie, who'd been torn apart by that white leopard up on Dark.

The only ones I noticed that weren't crying were Clare and Janny, who had to feed their babies, and Jeff, who was lifting the bags off the back of his precious Def and smoothing down its fur.

I wasn't crying either. I felt sort of numb. I sat on a stone and rubbed my feet.

'At least now there'll be a story to tell,' I said to myself.

If we'd all died up there on Dark, then the only story about us that would remain would be the story they'd tell about us back in Family, and what kind of story would that be? It'd be a story about a bunch of stupid kids who wouldn't listen to Council and Oldest and their own mums, and walked away from Family and were never heard of again. And that would have been where it ended, like the story of the Three Companions ended when they said goodbye to Tommy and Angela. But now that wasn't how it was going to be. It hadn't looked that way for a bit, but our story was still going on.

It wasn't the story I'd been expecting, though, because when we came down into Tall Tree Valley, it wasn't me that was leading everyone, it was Jeff. That was how things had turned out, and that was how the story would be told in the future. People whose parents and grandparents weren't yet even born would hear how the little clawfoot boy on his shining buckhorse came over the ridge to save his friends. They'd laugh and cheer when, up on some silly pretend mountainside, someone appeared on a pretend buck, playing the part of Jeff.

~ ~ ~

When Jeff had smoothed down Def's fur, he led it to the stream where it could graze, and then hobbled back to be among the others.

'Oh Jeff, Jeff, you did *brilliant* brilliant!' one after another of them told him. Even the Fishcreek brothers thanked him through their tears.

'Thankyou thankyou, Jeff! We'd all have died up there like Suzie did, if you hadn't come.'

I'd lost something, and Jeff had gained something, that was obvious. They'd all heard me get scared. They'd all heard me admit that I'd taken the wrong direction. They'd all been there in Dark where I'd led them, and known that I had no idea where to take them next. Jeff had come and saved them.

And now of course they were all over him, praising him, kissing him, hugging him, shaking his hand, patting his back. He'd probably never had so much attention before in his life, but he looked like he wasn't sure he really liked it. I think maybe he felt a bit like I'd done that time we brought the dead leopard back into Family through Batwing gate.

It was quite some time before anyone thought about me, sitting there by myself on my stone, watching them and rubbing my feet. But after a bit, Gela Brooklyn looked over and noticed me, and she came over and gave me a hug.

'You did good good too, John, to get everything together,' she said. 'You worked hard hard for a long time back at Valley Neck, when none of the rest of us really believed we'd ever have to come up here.'

Gela was one of those people who seem like grownups even when they're little kids, and now she made me feel like a kid who a grownup's being kind to.

'*And* you figured out how to drive away the leopard too,' she said.

Tina saw Gela talking to me, and she came over and gave me a hug too, though it was a hug just like Gela's, like the hug people give each other when they are just friends or groupmates.

More of them came to talk to me after that. Dix shook my hand. Jane kissed me. Silly Martha London threw her arms round me and sobbed and sobbed. But some of them stayed away. Mehmet didn't come near me, and nor did Dave and Johnny Fishcreek, whose sister had died because of my plan, nor Angie Blueside, whose cousin would never have been clubbed to death by Harry if I hadn't split Family in two, nor her groupmates Julie and Candy.

Even the ones who did talk to me soon walked away again, all except for Gerry, who squatted down and stayed by my side. And even with him things were different now. He knew I'd lost something too, but he was letting me know he'd stand by me anyway. He was always a kind boy, but he'd never had to show *me* that sort of kindness before, except maybe that time when I came out of Bella's shelter, and most of Redlantern looked the other way.

'I know you feel bad bad about what happened to Suzie and about us getting lost,' he said, 'but you did get us up on Dark. You got us sorted back at Valley Neck. You made sure we got all the stuff together.'

'Yes, I did get us up on Dark, but it was your little brother that got us down.'

And even while I was saying that to Gerry, half my mind was already thinking and thinking about how I should deal with Jeff.

~ ~ ~

Weird clever Jeff: I'd known him since he was born, and me and him and Gerry had shared a sleeping shelter back in Redlantern for wombs and wombs. He'd never been a trouble to me (at least not apart from his clawfeet) but now he suddenly was. I was tired tired of solving problems, but he'd become yet another problem that I had to figure out how to fix.

I don't mean I thought Jeff would try to take over from me. He wasn't like that. He wouldn't even be interested in playing the part I played. But people were going to listen to him more from now on, and they might quite easily decide that what he said was worth more than what I said. And that wouldn't just be a problem for me, it would be a problem for everyone, because they needed me to bring things together and make things happen, and to do that I needed them to go on believing in me.

But how could I get that back? Apart from having saved us all, Jeff had another advantage over me, which actually came from the fact that he wasn't interested in doing what I did. To do my job, you had to wear a mask and hide your feelings, you had to choose carefully what you said and what you kept inside. People could see that, and it made them wonder what it was that you were holding back. But Jeff could just be himself, and no one would ever doubt that what he said was what he really meant. So not only had he saved them all after I'd got them lost, but he'd always seemed easier to know, and gentler, and more genuine than me. Tom's dick, how could I compete against *that*?

I couldn't fight him, that was for sure. I couldn't push him away. I couldn't put him down. I couldn't turn the others against him.

'I'll just have to get closer to him,' I decided. 'Stop thinking of him as little Jeff and make him my friend. I'll have to . . .'

But then I made myself stop. It was stupid thinking about this now. Jeff would keep for another waking. There were other things I had to do right now, and I needed to save my strength for them.

I stood up.

'I need to talk to everyone together now,' I muttered to myself. 'Get things sorted so we can eat and sleep.'

~ ~ ~

The others were sitting by a small stream, many of them still crying, and many still with arms round each other. I went to a rock that stood above them all, next to the stream, and climbed up onto it. Tom's dick, I was weary weary of having to be John Redlantern. Bad bad things had happened since I stuck my spear between the ribs of fat old Dixon Blueside, and I could have done with a rest. But at the same time I knew this was one of those moments yet again, one of those leopard moments.

Michael's names, there were so bloody *many* of them! So many! One after another after another!

'Hey, everyone, listen up!'

I was scared that they'd take no notice, or even that they'd shout me down: 'You? Why should we listen to *you*?'

But that didn't happen. They might be disappointed in me and some of them might even hate me, but they all did what I asked and went quiet.

'Well, we *got* here,' I said. 'Maybe not to the other side yet, but to a new place. All of us except poor Suzie. And we would never have made it if it wasn't for my *smart* smart cousin Jeff who thought of turning bucks into horses, and came back to find us when – let's face it – we were *lost* lost. He got us there. He saved us. So thankyou, Jeff. Thankyou.'

Everyone cheered and yelled and clapped for Jeff. He smiled, and then suddenly laughed like it was all a big joke.

'And what will save us in the future,' I said, 'what will keep us going and keep us moving along, is new ideas, like Jeff had when he decided he could turn bucks into horses.'

They weren't so keen on that bit, with its hint that we would be moving on again.

'What will save us in the future, John,' Mehmet called out, 'is not going up onto Snowy Dark without knowing what we might meet or where we're going.'

He looked around, expecting some support, but everyone was silent. That had been a *bad* bad time up there in Dark, feeling our way along, not knowing whether snow leopards were out there ready to pounce, and I guessed it would probably keep coming back to all of us all our lives, over and over, in our dreams and when we were awake. But it had been too big big a thing to turn so quickly into quarrelling.

Mehmet shrugged, and crossed his arms, and kept quiet.

'We need to sort out a few things,' I said, more confidently now, 'like lookouts, and building shelters, and hunting and making a fire. And we need a funeral for Suzie and that poor baby of hers that never got to be born. It's sad sad we can't bury their bodies, but we can still have a funeral. We can still make a pile of stones and write Suzie's name on a stone.'

'Yes, but when Earth comes,' said Suzie's brother Dave, in a flat flat voice, 'Suzie's bones won't be there to be taken back to Earth, will they?'

'So she'll be left alone on Eden forever when everyone else has gone,' Johnny said, 'all because of what happened up there. Because of the path you took us on, John.'

'It did sometimes happen back in Family, didn't it,' I said, as gently as I could manage, 'with leopards and things like that, that there was nothing left for us to cover up with stones? We don't really know what happens when we're dead, do we? There are some, aren't there, who say our shadows always return to Earth when we die, even when our bones stay here in Eden? But we don't know. And of course what we'd all want, when we die, is for our bones to be kept in a place where Earth could find us. I'm sad sad for Suzie that we couldn't do that for her.'

Mehmet gave an angry snort.

'The way we're going, there's not much chance that *any* of us are going to find our way to Earth, dead *or* alive.'

A sort of sigh went up. Several people murmured in agreement with Mehmet and for a moment I feared again that I'd lost them. But I found I still hadn't. Dave and Johnny were standing near Mehmet, along with Angie Blueside and Julie and Candy, and their eyes were cold, but yet they were all still watching me, expecting me to carry on, even Mehmet himself. Whatever their private thoughts and feelings, they were all still waiting for me to tell them what was going to happen. That was what my job was, and, though they might not *like* me for it, they still agreed it was my job.

But I knew that they needed more from me now than just a plan, so I took out Gela's ring again.

'Remember that Gela is with us,' I said. 'Not with Old Family but with *us*, with this new little family of ours, which is trying to make the best of dark Eden, just like she did herself. Gela is with *us*. She's not with the ones who just sit and wait for sky-boats to take them home. She's not with the ones that try and prevent anything new from ever happening. She's with the ones who set out across Dark, not knowing what they'd find. And she is proud *proud* of you all. *You're* the ones doing what she wanted her children to do.'

I looked out at them. I saw Janny frowning, trying to figure out whether she agreed with me. I saw Lucy London, her face all smeary with tears. I saw Tina with her arms folded, waiting to see what trick I was going to play this time.

'And when sky-boats *do* come from Earth,' I said, 'they'll come looking for us right across Eden, because they'd *expect* us to make the best of our time here, and not skulk away our lives in Circle Valley until all the food is gone. After all, Earth folk themselves left even the solid ground behind, and travelled far far further than we've done, right across Starry Swirl.'

It was funny. I hadn't known myself what I was going to say when I started out, and I heard my own argument like it came from someone else. But it persuaded me. Yes, I thought, that really does make sense. It really *is* what Earth would expect! And I felt *relieved*

relieved, because there was doubt nagging in my own heart too.

But Gela Brooklyn, Tina's closest friend, questioned what I said, not in an angry way like Mehmet might have done but in a slow and puzzled way, like she was really trying herself to understand.

'Yes, John,' she said in her deep voice, 'but Angela was the one who always chose *not* to cross Starry Swirl when she had the chance. It was the Three Disobedient Ones who made her come to Eden, when she wanted to stay near Earth. And she and Michael did their best to make the three of *them* stay near Earth as well. Yes, and later, when she was here in Eden, she chose to stay here rather than cross back over Starry Swirl again with the Three Companions. She chose to stay and wait for Earth to send a new boat, rather than risk the old one, knowing that it might well sink.'

I felt a scary stab of doubt, like the one I'd had when we first started out over Dark. Maybe Gela was right. Maybe what we were doing really was *exactly* what Angela had warned against. But I kept my face firm and certain. Whether we'd done the right thing or the wrong thing, we'd done it now and we couldn't undo it. Our little group needed to feel that the choice we'd made was the right one, and I had to persuade them, as best I could, that it *had* been, whatever my own secret fears. I needed to put on a mask, and be certain certain certain. That was my job. That was my part in this story.

'Yes, Gela,' I said, 'but she herself chose to go up into sky in the Police Veekle, didn't she? And if she'd *really* been so set on not straying from Earth, she'd have tried to go back to Earth straightaway with the Companions, wouldn't she? But she didn't. She stayed here in Eden, because she was someone who took each situation and tried to make the best of it. And that's what she wants us to do too.'

I could see that a lot of them were looking puzzled and worried – I felt worried myself – so I quickly slipped the ring off my finger and held it out to them.

'Gela is with us, remember. She didn't give the ring to Caroline.

She didn't give it to David. She didn't give it to Oldest. She gave it to *me*. Yes, and she told me she wanted us to spread out over Eden, and find new places to live, and new hunting grounds. She *told* me.'

And it was weird weird, because I didn't even ask them to, but one after another of them came forward to touch the ring in my hand, pretty much all of them, except only for Mehmet, and Tina, and Jeff.

35

Tina Spiketree

We stopped there in that spot next to the stream, at the edge of Tall Tree forest. We got lookouts sorted, spread our wet wraps out to dry and gathered up some wood for fire. After that, most people crept off to sleep in whatever places they could find.

But John stayed awake with Harry and Dix and me to take turns with the fire sticks. Tom's neck, it took *hours* of rubbing them together to get a spark that would light anything. Our hands were all blisters with trying before we did. But even when we'd finally got some fires lit, John still wasn't ready to sleep. He stood up and called to the lookouts to keep the fires stoked up, then he said he'd go for a walk.

'I'm tired tired,' he said, avoiding looking at any one of us, 'but I'm going to find a pool to swim in before I lie down.'

Dix glanced at me, but I stood up with John, and gave Dix a little sign that I'd be back to see him later. It would be good to feel Dix's friendly arms around me before I let myself sleep, but I could see that John was carrying a heavy heavy load and it seemed unfair to leave him to do it all on his own.

~ ~ ~

This forest was different different from the one we had grown up in. That great lonely empty space under the lowest branches was three four times the height of a man, so the bats and flutterbyes weren't swooping and diving all around us like they did back in Circle Valley but were far far above our heads. Only sometimes a bird came blundering along at low level, squawking and screeching.

'Makes me think of those Earth stories,' I said. 'Remember those ones about huge shelters that went up to sky, straight straight, as big as mountains? Skyscrapers? Walking underneath those things must be a bit like walking under these trees.'

John didn't say anything for several minutes. He didn't even show that he'd heard me. In that way that he had, he was completely sunk down inside his own thoughts. But later, when I'd pretty much forgotten what I'd said, he spoke.

'Yeah. They were made of metal and rock, plus a kind of glass you could see through like water.'

'What?'

'Those giant shelters.'

He looked *tired* tired. He was so worn down I could see quite clearly how he'd look when he was a trembly blind old man. I suppose I didn't look much better.

'You did do well, John,' I said.

I reached for his hand, but he didn't respond to this in any way, so I dropped it again.

'I did well, you reckon?' he said. 'I lost Suzie, didn't I? And her baby. If it wasn't for Jeff I'd have lost all of us. Gela's eyes, Tina, when we were up there in the blackness . . .'

His voice was getting shaky and he broke off.

'When we were up there,' he began again, 'I thought about how I'd taken all these people away from Family, from their mums and their uncles and their brothers and sisters and all that and for what . . .?'

He glanced round at me, but I looked away. I didn't want to see him like that. It was just like the time he began to cry up there in Dark when that giant slinker nearly got the bat. I don't know why, but I just couldn't bear that side of him.

Off under the great trees to our left, where the ground began to slope up towards Dark, a herd of six seven woollybucks were grazing on starflowers. That was one good thing: we were *not* going to go short of meat.

'Do you really believe that Angela stuff, John?' I asked him after a bit. 'Really and truly? Only it doesn't sound like the sort of thing that you'd . . .'

'I saw Angela,' he said in a stubborn voice, not looking at me. 'Over by Deep Pool. I saw her sitting there by herself, crying. She didn't want to be in Eden. She never wanted to leave Earth. But she knew there was no point in going on about it. Eden was where she was now, and she'd have to make the best of it. And that's what she did: hope that Earth would come and get her back, of course, but meanwhile make the best of it. And she was right, wasn't she? If she'd just sat and pined for Earth, she'd have wasted her life, wouldn't she? Because she died before Earth came.'

'But you actually *saw* her?'

'Yeah.'

He glanced sideways at me and looked quickly away again, like a kid expecting to be challenged.

Well, there were lots of questions I *could* have asked him. Was he saying that he'd *really* seen her, like a real person, or was he just saying he'd imagined her in his mind? Was he saying that Gela really *talked* to him? Was he saying that she was really with us now? But I knew how it was when people start to talk about the Shadow People and all of that. You just can't pin them down. They talk like a thing can be true and not true at the same time, or both there and not there. I couldn't be bothered with it, and I'd always thought John couldn't either.

'Well, you never told me about it at the time,' was all I said.

'Gela's eyes!' he burst out. 'Make up your mind what it is you want from me. To share things with you or to bloody hide them?'

Well, I could sort of see that he might have a point there, but I was too tired to think about it, so I didn't say anything.

Haaaark! Haaaark! A bird was looking down at us from a branch high above us. We'd never seen a bird like it. It was a bird with no name, a bird that Michael Name-Giver had never seen. It was right beside a whitelantern flower so we could see the long shiny green wings it was smoothing down with pale long-fingered hands. Its hands and feet had long long red claws. *Haaaark! Haaaark!* It flew off through the trees.

'People need things like the ring,' John said after a time. 'They need a story. They need to have something from the past to hold onto when they go forward into the future. Like when you're climbing high up in a tree, you need to hold tightly onto the branch you are already on until you're sure you've got a tight grip on the next.'

'Well, some people might say that's exactly what Circle was for. Most people, in fact.'

'Circle was different. Circle was *stopping* us from going forward. It was making us stay in the past. Because it was fixed in that one place.'

He had the ring on his little finger (it didn't fit on any other). There was no need to hide it now. He stopped, took it off and passed it to me to hold. I must say, it was *perfect* perfect, so smooth and heavy in my hand, with those tiny little letters inside it. And it did prove that, whether John had truly seen her or not, there really had *been* an Angela, and she really *did* come from Earth. No one in Eden could make anything like that ring.

'Just think, Tina,' John said. 'When Angela first wore that she wasn't here in Eden at all, she was there on Earth. Imagine that! This

309

thing, this bit of metal you're holding in your hand, was there on Earth, with light shining down on it from sky!'

He took the ring back from me, replaced it on his finger.

'Probably everyone there has metal rings like this with tiny words on them, given them by their mums and dads.'

'Maybe.'

'I don't want us to keep wishing ourselves back on Earth, though. Earth will come when it's ready, and most probably not for a long long time. But meantime we should aim to make Eden more like Earth with rings and sky-boats and lecky-trickity and telly vision. Coming over Snowy Dark was just a start, Tina. It was just the beginning of what we need to do. And Gela's heart, we haven't even finished crossing Dark yet. We've still got to get down the other side.'

'Forget that for now, John,' I said sharply. 'Alright? Forget that *completely* for now. This place is fine. No one's going to want to move for a *long* long time. No one's even going to want to *talk* about moving.'

We'd reached a spot where a stream had come up against some rocks and made a pool, four five yards across and two three deep, shining with wavyweed. John took his wraps straight off and dived in without saying a word in answer to me.

'Tom's dick, it's *cold* cold.'

He came to the surface spluttering and laughing, swimming as quickly as ever he could to the bank and hauling himself straight out. Wet and freezing cold as he was, I put my arms around him and gave him a hug. I hadn't seen him laugh for a long time.

Then he shook himself dry, put his damp wraps back on and we went back towards where the others lay cuddled up in twos and threes round the fires. Just before we reached them, John found a place to lie down between the warm roots of a tree, and he gestured to it, inviting me to lie there with him. I hesitated because I knew Dix was waiting, but then I nodded and we lay down together. He put an arm round me.

'I've been thinking about the Three Companions lately,' he said. 'I've been thinking about how their story doesn't really have an ending, or not as far as we know anyway. That's a sad sad thing, isn't it? Not to have a story that carries on. But if they'd managed to get back to Earth and fetch help for Tommy and Angela, well, then their story would have been the *big* story about Eden, wouldn't it? Tommy and Angela would only have been a small small part of it, because they wouldn't have had kids together and they'd just have been ordinary Earth people again, not the Mother and Father of a whole world at all.'

He thought about this for a moment.

'And you and me wouldn't exist,' he added, 'and nor would anyone that we know.'

'I guess.'

Gela's tits, why did he want to talk about this *now*? We were so tired. We'd been through so much. I'd thought he might want to slip with me before we slept, and I'd sort of wanted that too. But now I wished I'd gone back to Dix. Dix wouldn't have wanted to go on about people who were dead long before we were born. He would have wanted *me*.

'Do you often wonder about the Three Companions?' John asked.

I shrugged.

'Not a lot.'

'They say Dixon – first Dixon – was the one who first suggested to Tommy and Mehmet they disobey President, don't they? He was the one that wanted to take *Defiant* across the stars. He thought that Jesus Juice was telling him to do it, whoever Jesus was.'

'Claiming to get instructions from some old dead person. Now what does that remind me of?'

He didn't respond to that. He didn't even seem to notice it.

Typical of John, I thought, to have a soft soft spot for his great-great-grandmother who was buried under stones long before he was born.

Having a soft spot for someone you never knew was another way of not having to be with equals, wasn't it? Dead people can't talk back, and you can choose what you want to hear them say, and know they'll never tell you you're wrong. Lucy Lu found *that* out, long long before John ever did.

But I didn't say that to him.

'And first Mehmet,' he went on. 'His group was called Turkish, wasn't it, and it's said he was funny and kind and he was the one that Angela loved best. She said that once to Tommy, didn't she? "Why couldn't it have been Mehmet that stayed, not you?"she said. "Mehmet I could *really* have loved."And then Tommy hit her, in front of all their kids, and called her miserable and cold and cruel. Remember that story? *The Big Row*. They used to act that one out sometimes, do you remember?'

'Yes, of course.'

'And first Michael. He was gentle and quiet, they say. He was with Angela at first in that other little sky-boat. They were called Orbit Police, weren't they? Their job was to make sure people followed the rules of Earth when they were up there in their boats in sky. He was like Angela. He didn't want to come here. He wanted to stay in sky of Earth . . .'

He broke off.

'Someone will come from Earth eventually,' he said after a bit. 'I mean, we know the Companions went up to *Defiant*, don't we? Okay, I know it was damaged. I know it was like a boat whose skins are beginning to come off. But the story doesn't say it couldn't make another Hole-in-Sky and fall through it, does it? The story just says that falling through most probably would have done for it, and for the Companions, and that means the remains of it would still have ended up somewhere near Earth. Sooner or later Earth people would have found them, even if the RayedYo was broken and didn't call them. You've got to remember sky round Earth was busy as Greatpool, Tina, full of sky-boats doing this and sky-boats doing that. Just like Greatpool with all the groups out fishing. One of them would have found it. I mean, there were Police Veekles and . . .'

I thought at first that he was just trying to remember what other kind of boat there'd been.

' . . . and Sat Lights?' I suggested.

But he didn't answer me. Pretty soon he began to snore.

36

John Redlantern

I didn't like Tall Tree Valley one bit. I knew that when we first followed Jeff down from Snowy Dark. I knew it when me and Tina and Harry and Dix sat up trying to get a fire going. I knew it when I lay down to sleep with Tina. And I *still* knew it when I woke up again on my own.

There was a smell of roasting buckmeat, and I could hear people already awake, but first thing I did was walk up the slope a bit, up near the bottom of the snow, so I could see out over the valley.

'No,' I said out loud as I looked down at this little bit of forest with Dark high high above it on every side, 'there is *no* chance that I'm going to settle for this place.'

Tall Tree Valley wasn't anything like a good enough trade for Bella's death, and for bringing killing into the world. It might make us feel tiny tiny like ants under those big trees, but it was *small* small itself. You could walk from one side to the other in one two hours. And how many people could a place that size support, when there was hardly enough meat in whole of Circle Valley to feed Family? There might be lots of bucks here now – I could see five six of them just standing where I was – but there'd been lots back in Circle Valley too, hadn't there, before Family did for most of them.

And anyway, who wanted to stay in a place where you had to cover up your skin just to keep warm?

I walked back down towards the others. They were already busy. Tina and Gela had been giving people jobs to do. Someone had done for a little buck and roasted two of its legs, and Jane Spiketree was cutting off strips of greeny meat with a leopard tooth knife, and tossing them onto a bark plate that Harry was holding out for her. Mike Brooklyn and Candy Blueside and Gerry were dragging branches over for a simple fence. Dave and Johnny Fishcreek, with those awful shadowy faces people have when someone they love has just died, were slowly slowly spreading out a pile of fading starflowers to dry, with Angie and Julie helping them. Jeff was sitting in front of Def, offering it handfuls of wavyweed from a heap he'd gathered from a pool. The woollybuck prodded and stroked each handful with its feelers before it gulped the stringy stuff down.

Sound carried a long way in the empty space under the trees, and I could hear them all talking when I was still ten twenty yards away.

'There's bucks everywhere in this place, aren't there?' said Janny. 'Getting meat is going to be *easy* easy from now on.'

'We'll just wear a few more wraps than we used to and it'll be fine,' said Tina's sister Jane.

'Yeah,' said Gela, 'and we should be able to make shelters a bit stronger than usual to keep out the cold.'

'Plenty of starflowers everywhere, I must say,' said Julie Blueside.

'But fruits are too high to reach to reach, though, aren't they?' worried Lucy London, looking up at the trees with her bulging eyes.

'Yeah,' said Tina in a bright bright voice that didn't sound like her normal way of speaking at all, 'but we can use ropes, or make nets, can't we? We'll have plenty of time for jobs like that, when meat is so easy to get.'

That was the story they were telling each other: Tall Tree Valley was going to be *fine* fine. And if one of them started to tell another story, then someone else would straightaway put them right.

'Whole time we've been here I've not heard one leopard,' Janny said. 'That's a good sign, isn't it?'

'We're going to miss Family,' sighed Lucy London. 'I wish we weren't so far from them.'

'But we've got each other, haven't we?' Jane said quickly. 'We've got each other. And we're nearly grownups after all, aren't we?'

'Do you reckon those snow leopards come down here?' asked Lucy Batwing. 'I couldn't cope with them again.'

'I don't see why,' Gela told her, in the same bright bright voice that Tina had used. 'They didn't ever come down into Circle Valley, did they? Not even as far down as the hills. If they did, we would have known about them before, wouldn't we? And like Janny said, we haven't even heard an ordinary forest leopard here, and you'd think we would have done by now, if there were any, wouldn't you?'

'I *like* it here,' Tina said firmly. 'I like these tall tall trees.'

'Yeah. And did you see those flying monkeys?' asked Mike, coming over from his work on the fence to get some meat.

'I'm scared about having my baby here,' said Julie Blueside, 'with no oldmums near to help.'

'We've got Clare and Janny,' Gela said in that bright bright voice. She had a baby inside her too, and so she must have been worried about the same thing. 'They might not be oldmums, but they've been through it, haven't they? They'll know what to do.'

'But they had help from their mums over by Lava Blob, didn't they?'

'Try this buckmeat, Mike,' Jane said loudly, 'it's *good* good.'

'Harry loves it! Harry loves it! It's the best meat ever.'

Of course they could all see just as well as I could that Tall Tree Valley was small and cold and lonely, but they didn't want to let thoughts get into their heads about setting out again for somewhere else, not after what had happened up in Dark. So they were trying to squash each other's doubts and fears, and talk themselves into feeling at home. But it was *thin* thin, this hopeful talk of theirs. It was thin thin thin. Just underneath the surface of it was the memory of that horrible cold dark place where Suzie Fishcreek died, and where they'd *all* almost died, groping their way like blind oldies through darkness and ice. Harry's dick, they'd have talked themselves into any damn thing rather than face that again.

I walked up to the fire.

'Hey there, John,' said Tina and some of the others, but Mehmet busied himself with sharpening the tip of his spear and didn't look up.

'Yeah, we can definitely make something of this place,' he said, carrying on with the talk they'd been having as if I hadn't arrived.'We were lucky lucky to stumble on it.'

I fetched some starflowers and buckmeat for my breakfast, and sat myself on a stone next to Janny, whose baby Flower was sucking at her breast, almost hidden away inside the buckskin bodywrap that she'd made specially with an opening at the front. When I'd swallowed down the flowers and the meat I stood up.

'We need to find out more about this valley,' I said.'We need to see if there are ways out of it, and what lives here, and we need to check out the possibilities and the dangers before we dig in too deep in this one spot. I know we can't spare many people from the jobs we've got on here. But I'm going to walk once round the edge of this place.'

I saw Tina look at me, wondering if I was going to ask her to go with me, and hoping hoping I wouldn't. I saw Gerry looking at me too, *part* of him wanting me to ask him to come, but a bigger part hoping I wouldn't take him away from the rest of them.

But I'd already made up my mind to take Jeff.

~ ~ ~

Me and Jeff took a spear, and a bow and some arrows, and we went up the slope a bit so we could get a view and then made our way

round the valley at that level, me walking, him riding beside me on
his buck. It felt weird being just with Jeff. He'd always come as a pair
with Gerry. And it felt awkward because of course he knew quite
well that I'd chosen to go with him alone for a reason.

'There must be an exit from this valley,' I said after a bit. 'Or all this
water from the snow would have turned it into a giant pool.'

I looked out over Tall Tree forest, with its white and yellow lanterns
shining at the bottom of that steep dark bowl. Clouds of fug were
rising up from middle of it, lit up by the lanternlight. Here and there
the odd bird or bat was flying above the trees.

'I know what you're hoping, John,' Jeff said, smiling. 'You're
hoping that you'll find us a nice wide exit full of bright trees, so we
can just walk easily down to whatever's at the bottom, and you won't
have to try and persuade us all to go back up over Dark.'

I didn't answer that.

'I can't see a gap anywhere, can you?' I said. 'Dark seems to go all
the way round without a . . .'

I broke off because I noticed three of those monkeys watching
us from a tree. One by one they jumped out into the air. As they fell
they reached out forward with their front hands, backward with their
back hands, and straight out to the sides with their middle hands, so
that their loose wrap-like flaps of skin were stretched out tight like
the skin of a bat wing. They glided fifteen twenty yards and landed,
one after another, on another treetrunk, with a little *clack – clack –
clack* each time as their claws took hold.

'That stretchy skin could be useful stuff,' I said.

I put an arrow on my bow and lifted the bow to take aim . . .

But Jeff leaned over from Def's back to push my arrow towards
the ground.

'Leave them be, John!' he said, laughing. 'You don't have to make
everything serve your purpose all the time.'

Gela's tits, who was he to tell me what to do? He might have saved
us from Dark, but he was still only a funny little clawfoot kid, with no

new hairs even, except maybe a first bit of fluff above his dick.

'You don't get it,' I said crossly, lifting my bow again. 'We've got to use everything we can if we're going to . . .'

But the monkeys jumped off again – one, two, three – down towards main forest. As soon as the last one had landed, the first one was off again, and then they were gone.

As I lowered my bow, I noticed I felt relieved that I hadn't had to try and shoot them. I wouldn't admit it to him of course, but bloody Jeff was right. It did feel good to just let things be for once. I took the arrow off the bow, and for a little while me and him stood there quietly, looking out over the valley.

'There *is* a big waterfall somewhere,' I said. 'Can't you hear it? That faint faint roar, under the sound of the trees?'

~ ~ ~

But though we went right round until we could see the smoke from the fire ahead of us again, softly lit up by forest, we found no break in the wall of rock that surrounded Tall Tree Valley. Where did the water go? Where was that waterfall roar coming from?

'Do you remember once when we were little kids,' I said, 'you, me and Gerry used to make those little boats with dry fruit skins? We used to grease them to stop them going soft.'

'Yes, of course. All the kids played with those.'

'Remember one time we dug out our own little pool for them? But the water sank into the dirt and turned to mud, so we had to keep filling it up again, and in the end we gave up. Me and Gerry chucked stones into the mud, remember? Each one went *splat* and made a neat little hole with a ridge round it in a circle. This valley's just like that, like a giant stone splatted it out.'

'Well, that's what probably happened,' Jeff said.

'Don't be dumb, Jeff. A stone would have to be *huge* huge to make this.'

'There are much bigger stones than that in sky, aren't there? Eden is one, isn't it, and so is Earth. Sky is full of stones.'

It was weird. I knew all that stuff, the same as he did. It was part of the True Story. But I'd never once before thought of those stones as really being in the same world as me.

'Let's follow a stream,' Jeff said, 'and see where the water goes.'

He led the way downhill. Soon we heard the waterfall roar quite definitely ahead of us beneath the humming of forest. A bit later we started to feel drops of spray on our faces. And then, in the lowest part of the valley bowl, forest just stopped and there was a huge jagged hole right in front of us, with water pouring into it over steep cliffs from streams on every side, and warm steam rising up from below.

The bottom of the hole was full of steam, but, as we stood at the edge of it looking down, the steam thinned out for a few seconds, enough for us to make out the blurry lights of trees far far down below, red and blue and yellow and white.

'Michael's names,' I murmured.

It was a way down into Underworld, where all life on Eden began, all life except for us.

Def was restless with all the noise, and Jeff was stroking its head to calm it down, all the time looking down into Underworld. I saw his lips move and, though I couldn't hear him, I knew quite well what he was saying.

'We are here,' he was murmuring to himself. 'We really are here.'

Then he pointed. Four monkeys had gathered on the edge of the cliff over to our left. They were peering down into the steam with their flat Eden eyes, and, strangely, each one of them had shoved a big stone right up to the edge. Suddenly they jumped into the hole, not stretching out their arms to fly like the ones we'd seen in the trees, but grasping their stones beneath them with all six hands, so that the flappy skin puffed out between their arms and slowed their fall as they disappeared into the steam.

'We could do that,' I said to Jeff, after a bit. 'We could sew up skins and make something like that to break our fall.'

That made him laugh. He laughed and laughed, until even I couldn't help smiling.

'I never give it a rest, yeah? Is that what you're thinking?'

'No, you bloody don't, John. It's like everything in the world is just stuff for you to use for your plans.'

He carried on stroking Def, and watching the water dropping down through the steam.

'And anyway, how would we get back out again?' he said after a bit.

'We could make ropes.'

This made him laugh again.

'Big big ropes they'd have to be.'

The woollybuck groaned and snorted, and Jeff turned to attend to it. I leaned over the edge to look straight down. The steam had cleared a bit again, and I could see those shining trees again, way way down below: red and blue and yellow. And then I saw something moving down there, a row of ten twelve red lights weaving through the lights of the trees.

'Jeff! Quick! Look!'

But steam blew back before Jeff had a chance to turn away from Def, and when it next cleared the moving lights had gone. It was only me that saw that long long creature winding its way through the trees.

'What did you see?'

'Just those trees down there again,' I said.

Suddenly I jumped to my feet with a gasp and backed away from that dreadful hole. It was weird. I was shaking. It was like it had almost sucked me in.

'What's the matter, John?'

'I don't like this place.'

'This hole, do you mean? Or Tall Tree Valley?'

'Neither.'

'You really don't, do you?'

Still standing with Def by the edge of the hole, Jeff looked back at me and smiled.

It was horrible to think that, even for a moment, I'd suggested we might go down into that hole. It was like Underworld had been trying to trick me, to suck me away from sky and Earth.

'We can't stay here, Jeff. We'll have to go back up on Dark and carry on to other side.'

'No one will go up Dark with you now, John,' Jeff said, climbing back onto Def's back. 'Not even Gerry.'

I pulled off Gela's ring and started to twist and turn it between my fingers.

'Okay, so I'll just have to wait till the time's right. But we can't stay here forever, Jeff. We can't!'

He didn't answer. He just watched my fingers playing with Gela's ring.

After a bit, feeling calmer, I passed it to him to hold. He studied it for a few seconds and then handed it straight back to me, the ring that Angela was given on Earth by her mother and father, like it was nothing more than a nice stone or a pretty bit of shell.

'If we were there on Earth,' he said, 'then we'd call Earth *here*, and it would be the ordinary dull place we were stuck in, and Eden would be the strange wonderful place that was far far away.'

'I don't get you.'

'I mean, wherever you are, that's here, and that's the only place you can be. Here or nowhere.'

I put the ring back on my finger.

Another monkey pushed a stone to the edge of the hole and dropped down through the steam.

'Are you with me, Jeff?' I asked.

Jeff laughed.

'Yeah, of course I am.'

'No, I mean are you on my side?'

'Your *side*?'

I could see straight away that it wasn't the right question to ask him. I always wanted to narrow things down, shut things out, concentrate all my effort on one point so as to get things done, but Jeff was the opposite of that. He was always reminding himself to lift his eyes from the things we all got absorbed in, and to see the wide world beyond. He'd never settle for seeing only one side of a thing.

'I mean, are we friends?' I finally asked lamely.

This made him laugh and laugh.

Then we heard a scared cry from back where the others were. We hurried back to find that Julie Blueside's baby was on its way.

37

Gela Brooklyn

It took two whole wakings for Julie's baby to be born. It seemed to be stuck inside her, no matter how hard she pushed, and she screamed and screamed, and we all thought she was going to die. There were oldmums back in Family who knew how to help with things like that, but none of us did. None of us had any idea. Everyone cowered down inside themselves while Julie screamed and screamed and screamed, and even while I tried to comfort and reassure her, I felt my own baby growing inside me, and wondered if this was going to be how I died too.

And then something shifted somehow, and the baby came out. It was a tiny tiny little batfaced boy and it was dead and blue and shrivelled up. Another death to add to Suzie's and her baby's and make Tall Tree seem even more like a place of loneliness and sadness, however much we all tried to tell each other that it was fine.

~ ~ ~

After we'd buried the baby under stones, we stayed up by that stream at the edge of forest for a couple of wakings. Then Tina and me persuaded everyone to move further down into forest and we all built shelters and a new fence down there next to a small pool.

Me and Tina pretty much ran things after that, just like we'd done back at Valley Neck. John might have been the one that brought us here, but now he was busy busy again with his own things: trips up to edge of Dark, sewing new wraps and greasing them and storing them in logs, cutting new snowboots from bark, drying wavyweed and twisting ropes, trying out new kinds of footwrap with different mixtures of grease and sap and buckfoot glue.

We'd been living there for some time – two three periods – when we heard the lookouts calling out during a sleep, and crawled out of our shelters to find snow falling. It fell and fell and fell all across Tall Tree Valley, until the ground was white with snow everywhere, and the lanterns on the trees shone out through lumps of snow, and icy water came drip-drip-dripping from every branch as the snow melted on the warm bark. Even when snow had covered everything, it still kept falling falling from the black sky, until it lay two three feet deep, and our shelters were smooth white heaps. A couple of them collapsed under the weight.

'Snow! Snow! I hate cold snow,' whimpered Harry Spiketree. 'Why won't it stop? I'm scared. Why won't it go away?'

As usual people yelled at him to shut up, but really all Harry ever did was say out loud what everyone felt inside. It *was* scary. I thought so too. It was like we'd come down here to this dismal bloody place to get away from Snowy Dark, but now Dark was following after us.

We built up our main fire quickly, before the snow could put it out, dragging logs out from under the snow that had covered our big log pile, and then we huddled round the flames with greased buckskins over our heads, trying to keep as warm and dry as we could.

I felt something squirm inside me. It was the little baby in my womb. My first baby.

'Hey!' I said. 'It's started to . . .'

But I never finished telling them. A cry had come from somewhere on the slopes above us.

Aaaaaaaah! Aaaaaaaah!

A snow leopard. Gela's heart! Lucy London burst into tears, and quite a few of the others began to sob and moan and rock.

'We'll be alright,' I told everyone. 'We'll be alright. Even forest leopards don't like fire, do they?'

'That's right,' Tina said straight away. 'And snow leopards aren't used to *any* sort of light, are they? So they'll be even more scared if anything'

We were *trying* to be cheerful, but weirdly John suddenly seemed like he *really was* happy happy.

'Snow. Cold. Leopards,' he said cheerfully, jumping up to get more wood for the fire. 'It's like Dark's come down to get us, isn't it? It's like we haven't really got away from it at all.'

He chucked a log onto the flames and looked around at us with a big smile on his face.

'The fire *should* scare them away,' he said, 'but better get a few bows and spears ready, just in case, eh?'

The slinker! He was hoping that this would put us all off Tall Tree Valley for good.

Actually, even though I'd felt scared at first, I didn't think the snow would really harm us. Even back in Circle Valley it happened occasionally that snow fell, and sometimes it even settled for a waking or two in forest on slopes of Blue Mountains or Peckham Hills. I guessed it would be the same here. It wasn't going to be fun, but we wouldn't freeze. We had a huge pile of wood to burn and keep us warm till the snow had passed, and we had a fence round us, and I'd never heard of any animal that would come close to a big fire.

'Trouble with Tall Tree Valley,' John said, 'is that it's still in Dark. It's not really so different from that place up there where we saw the giant slinker: just a little warm patch in middle of Snowy Dark. We won't *really* get away from Dark until we're right across and down the other side.'

If he'd said that a waking earlier, we'd have all been mad at him, but now, our shelters buried and leopards wailing on the slopes, I could see people listening to him and thinking and taking it in, and I could see them remembering all the things that they didn't like about small, cold, lonely Tall Tree Valley, the things that people like me had been trying to push away with our cheerful chatter about how easy it was to find bucks, or how nice the bloody starflowers tasted.

Huddled up all wet and cold with a buckskin over my head to keep the snow off my hair, I thought about what it would *really* be like to stay forever under these lonely high trees, and deal with snows like this every couple of periods.

'Yeah, you've got a point, John,' I said. 'Tall Tree Valley just doesn't feel like a place where people are meant to live.'

Mehmet laughed angrily.

'Tom's dick and Harry's, what *is* this? People lived on Earth in places where it snowed for wombs on end, Gela. Didn't you know that? And as for you, John, what is your problem? You *know* this snow won't last, and you know quite well we could manage it easy easy if we put our minds to it, with bigger fires and better shelters and thicker wraps. So what is it you're trying to do? Are you *determined* to do for us all?'

I'd never liked Mehmet much, but I had to admit he was learning. He used just to moan at everything John did without offering another plan of his own, but now for the first time he was proposing something that could actually work. We *could* stay in Tall Tree. We *could* build stronger shelters. His hands were shaking and his voice was wobbly, but finally Mehmet was offering an alternative to John.

He didn't have long to wait either for someone else to take his side.

'No way am I going back up there where my sister died,' said Dave Fishcreek. 'And no way am I going to let you lead me anywhere again, John, not after what happened last time.'

His voice was shaking too. I'd tried a few times to point out to Dave and his brother Johnny that nobody made us go over to John from Family, and nobody forced us to follow John up onto Dark. I'd tried to point out that none of us could have have known that there was such a thing as snow leopards, and that John's quick thinking had at least saved the rest of us from what happened to Suzie. I'd even tried reminding them Suzie was my friend, and that I loved her and grieved for her too, but she wasn't the sort of person that would want them bitter bitter like this. But they'd never been willing to hear what I said.

Johnny backed up his brother straight away. He wasn't going to leave Tall Tree Valley and that was that. And as soon as he'd spoken, the three Blueside girls, one by one, said the same. And then the six of them – Mehmet and his five followers – looked around at the rest of us, hoping for more support. But everyone else stayed silent. Hunched under our buckskins, we peered up at the falling snow and *wished* wished we were somewhere else. And John was telling us we *could* be.

'I'm getting tired of living in this little patch of trees up in Snowy Dark,' John said. 'I'm going to try and get down the other side to a proper forest, and if anyone wants to join me they can. It'll mean going through more snow, I admit, but look around you. We're in the snow already!'

Mehmet jumped to his feet.

'Harry's dick, John. Don't pretend this is the same as it is up on Dark. We can still *see* here! We can still find things to *eat*! We can still make *fires*! There's firewood everywhere! And if we just built bigger and stronger shelters we wouldn't even need to get wet.'

I looked across the fire at Tina. I knew she'd be annoyed with John for once again springing a whole new plan on everyone, but when I mouthed the question to her 'Will you go?', she nodded, and I nodded back to say 'Me too'. Then I looked at my sister Clare and asked her the same thing, and she nodded as well. So did Lucy Batwing. So did Janny and Jane and Mike.

Aaaaaaaah! cried the leopard again, not so far up above us. Lucy and Martha London started crying again and said they couldn't bear to live any more in this cold snowy place. I looked at John and saw the old slinker was having a job not to smile.

~ ~ ~

Something came into my mind then that my mum made me learn when I was fourteen fifteen wombs old. It was a secret thing that I wasn't to talk about. It was words that had passed from mother to daughter all the way down from First Angela, who I was named for. And Mum said I should remember the words exactly and pass them on in turn when I was older to any of my own daughters who would be able to remember them carefully, and keep them to themselves.

'It's not that these things are such a *big* big secret,' my mum said. 'But if everyone were to tell these words to each other all the time, they wouldn't stay the same. They'd change in the telling in the way that the True Story does, and we wouldn't remember any more what Angela actually said.'

There were a lot of words from Angela that Mum taught me, but the ones I remembered now, as John and Mehmet were fighting over whether we should stay in Tall Tree Valley or whether we should go, were these:

'Some men want the story to be all about *them*.'

It was so true of John, I thought. As soon as things got quiet, and everyone was just getting on with things, he got uneasy because life stopped being a story about anyone in particular, and certainly not about him.

But it was true of Mehmet too.

~ ~ ~

'John doesn't know the way to another forest,' Mehmet hissed now, his face all blotchy with anger. 'He doesn't know it any more this time than he did before. Michael's names, what's the matter with all of you? This snow here won't kill us, but *that* snow will.'

It would have been nice nice, I thought, if this didn't have to be about John *or* Mehmet, and could just be about deciding the right thing to do, but there weren't any other choices apart from what the two of them were offering. It was the same when I first came over to John at Cold Path Neck: only that time the choice was him or ugly old David Redlantern.

'We can stay up here in middle of Dark until we die,' said John, 'or we can finish off the job we started and find a place on the other side. Do we want to live the rest of our lives in the warm wide forests that we know are over there, or do we want to huddle up forever in this small cold place?'

Aaaaaaaah! came the cry again from the slopes up to Dark.

For a few seconds everyone was silent. Then Mehmet spoke.

'And what about leopards, John? Want to explain to us why it makes sense to go up there among those white leopards all over again?'

John laughed.

'What makes you think they're up there, Mehmet? They can throw their voices, remember? Tom's dick, it was you that first figured that out! They could be down here in forest now. They could be just a few yards away. We're *in* Snowy Dark, remember. We're still in it, and we will be until we get down the other side.'

'Oh that's just a load of . . .' Mehmet began angrily, but John cut him off.

'Snow leopards cry out before they attack, the same as forest leopards sing. We know that now, don't we? They cry out to confuse their prey about where they are. And we know now that if we hear that sound up on Dark, we just have to yell and scream loud enough, and we'll scare them off.'

He looked around at the faces in the firelight, half-hidden under buckskins.

'In fact those leopards up there are a *good* sign. I'll bet you anything they're there because the bucks are climbing out of Tall Tree Valley to find their way down to lower ground, like we know bucks do in cold dips.'

He made all of us to walk to the edge of forest so we could look up and see for ourselves. He was right. The snow was barely falling now, and, on the huge dark slopes all round us, we could see the headlanterns of bucks moving in long lines up out of Tall Tree Valley.

'You see?' he said. 'Look at them! Heading off for the big low valleys! Those ones over there are going back towards Circle Valley, aren't they, but look at these ones here! Where are *they* going, Mehmet? What does that tell you?'

'It tells me you're crazy, John. It tells me that, if we let you, you'll go on until you've done for all of us.'

Mehmet turned to the rest of us.

'Harry's dick, can't you see it? He's doing it again! He's trying to control our minds. He's trying to make us think that the way he sees things is the only way to see things!'

'You don't have to . . .' began John.

'Oh, just shut up, John, will you, shut up and give us all a rest!'

Mehmet had come right up in front of John. He was the shorter one of the two and he glared up into John's face, and then shoved him, hard hard, so he staggered and nearly fell.

But John was nimble. He recovered his balance quickly quickly, and, in one single movement, he passed his spear from his right to his left hand, grabbed Mehmet by the neck and flung him down into the snow. And then he was over him. Mehmet's body wrap had fallen open and John pressed the tip of his blackglass spear into the smooth skin of Mehmet's chest. Both of them were panting panting for breath. A bead of red blood trickled across Mehmet's skin and under his wrap.

'Gela's heart, John, what are you doing!' I screamed.

'John! Stop!' yelled Tina.

And in the same moment she cried out, a leopard cried out too above us.

'Go on then John,' jeered Mehmet. 'Do for me, like you did for Dixon Blueside. It's getting to be a bit of a habit, isn't it? That'll make five, at my count, dead because of you. Or should that be seven, with the two little ones?'

Tina stepped forward, yanked away the spear. I pulled Mehmet roughly up to his feet. The two of us pushed them apart.

'It's a choice,' Tina hissed at Mehmet. 'It's a free choice. People can stay with you or they can leave with John. What's so hard to understand about that?'

No one spoke. The Fishcreek boys and the three Blueside girls went to stand by Mehmet, the boys clutching their spears tightly. The rest of us walked back to our camp and began to dig out our storage logs from under the snow, to get out dry food and spare wraps.

I could see the six of them wavering as we loaded up. I could see them wondering what it would be like to be by themselves in this cold bleak place. I wondered if, at the last minute, they'd crack and come with us, as Mehmet had always done before. But they stayed.

'Don't think you're the brave ones,' Mehmet jeered after us as we set off behind John and Jeff and Jeff's woollybuck, Def, 'just because you're the ones that are going. Angela stayed, remember, when the Three Companions left. She stayed in one place and made a go of things, like we're doing. But you, John, and all of you that follow him, you just run run run.'

38

John Redlantern

There were lights below us! There were lights and lights and lights, on and on, as thick as stars in Starry Swirl.

'Gela's heart, Jeff,' I whispered, 'this is the best moment in my whole life, the *best* best moment!'

Bright bright lights, on and on, and not just ahead but to the left too, and to the right: red and green and yellow and blue and white. We'd never seen such a thing. We'd never seen a forest that bright and that big.

I turned to shout to rest of them still toiling up the slope behind us in the darkness. We'd been walking through Dark the length of two long wakings. We'd twice heard leopards and had to scream and yell to scare them away.

'Quick! Quick!' I yelled down. 'We've done it! We've made it! We're okay!'

I turned to look down again at forest below us.

'Just look at it, Jeff. Tom's dick, just bloody *look* at it! On and on!'

As each of the others reached the top, they shouted angrily.

'You two were *way* too far ahead! You should have bloody waited for us! What would have happened if a leopard had come?'

But, when they saw what was laid below them, they fell silent, just like me and Jeff had done.

Never mind little Tall Tree Valley, this made *Circle* Valley look tiny and closed-in. Both those places were really just little splat holes in Snowy Dark. But this wasn't a splat hole. It wasn't just another valley. It was a whole world. Everyone could see that. Everyone.

'Weird to think Family stayed in that one little place for a hundred and sixty bloody *years*,' Gela Brooklyn said, rubbing her pregnant belly, 'when all of this was so near.' 'Tom's neck, John!' Gerry shouted excitedly, coming up next to me, putting his arm round my shoulders and leaning his head against mine. 'You did it! You bloody did it! You are brilliant brilliant, John. You're great.'

He was proud of me again, as proud of me as he had been when I did for the leopard.

In fact they were *all* proud of me.

'You made this happen,' Tina said, coming over beside me too, and slipping her arm round my waist. 'You started this all by yourself and made it happen.'

We still had our headwraps on to keep out the cold, so we were like some kind of weird two-legged bucks standing up there in the snow, and it was dark dark too, but in the light of Def's headlantern I could see Tina's shiny eyes looking at me out of the holes in the buckskin.

'You bloody did it, John!' said Gerry again.

'To think I was about to say we should turn back,' said Janny, looking down at the thousand thousand lights below. 'To think my Flower could have grown up in bloody old Tall Tree Valley, when all this was waiting for us.'

And then suddenly she pulled off her headwrap and mine too, so she could give me a wet batface kiss.

'Well, if Janny's going to kiss you, I will too!' Tina said, yanking off her own headwrap. Our skins were all pink and sticky from being inside the wraps, and she kissed me slowly with her mouth open, like a kiss before a slip. The others cheered us on.

They'd never been pleased with me like this. Even when they first came over to me at Valley Neck – and that was long *long* before Suzie died, long before I'd got them lost and Jeff had had to save them – they'd grumbled as if I'd *made* them come, as if all that they'd given up was my fault and nothing to do with them. But now, when me and Jeff had forced them to keep going and risked their lives by pushing on ahead with their only source of light, they were pleased pleased pleased.

It felt good good, but even better than their praise was the sight of Wide Forest itself stretching away down there, with no Dark to make an edge to it, except for the Dark we were standing on.

Far off in the distance, I noticed, the light of Wide Forest changed. There was a kind of winding edge between the twinkly light of the trees below, which was like the light of Circle Valley, and a softer, smoother, more even light, which was more like the light that comes out of a stream or a pool.

'That couldn't all be water over there, surely?' I said to myself. It didn't seem possible, and yet I remembered stories of such a thing on Earth, a pool that was bigger than all the dry ground put together. The C, it was called for short, but no one in Eden knew any more what that had stood for.

'Think of bloody old Mehmet and the other five,' said Dix with a snort of laughter, 'stuck back up there on their own in Tall Tree Valley, figuring out how to keep warm next time it snows.'

'Yeah,' shouted Harry. 'Ha ha! Sitting by themselves in the snow.'

He laughed and laughed, as Harry sometimes did, going on until it was almost like it was hurting him or he was having a fit. It often got on people's nerves so much that they ended up telling him to bloody shut up, and then he'd get upset, which was even noisier and more annoying than his laugh. But this time everyone joined in with him happily, laughing and laughing up there on that ridge in Dark, with the wide bright world below, all glittery and fresh and new. No more snow and dark and snow leopards. All of that was behind us. No hungry wakings. No having to eat bats and slinkers because there wasn't enough buckmeat. A new start for us, a new world, and all the space we could possibly need for generations and generations and generations.

We started down the mountain. In a couple of hours we were walking by a stream with trees humming all around us, and their lanterns lighting our way, white, blue, pink, yellow. Herds of stonebucks lifted up their heads from the shining starflowers and watched us pass. They didn't even try to run away.

39

Tina Spiketree

So now we'd crossed Snowy Dark and found Wide Forest, the wide wide space that John had always insisted would be there. And in some ways life was easy easy, easier than it had ever been back in Circle Valley. There was so much fruit and so many birds and bucks – stonebucks and woollybucks and a new kind of buck we called a widebuck, big like a woollybuck, but with smooth smooth skin – that we could get together the food for a waking in just an hour or two. You didn't need to have everyone working working all waking long just to get enough to eat, like we used to have to do back in Family. John said we should start School again when our children were a bit bigger, and teach everyone to write and do sums. He said we should use all that extra time to learn things and find out new things, like they did on Earth.

We found a place to stop, a quarter waking's walk from bottom of Dark. It was next to a long warm shining pool that bent round like a knee or a letter L, so we called it L-pool. It was full of fish and oysters and ducks. Trees grew round the edge of it and out into it too, waist-deep, and their big bright lanterns hung down over the water, white and green and yellow, giving out a thick sweet scent. The water gave us protection from leopards on two sides, and we quickly made a short fence out of branches near where the two sides of the L joined, so as to make ourselves a little safe triangle. Inside this fence we built a half-circle of shelters, and two big fire holes in middle, deep deep so as to be sure that there'd always be red embers glowing there.

'Right,' said John, as we sat round the fire inside our newly finished triangle fence. 'We're safe from leopards now, so let's start building a *proper* fence.'

He wanted to enclose a big big space, big as whole of Family area back in Circle Valley, so that it would give us enough room to grow as big as Family itself, and he wanted us to help him build a huge L-shaped fence so as to make a square with the two whole sides of L-pool.

'But why do we need that, John,' Gela asked him, in her sensible way, 'when there are only fourteen of us plus a couple of babies?'

'This is a new family,' John said. 'This is a beginning again, free of all the bad things that happened in Old Family. Clean and fresh and new. Without Oldest. Without Circle. Without Council. Without David Redlantern and his crew. Without Any Virsries where only Council can speak.'

He looked round at us.

'A new family without all those things, yes, but still one that will grow as big and strong as Family itself. Bigger, even. Stronger.'

Harry jumped up and danced a silly jig. He could tell that John wanted us to be excited about his idea and he was trying in his own way to get us going.

'Harry's happy! Harry's happy!'

I suppose it looked cute when he was a little boy, before I was born, and I guess back then everyone laughed and encouraged him, but it didn't look cute now, not when he was older than anyone else there. No one joined in and no one laughed.

~ ~ ~

And we weren't so crazy, either, about that 'fresh and new' thing of John's any more. We helped work on his big fence from time to time, to keep him happy and because it wasn't such a bad idea to stop leopards from coming in too close to the little fence around our shelters, but mostly we just got on with doing the ordinary things we needed to do to keep ourselves going.

Life was easy in one way, but in another way it had turned out hard. Sometimes I felt lonely lonely. There were so *few* of us. Okay, there was my Dix, and his mate Mike, and my good friend Gela, and my batface sister Jane, and little sharp Clare, and cheerful Janny, who was always up for a laugh and a joke. And Gerry was alright, I suppose, boring but alright, and so, in his own funny way, was clever weird Jeff. And bloody old John was okay too, at least some of the time, and I guess I cared about my brother Harry, or I felt responsible for him anyway, though it drove me nuts having to sort things out for him when he annoyed people with his noisy stupidness. I even got on alright with Lucy Batwing, and the two London girls.

But that wasn't a lot of people to fill a whole world with, not when there was forest forest forest stretching away on both sides of us for miles and miles and miles. Thousands and thousands of trees shining and pumping – *hmmph, hmmph, hmmph* – thousands of flutterbyes and bats and bucks and treecats and slinkers and leopards, all with their flat eyes and their two hearts and their greeny-black Eden blood, taking no notice of us, carrying on with the things they'd been doing for hundreds and thousands of wombs, ever since they first came up from Underworld: it was lonely lonely when you thought too much about it. So much space, so much life going on that didn't know or care we existed – and then us, just us, us few human beings, by ourselves in the middle of it all.

We made babies as quickly as we could. Even *I* worked on making babies, though I was never that keen on being a mum. I slipped with Dix, I slipped with John, I even slipped with Mike once twice. And often I found myself doing it like a broody oldmum back in Family, not really thinking about the thing itself and what it felt like, just waiting for the job to be done, and then laying back after the bloke was finished, whichever one it was, and trying to keep his juice inside me. All the girls did the same.

'Slipping should be a special thing,' John said one time, when a bunch of us were together by the fire, scraping buckskins clean. 'Not just something you do with anyone you feel like, or anyone needing a bit of juice. We should go back to how it was on Earth. One man just slips with one woman, so he knows which kids he was the dad of, and a kid knows which bloke is his dad. This way of doing things we've got into on Eden, where everyone slips with everyone: it only began here on Eden in First Harry's times, when there *was* only one man in the world and it was him.'

He looked straight at me as he said it. He hated that I slipped with Dix, and he knew I knew that he hated it. And in a way I understood what he felt, because I didn't used to like it much either when he slipped with the oldmums back in Family. Back then I wanted him for myself, and now he wanted me to be just his alone. But how could I agree to that with a bloke like him, who wanted to slip with me one waking and then, for wakings and wakings after that, wasn't even interested in even *telling* me anything, let alone touching me?

'How would that work, though, John,' Janny Redlantern asked, practically, 'when there are eight girls here and only six blokes?'

'Yeah,' said Clare, lowering her voice and looking round to make sure my brother was out of earshot, 'and out of the six of us that *did* get a bloke, how would we decide which one got bloody old Harry?'

They all laughed at that, though a couple of them looked guiltily at me and my sister Jane.

Even John laughed.

'You've got a point there, Janny,' he said. 'I admit you have a point.'

Five six wakings later I came across him in forest with ugly merry Janny Redlantern, giving her a slip from behind, while she chattered away to him, just like some oldmum back in Family. He looked up and spotted me. Gela's heart, I could tell how much he hated that I'd seen him. And soon afterwards he took his spear and a leopard tooth knife and a rope, and went off into Wide Forest on one of his long lonely trips.

~ ~ ~

He was always going off into forest and, if he wasn't in forest, he was toiling and toiling away on the big fence, dragging up branches, hacking at trees, all by himself if no one would help him, to enclose that stupid massive space that we wouldn't need for bloody generations.

He was restless *restless* all the time.

Gela's tits, he'd broken up Family, he'd killed Dixon Blueside, he'd led us though ice and darkness, he'd lost Suzie and nearly killed the lot of us, all because he wanted to cross Snowy Dark and start again on the other side, but now we *were* here, it wasn't enough for him, this little group of familiar faces, this ordinary waking-by-waking routine of hunting and scavenging and cooking and mending spears and scraping skins. It didn't leave him with any outlet for all that energy of his, squeezed tight up inside him, like sap inside a tree.

40

Sue Redlantern

Paaaaarp! Paaaarp! Paaaarp!

I'd just got off to sleep when the horns started for another bloody AnyVirsry: one hundred and sixty-sixth. Of course I knew it was coming but, Michael's names, I'd been dreading that sound. I didn't care much how many years it was since Angela and Tommy came to Eden, but what I hated *hated* was that each AnyVirsry was another year since my two boys Gerry and Jeff and all those others disappeared from Cold Path Neck and never came back.

Paaaaarp! Paaaarp! Paaaarp!

I crawled out of my shelter to make sure everyone was moving, and to help the youngmums with the little kids. Fox was out there already hurrying people along. He was Redlantern group leader now. It had been David for a bit, but then he became Head of Guards, and he moved out of Redlantern and set up his own fires and shelters with the other Guards over beside Greatpool, like a group all of their own with only men in it, a group over all other groups.

Paaaaarp! Paaaarp! Paaaarp!

'Come on, darling, don't cry, mummy'll be back out for you in a minute when she's got your baby brother . . . Gela's tits, Fox, give them a moment. Kids can't wake up just like that. It takes them a bit of time . . . Here's mummy look, darling, coming out of her shelter now . . .'

Paaaaarp! Paaaarp! Paaaarp!

'Yeah, yeah. We know, we know, give us a break. It's all fine and easy if you're on London time, but we were deep asleep over this side . . . Come on, sweetheart, you can't go back into your shelter now. Wait till we get to AnyVirsry, eh, and then you can lie down and have a little kip again . . . Michael's names, but you are a big big boy, Dixie, aren't you? You look like you're ready for a leopard hunt, mate, never mind an AnyVirsry. What do you reckon? You could go out and do for a leopard easy easy, I'd say . . . Yes I know, Fox, but the Guards won't kill you for giving the littles a few minutes to sort themselves out before they go.'

Paaaaarp! Paaaarp! Paaaarp!

'Yes alright, Roger, you can lean on me. But don't get any ideas, alright?'

And off we went, whole Redlantern group – Fox, blind Old Roger, Lucy Lu, Jade, all of us – through Spiketree (who were still getting themselves together) and Brooklyn and across Stream's Join to Circle Clearing. I was doing my usual job of jollying people along – Fox might be leader but he hadn't got a clue about all that – but inside me all the time it was cold and empty and dark, because I knew too well what I was going to have to see and what I was going to have to hear and what I was going to have to swallow.

There was a fug sinking down over us. It was warm and close and the rain was coming, just like it did that Strornry after one-sixty-three, when John destroyed the Stones. Such a terrible time that seemed then, the worst time, like everything was poisoned and spoiled: Gerry and Jeff and the others going off after John and Tina, Bella hanging herself like Tommy from a tree . . . But, looking back on it now, it wasn't really *so* bad after that Strornry, not for about a wombtime. A lot of newhairs were outside of Family over Cold Path Valley way, it was true, and we missed them and things were tense.

But we could still see them at Lava Blob and in forest round there, still see them and get news of them, and still look after them in a way.

But then, not long before one-sixty-four, horrible Dixon Blueside went off with our Met and with John Blueside and the three of them never came back.

Well, David obviously knew something that we didn't know, something about where they went and what they meant to do. He and a bunch of his newhair boys – we didn't call them Guards then, but that was what they were becoming – they all rushed off into forest with their spears and their clubs and their angry puffed-up faces. They found the bones that the foxes and starbirds had left – *this* side of Lava Blob, they all insisted, *this* side – and then they went on to the camp that John and the others had started over at the mouth of Cold Path Valley. They found all of them gone. It was obvious, David told us: they'd all gone up onto Dark to die of cold with Juicy John and Teasy Tina. 'I'm sorry for those of you who've lost your kids,' he said, 'but didn't I *tell* you we should have spiked that John up like Jesus? Didn't I say it? "Spike him up until he burns," I said. But you all said I was being too hard.'

He said the same things again at one-sixty-five and I knew, I knew, I *knew*, he'd say the same things again now, at one-sixty-six: they were all dead up in Snowy Dark, they were fools for following John, we were fools for not doing for John when we had the chance.

~ ~ ~

Anyway, here we were back in Circle Clearing in the space between the trees and the stones – the *new* stones: they've never seemed the same to me as the old ones – and there was Caroline inside Circle looking sort of tired and shrunken and old. Mitch was beside her, the last of Oldest, the last one of Tommy and Gela's grandchildren, with his scrappy white hair and beard, and his blind eyes, and his hands that grabbed and groped around him all the time, like he was frightened he was sinking into the earth. Just outside Circle, Secret Ree stooped over her bits of bark.

Paaaaarp! Paaaarp! Paaaarp! The Council helpers were still blowing those old hollowbranch horns because the most important people hadn't yet arrived and the meeting couldn't start without them.

Paaaaarp! Paaaarp! Paaaarp!

Parp–parp–parp–parp! came the reply at last, and then into the clearing rode David Redlantern, the Head of Guards, in all his ugliness, up on the back of the woollybuck they'd managed to train for him over the last year. He glared round at us, and behind him his Guards, thirty forty young men, grinned and smirked at each other with their big blackglass spears over their shoulders. And he led them right round the clearing, right round the edge of Circle, so we could all see who were really the ones that decided things around here: the ones that could arrive as late as they liked at AnyVirsry and still everyone would wait for them and not complain, however long they took. It wasn't tired old Caroline any more who was in charge.

And then, when they'd made that point, they all stopped in a group together in the space between Circle and the rest of Family. Two of them helped David down from his buck, and they all squatted down, and David gestured to Caroline to carry on.

Tom's neck, how did he *get* all that power? Why did we let him take it? He was only a Redlantern boy after all. I remembered him when he was a little kid and I was a newhair. I didn't like him much even then. He was sort of loveless from the start, but when I was little I used to keep an eye on him. We batfaces took a lot of stick and we had to stand up for each other. I didn't expect him to grow up into anyone nice or special, and I was right: he didn't. He grew up into a sour sarcastic lump of misery. But sour and sarcastic is one thing, this was another. Who could have imagined *this*?

But anyway, it was time for the count. The leaders came out from their groups to report how many in their group were here now, and how many were out hunting or scavenging and all of that, and Secret Ree scratched the numbers down with a shaky hand, though she was nearly blind. Then we waited while they added up the group counts and worked out the count for whole Family. It went on and on, like it did every time. Harry's dick, how hard can it *be* to add up the numbers from eight groups? Babies cried. Newhairs gave each other looks.

Then at last Caroline stood up.

'There are five hunded and eighty-one people in Family,' she announced, 'more than ever ever before!'

My clever Jeff wasn't in that count, was he? Nor my Gerry, nor Janny Redlantern, nor John. They weren't part of it any more. And yet, even without them, the number had gone up. It was like they didn't matter somehow, like they made no odds at all.

Caroline yelled the number into old Mitch's ear, and they levered him up his feet, and he began to quaver on about rememfer this and rememfer that, and how a big round boat came down from sky, and how there were only thirty people when he was a kid, thirty in whole world.

We were supposed to be impressed or feel sorry for them, for managing to keep going when they were so few. But there were only *twenty* with John that went up on Dark.

How does David know they died? I thought. How could he really know? John believed it was possible to cross right over or he wouldn't have led them there, and who's to say he was wrong? He was no fool. He figured out how to make warm wraps. And my own Jeff figured out how to turn a buck into a horse for them to ride. (David would never have thought of that, never, not if he lived for a thousand wombs, though he was happy enough to steal the idea from Jeff.) So who was to say that they didn't make it over to the other side?

There was a new part in Any Virsry now. There was a special bit where bloody old Lucy Lu got up and started telling us the messages she'd had from Angela and Tommy and dead Stoop and all the other Shadow People.

'John is with them now,' she told us, 'John Redlantern, and all his little gang. They froze up on Dark and now they're Shadow People with the rest of them. But none of the other Shadow People . . .'

She broke off here, rolling her eyes and screwing up her face as if she was in terrible pain. That woman has always been a liar and a faker, ever since she was a little kid.

'Gela's heart,' she cried, 'Gela's dear good heart, but they are *lonely* lonely. None of the other Shadow People talk to them because they broke up our Family. And they *know* now they did wrong. They know it, because all is revealed in the Shadow World, *all* is revealed. And they feel ashamed ashamed, and they hate themselves and they hate each other, and that's how it'll always be for them, poor things, poor poor things, for ever and ever and ever.'

David stood up, one hand on the back of his buckhorse. Michael's names, I *hated* all this. It was *my* boys they were talking about, my boys and their friends. How dare they talk about them like that? But I knew from the past what would happen if I tried to speak out. Everyone would yell at me and shout at me. People would warn me I'd end up being an enemy of Family too if I wasn't careful. People would ask whose side was I on. People would hiss that they could see where my boys got it from. So I kept quiet, with only silent tears to show how I felt inside.

'Yeah,' David said. 'Dying in the cold and hating themselves forever. That's what you get for trying to break our Family, and that's why we have Guards now to make sure it never happens again.'

'Oh I know, I know,' wailed Lucy Lu, 'I know it has to be. But when you see them as I see them, you can't help feeling sorry for them: always lonely, always miserable, always with the cold of Snowy Dark creeping through them and always . . . always . . .'

She stopped because we could hear shouting voices coming from forest behind us on the Peckham side of the clearing. In came three more of David's Guards, dragging along another young man, with a buck on a rope following behind them.

The Guards didn't take any notice of the fact that an Any Virsry was going on, and they paid no attention to the person in middle of Circle who was supposed to be Family Head.

'David! David! Look who we found skulking around outside Family. Look who it is!'

Who *was* it? He looked familiar – that narrow, clever face with the wispy blond beard – but we hadn't seen him for a long time, and he'd grown, and we'd never seen him looking so scared before. But Gela's sweet heart, it was one of them! It was one of our lost kids!

'Let go of me,' snapped Mehmet Batwing, 'I wasn't skulking. I came down here to talk to you. I've got things you might want to know about.'

'Talk then!' growled David. 'Talk!'

'Never mind David, Mehmet,' I yelled. 'Talk to *us*! Where's our kids? Where's Gerry? Where's Jeff? Where's John?'

Other people started calling out and coming forward too, mums, sisters, brothers. The Guards quickly stepped in to keep us back and away from Mehmet and David, but they couldn't stop us calling out.

'Where's Tina and Harry? Where's Jane?'

'What about Dix? Dixon Brooklyn, I mean? And Gela and Clare, are they alright?'

'No, talk about Lucy first. Lucy Batwing. Tell us about her!'

David raised his hands for quiet before Mehmet could answer.

'One at a time, one at a time!'

He turned to me.

'And you can forget John,' he said. 'He's not part of Family any more. He's none of our business.'

'That's right,' chipped in Lucy Lu, staring at us all with her weepy eyes. 'Tommy and Angela told me themselves, remember? They told me we should forget that John Redlantern ever existed, and never speak of him again.'

'Oh shut up, Lu, you silly woman, you just told us they were all dead!' said a big Batwing woman called Angie. She was Mehmet's auntie. It had been her who'd raised the boy up after a leopard did for his mum. 'You come here, Mehmet my pet. Come to Auntie Angie.'

'Yes, and I *want* to hear about John,' called my sister Jade, 'I want to hear about him!'

And she looked at me guiltily, as if she doubted her own right to get involved.

'Gela and Clare Brooklyn,' someone else was calling. 'Are they alright? Tell us that they didn't die in the snow!'

'What about Julie Blueside? And Angie and Candy?'

Everyone was pushing forward, crowding round Mehmet and David and the Guards.

'What about Dave and Johnny and Suzie Fishcreek. How are they? Suzie's alright, isn't she?'

It was weird. Even before I heard Mehmet's answer I knew what it would be. Everyone was yelling yelling at the same time, but when Suzie's mum called out, a kind of hollowness suddenly opened up in middle of all that noise.

'No,' Mehmet said, 'Dave and Johnny are still alive, but Suzie is dead.'

And whole Family was silent then, completely silent. You could hear the *hmmmmmmmm* of the misty forest all around us, the *hmmph, hmmph, hmmph* of the trees nearby.

'Dead?' said Suzie Fishcreek's mum, smiling broadly like he'd just told a joke. '*Dead?* No, that can't be . . . You just told us . . . Well, you didn't *tell* us but the fact that you're here proves that . . . Well . . .'

She giggled.

'No, not dead,' she said firmly.

Poor woman. Mehmet had brought her sons and her daughter back to life for her when he came into the clearing, just like he'd

brought Jeff and Gerry back to life for me. Suzie had leapt out of
Snowy Dark for her, alive and well. And now, a few minutes later,
she was dead again.

'Yes, dead,' said Mehmet. 'That fool John led us up onto the snow.
He had no proper plan. He didn't know what to expect. It's only
luck that we didn't all die. But Suzie *did* die. There's a terrible kind of
leopard up there, a white leopard that can throw its voice from one
place to another. It did for her up there, her and one of our bucks,
and it drove off the other one with Jeff on it, so we were all left in
Dark.'

My heart went cold. The world closed in round me. I felt like I
couldn't breathe. Was Mehmet going to kill off *my* child as well?

'Jeff?' I cried. 'It drove Jeff off? What happened to him? Did he
come back? Is Jeff alright?'

'He was alright last time I saw him.'

'Well, so's Suzie then,' said Suzie's mum, smiling round at the
people around her. 'She's not dead. Mehmet's here, isn't he? Mehmet
is here to prove that they're all okay!'

'Suzie died,' Mehmet said. 'Last I heard all the others were alive.
Dave Fishcreek was with me earlier this waking. He came down with
me from Tall Tree Valley, but he ran off when you guys started yelling
at us and waving spears. Johnny Fishcreek, and Julie and Angie and
Candy Blueside, they're all back up there in Tall Tree Valley. We've got
our own little Tall Tree group up there. Three babies too.'

'And Jeff? And Gerry?'

'All the others stayed with John. He had to keep going, didn't he?
Tall Tree Valley is a good place – all the bucks you could wish for – but
he had to go back up onto Dark again, trying to find the way across
to the other side.'

So of course me and all the other mums and sisters and brothers
and friends were calling out to know more again.

'It gets cold up where we are sometimes,' Mehmet said, 'and snow
comes down. But it doesn't kill us, does it? It's not cold like up on

Snowy Dark. And it's not dark either. But, first time the snow came down, off they all went, the bloody fools, Tina, Dix, Janny, Gerry, Jeff, dumb old Harry, all that lot, following that crazy John, that crazy killer John, back up onto Dark where Suzie died, and where we all *nearly* died, and would have done too if Jeff hadn't come back for us. Good luck to them, they'll need it.

'But me and Dave and Johnny and the Blueside girls, we figured we could work out how to deal with a bit of snow. We *have* figured it out too. We wear thick wraps. We make strong shelters and big fires. We turn bucks into horses. It's a good life up there. We get all the buckmeat we could ever want, and all the . . .'

'My Jeff came back for you, you said,' I called out. 'What did he do? Where had he gone? Where did he come back *from*?'

But David stepped in before I got an answer.

'Never mind that now. Tell us what you mean by *killer* John?'

Mehmet gave a weird little smirk. His head was cradled against his big fierce auntie's enormous breasts – she'd pushed her way through the Guards like they were little kids – and he had other Batwing people standing round him, stroking him and touching him like they couldn't believe he was real. He could tell he wasn't in danger now and he was enjoying the attention and the power he had over us all.

'Oh, didn't you know, David?' he asked. 'Didn't you know that John did for your friend Dixon Blueside? Speared him from behind when he was trying to get back here. And Gerry and Harry – you know, Gerry Redlantern and big old, dumb old Harry Spiketree – they did for the other two that Dixon had with him. Harry did for John Blueside. And Gerry, well, I'm afraid Gerry did for his own groupmate Met.'

Oh Gela's crying eyes! What a thing Mehmet had let loose! We'd guessed that something bad had happened, something bad enough to make whole bunch of them suddenly head off up to Dark, but we'd never known what that something was. Now John Blueside's mum, and all the rest of Blueside group too, began to yell and bellow across the clearing at Redlantern and Spiketree, pushing forward against Guards, who held them back with the sticks of their spears.

And Met's mum, my own cousin Candice, turned on me.

'*No, no, no, no, no, no!*' she screamed. 'I hate Gerry, I hate him, I hate him, I hate him.'

She snatched at my eyes with her nails like a tree fox, scratching my face so I bled. People pulled her off me then, but she carried on screaming. Other people were joining in too, screaming and screaming: Blueside people screaming at Spiketree and Redlantern people, Redlantern people screaming at one another, all in the little fuggy space of the clearing with the thick fug all around and the fake Circle in middle of it all.

And then Suzie Fishcreek's mum finally heard in her mind what her ears had heard a little while ago. Suzie was dead. Her daughter had been torn apart by a white leopard that lived in Dark and the snow. Over all the other screaming and shouting, she let out one single horrible high-pitched shriek.

'*Silence!*' bellowed David.

Everyone was quiet.

'Silence,' he said again, glaring round at us.

Gela's eyes, I'm a batface too and I'm no beauty myself, but he looked ugly *ugly*.

'Screaming and yelling won't solve anything,' David said. 'What's needed now is to get that killer John and spike him up, just like I always said we should. Him and his creepy friend Gerry and that baby-man Harry. You all thought I was being hard, but if we'd spiked Juicy John up when I first suggested it, there'd be four people alive now who are all dead. This time we're going to do it my way.'

'Yes, but they're right across the other side of Snowy Dark,' I whispered to myself. 'Thank Gela, they're *far* away from here. David is only play-acting. There's nothing he can really do.'

'Yes, John is a killer,' Mehmet said. 'He could have killed any of us.

That's the only reason I went with him over the top in the first place. I didn't want to go. I spoke out against it. I told him I didn't agree with the killings. But . . .'

David took no notice of any of this.

'You bring us down some of those buckhorses of yours, Mehmet, if you really want to be our friends. And bring us some of those warm wraps. And show us the way the others went over the mountains.'

'Oh yes, I will,' Mehmet said. 'I surely will. I don't want to break with Family. We Tall Tree people don't want to break with Family. One of us was a cousin of John Blueside, don't forget, and three of us grew up with him and Dixon Blueside in their group. We want to get back at their killers as much as you do.'

'Then maybe we can sort something,' David said, 'us and you. Maybe you can be part of Family again.'

'I don't think that's down to you, David,' came Caroline's voice from behind him. 'It's for Council to decide things like that, Council and me as Fam . . .'

'Bucks and wraps and information,' David said to Mehmet, completely ignoring Caroline – and from that moment on, we lost any last notion we had that her or Council counted for anything at all – 'bucks and wraps and information. That'll show us which side you're on.'

'Gela is talking to me,' cried Lucy Lu. 'Gela is talking to me now. She's explaining things. And I see now why I thought that John and the others were dead. The truth is that they're *worse* than dead. Even to the Shadow People they seem dead. Even to the Shadow People, think of that! In one way I misunderstood what the Shadow People were telling me, that's true, but in a deeper way, I did understand, I understood *too* well. That's what Angela says. They're not just dead. They're *worse* than dead.'

'John says he talks to Gela too,' Mehmet said.

Michael's names, you should have seen how Lucy Lu changed when she heard that! All the dreaminess and weepiness disappeared in a moment. Her face went all twisty. She looked like she was crouching ready to pounce. She looked like a hunter about to make a kill.

'Him?' she snarled. 'Him talk to Angela? Ha! Don't make me *laugh*.'

'Yes, but listen to this. He fools people *because he's got Gela's ring*!'

There was a gasp from whole Family.

'What do you mean?' demanded David. 'What do you mean, her ring?'

'The lost ring, like in the story. The one she lost and then cried and cried for wakings afterwards. I've seen it myself. You can tell it comes from Earth easy easy. It's made of metal – it's smooth smooth, and shiny – and it's got tiny writing inside it: "*To Angela with love from Mum and Dad*", that's what it says. I've seen it myself. John found the ring in forest near here and told no one, kept it all to himself, and then he destroyed our Circle.'

'You went over to him after he destroyed Circle, Mehmet,' I called out. 'Stop trying to pretend that you . . .'

But people yelled at me to shut up. They didn't want to think about that. They didn't want any complications. They wanted to think about the wonderful ring from Earth, the lost ring in the story, being found again, and they wanted to be angry angry with the arrogant newhair who'd destroyed Circle but kept the ring. He'd taken away *our* bit of the past without even asking us, and kept *his* own bit without even telling. He was my nephew and I loved him, but even I thought that was selfish and bad.

'This is Gela's Family,' David said. 'We're her children. That ring belongs to us.'

'Gela says we must get it back,' Lucy Lu confirmed, rolling back her eyes so you could only see the whites of them. 'I hear her now. Gela says we must get it back. Get the ring and punish wicked wicked John, who says he speaks in her name when he doesn't, he doesn't.' Her voice rose into a shriek. 'How *dare* he? *He doesn't! He doesn't! He doesn't!*'

She began to shake and tremble, like people do when they're having a fit.

'He must be killed. He must be killed like a slinker,' she hissed. 'Him and Gerry and Harry, all three of them. Kill them! Kill! Kill!'

Other people began to yell out the same thing, 'Kill! Kill!' and gradually it turned into a chant:

'*Kill! Kill! Kill! Kill! Kill! Kill!*'

Jade reached out her hand to me and we held onto each other while the crowd around us shouted for the death of our own sons.

'*Kill! Kill! Kill! Kill! Kill! Kill!*'

Mehmet had a strange look on his face. Standing there with his auntie's arm still around him, he looked half-pleased by the effect he had had, half-scared by what he had set off. He had done a terrible thing, coming down from Dark, and feeding our fear and hate to serve his own ends. But all the same, you couldn't deny – even I couldn't deny – that it was John who'd started it, John who'd killed another human being for the first time ever in Eden. And that was like the spark that lights a fire. There would be no end to the killing now, no end, not unless it killed us all.

41

John Redlantern

I'd destroyed Circle of Stones. I'd got a bunch of people over Dark. I'd proved that human beings didn't have to live forever in Circle Valley. I'd done all those hard hard things, but what was left for me?

Did I do all that, I thought, just to live quietly quietly in our own little family, hunting and scavenging and raising up kids?

Everyone could hunt and build shelters and raise up kids, that was the thing, and some of the others could do all that a lot better than me. Dix was a better hunter. Harry was stronger. Gela was better at sorting out quarrels. Jeff was best at turning baby bucks into horses that would let us ride them. The one thing I was good at, the one special thing about me, which no one could do even *half* as well as me, was breaking out of something old and making something new. Was I going to accept that I'd never do any of that again, when I was only barely grown up, and that from now on other people were going to be better than me at doing everything?

Tom's dick and Harry's, no I wasn't! I *needed* to make something else happen, and, what's more, *they* needed me to do it too, even if they didn't know it themselves, because otherwise they would get bored bored bored. That's why people let me lead them, because I knew what they needed even before they did, and because I saved them from getting bored.

'We should go further,' I said to Tina, sitting at the end of a waking on the bank of L-pool. 'We've been here for two wombs now, less than a waking's walk away from bottom of Snowy Dark, with whole of Wide Forest out there waiting for us.'

'We're far enough from Family already, John,' she said. 'No one wants to go further than this from their friends and their mums and everyone.'

'Okay, well, maybe we should go back to Family, then? Go back over and get some more of them to come and join us.'

'John,' Tina said, almost like she was explaining something to a kid. 'You destroyed Circle, remember? You broke up Family. You did for Dixon Blueside. Okay, Family doesn't know what happened exactly but they know something did, and they're not going to forgive us for it, are they? David Redlantern isn't, that's for sure. Come on, you know that!'

'Of course I know but . . . I reckon we could sneak up on Family without him knowing. See if more of them want to come and join us?'

Tina snorted. 'Yeah, we could try, until it ended up being *us* with spears stuck through us and *our* heads cracked open. There's a lot more of them than us, remember, John.'

I sat with my feet in the water, with tiny shining fishes nibbling at my toes. Three four yards out, beyond the trees that grew up out of the edge of the water, I could see pink oysters shining, and I thought of suggesting we dive for them like we'd done back at Deep Pool.

'Or maybe David and his mates would decide *not* to do for all of us,' Tina said. 'Maybe they'd keep some of us girls, and do to each one of us what Dixon Blueside tried to do to me.'

She chucked a bit of stone out into the water.

'Yeah,' she added, glancing round at me, 'and come to that, maybe they'd do to you what David first suggested they do. Remember? Tie you to a spiketree to burn, the way hunters cook meat.'

'Yeah, well. It's just something to think about, that's all. Either going back to Circle Valley to get more of them to join us, or pushing forward ourselves. There's no point in just sitting here.'

She didn't even answer that. She pulled her feet out of the water and turned to face me. Her face was tired but she managed to smile.

'So do you want a slip, then? Have a go at making another baby?'

I said yes, but, once she'd got my juice, all Tina wanted to do was go back to the shelters and sleep.

I couldn't rest, though. I got my spears and my hunting bag and went out into forest alone. I'd often gone out on long trips, for two three four wakings. Sometimes Gerry came with me, sometimes Jeff came, riding on the back of Def, sometimes one two of the others, but often I went on my own. I'd scald my meat on a hot spiketree, and sleep between whitelantern roots with my spear ready in my hand.

~ ~ ~

Once, thirty forty wakings after we first came down into Wide Forest, I'd been been out on my own like that, a waking away from L-pool, when I woke up from a short sleep to hear a snuffling scrunching sound ahead of me. Thinking it would be bucks of some kind, I crept forward on my belly through starflowers to try and do for one of them. Buckmeat would be too heavy to carry, but I reckoned I could manage to take back a skin.

I was almost on top of the creatures before I saw them, and realized they weren't bucks at all. They were tall as trees, standing on four legs that were each the height of a man, and black all over, *black* black like leopards. They had long long necks, and at the top of their necks, just below their big long heads, they had two strong arms with hands. Two of the animals were slowly feeding from the trees, pulling the branches towards their mouth feelers with their hands and biting off the shining lanternflowers. A third one had its neck bent down to the ground, and was pulling up starflowers in armfuls and feeding them to its slowly scrunching mouth.

I put an arrow on my bow, but I found I couldn't bring myself to shoot. It seemed wrong somehow to try and do for something that had grown so big. And anyway, what could one person do with a thing that size? So I lowered my bow and, instead of shooting, I called out to the creatures.

'Hey, big guys! Look at me!'

All three of them stopped. The one with its head down lifted it a bit, the two with their heads up lowered them, and the three of them together stared at me with their round, flat, flickering eyes, snuffling and blowing and chewing. One of them gave a belch – I could smell the sour stink from where I lay – and then all three of them just carried on eating as if I wasn't there.

I found that they'd left a wide strip of darkness stretching away through forest where they'd been. It was twenty thirty yards wide, a wide dark strip with no lanterns or starflowers growing in it. Even flutterbyes left it alone. I followed it for half a waking, further away still from L-pool and all the others, thinking to myself that this was what it would be like on Earth to walk in a forest at Night.

But then, ahead and over to the right, I saw a new light shining through the trees, smooth and soft like the light of pools and streams. I knew straight away that it was that smooth watery light we'd seen from the ridge, and ran towards it.

Gela's sweet heart, I came to the edge of the trees, and there it was: a huge shining pool, so big you couldn't see the other side, and deep deep, with giant wavyweed shining down there, like another Wide Forest under the water.

I stood there for a long long time, looking down on it from a low cliff. Fishes swam through its branches like bats and birds. Little hills of water moved steadily across it until they toppled over on the shore. I couldn't see the ends of it to the left or the right.

'You can't see the other side!' I shouted to the others as soon as I got back. 'You can't see the ends of it! It's like that C back on Earth. Worldpool, we should call it. It's another whole world, like Forest, or Dark, or Underworld! Think of that! Maybe we should leave this place, move over there, make strong boats and go and see what's on the other side!'

But Gela just laughed.

'All that work you put into building that wide fence here, John, and now you want to leave it all when you haven't even finished.'

'And how would Earth find us when they came?' asked Dix.

It had been two three wakings before I'd even managed to persuade any of them to come over to Worldpool and look.

~ ~ ~

Remembering that made me feel me feel angry and sad as I headed away from L-pool and back to Worldpool again. I must have been there twenty thirty times since my first visit.

Somehow I needed to get them all to move again. And at some point, somehow, we'd need to get back in contact with Family. Okay, Tina was right, we might end up being speared, or spiked up on a tree, but everyone had to die some time. People drowned, and got eaten by leopards, and died from infected slinker bites, and cancer, and sap-burns. Babies got born that couldn't suck, and starved while their mothers' breasts ached with milk. *Everyone* had to die, and death was usually nasty nasty, but there were still choices in life, it could still be better or worse.

I slashed out at a jewel bat swooping down in front of me.

'Tom's neck, I didn't split up dozy Old Family just to make another dozy Family on the other side of Dark. I did it to make things *new*.'

But the only one of the others that was still trying to make new things happen was Jeff with his baby bucks.

42

Tina Spiketree

My first baby I called Peter. He was a little batfaced boy, who looked like my sister, and I knew for sure his dad was Dix.

My next baby was a girl and I called her Star. I didn't expect this, but John loved her straight away. He was always picking her up. He was always offering to take her over to the pool to bathe her. And for a while he even stopped wandering off on his trips through Forest over to his precious Worldpool.

I thought for a little while that he'd finally learnt how to be at ease with ordinary life, and then I remembered how John found it hard to be with his equals, and thought maybe *that* was why a baby was easier for him. A baby doesn't answer back, does it?

'I *am* Star's dad, right?' he asked me, when Star was five six periods old. 'We made her that time we slipped next to the pool, didn't we?'

We were by the pool now, in pretty much the exact same spot he was thinking about. He was holding Star in the water, and she was kicking her little fat legs.

I wished he hadn't asked me. I knew he longed for me to say yes, and I thought, Shall I lie and tell him he's the dad for certain? But I didn't like lying, and nor did John, so I told the truth.

'She could be yours, John, but she could be Mike's too. Not long

361

before I fell pregnant with her, I slipped with him once twice while we were out scavenging, and you were way away over bloody old Worldpool or somewhere.'

When he heard that, he lifted Star out of the water, handed her over to me and went off into forest for half a waking. I wished then that I'd told him a lie. It wouldn't even have been a big lie, because it *could* have been him that was Star's dad, and I felt I'd been mean to him, insisting on the truth. I could see how it would be a special thing for someone like John to have a little girl or boy that he knew for certain was his own.

'It probably was you, John,' I told him when he got back. 'It really probably was you that time by the pool.'

I tried to reach and kiss him but he sat stiffly and wouldn't relax into it. He nodded, and ruffled Star's head, and then turned and gave me a little stiff smile.

'It doesn't matter anyway,' he told me. But I could see it did. All the restlessness had come back into him.

And at the end of that waking, when we were all eating fruit and stonebuck meat round our fire, with bats swooping overhead, he announced that he was planning to go back up Tall Tree Valley.

'*Why?*' I asked.

'No point in cutting ourselves off from Mehmet's lot, is there?' he said. 'We all set out together across Dark, didn't we? There's no reason why we can't be friends. They might even want to come down here with us, if we told them what it was like.'

'But wouldn't this just be stirring up an ant's nest?' Janny said.

'Yeah,' Jane said, 'it's been three wombs since we left them. What makes you think they'd want to see us now?'

'And do you really think Mehmet will be so glad to see you, John?' asked Gela, looking up from her second little one sucking at her breast. 'Let's face it, he wasn't exactly crazy about you even *before* you left him up there with just the other five for company.'

'Who's Mehmet?' asked little Fox.

His mum Clare laughed. She had three kids around her now. Our little group had grown. The fourteen who'd walked here from Tall Tree Valley were all grownups. The two babies that came with us – Fox and Flower – were little kids. And there'd been another ten new babies since, ten that had lived, with more on the way.

'I think they'd be glad to hear from us up there,' Clare said, 'I reckon they'd be glad to see anyone after all this time. I mean there's not so many of us here, but there were only *six* of them up there, remember. They must be going completely nuts if they haven't already done for each other.'

'That's true,' Gela admitted, 'and they'll have had kids too. It'd be nice to see their kids.'

'It would be nice to see anyone at all that wasn't us,' Janny said.

'It could be they've all gone back to Family,' said Jeff.

Jeff had grown his new hairs now and he had changed. He was *beautiful* beautiful, with fine features and a strong slim body to go with his big deep eyes. All the other seven girls wanted to slip with him and he obliged them just as much as they wanted, like he was making up for all the time when no one would accept him as a proper boy, only as a clawfoot who was outside all of that. For myself, though, somehow I couldn't quite forget Jeff the funny little kid whose sore feet I'd washed back at Cold Path Neck.

'They'd never do that,' John said with a snort. 'Go crawling back to Family after what happened to Dixon and Met and John Blueside? They wouldn't dare.'

'They might, though,' Jeff said. 'It wasn't any of them that did for those three. Remember how Mehmet liked to remind you about that?'

John shrugged.

'Only one way to find out.'

He stood up, looking back towards Snowy Dark.

'Eventually we'll need to get back in contact with Family itself anyway. Not now, obviously, but when we're strong enough.'

We all looked at each other. Gela's tits, was this man never going to leave anything alone? Must he constantly be poking and meddling around with the lives of everyone on Eden? 'You'll get us all done for, one waking,' said Lucy Batwing. 'The way you keep putting us in danger again and again.'

'Well, I'm not suggesting we get in touch with Family *now*, am I?' John said, laughing. 'I'm just suggesting going up as far as Tall Tree Valley, to see Mehmet and the others. Surely there's no harm in that?'

43

John Redlantern

Me and Gerry and Jeff went back to Tall Tree Valley. It meant going up over Dark again, but crossing Dark wasn't the same as it had been before. It didn't seem so far when you knew for certain there was something there to get to and you knew how to find it. (And that made me realize that it wasn't really so far back to Circle Valley either. This journey that everyone had said was impossible for five six generations: you could walk whole of it easily in six seven wakings.) We each had a fullgrown woollybuck of our own to ride on now, and we each pulled a big snow-boat behind us. Mine was loaded with food and spare wraps for us. Theirs were piled with things to trade with the Tall Tree people: smooth widebuck skins that they'd never have seen before, and fruits you couldn't find up there.

It was weird weird when we'd got over the high Dark and dropped down into Tall Tree Valley to find Mehmet and Johnny and Julie still up there near the place where we'd all once lived together after Jeff saved us from Dark. And they were men and women now, young men and women, not newhairs any more, and they had five six little kids running round, and strong strong shelters they'd made with stones. They'd covered them over with branches and sealed up the roofs and walls with mud and buckskins so they'd keep out the cold, even in the snow.

Tom's dick, they were *surprised* surprised to see us, surprised and scared, like we were Shadow People or something, come back to life again from death.

'We thought it might be time to make friends again,' I told them.

Mehmet stared at me for a moment, and then suddenly he smiled.

'Friends! Yes, friends!' He rushed forward to shake my hand. 'That's right, John, we should be friends. We're grownups now, after all, not newhair kids. We should put our little arguments behind us, like kids' quarrels.'

And he hugged me and gestured to the other Tall Tree people to come and do the same.

'Let's get a buck roasting,' he called out to them. 'Let's get the fire built up, get a good blaze going for a big roast.'

Julie kissed me and Gerry and Jeff.

'Wow, look at *you*, Jeff!' said Julie. 'Wow! You look *fine* fine. I can't believe how you've changed.'

Who would have thought weird little Jeff would turn out to be the one that girls wanted to slip with as soon as they saw him, clawfeet and all?

'The others still around, are they?' I asked. 'Dave Fishcreek? Angie? Candy?'

'Candy died having her baby,' Julie said shortly. 'The others are out hunting with . . .'

Mehmet hastily interrupted.

'Yes, I should explain, John. We've got a couple of visitors up here from Family. Don't worry,' he gave an awkward laugh, 'it's not David Redlantern or anyone like that. Just a couple of Fishcreek people, come up to trade a few bucks for some blackglass. I don't know how you're fixed where you are, but we haven't got any blackglass up here and we kind of need it.'

And then he sort of *peeked* at us, like he was in a hiding place and peering out, and not really standing right there in front of us at all.

'You got blackglass at all where you are?' he asked.

'Come to think of it,' he said, without even waiting for us to answer that first question, 'where *is* it exactly that you're staying now? Is it far from here?'

'Not really,' began Gerry, 'just over the ridge there and then . . .'

Mehmet was leaning forward, listening intently.

'Oh, it's a fair distance,' I said, to cut Gerry off, 'quite a few wakings' journey. That's why we've never been up before.'

Mehmet looked between Gerry and me and smiled his complicated smile. And presently Angie and Dave Fishcreek came back with a couple of young Fishcreek men called Paul and Gerald. Harry's dick, those two's faces looked even *more* like they thought we were Shadow People come back from the dead than the faces of the Tall Tree people had done. As soon as they saw us, they stopped dead where they were, their muscles tensed up, ready to fight or run, and their fingers tightened around their spears. But Mehmet ran over to them, gabbling excitedly.

'Who'd have thought it, eh? We thought maybe the rest of them hadn't made it through Dark, after they left us here. But it's John, look. Old John Redlantern himself, and Gerry and Jeff with him. Nice to see them, eh? Nice to have a chance to put old troubles behind us.'

'Er . . . yeah . . .' said Paul Fishcreek and Gerald Fishcreek, uncertainly, still fingering their spears.

'So how is Family these wakings?' I asked them. 'Caroline still Head, is she?'

'Caroline? Um. Yes,' said Gerald, looking at Paul.

'How about our mum?' Gerry asked. 'Sue Redlantern. She okay, do you know?'

'Yeah. She's good,' said Paul.

'You guys still hate us down there, then?' I asked.

Gerald and Paul Fishcreek looked at each other like they were in agony.

'Oh no, no . . .' they both began.

Tom's dick and Harry's, there was weird stuff going on, *weird* weird, but I couldn't tell exactly what it was. When we'd eaten Tall Tree's buckmeat and the Tall Tree people had got to their usual sleeping time, I refused Mehmet's offer of a space in one of their shelters and found somewhere else a little way from them, where me and Jeff and Gerry and our bucks could get some rest with solid rocks against our backs, and could get a good view of anyone that came near.

'It's not so cold that we need a shelter,' I explained to the Tall Tree people, 'and of course we've been keeping different wakings to you. We'll be more comfortable out there where we can talk and get up and move around without disturbing you.'

I told Gerry and Jeff I'd keep the first lookout, but none of the three of us had actually gone off to sleep when, after an hour or so, we heard someone creeping up. We grabbed our spears ready. But it wasn't Mehmet or Dave or Johnny or the Fishcreek blokes, which I'd truly thought it might be, sneaking up on us with leopard tooth knives. It was Julie.

'Hey, Jeff, do you want to slip with me?'

I suppose life wasn't much fun for them up there. It was cold, and nothing happened, and, when they didn't have visitors, each of them only had four other people to talk to, apart from the little kids.

'That would be good, Julie,' Jeff said.

And he did it with her, right there in the space beside the rock, slowly slowly and gently – and quietly quietly like you do when other people are near – and afterwards he held Julie in his arms on the sleeping skins and they talked, softly softly so as to let me and Gerry sleep if we wanted to. But I didn't sleep. I lay there listening to the sound of their talking, while the strange tall trees hummed all around us.

Most of the time, it was too quiet for me to hear the words, but once Jeff raised his voice slightly, not in anger (he was hardly ever angry) but firmly to make a point.

'They were protecting me and Tina, Julie!' he said. 'They didn't just do it for no reason! You know that!'

I didn't pick up any more of what they said after that but after a while I heard Julie begin to sob and Jeff comfort her. That's why girls loved him, not only because of his beautiful eyes and his face and his golden hair and his long fine fingers and the way he could slip on and on until they'd had enough, but because he was kind.

Maybe an hour later a kid began to cry over in one of the stone shelters, and Julie recognized it as her own.

'Michael's names, Jeff,' muttered Gerry enviously, after she'd gone. 'How do you bloody *do* it?'

But Jeff had more worrying things to talk about.

'John, Gerry, listen to this,' he whispered. 'Mehmet has been down to Family. It wasn't so long after we left Tall Tree last time. Apparently David Redlantern is the only one who really decides what happens in Family now. He's got a whole bunch of young guys called Guards, who make people do what he wants, and Caroline doesn't matter any more. Julie says Mehmet's done a deal with David to get the friendship of Family back. She doesn't know what the deal is exactly, and she's sure that Mehmet hasn't told them whole story, but she reckons he's promised he'll help them to get to you. One thing Mehmet has told her and the other Tall Tree people is that David still wants to kill both of you two, and Harry as well. He still says he wants to spike you up to burn like Jesus, for killing Met and Dixon and John Blueside. And Julie says Mehmet's told David about Gela's ring. Apparently David hates you for that too, he hates you for keeping it for yourself.'

'Bloody Mehmet Batwing,' I said, taking my spear and jumping up. 'That treacherous little slinker.'

In my mind I saw that giant bat on the top of the tree, with the slinker creeping up towards it through the steam.

'I'll go and do for him now,' I said. 'I'll kill him before he can do any more harm.'

'That won't work,' Jeff said. 'Just killing another person won't work.'

Well, no, I had to admit it wouldn't. Not unless I killed *everyone* here: the two Fishcreek guys and Johnny and Dave and Angie and Julie and all their kids. Otherwise there'd still be someone left to tell Family that we'd been here and that our camp wasn't so far away, somewhere just over the ridge.

'Not all of Family is your enemy,' Jeff reminded me. 'And not all of these people here are either, not any more. But if you killed again you'd make *more* enemies, wouldn't you? You'd make it easier and easier for everyone to see you as nothing but a killer, like a leopard that needs to be hunted down. You were the first one in Eden to kill a human being, after all.'

Gerry just sat on his sleeping skin looking up at us. This was outside of his reach. This was difficult grownup stuff between me and his little brother.

'Gela's eyes,' I muttered, after I'd thought about it for a bit. 'I've got it all wrong, haven't I? Things weren't perfect before I chucked those stones into the stream, but look at it now! I've taken Eden and broken it up into pieces.'

There are lots of different stories branching away all the time from every single thing that happens. As soon as a moment has gone, different versions of it start to be remembered and told about. And some of them carry on, and some die out, and you can't know in advance which version will last and which won't. It had never occurred to me before that the story of John Redlantern might end up as the story of a famous killer, the first one in Eden ever to do for another human being. But now that story suddenly took shape in my mind.

I could see it being acted out in the future. *John the Leopard-Man*; John who killed a leopard and ate its heart and somehow the heart crept into him and became his own; John who sang sweetly and treacherously like a leopard does, and promised wonderful things, and made people leave everything and walk towards him, but really all he did was to lead them to their deaths. Death followed after him. It spread out from him across the world like ripples across a pool, like evil ripples. But then at last brave David Redlantern hunted him down, just like you'd hunt down a leopard that had taken to prowling around outside the fence and watching the kids playing inside. Brave ugly David hunted him down with his Guards, and then the world was safe again and Family was whole once more.

'No, John, you didn't break it, you opened it up,' Jeff said. 'That was why we followed you. It needed to be opened up. It needed to happen.'

He looked at me with his big deep eyes, putting his hands on my shoulders. I'll tell you, I was pretty near to crying.

'Still,' he said, 'that's not to say that you don't sometimes make mistakes.'

I nodded.

'We'd better go then,' I said. 'Let's just get straight on these bucks and go back over Dark.'

Gerry looked at his brother, his eyes big and as gentle as Jeff's but without the depth, waiting to hear Jeff's judgement. Jeff shook his head.

'That won't work, though, will it, John? That'll tell Mehmet we know something. It will tell him that someone here has told us something that worried us enough to make us leave in a hurry. If we don't want that, we should stay till everyone wakes. We should let them have the widebuck skins and the fruit we've brought for them, trade them for some of the blackglass they get from Family. And then we should tell them we'll come up and see them again soon soon, and hug and kiss them, and say goodbye, and go.'

Gerry looked at me.

I laughed.

'I didn't know you were capable of being so devious, Jeff.'

To my surprise, Jeff hung his head. He really hated lies and tricks.

'I know. But I don't think we have a choice.'

We looked out at the strange tall trees, humming and shining, with the bats and flutterbyes diving and swooping among their high branches.

'We are here,' Jeff muttered, as if to remind himself of a truth that stayed true no matter how much we lied and tricked each other. 'We really are here.'

I touched Gela's ring on my little finger, felt its hardness, turned it round a bit. We were brothers and sisters really, all of us, that was the weird part. Me, Mehmet, David Redlantern: every one of us in Eden came from the same mother and the same father.

~ ~ ~

So when Mehmet and the others began to stir and poke up their fire and get things ready for another waking, we went down to them, pretending that nothing had changed.

'We need to get back to our own people,' I told Mehmet. 'It took us a long long time to get here, and they might think a snow leopard has got us if we don't show our faces soon. But maybe you'd like to trade with us a bit before we go? We've got these skins, look, like woollybuck skins but smooth. And fruit, like you get down in Circle Valley. What can you trade us for this lot?'

And then we were off again, up over Dark, till we came to the ridge looking out over the Wide Forest.

'Look at that!' I said. 'Even from here you can see the smoke of our fire down there. They could easily find us.'

The air was still, and the smoke went straight up like a tree trunk, lit up clear and white by the lanternlight of Wide Forest.

'Yes, and look at *that*!' said Jeff, pointing back.

I looked round. On the snowy slope behind us were three patches of light from the headlanterns of three woollybucks. It was Mehmet and a couple of the others. They'd been behind us all the way, following to see which way we'd go. They'd only need to come as far as this ridge we were on now to see Wide Forest below them, and the smoke rising up from our fire, all lit up by the firelight and by the lanterns all around it. And then Mehmet would know where we were living and he'd know we'd been lying when we said our camp was far away.

44

Tina Spiketree

When he came back down from Tall Tree Valley John was full full of himself, like he hadn't been for a long long time. He had all his authority back. He knew exactly what he was doing and how to carry everyone with him. And the funny thing was, he didn't have good news at all. He had *bad* bad news, but he was happy happy happy. It was just like when the snow came down into Tall Tree Valley: he liked having trouble to deal with.

'We need to leave this place,' he told us. 'David Redlantern and his lot could soon be down here after us. We need to get far enough away from here that they can't see the smoke from our fire from the top of the ridge. Where we are now, they could be here within twenty wakings if they put their mind to it.'

He looked back the way the three of them had just come down. There was a dip going on and Starry Swirl was filling up sky, bright bright and big as whole world, with the black shadow of Snowy Dark sharp up against it.

'We won't always run from them,' he told us. 'Time will come when we'll turn round and face them. And, if we need to, when that time comes, we'll fight David and his lot and beat them. But we're not ready for that now. There's only sixteen of us here, not counting little kids, and he could bring maybe fifty sixty grownup men and newhairs with him over the ridge, with blackglass spears and bows and everything. We're not ready for that. But a waking will come when there'll be more of us, and we'll have found our own blackglass, and then . . .'

'And then,' said Gela with a sigh, 'there'll be a lot more killing. There'll be lots and lots more red red blood. Harry's dick, John, you don't have to apologize for telling us to run away! Surely there's enough space in Eden for people who feel like doing for each other just to move apart and keep out of each other's way?'

'Yeah, and let's stop talking about killing, if you don't mind,' Clare said. 'What's poor Fox and Flower going to make of it, eh?'

The two children were both listening intently, their faces stiff. Poor things. It was never like that when *we* were littles. We might have been scared of leopards or slinkers sometimes, we might even have felt scared of grownup people who were angry or unkind, but we never never thought that other people might come and do for us on purpose.

'We need to take everything we can,' John said, 'skins, wraps, blackglass, spears, everything. Load it onto bucks, or carry it. We'll go that way,' he was standing facing Dark, and he pointed behind and to his left, 'along between the hills and Worldpool, but making our way over towards Worldpool till we're going along the edge of it. We'll keep going for ten wakings. That'll take us far enough from the ridge. After that we won't have to move so fast, but we'll still keep moving on every few wakings for a while, to get us a good long way away. We should be safe then for wombs and wombs, by Worldpool somewhere, far off from here. We could even make boats, if we wanted, make boats and figure out how to cross the water. Then we'll have somewhere else to go to if we have to get away again.'

Yes, we *could* be safe, I thought, but you won't like that, John. You'll get bored again. You'll do something to make things more exciting, just as you've just done by going up to Tall Tree Valley and stirring up an ant's nest, just like we feared would happen.

But I didn't say that then. We needed to move. Tom's dick, I did *not* want to be around when David Redlantern and his lot came over Dark, and I certainly didn't want my little ones to be there to see what they did to us. We needed to move. And of course I had to admit John was good at getting things moving.

We started to pack stuff up, sort things out, figure out just how much we could carry on our backs or load onto the seven woollybucks we had now managed to turn into horses. It wasn't all that much we could take with us when it came to it, not when Jeff had to ride on one buck, and we had twelve little ones to bring along with us, and we needed to take embers on a bark so we could make fires again without spending whole wakings trying to get a spark from twigs. Within a waking we had loaded up everything we could carry and were ready to leave our camp at L-Pool behind us, that big empty space inside John's fence that we'd hardly begun to fill up.

'The annoying thing is,' said Gela, 'that when David's lot do come over the top they'll find this place and make it their own. We've done all the work for them.'

It was probably true. From what John and Gerry and Jeff had heard up at Tall Tree, Family had been happy to steal all the ideas that John and the rest of us came up with, even though they condemned us for having them in the first place: they were turning bucks into horses over there now; they were making footwraps and headwraps and bodywraps. Why wouldn't they start their own camp in Wide Forest?

But who cared, eh? We'd be long gone when they arrived here.

~ ~ ~

Hunting and scavenging as we went along, we moved slowly through forest. The trees went *hmmmmmmm* all around us. Starbirds called to each other. Two three times we heard a leopard singing in the distance. Once we passed two of those huge slow animals that John had named Nightmakers, and three four times we crossed the wide dark paths they made through forest as they slowly munched up every shining flower on the trees and the ground. You could tell how old the paths were by the number of flowers that had grown back.

We went slow slow. There was a lot to carry, including all the little kids except for Fox and Flower, who'd walk a little way, and then ride up together on a buck, and then walk a little more.

About three four hours into the second waking, I went up to the front with my little boy Peter riding on my back in a buckskin sling. John was up there already walking next to Jeff on Def, with Gerry following on just behind them. John had Star in his arms. She was fast asleep and he bent from time to time to kiss the top of her head. Now that things were moving on again for him, he seemed to have forgiven her for maybe being Mike's kid and not his own, and he loved the sweet fresh smell of her hair.

'Why do we need to stop in one place at all?' I said to John. 'We could just keep moving on slowly forever.'

John beamed round at me. He was in a *good* good mood, relieved relieved to get away from that little place we'd made for ourselves by L-pool. Tom's neck, he'd worked for wakings and wakings on that big fence, scratching and cutting himself, wearing himself out, but now he'd left it behind without even a moment of regret. Moving was what he liked to do best.

'Now you're talking, Tina,' he said laughing. 'It *could* work, couldn't it? Just going a few hours further on each waking, perhaps, so we had time to hunt and scavenge and rest. We'd just need a few more bucks to ride on and carry our stuff, and we'd be fine, we'd never need to stop anywhere.'

We walked on a bit.

'You know,' John said after thinking for a little while, 'you really are right, Tina. It *would* be good to keep moving.'

I'd hardly ever heard him so willing to discuss anything that another person had suggested to him.

'But not heading *away* all the time,' he went on. 'Sooner or later we need to turn and face them. When there's a few more of us, I mean. When we're stronger. When we're ready. It's not good just to keep running *away*.'

I shrugged. Why *should* we ever turn round? Why *should* we face them? Eight nine wakings' journey from here, back in Circle Valley, Mehmet had probably already talked to David Redlantern. Now, or soon, David and his Guards would be gathering themselves together – their blackglass spears, their horsebucks, their bows and arrows, their knives, their clubs – and making their way up to Tall Tree Valley and on to the ridge beyond. And when they got there, they'd look down on Wide Forest as we had done. They'd be amazed amazed, like we'd been, and, for a while, their mouths would water at the thought of all that space and all that easy meat. But then they'd remember why they came, and they'd stop admiring Wide Forest for its own sake, and start searching searching searching for signs of us.

They'd have ridden on the backs of bucks, which was Jeff's idea, and they'd have followed the route that no one would have taken if it wasn't for John, but that wouldn't make any difference to them. They'd use the things we'd found, to hunt us down for daring to find them.

I didn't doubt, now Caroline was out of the way, that David Redlantern really would stick John onto a spiketree if he could, and let his skin burn off on its scalding bark, just as he'd always said he would. And I didn't doubt that if he got hold of me, he would do to me what Dixon Blueside would have done if John and the others hadn't come back to stop him. He'd hold me down and force himself up me and spurt his juice inside me, just to show how much power he had, and how little I had, however pretty I might be and however horrible and ugly he was. And if there was no one to stop him he wouldn't just do it once. He'd do it again and again and again, until he'd used me up, and he could chuck me aside, like the empty husk of a whitelantern fruit with its sweet flesh eaten away.

Why *should* we face all that, any more than we would choose to stick our arms down an airhole with a slinker hiding in it or pick up a piece of shit and force it down our throats? No, I thought, we should just go on and on and on. I even began to think that I'd go along with paddling out across Worldpool, if that's what it took to keep us safe. In fact I could see myself agreeing to any plan at all that would distract John from his idea of turning round and facing David.

But then my mood changed, and I thought that the further away we travelled from Circle Valley, the further we left behind all those other human beings too, the nice ones, like my mum, and nice batfaced Sue Redlantern, and all those others back in Family who weren't like David Redlantern at all. And even though we hadn't seen any of them since we left Cold Path Neck, it was sad to think that we might go so far far from them that there stopped being any possibility of contact again.

Yes, and there was Earth to think about too of course. It was dreadful dreadful to think of Earth coming for us and not being able to find us because we'd gone too far, so that David and all the others went back to that world of light, and we few were left behind here like Tommy and Angela had been, all alone in dark dark Eden.

And now I understood why John wanted to turn and face them. It wasn't just about fighting and killing. That was part of it, but it wasn't whole thing. It was also about staying *connected*. Even fighting was.

'Jeff was just saying that maybe we could get some baby leopards somehow and train them up like bucks to protect us,' John said, looking round at me for my opinion. 'Sounds worth a go, don't you think? If it works with bucks, why wouldn't it work with leopards too?'

He wasn't expecting it but I put my arm round his neck and kissed him. And he let me this time. He relaxed and laughed and kissed me back.

'And another idea me and Jeff had was about *cars*,' he told me. 'Do you remember that model Car that Oldest kept back in Family, with its four wheels? I reckon we could figure out how to make a kind of snow-boat with wheels that we could get bucks to pull along with our stuff on, even if there wasn't any snow.'

And then he talked about catching a baby nightmaker and turning that into a horse.

'Think of the load a thing like that would carry!' he said, looking round at me again to be sure that I was as excited about it as he was.

I laughed and kissed him again, and then fell behind a bit to see Dix, and ask him to take a turn with Peter, who was getting big now and was hard to carry for too long.

~ ~ ~

In two more wakings we reached Worldpool.

I'd been to the edge of Worldpool three four times since John first found it, but just seeing it was a different thing from walking along next to it. This way you really got a sense of how *big* big it was. It was a pool that you could walk alongside all of one waking and still not reach or see the end of it, a pool with ripples on it half as tall as a grownup, like moving hills of shining water, which you could look into and see shining fishes swimming inside, before they came toppling over to swirl round the rocks in white bubbles that caught the light from the plants and creatures below. It was a pool that stretched away from us, softly shining into the distance, but didn't reach another bank, like all the other water we'd ever seen, but stretched out instead to a far-off place where it seemed to touch the edge of the black black starry sky in a long straight line. But it wasn't really touching sky. That line was Eden itself, our own dark Eden, curving down and away from us, hiding even more wonders from our sight.

After we'd walked for half a waking, we came to a place where a river, thirty forty yards wide, had cut through the cliff and was pouring out into Worldpool over a shallow bed of stones. We and our bucks had to wade across it – it was waist deep in the middle – carrying our kids and all the stuff we had with us. Dix and Gerry carefully lifted the fire-bark above the water, with the embers glowing on their flat stone.

'Hey, look at this!' shouted Lucy Batwing in the middle of the stream.

She'd noticed something that was floating by. She caught it and brought it to shore to show John. It was a little toy boat made of a dry fruit skin rubbed with grease, like the ones little kids used to play with back in Family. But, Michael's names, how could a little thing like that end up here on the edge of Worldpool?

'Well, this must be Main River,' Jeff said. 'This must be where Main River comes to from the bottom of Exit Falls.'

It was strange strange to think that this exact same water had flowed down from Dixon Snowslug, and Cold Path Snowslug and all the other snowslugs and streams that fed into Circle Valley, strange to think it must have come through Deep Pool where me and John had dived for shining oysters, and through Longpool and Stream's Join and Main Stream, and on through Greatpool. It was strange to think that some little kid in Family, some kid probably not even born when we were back there, had played with this little boat up there, just like we used to do, among all those old familiar places. It can't even have been all that long ago. Grease or no grease, those little boats didn't last many wakings before they turned to mush.

'We'll come back here one waking,' John said, 'and follow the water up towards Dark. Maybe this is another way back into Circle Valley. Maybe we could climb up Exit Falls from below.'

Tom's dick, did he *never* let up?

~ ~ ~

There was a warm wind blowing in from Worldpool as we continued along the cliffs. It had a strange scent to it, rich and pungent, a bit like the way wavyweed smells when you spread it out on branches to dry it out for rope, but sweeter and more complicated. Birds and long-winged bats of kinds we'd never seen before gave out strange hoots and cries from little hiding places in the cliffs below us, and looked down at us from high high up under Starry Swirl.

We came across a completely new kind of creature lying below us on the rocks beside the water. There were twenty thirty of them, as big as widebucks and with a buck's mouth-feelers and big flat eyes, but they had no legs at all, only two little arms at the front with webbed hands on them like a duck, and four long fishy fins. They were *slow* slow when they were moving about on the rocks, just like a woollybuck or widebuck would be if it lost its legs and was trying to wriggle around without them. But in the water, among the wavy trees that swayed down there with their watery lanterns shining yellow and green, those great fat things swooped and dived as quickly and gracefully as bats hunting flutterbyes among the lantern trees in Circle Clearing.

Dix shot one of the creatures with an arrow. What a screaming and a yelling it made! *Eeeeeeee! Eeeeeee! Eeeeeee!* And then all of the other ones started up as well. *Eeeeeeee! Eeeeeee! Eeeeeee!* they screeched as they wriggled to the edge of the rocks, tipped themselves into the water and then shot off down into the depths like they'd suddenly become arrows themselves, shot from a powerful bow, heading down and down and down.

Dix and me and John and Gerry put down the kids we were carrying and scrambled down the rocks to finish off the squirming thing with clubs and spears. We skinned it and cut it into pieces. We didn't cook it on a fire, because we didn't want to make smoke, but we cut the meat in strips and scorched it on a spiketree. It was rich fatty meat. It filled you up quickly and lay heavy in your stomach for a long time, and it made a couple of people get sick. But, Gela's eyes, that was good thick fat, and, like John said, if you needed fat for snow-wraps or to seal up a boat, those creatures would be the place to go to get it. So we called them fatbucks.

~ ~ ~

Next waking, John went out in front as usual, this time with Jeff and Gerry and Harry, excited and keen to find more new things. Pretty soon they were so far ahead of the rest of us that we could hardly see them at all. The brightness of Worldpool made the cliffs along its edge look dark by comparison and we could just barely make out the four of them – John, Jeff, Gerry and my big dumb brother – as little dark specks on top of that dark mass of rock, with the shining water on one side of them, and the shining forest on the other. Far off ahead of them – so far off you couldn't tell if it was in forest or out in Worldpool or in Dark or what – a volcano was burning. You could see its dark red flame where Eden's shadow met sky, and then, above that, the stain of black smoke trailing across Starry Swirl.

The rest of us plodded along steadily behind for some time, until suddenly we realized that the ones in front were yelling and hollering. We couldn't tell what they were saying, or whether they were excited or scared – the warm wind coming off the water was blowing in our ears and buffeting our faces – but John and Harry and Gerry were waving and jumping up and down on the cliff like they were crazy. Only Jeff was still calm, sitting up on the back of his buck and watching the others shout and yell.

Gela's tits, what *was* it? What could they have found?

We began to run forward.

As we drew nearer we saw they were standing in front of some big solid thing lying in the trees some ten fifteen yards back from top of the rocks. At first it looked like a boulder of some kind, a *big* big boulder, almost a hill. And then – Tom's neck – as we got closer we began to see why their cries had sounded so strange. They didn't *know* if they were excited or scared. They didn't *know* if this was good

good or bad bad, because it was something we'd never seen before. We'd never seen anything that was even a bit like it.

You had to stand and stare at it a long long time before you could even get your eyes to tell you what sort of shape you were looking at. Even the stuff it was made of was something new, not wood or rock or earth or anything like that at all. It was smooth and shiny, like . . . like *metal*. But it was hard to believe so *much* metal could be all together in one place, because this thing wasn't the size of the little metal ring on John's finger, it was the size of Circle of Stones itself!

It was that shape too. It was a huge *huge* circle of metal, tipped a little bit on its side with the lowest part of it sticking into dirt of the forest floor, all mashed and broken up. It was like this huge thing had somehow *fallen* there, or been thrown down hard into the edge of forest, like you'd throw a lump of stone. But what could possibly have thrown a thing as big as that?

We went up to it. We gingerly touched it and then, when it didn't sting or burn, we felt it all over. It really was metal, hard like stone but colder, and smooth smooth all over, with no grain in it, no roughness, no texture, only from time to time straight lines that divided the surface up into square shapes, and straight rows of little round dots. But the metal was only the beginning of the strangeness of it. At the top of it, in middle, there was a smooth shape sticking out like a bowl that you might use for water but twenty thirty times the size and made of what looked like smooth ice, so clear that you could see Starry Swirl shining right through it.

Dix was nimble. He climbed up there and touched it.

'It's not ice,' he said. 'It's warm and dry. And it's smoother even than metal, smooth smoo . . . Oh Gela's tits!'

He came scrambling and tumbling down like he had six leopards after him.

'What *is* it? What *is* it?' we were all yelling at him.

'Faces,' he said, 'faces inside that ice thing looking out. White grinning faces with huge eyes!'

Lucy and Clare and Mike grabbed their kids and started to run. The little ones began to scream. But John and me climbed up the top and looked in. It was dark inside, but there was just enough light from forest and stars for us to make out two white faces staring up at us, with big dark eyes and toothy gaping mouths.

'They're just skulls,' said John, 'that's all. They're just human bones.'

Human bones weren't something we saw too often because we always used to bury dead people back in Circle Valley under stones. In fact I'd only ever seen the clean white bones of a person once before, when a bunch of us found the remains of an old Batwing bloke called Johnny in forest when I was a little kid. (He'd been out there scavenging by himself and he'd died for some reason – maybe a heart attack or something – and had the flesh eaten off him by starbirds.) I looked through the smooth hard icy stuff at the faces looking out at us. Their mouths hung open like they were roaring with laughter. Ugh!

'Just bones,' John called out. 'They can't hurt us.'

The others who'd scattered in panic came reluctantly back to the metal thing.

'Hey, look here!' Gela called. 'There's a hole under here. You could get inside.'

John and me jumped down to look. It was only a small hole, but certainly big enough to crawl through. John wriggled straight in there, with faithful Gerry following him and then me and Jeff. The rest of them seemed to think it was our special job, mine and Gerry's and Jeff's, to be the first to follow John into strange and scary places.

There was a hollow cave in there under the hard ice-like stuff, a tilted-over cave that smelt like a kind of mud. Three skeletons were sitting in there on special seats made of some soft dark crumbly stuff that we'd never seen before. We hadn't noticed the third skeleton from outside because its skull had fallen off its neck and had rolled down to the bottom edge of the cave with its skull eyes looking away from us. The skulls and bones stood out because they were white, but it was too dark to make out much else. I went back to the opening and called for someone to pull down some branches of whitelanterns for us to see by.

When I went back inside to the other three, I reached out for their hands. We were all shaking. I don't honestly know if it was fear or what. We really didn't know what to think or feel.

Then Gela crawled in with three four bright whitelanterns on a bit of branch, and now we began to see just what a *weird* weird kind of cave this was. All round us were strange brown surfaces covered with rows of little shapes. They reminded us of the Kee Board and the Screen that Oldest brought out to show us on Any Virsries, but there must have been thousands of those little square shapes here, dozens of different screens. We didn't really know what to do next, so we began to touch the little springy squares, pushing them in and out like we used to push them in and out on the Kee Board as little kids when Oldest's helpers carried round the Mementoes at Any Virsries.

More people were trying to get inside now. Mike was crawling in, and Clare, and even little Flower, and the metal thing rocked slightly with the weight of us all moving around inside it, and creaked like a tree does in the wind.

'It's the Three, isn't it?' John said. 'It's the Three Companions. This is Dixon and Mehmet and Michael. The *first* Dixon, I mean, the *first* Mehmet. And Michael . . .' He could hardly bring himself to say it, and when his words came they were all shaky and wobbly. 'And Michael Name-Giver.'

We didn't answer him out loud.

'And this is their sky-boat,' Jeff said after a while. He spoke quietly, but more calmly than John. He was interested interested in everything, but he didn't easily get excited or upset. 'This is the Landing Veekle. They never made it back to *Defiant* at all.'

In the fading light from the branch of whitelanterns, we could

see the three skeletons more clearly and we could see that they still
wore wraps around them, wraps to cover their whole bodies, like
Tommy and Angela's wraps that Oldest still kept bits of in the hollow
log. The two skeletons with heads had white wraps, the headless
skeleton had a blue one. And there was *writing* on the wraps. Gela's
eyes, once we'd got some fresh whitelanterns in to give us more light,
we could see their names written there – *Mehmet Haribey, Dixon
Thorleye, Michael Tennison* – names from that old old story which
was so old that, though we believed it was true, we didn't *really*
believe it happened in the same world as us. But here they were, not
in a story world at all, but right in front of us.

Michael Tennison was the one whose head had fallen off. I picked
it up now, that hard hollow thing with its white stony mouth that
had first spoken the names of the animals and plants of Eden, all
that long long time ago.

'Just think,' I said. 'When we say "Michael's names" this and
"Michael's names" that, this is the Michael we're talking about!'

People had got tired of pushing on the little squares by now
and most had stopped doing it, but little Flower was still at it. She
pushed in a square and suddenly – Tom's dick, it was hard to believe
– suddenly there was a voice speaking to us and a face looking out at
us from a screen. Flower screamed, everyone shouted and yelled and
jumped back, and the sky-boat rocked back and forth once again.

'Be quiet!' John yelled furiously. 'Gela's eyes, be quiet and listen!'

It was a man's face, a man with fair hair and tired grey eyes but no
beard at all, his shoulders covered in a bright blue wrap.

' . . .Tennison,' his voice was saying, but it sounded all thin and
strange, like he was half-buried in the ground, and he spoke his
words in a funny way that we could hardly understand, like he was
speaking right up at the front of his mouth. 'Michael Tennison. I'm
afraid it looks as if the Landing Veekle must have been damaged
when we . . .'

And then the voice stopped, and the face disappeared, and the screen went black like all the others. And we pushed every one of those hundreds of little squares over and over again, over and over and over. We even got Flower to push them all again, in case there was something about her touch that made a difference, but we could not get the face or the voice to come back again, however hard we tried.

45

Sue Redlantern

I was grinding up seeds to make some cakes for dinner when a Batwing kid came running into Redlantern area, shouting out that Mehmet Batwing had come down again from Dark. He'd come down with two Fishcreek boys, Paul and Gerald, who'd been the latest two sent up by David across Dark to the place called Tall Tree Valley where Mehmet and his lot lived. Mehmet, Paul and Gerald had gone straight to Guards up along Greatpool, without walking through the rest of Family at all. But one of the Guards had told his sister about it, and news was spreading from her across Family about what had happened. Apparently Paul and Gerald had met John up there: our John, John Redlantern! He'd been visiting Tall Tree too, but from the other direction, from some other place on the far side of Dark, some other forest.

Harry's dick, how many different places *were* there in the world?

Not that I was worrying about that just then. As soon as I heard the news I knew something *bad* bad was going to happen and I ran straight over towards Guards, yelling out the news on my way to everyone I saw.

'They've found out where John and his lot are!' I called out. 'They'll go over after them unless we stop them! Go after our boys and girls. Spread it about! Quickly! Come over to Guards now!'

It was already busy busy in Guards. They were getting out warm wraps for the snow and rolling them up. They were tying up bunches of arrows. They were taking out their strongest blackglass spears and their best leopard tooth knives.

'What's happening?' I bellowed at them. 'What in Gela's name is going on?'

Guards laughed and went on gathering their things together and tying them onto their backs with string and buckskin straps.

'Get out of our way,' David said, stuffing some wraps into a bag. 'We're busy. We've got a job to finish, and we'll have no time spare until it's done.'

Mehmet was there beside him, already up on the back of his woollybuck, ready to lead the way back up Dark.

'What job?' Jade asked David.

I looked round, surprised. There were ten eleven mums there, and Jade had come running up with the rest of them.

'You *know* what job, Juicy John's mum,' David told her. 'You know perfectly well what job. We've found out where your juicy boy is hiding out with his chums, and we're going to do what we should have done long ago.'

'They're *our* boys and girls,' I told him. 'They're Family's. They're not yours to do what you like with!'

David came over to me and sneered into my face.

'*They're our boys,*' he simpered in a fake little whiny whiny voice. '*They're part of Family. They're not yours to do what you like with.*'

Then he snorted and stepped back from me so he could talk to all us women together in his normal rough hard voice.

'Everyone listened to that talk before, didn't they? All that stuff about how dear sweet Juicy John was *our* boy, how he was one of us, how we mustn't hurt him. And look where it got us, eh? Four people dead who'd be living and breathing now if it wasn't for him! Four people! And a baby inside its mum's womb. Now get out of my way, and don't talk to me about being sorry for people.'

I ran forward and grabbed hold of his arms.

'Listen to me, David Redlantern, I've known you since you were a little boy. I looked out for you. You know I did. I told you stories. I comforted you when the other kids teased you. I looked after you. So listen to me. You owe me that, and I'm not letting you go until you . . .'

He turned and called over his shoulder.

'Mike! Get her off me and keep her off me.'

A hard young London boy called Michael came with his mate and dragged me roughly off David.

'You're in charge here until we get back, Mike,' David said. 'Meantime keep these blubbering oldmums out of our way so we can finish getting ourselves together and go.'

David had his Guards divided into two groups. One group was to go with him up over Snowy Dark, with Mehmet Batwing as their guide. The other group – about twenty of them, all with spears and big clubs – was to stay back in Family with Michael London in charge, so as to hold us back and to keep us under control while he was gone. But of course all of this lot that had been told to stay and control us were men and newhairs that we'd known for wombs (as were the lot that went with David over to Dark), and quite a few of them were cousins and uncles and even brothers of the group of kids who'd gone over to John all those wakings ago.

'Back off, all of you!' shouted Michael London, prodding at us with the butt end of his spear. This silly self-important kid was no older than my Gerry. But he was determined that if he was going to miss all the excitement across Dark, he was going to have fun back here instead.

'Back off or we'll use these clubs on you!'

And meantime David and the other lot of Guards – another twenty men and newhair boys – climbed onto their buckhorses with their weapons and their snow-wraps, two Guards on each buck, and started to head off Peckhamway.

'David!' I yelled after him. 'David! Please stop!'

He didn't even look back.

'*Mehmet!*' I shouted then. 'Don't lead him to them! He wants to do for them all!'

Mehmet Batwing *did* look round, and his face was strange strange because it was two things at the same time. He was trying to look cold and hard like David – and part of him really *was* enjoying the power he had – but part of him was troubled too. It was like he was only now really understanding what it was that he'd set loose, now that it was too late to stop. He had got a *sort of* power, a sort of importance, but he'd only got it by giving up having any real power at all.

'Mehmet!' I shouted, as he turned quickly away again. 'You don't want to do this, so *don't* do it! We'll back you up.'

All the other mums were yelling now, and other people were still arriving from groups, and they were yelling too, calling out to David, calling to people they knew among the twenty Guards on buckback: 'Johnny! Mike! Dixon! Mitch! Pete! Don't go with them! Don't go!'

And some of the Guards looked back from the backs of their bucks, and some didn't. But, either way, what could they do? They were in the same position as Mehmet. They'd gone too far. If one of them turned back, it would be *him* that the others would be spiking up next.

We turned our attention to the Guards who were holding us back:

'Let us go! Let us bloody *go*! They're going after our boys and girls. They're going after people that used to be your friends and your groupmates. They're going to kill them! Is that really what you want?'

They just shrugged. A few laughed mockingly but you could see a lot of them were troubled by what was happening. It made no difference, though. They still wouldn't let us get past them. How could they? It was the same for them as it was for their mates riding out towards Snowy Dark on their bucks. If they didn't do what they were told, they were at risk themselves. So they frowned and avoided our eyes and prodded us and hit us with clubs and spearbutts if we pushed forward or tried to get round them. And then, pretty soon, it was too late for us to catch up with the bucks anyway, so they shrugged and let us go.

'Do what you want,' said Michael London. 'Just get out of Guards area and stop that bloody yelling. You're making my head hurt.'

And they turned their backs on us and walked off in different directions, pretending that they were busy and didn't have time for our nonsense, but really just trying to get away from all of this, so as not to have to face us, or think about what they were doing.

Some of the mums ran straight off into forest after David and his lot, but there was no point in that. People can't run as fast as bucks, and David had made sure sure that no one in Family had horsebucks to use except only for Guards. So I ran instead after the two boys, Paul and Gerald Fishcreek, who'd come down with Mehmet from Tall Tree Valley and were now part of the group of Guards who'd been told to keep us under control.

'What did you see up there? Who did you see? What did they tell you?'

They looked at each other guiltily, and then looked round to see if anyone else was near.

'John and your boys came up while we were there,' Gerald said, with a silly fake shrug, pretending it was all nothing to him. 'Gerry and whatsisname . . . Jeff.'

'Gerry? Jeff? Both my boys?'

I was shaking now. It was weird weird, to be talking to someone who'd seen my two sons only a few wakings ago, but there wasn't much comfort in it, not with David and his lot riding towards them.

'How were they?' I asked him.

Again Gerald looked at his groupmate. Then he shrugged again.

'Okay,' he said. 'Pretty good. They've grown. Jeff's a big bloke now, with a beard and all. Quite a looker, actually.'

'Do you hate them?'

Gerald glanced at Paul.

'Well, no,' he muttered. 'Of course not.'

'But yet you came back here with Mehmet Batwing to tell David about them, knowing how badly David wants to spike them up to die?'

'We didn't . . .'

'Come on, Gerald. You knew David would be after them the moment he got the news. Don't try and tell me you didn't.'

Gerald looked desperately at Paul. I looked at Paul too. I gave him the look I give to naughty children, and he looked guilty and scared for a moment and then straight away he frowned, making his face hard hard hard, a proper Guard's face. It was like he was putting on a mask.

'Back off, Sue Redlantern,' Paul said. 'Back off or I'll use this club on you, alright?'

'What?' I hissed at him. 'Club me for asking you why you want to do for my own sons?'

He cowered like I'd just hit him, but held his club tight in his hand.

I let them go, the silly weak kids. And then I cried and cried. I cursed First Tommy and First Dixon and First Mehmet for bringing human life to Eden. I cursed Tommy and Angela for deciding to stay here and slip together and so bring all of us from peaceful peaceful nothingness into this cruel dark world. This was a *bad* bad place. People weren't meant to live here. People were meant to live on Earth where it's fresh and bright and new as the inside of a lanternflower. This place was only good for creatures from dark dark Underworld, with flat eyes and green-black blood and six limbs with claws. Nothing good would ever come to us in this miserable dark Eden. Never. Never. Never. There would only ever be pain and misery and blood, blood, blood.

'Sue,' a voice whispered behind me. 'Sue.'

CHRIS BECKETT

It was Gerald Fishcreek back again, without his brother, without his spear.

'Julie warned them, Sue. She slipped with Jeff up there, up at Tall Tree, and she warned him about David and Mehmet. She told him Mehmet would talk to David, and what David would do when he found out where they were.'

'How do you know that?'

'Because I spoke to her. You're right, I don't hate John and your boys. In fact when we met them up there I really liked them, specially your Jeff. And after the three of them had gone and there was no one else near, I said to Julie that I wished I'd warned them what was going to happen. And she said, "Well, don't worry, Gerald, because I did."'

Well, I hugged him, and then I hit him hard hard round the face, because if John and the others were saved by that warning from Julie, it would be no thanks to *this* cowardly little slinker, whose conscience only started to prick him after it was too late, so that he could reassure himself that he wasn't really bad without the trouble of actually doing anything that was any good. And then I hugged him again anyway for telling me.

He pulled away from me, looking round guiltily. And now he put on his hard Guard face too, just like his groupmate Paul had done.

'Don't ever speak to me about it again, alright?' he said. 'Don't ever tell anyone I spoke to you, because I'll call you a liar if you do.'

'Did they say what it was like over the other side?'

He looked round again. He wanted to go. He was scared scared someone would see him talking to me.

'Big,' he said, 'a big big forest. So big, they said, that you can't even see where it ends. And there's a pool there that's just the same. You can't see the ends of it. You can't see across to the other side.'

Off he ran. I sank down against a whitelantern trunk and cried some more. But it was a different kind of crying now. I was crying with relief. They still had a good chance of getting away from

David, into that big big forest, which they knew and David didn't.

Yes, I thought, but it's an odd thing, isn't it, a sad sad thing, for a mum to be relieved that her sons can go further away from her, and hide in a place where she may never see them again?

46

John Redlantern

We spent one two hours in there, just trying to get the talking face back on the screen. All the time people were pushing to get in, pushing each other out of the way, pushing the bloody little squares, pushing past the bones of the Three Companions like they were just dead twigs in forest.

'Watch what you're doing!' I said. 'You'll knock the others' heads off as well!'

No one was even listening.

'Try that one there!' someone said.

'No, try pushing the ones that Flower pushed!'

'No, don't do *that*! What's the point of that? We've tried that a hundred times. Leave those alone and let me try *this* one.'

'Hey! Back off and let me through, I've got some more lanterns here. Let's get some light on this!'

The strain in people's faces! The desperation to get someone they didn't know to appear for one moment more on that screen and speak words to them that they could hardly understand! That one thing, the screen with its voice, had taken over from all the other wonders here: the dead Companions, the Landing Veekle itself. Perhaps they just didn't want to think about what all this really meant.

I crawled back out through the hole and left them to it. Jeff and Harry and Gela were already outside. Gela and Jeff were looking after a couple of babies plus five six littles who didn't want to stay in the sky-boat because they found it scary. And Harry agreed with them about that. He didn't like the bones or the metal cave, and he'd hated hated the strange voice that spoke to us from the screen. Now he was pacing around and muttering and moaning to himself, wanting to get away.

'Harry doesn't like it. Harry wants to go.'

Tina came out soon after me, then Janny, then Dix, all looking kind of shaken and a bit ashamed, like they'd let something bad come inside them and take them over, and now they regretted it.

'I reckon we should stop this,' I said. 'I don't think the talking face will come back.'

Tina nodded. I stood up.

'Come out now! Everyone out!'

No one argued with me. They all emerged one by one through the hole in the boat – Gerry, Lucy Batwing, Mike, Clare, Jane, little Flower, Clare . . . with Martha and Lucy London coming out last of all, both of them crying bitterly.

'Listen up, everyone!' I called out.

~ ~ ~

They all went quiet quiet, standing there next to the Veekle under the bright whitelantern trees, with the smooth soft sheen of Worldpool nearby.

I looked round at their faces, grownups and children, excited, scared, hungry for something that they didn't even understand, and I tried to figure out what I ought to say. It was hard hard because I'd been excited too, and I'd felt that same hunger, and, like all of them, I was still dazed dazed by the face of Michael Name-Giver himself talking to us from the screen. (Who could believe that such a thing would ever happen to us?) But somehow I needed to help the others make some sense out of it, when I hadn't really made sense of it myself.

'So . . .' I began. 'So now we know how the story of the Three Companions ended. After all this time. After . . . all these wombs, and . . . and all these generations.'

I talked without knowing what I was going to say, but something was creeping up into my thoughts. It was like when you first spot a leopard in forest. To start with you're still not sure if it really is a leopard or if it's only a patch of flowers, and then you're pretty sure it is a leopard but you still can't quite make out its exact shape. And then you *see* it.

'And that means, doesn't it, that they . . . That means they never got back to *Defiant*. And . . . *that* . . . means . . .'

Oh Gela's heart, that meant . . .

I looked at their faces. I could see some of them getting it too: Gela, Tina, Dix, the quicker, stronger ones. I took a deep breath to try and get control over my voice.

'And that means that *Defiant* never left Eden at all. I . . . I suppose it must still be up there in sky somewhere, too high up for us to see. All this time, we've imagined it somewhere far out across Starry Swirl, but it's been up there all the while. And that means . . .'

'That means they'll *never* come for us,' wailed Lucy London. 'Never, never, never!'

Pretty well everyone was crying – grownups, kids, men, women – crying and crying for that old old dream that would never never come true. Tina was crying, Gela was crying, Gerry was crying, Martha London was wailing wailing and rocking back and forth like a mum that's lost a child. And there were tears running down *my* face too, even while I tried to get us past this. Only Jeff wasn't crying. I think he'd understood what this meant from the moment we saw the Veekle, and now he was calmly watching everyone with his gentle interested eyes.

(Right behind him, on a whitelantern branch, a bat was watching too. Its head tipped slightly on one side, it watched, and fanned its wings and scratched its ear thoughtfully with a single thin black finger.)

'That's right,' I said. 'It means we have to give up on the idea that we're waiting for Earth folk to come for us and take us back again to . . . back to . . .'

It took me three tries to get out the words, I was so sad sad. And yet it was me that that had destroyed Circle, me that had said we shouldn't just sit and stew in Circle Valley, waiting for help from Earth.

' . . .back to that place where the light comes down from sky, bright as the inside of a whitelantern, and where they see clearly when we're blind, and know about all those things that we have to try so hard hard hard to figure out.'

I was getting some control of myself now. I was pleased about that. And I could see them all looking at me, waiting for me to make it better for them, and I was pleased about that too.

'But listen, everyone. We're no worse off than we were before we found this thing. We've still got each other. We've still got fruit and meat to eat. We've still got Eden, just the same as it was last waking and all the wakings before, for all those generations. Nothing has changed except for one thing, and in a way it's a good thing. Now we know for sure we can just get on with things and don't have to wait around for Earth.'

I looked at Tina, and that reminded me of something she'd said to me once by Deep Pool, when we were newhairs back in Family.

'It's like when a kid gets lost in forest. The kid's mum can't rest, can't get on with anything but searching and crying and searching, until they find the bones. And when they do find the bones and bring them to her, she's sad sad, and she screams and cries and rocks and tears her wraps. But at least she knows there's no point in searching any more, and slowly slowly she gets back to her life as it was before, and back to her other kids, knowing there's no need to look out any more for the one that's gone. We've always known that Earth might never come. We've always known that, even if Earth did come one waking, it probably wouldn't be while we were alive. I mean, that's what decided Tommy and Angela to stay here in the first place, isn't it? But we've always deep down secretly hoped that Earth would come soon and carry us away from all our sadness and trouble, even if the odds were against it, and even though we knew – don't forget this either – even though we knew that Earth had *bad* bad troubles of its own. We just couldn't help it. We didn't fully give ourselves to Eden because we were dreaming about that other place full of light. But now we can *really* be here.'

Jeff recognized that I'd got that last bit from him, and he gave me his funny little smile. Tina nodded. And Gerry, even though he was still crying crying, looked proud of me, and that always felt good. I nodded to myself. I thought I'd done well. I was pretty sure I'd got through to most of them.

I wiped tears from my own eyes and finished what I had to say.

'We can't stay here,' I told them, 'we're still too close to Tall Tree ridge. And we can't take this sky-boat with us. So we'll just have to leave it behind us here. But it's good that we found it. It's good good. Those three have been sitting in there all this time like they were still trying to cross sky and finish their story, but now we've found them, that's all over. They're back in *our* story again and we can let them rest.'

They *were* back in our story. They existed again, and I was pleased about that, in spite of the sadness and loneliness of knowing they never even made it to *Defiant*, and the horrible sadness of losing even the hope of Earth.

For a moment I had a sense of people from the future all around us, generations and generations of them, watching this scene, calling to us in their faint thin voices. But I couldn't make out what they were saying because living people right in front of me were shouting things out as well.

'What will we do with the bones?' asked Tina.

'We can't just go,' sobbed Martha London, arm in arm with bulgy-eyed tear-stained Lucy. 'There's telly vision here, and lecky-trickity, just like Earth.'

'We should take the bones out of the Veekle and bury them properly with stones,' Gela said. 'Give them a funeral.'

'No time to find stones,' I said at once, pulling myself back into the moment. 'And anyway, remember why we buried people under stones when they died? It was so Earth could find them and take them home. And that's . . .' I stopped to steady my voice. 'Well, like we've just talked about, that's not going to happen, is it?'

Several people started to sob again at the thought that even our bones would never return to Earth. But one or two were already trying to figure out a new way of dealing with our dead.

'Maybe we should just take them out and lie down them here, then,' said Janny.

'What?' said Gela. 'So David's lot can find them and take them back for Lucy Lu to drool over?'

'I know what we'll do,' said Tina. 'We'll put them in Worldpool, and all that swirly water will take them away.'

That was what we did.

Clare scratched their names on stones, with her tongue hanging out just like Secret Ree's, and we laid them on the ground next to Veekle like the stones in Ash Clearing back in Circle Valley:

FIRST DIXON, ASTRONORT
MEHMET, ASTRONORT
MICHAL, ORBIT PLICE

Then we carried the bones down the rocks, and waded two three yards out to the place where the bottom of Worldpool dropped down into a deep deep waterforest. And we let them fall, twisting and turning and falling apart as they sank through the water lanterns and the shining shoals of fish, deeper and deeper into Eden.

We all clapped and cheered, except for sobbing Lucy and Martha London, who were still grieving for the telly vision and the lecky-trickity. And then we went back up the rocks and everyone started loading things up again onto the bucks. I didn't even have to ask them to do it.

~ ~ ~

'John? Alright? Everything's ready now. Shall we go?'

Tina spoke in that pained voice she used when she could see I was troubled about something. Bloody old Tina, it was always the same: she wanted me to show myself more, but she wanted me to hide myself more as well, both at the same time.

'Just a moment,' I said. 'Just give me a moment.'

I walked over to the edge of the cliff. The shining water of Worldpool was bright bright and three big fatbucks were swooping and swerving through the swaying branches and coloured lanterns of underwater trees.

I took Gela's ring off my little finger and turned it around in my hand. Of all the things we had in Eden that came from Earth, this was still the most perfect and the most beautiful, this little ring with the words inside it: '*To Angela with love from Mum and Dad*'. But we were saying goodbye to Earth here, weren't we? So perhaps I should leave it behind here, or throw it out into Worldpool, along with the bones of the Three Companions?

'No! No! No! Don't leave it!' called out the voices of future people, looking in on our story, appalled. 'It's the most precious thing left! You will never, never be forgiven!'

But other voices said the opposite:

'Leave it! Leave it behind! It'll just bring trouble, trouble, trouble, and more blood. You destroyed Circle, you're leaving the sky-boat behind, so why not leave Gela's ring as well and be done with it all?'

I turned the ring round in my hand. I held it up close to my face so I could read the message written inside it to the woman who was the mother of everyone. Everyone's mother, even mine.

I looked back towards the others waiting beside the broken sky-boat.

I slid the ring back onto my little finger.

Starry Swirl shone down. It shone down over everything: the wide forest with its thousand thousand trees, the fatbucks gliding through the shining water, the black black shadow of Snowy Dark, the distant volcano burning red . . . It even shone down over David and his Guards somewhere out there, still far away, but creeping towards us like little angry ants over the great face of Eden.

Tina and Gerry came over to me, and so did handsome gentle hobbling Jeff.

I smiled. These were *my* Three Companions, I thought, these were my First Three, the ones who were with me from the beginning of all this.

As he reached me, Jeff opened his mouth to speak.

I put my finger to his lips.

'I know, Jeff, I know. We are here. I just said it back there, didn't I? I said it for you. We really are here.'

And Tina laughed her sweetly mocking laugh.

~ ~ ~

Hoom! Hoom! Hoom! went a starbird out there in forest between us and Tall Tree ridge.

Aaaah! Aaaah! Aaaah! another one answered back.

'We should pick up those loose bits of metal there and take them with us,' I said. 'They'll be useful for spears and knives.'